M000306453

SINCE

YOU

WENT

AWAY

SINCE YOU

WENT AWAY

Part Four: Fall

Nan
McCarthy

RAINWATER
PRESS

Since You Went Away by Nan McCarthy

Part Four: Fall

Rainwater Press

www.nan-mccarthy.com

Cover design & illustration by David J. High, highdzn.com
Interior design by Kevin Callahan, BNGObooks.com + David J. High
Cover art from Shutterstock illustrations by rudall30, Radiocat,
Lana_Samcorp, & Kevin Sanderson
Author photo by Kelly Anderson Cole

Published in the United States of America by Rainwater Press. For information please use the contact form on the author's website www.nan-mccarthy.com/contact/.

ISBN 978-1-888354-15-7 (paperback)

ISBN 978-1-888354-19-5 (ebook)

First Edition: November 2020

for Pat, Ben & Coleman

Contents

Characters & Places

Liam Mahoney   Emilie's husband, Finn & Rory's dad, colonel, U.S. Marine Corps

Emilie Mahoney   Liam's wife, Finn & Rory's mom, high school In-School Suspension supervisor

Finn Mahoney   senior in high school / freshman in college, Liam & Emilie's older son

Rory Mahoney   freshman / sophomore in high school, Liam & Emilie's younger son

Soda   Mahoney family long-haired Chihuahua mix (rescue)

Brig   Mahoney family Highland Terrier mix (rescue)

Smedley   Mahoney family cat, gray long-hair mix (rescue)

Button   Mahoney family cat, calico mix (rescue)

Daly   Mahoney family cat, tan short-hair mix (rescue)

Ozzy   Rory's bearded dragon lizard

Elvis   Rory's goldfish

Ahmad   Iraqi interpreter living in U.S., friend of Fakhir and DeYoungs

Fakhir al-Azzawi   Iraqi interpreter living in U.S., friend of Wade, Liam, and Ray

Farah al-Azzawi   Fakhir's youngest sister

Arifa al-Azzawi   Fakhir's mom

DeYoungs   Marine Corps family hosting Ahmad

Ray Salazar   works with Liam, husband of Janet, major, U.S. Marine Corps, original hosts of Fakhir

Janet Salazar   wife of Ray, friend of Emilie, original hosts of Fakhir

Agnes Hawkins   neighbor, wife of Eugene, mother of Ethan, book club member

Eugene Hawkins   neighbor, husband of Agnes, father of Ethan

Ethan Hawkins   neighbor, son of Agnes & Eugene, friend of Rory

Crystal   Finn's date to Turnabout dance, friend, bandmate

Ashley   Rory's date to Turnabout dance

Wanda Reszel   neighbor, wife of Vince, friend of Emilie, book club member

Vince Reszel   neighbor, husband of Wanda

Wade Miller   family friend of Liam & Emilie, friend of Fakhir, major (ret.), U.S. Marine Corps

Isabel Miller   Wade's 2nd (& current) wife

Chloe Miller   Wade & Isabel's baby girl

Mrs. Nardi   Wade & Isabel's neighbor

Shelley   Wade's 1st wife

Rourke Mahoney   Liam's dad, retired Marine, Korean War veteran, deceased

Mary Mahoney   Liam's mom

Lucia Caputo   ISS student

Raquel Caputo   Lucia's mom

Carmen Caputo   Lucia's dad

Andy, Arthur, Angel Caputo   Lucia's three younger brothers

Mr. Lavin   Finn's piano teacher

Ken Phillips   fellow colonel who works with Liam, husband of Tammy

Tammy Phillips   Col. Phillips' wife, friend of Emilie, eventual book club member

Tiffany   Emilie's coworker

Neil Harris   Finn's high school friend and bandmate

Suzanne & Mike Harris   Neil's parents

Darryl   Finn's high school friend and bandmate

Josh   Rory's friend, lives in neighborhood

Aunt Dottie   Emilie's aunt (sister of Emilie's deceased mother)

Joey   Aunt Dottie's boyfriend

Wally   Aunt Dottie's 1st husband, deceased

Jacques   Aunt Dottie's Jack Russell terrier (aka Pol Pot)

Bonnie   Aunt Dottie's next-door neighbor

Fred   Aunt Dottie's boyfriend before Joey

Marcus Oliver   ISS student

Derek   ISS student

Chancee   Bunco hostess

Pamela   lives in the neighborhood

Dr. Hermey   Mahoney family dentist

Genie   book club member

Patty   book club member

Barb   book club member

Roxanne   book club member

Kim   book club member

Charlene   book club member

Dr. Amy Gouwens   principal at Finn & Rory's high school, Emilie's boss

Portia   yoga instructor

Coach Crowley   Rory's track coach

Mrs. Callahan   Lucia's Language Arts teacher

Mrs. Schaeffer   Lucia's History teacher

Mr. Zim (Zimmerman)   Finn & Lucia's Nutrition teacher

Brian   Lucia's boyfriend

Officer Sean Dempsey   high school resource officer

Mrs. Nelson   assistant principal at the high school

Gerald Lewis   Liam's commanding officer, brigadier general, U.S. Marine Corps

Virginia Lewis   wife of BGen. Lewis, facilitator of FSG

Jerri Jablonski   wife of Maj. Jablonski, head of FSG

Maj. Jablonski   husband of Jerri, Liam's coworker

LtCol. Dobson (Ret.)   director of MWR

"Mrs. Baez" (alias)   spouse at FSG meeting

"Mr. Baez" (alias)   service member who works in Liam's shop and is married to "Mrs. Baez"

Leah Gibson   previously known as "Mrs. Baez," friend of Emilie and Isabel, eventual book club member

Jacob Gibson   previously known as "Mr. Baez," Leah's husband, corporal, U.S. Marine Corps

Frank   ISS student

Ronny   head custodian at the high school

Colin   Liam's youngest brother

Carolyn   Colin's wife, Liam & Emilie's sister in-law

Donovan   Liam's oldest brother

Kurt   Rory's friend

Billy   Rory's friend

GySgt. Lee   retired gunnery sergeant (U.S. Marine Corps) at American Legion

Officer Andrews   police officer in Buell City Police Department

John   Emilie's brother

Stevens family   neighbors who live behind Mahoneys

Greg   Wade's 2nd counselor at the VA

Francis   Emilie's step-father, deceased

Ginna   Emilie's mother, deceased

Mel   Finn's college roommate

Riikka   Rory's hockey teammate from Finland

Fiona   Liam and Emily's niece

SSgt. Scott   Marine recruiter

Princess   Fakhir's family dog

Jane   Emilie's yoga partner

Dr. Crandall   Mahoney family veterinarian

Chesty   Wade & Isabel's bulldog

Maggie   Finn's girlfriend

Jenn   Mondo warehouse supervisor, Wade's boss

Louise   Joey's ex-wife

Stephanie   Joey's daughter

Jerry   ISS student

Mrs. Lescynski   Calculus teacher

Fawzia al-Azzawi   Fakhir's oldest sister

Farida al-Azzawi   Fakhir's second oldest sister

Faisal al-Azzawi   Fakhir's dad

Cooper   ISS student

Kenny (Jr.) & Kevin   Tammy & Ken Phillips' sons

Sgt. James   duty sergeant

Cpl. Roberts   Sgt. James' neighbor

Uncle Zareb   Fakhir's uncle who provides shelter for Fakhir's mom & sisters

Shelley Griffith   sophomore at Buell City High School

Mrs. Garner   Geometry teacher

Detective Dunhill   police investigator

Sabrina   ISS student

Sgt. Garnett   Marine sniper in Fallujah

Cpl. Cotten   Marine spotter in Fallujah

LtCol. Cromwell   speaker at Marine Corps Birthday Ball

Officer Clemmons   formerly known as Officer Pizza Roll

Mayor Gunderson   mayor of Buell City

Capt. Wilson   C-130 pilot in Vietnam

Capt. Hite   C-130 copilot in Vietnam

TechSgt. Vestine   C-130 engineer in Vietnam

1st Lt. Mandel   C-130 navigator in Vietnam

Uday Hussein   Saddam Hussein's eldest son

Yasin   Uday's chief executioner (fictional)

Buell City   fictional Midwest town where Mahoney family lives

Fidelia's   coffee shop where Finn works

Mondo   fictional company that sells things on the Internet

Peroni's   pizza place near Mahoney house

Smollett's   ice cream parlor near Mahoney house

Wakeville   fictional Midwest town three hours from Buell City & the site of a Mondo fulfillment center.

St. Elizabeth   Catholic high school Maggie attends

Alfalfa's   organic grocery store where Leah works

Woolley's Tavern   bar & grill near Mahoney house

The Cherry Lane Motel   establishment in downtown Buell City

Jack's   tavern near Mahoney house that serves wings

Manuel's   Mexican restaurant in town

Tony's   high-end Italian restaurant downtown

Walker County   the county that encompasses Buell City and surrounding area

Part Four

Fall

A note from the author:

*A glossary on page 255 explains
military terms & acronyms used in this story.*

Monday, September 22, 2008   3:39 a.m.

Fuck.

Fuck, fuck, fuck, fuck, FUCK.

What the fuck? What even the fuck? What the goddamn motherfuck? The fuck? Fucking fucks.

Fucked by the green weenie again.

Unfuckingbelievable. Motherfucking motherfuckitude.

Fucking hell. What kind of fuckside-down fucked up fuckery is this? Are we living in fucking Fucksville for fuck's sake? How the fuck am I supposed to even give a chicken-fried fuck anymore? Haven't I already given a fuckload of fucking fucks?

Fuck it. Fuck the fucking fuckers. Fucking fuckchops. Fucking fuckbuckets. Fucking fuckaholic fuckbrains. Fucking fuck-haired von fucksticks. Fucking fucknuggets dipped in fucksauce.

Fucking Jesus Christ on a pogo stick.

Fuck you, deployment.

Tuesday, September 23, 2008   9:09 p.m.

Was that really necessary? Sending not only Mrs. Lewis but also *General Lewis* to come over here and check on me? You could have just called Col. Phillips you know. Or even Fakhir. Either one of them would have told you I'm fine.

Or why didn't you just call me yourself? I guess you wanted someone who could make visual contact. I get it. But General *Lewis*? Really? Do you know how absolutely mortified I was when the doorbell rang last night and I found the two of them standing on our doorstep? Well shit fire and save the matches, as Dottie would say.

The only thing that made the situation even somewhat bearable was when I showed them the email. They were sitting on our family room couch, sipping decaf, and we'd been talking for about an hour. By that time I had mostly convinced them I was fine. They were being so understanding about everything. So I offered to show them the note that had caused you so much alarm. I grabbed my laptop and pulled up the email.

They'd been acting all serious and everything but once they began reading — well, it looked to me like they were trying not to smile. After they were done, the two of them exchanged glances. Gen. Lewis handed my laptop back to me and said, "That's quite an email, Emilie. I can see why Liam was ... concerned about you." He's looking at me real thoughtful-like, slowly nodding his head, as if he's thinking, ah yes, it all makes sense now. Finally Mrs. Lewis pipes up. "Bravo Zulu Emilie. Couldn't have said it better myself."

We had ourselves a nice little chuckle. Gen. Lewis said there's a word for what I did — lalochezia. (He also said I'm the sweariest non-Marine he's come across in his entire 30-year career. I think he meant it as a compliment.) I looked up the word after they left and basically it's the emotional relief a person gets from swearing. Who knew?

I confess, I did feel better after I wrote the email. But I shouldn't have hit Send. If I'd been thinking clearly, I would have just saved it in my Draft folder and gone back to bed. I apologize for not thinking how the email would affect you, Liam. I should've known it would worry you.

I'd been lying awake for hours after I got the email about your deployment being extended three months. I just couldn't turn off my brain and the anger and frustration and disappointment kept building inside me until I thought I was going to break. When I got out of bed and opened my laptop, I had no idea what I was going to write. The words just hurled themselves from my gut to the keyboard.

Still, that's no excuse. I'm sorry I sent it. Will you forgive me?

I understand the decision to extend your deployment is not something you have control over. I just really really don't like the Marine Corps right now. (Is this why they say the "H" in Marine Corps stands for happiness?)

Wednesday, September 24, 2008   6:26 p.m.

I haven't told the boys yet about your deployment getting extended. I need to find the right moment to break the news. When Gen. & Mrs. Lewis came over Monday night Rory was upstairs doing homework. Lucia was at work, and Fakhir, sensing we needed privacy, made himself scarce by taking the dogs out to the back porch. After they left I did tell Fakhir what was going on, and asked him to keep the news to himself until I have a chance to tell the boys. I think I'll have a sit-down with Rory first and call Finn at school after that. They may not take it well so I need to figure out the best approach. For once in my life I find myself at a loss for words.

It was unusually warm today so Rory went over to Isabel's after hockey practice to mow and edge. Isabel and Leah were in their usual spots on the patio, sipping mojitos and sunning themselves in their lounge chairs. I imagine they won't have too many warm days left to wear their bikinis. Chloe was on a blanket in the shade with Chesty. Rory thinks Chloe can say his name now — he swears she said "Wawee!" when she saw him. He also said he wasted a bunch of time looking for the key to the shed (where they keep the mower). The key is usually under the mat by the back door but it wasn't there and Isabel wasn't much help. (She had no idea where it might be and apparently didn't feel like getting her ass out of the chair to help Rory look for it.) After poking around a while Rory finally found it in the planter on the patio. Maybe Wade thought that was a safer spot for it and forgot to tell anyone he moved it. Luckily it didn't take long for Rory to mow since it hasn't rained much lately and the grass wasn't very long. He offered to pull some weeds from their flower beds and then played with Chloe a few minutes before heading home. This might be one of the last times he goes over there until next spring.

It appears Wade and Isabel are back on good terms again. I was a little worried after they had that kerfuffle Labor Day weekend over Isabel and Chloe moving to Wakeville. But when they came here for breakfast the morning after Finn's party, everything seemed fine.

Fakhir continues to be in daily contact with his mom. Everybody is scared shitless that whoever blew up their house in Baghdad is going to find Arifah and Farah hiding out at the uncle's house. And what then? Will they pull them out onto the street and threaten to set them on fire like they did with Ahmad's family? Or will they just go ahead and murder them since they've already given them a warning by annihilating their house?

Thank God Fakhir has Lucia to fortify him. I mean, we're all supporting Fakhir, but she has really stepped up to the plate. She massages his temples most nights when we're watching TV, and she leaves little notes of encouragement for him to find by the coffee maker in the morning. It kind of chokes me up just thinking about it.

Speaking of Lucia, I found another one of her bras laying around the house while I was searching for Soda's tennis ball. This one was on the floor behind the couch in the family room. Royal blue satin underwire. I didn't think she wore underwire but whatever. I went up to her room before dinner to return it. She was sprawled on the floor reading a copy of *Vogue*, her head resting on a pile of dirty laundry.

"Hi Lucia. I found another one of your bras."

"Thanks." She holds out her hand without looking up from her magazine.

I place it in her hand. "Don't you want to know where I found it?" I ask.

She tears her eyes away from her article long enough to glance my way. "Does it matter?"

"I don't know. It's just, we find your bras in the weirdest places. Do you suddenly decide you don't want to wear your bra anymore and then drop it wherever you happen to be sitting, or … ?"

She lets out an exasperated sigh. "I don't know Emilie. Honestly I don't even remember wearing this one lately." She tosses the bra toward the hamper and misses. "It's underwire and I don't really like it anymore. Last I remember it was in the back of my lingerie drawer. Or maybe at the bottom of one of these piles of laundry. What can I say? I have a lot of bras."

"Well, they sure pop up in the strangest places."

She shrugs. "What do you want me to do? Put a GPS on every piece of lingerie?"

"No need to get huffy about it," I say.

She sets down the magazine. "I'm sorry Em. I just find this obsession with my underwear rather strange."

"Who's obsessed with your underwear?" I ask. Then, "Wait. Don't answer that. I need to go check on the potatoes. Dinner will be ready in a few minutes."

"Thanks Emilie. You're the best. Even if you are a weirdo."

Thursday, September 25, 2008   11:17 p.m.

I almost didn't go to book club last night. Didn't feel like it. But I forced myself. Kim hosted *The Five People You Meet In Heaven* by Mitch Albom. Honestly, I was prepared to hate it. (Because, well, Kim.) But I didn't. Maybe if I'd read it at a different point in my life the skeptic in me would have written it off as sentimental sassafras. Instead it made me cry.

Specifically, it was a quote about sacrifice that got me:

"*Sometimes when you sacrifice something precious, you're not really losing it. You're just passing it on to someone else.*"

Maybe the extra three months you're serving over there will give another service member three months at home they might not have had. Thinking about it that way helps me feel better about the situation, even if it's probably not true. Besides, me being upset doesn't change anything. And you're the one who's sacrificing the most. We'll be okay — all of us. I mean, we have to be okay. We don't have any other choice, do we?

Speaking of sacrifice, Tammy told me they finally got word on Ken's deployment to Afghanistan — he's leaving sometime before the holidays. They don't know exactly when but — sheesh — couldn't the HMFICs at least let Ken spend Thanksgiving at home before he ships out?

Wanda was a little cool toward me tonight. I wonder if she's still butt-hurt about me ordering a pizza after I got home from book club at her house last month (the night she expected us to get by on orange slices and chia pudding)? Or do you think she's mad about something else?

It could be that I stopped accepting her invites to play Words With Friends. When we first started playing a few months ago I was mostly winning. (I *am* an English major after all.) And then suddenly she's coming up with these obscure two-letter words and getting ridiculously high scores. I'm talking non-stop winning! I like a tough opponent as much as the next person but it was pretty obvious she was googling words or something. I mean, she starts out as a fairly average player and then overnight becomes the Bobby Fischer of Words With Friends? Where's the fun in that?

Agnes seemed good. We didn't get into much personal chitchat — I don't think the rest of book club knows Eugene's been laid off, and I don't blame her for not wanting to talk about it. She did pull me aside to say how much she appreciated Rory inviting Ethan for a sleepover last month. Maybe I should invite Agnes out for coffee soon, or at least give her a call — we've had so much going on here at home lately I'm afraid I haven't been a very good friend to her.

Kim gave me some leftovers to take home even though I didn't ask for any. (Either everyone feels sorry for me because you're deployed or I've developed a reputation as a food hoarder.) On my way out the door she handed me a plate of her bologna roll-ups with cream cheese and a pickle in the middle along with some cold pigs in a blanket. I don't care how much we loved little smokies wrapped in canned dough when we were kids — those things need to stay in the '60s along with jellied chicken. When I got home, instead of hiding the leftovers in the back of the fridge like I normally do, I left everything out on the kitchen island for Rory, Fakhir, and Lucia to finish. It was still there when I got up for work this morning.

p.s. Leah didn't show up at book club last night which was odd. I texted her a little while ago wondering if everything is okay. She said she and Isabel had a few too many mojitos on the patio earlier that evening and she decided to spend the night. I told her she missed out on seeing Kim's & Charlene's matching outfits — maxi dresses with boho headbands — which were a total ripoff of Leah's outfit last month. (I also let her know they didn't pull it off nearly as well as she did.) I asked Leah if she'd wear something crazy to next month's meeting to see if those two copy it, and she said she's on it. I can't wait to see what she comes up with.

Friday, September 26, 2008   10:28 p.m.

After we got home from school today I finally worked up the nerve to tell Rory about your deployment being extended. He was sitting in the family room watching a "Full House" rerun, eating my bag of Lay's.

"Where'd you find those?" I ask.

"In Dad's footlocker in the garage," he says before shoving a handful of chips in his pie-hole.

"That's my secret stash."

"Well, it's not secret anymore now is it?"

"You're a smart-ass. Just like your father." I take a seat on the couch next to him. "Can I talk to you for a sec?"

He mutes the TV and turns to me. "What's up?"

"Well, I'm afraid I have some bad news to share."

"Is Fakhir's family okay? Those fuckers didn't find his mom and sister did they?"

"No, they're fine Rory. I wanted to talk to you about Dad — he's fine too. It's just that … his deployment got extended. By three months." I brace myself for his reaction.

Rory pops another handful of chips in his mouth and says, "I know."

"What do you mean, 'I know'? And don't talk with your mouth full. I raised you better than that."

He finishes chewing, and without an ounce of guilt says, "I sat at the top of the stairs when Gen. Lewis and his wife came over the other night. I heard the whole conversation."

"That's rude Rory. It's not nice to eavesdrop."

"I know. But I figured it had to be something important if Dad's CO is showing up at our house."

"Well, don't eavesdrop anymore, okay? If you were that curious you could have just asked me about it after they left and I would have told you."

"Okay. So, can I see that email you wrote to Dad — the one you showed the Lewises?"

"Mmmm, I don't think so."

"Oh come on Mom!"

"Maybe another time. I need to call your brother and tell him about Dad."

"Finn already knows. I called him after Gen. and Mrs. Lewis left. I filled him in on everything while you and Fakhir were talking in the kitchen."

"What the hell Rory?"

"It's fine mom. Finn is cool with it. He knows it's not Dad's fault his deployment got extended."

"Well. You guys are taking the news much better than I did," I say, looking down at my hands folded in my lap. I'm feeling pretty stupid right about now. Our sons are being more mature about the situation than their own mother. A teardrop falls from my lashes and lands on my jeans.

Rory leans over to put his arms around me. "We'll be okay Mom. We can do hard things, remember?"

"I remember," I say as I hug him back. "I used to say that to you guys when you were little. You're right. We can do hard things."

Saturday, September 27, 2008   8:36 p.m.

Thanks for the email. Now that I'm over the shock of your deployment getting extended, I can at least breathe easier knowing you've returned from Ramadi and are safely back at the base — for the time being. Life is a little less scary when I know you're on Camp Victory. (Even if you do get called a Fobbit for it — fuck those guys and the horses they rode in on).

It also helped that I went to yoga this morning. I keep saying this, but I really want to try to get there more regularly. I'm going to need to be in top mental and physical condition to last an extra three months without you.

Portia stopped me on my way out of class to ask how Wade is doing and to tell me she's starting a yoga class for veterans.

"He's doing real well. Likes his job a lot and might even get a promotion soon," I tell her.

"Wow. That's good to hear," she says. "Is he still coming back on weekends? I'm starting a class for veterans on Saturdays and thought he might like to come."

"I'll let him know," I reply. I don't have the heart to tell her Wade said he's giving up on yoga and taking up running instead. "That's great you're doing a class for vets," I continue. "I can totally see how yoga would help people dealing with PTSD." I nod encouragingly.

"It's PTS," she quickly corrects me. "We like to leave off the 'disorder' part. It's less stigmatizing."

It appears Portia has suddenly become an expert on this stuff. "That makes sense," I reply, shifting my weight from one leg to the other.

"We'll be focusing on mindful resilience. Things like self-regulation strategies to help class members cope with anxiety and other symptoms of post-traumatic stress," she explains.

"Wow. That sounds awesome. I'll be sure to mention it to Wade." I'm being sincere when I tell Portia the class sounds awesome. On that last part, I'm not exactly sure I'll be talking to Wade about it. The last few times I've mentioned yoga or anything related to Portia, he changes the subject. I know how to take a hint, even if Portia doesn't.

In other news, Fakhir found an apartment he likes and put down a security deposit today. He's moving in next weekend. It's just a few miles from here, so he won't be far. (This is me trying not to be sad about Fakhir moving out.)

He and Lucia went out to celebrate tonight. They're going to Peroni's for pizza and to the movies to see "Tropic Thunder." I guess you could say this is their first official date since they went public with their romance. Lucia looked gorgeous — her hair and makeup were perfect, and her new leopard-print blouse looked darling with black leggings and platform sandals. Fakhir was acting all formal and everything, opening the door for her and telling her how nice she looked. Those two are adorable.

I wonder … when Fakhir gets his own place, will Lucia start spending the night there? And if so, is it any of my business? This is all so confusing. I should give Raquel a call to see what their expectations are. Just to make sure we're all on the same page.

Rory and Josh are out on the back porch having a sleepover. They set up an air mattress out there and last time I checked they were playing electronic Battleship. I'm up in our room getting ready to watch "The Night of the Hunter" with Robert Mitchum and Shelley Winters. I've told you before how the Robert Mitchum character scares the hell out of me. He reminds me of my step-father Francis. That scene where the Reverend is chasing down Pearl and her brother reminds me of the time John and I hid in the laundry closet for several hours when Francis thought we'd been playing in his office and broke one of his ceramic clown figurines (we were, and we did). Thank God our mom was nothing like the Shelley Winters character in the movie. When Mom came home and found John and me hiding underneath the dirty laundry she told Francis to "back the fuck off." (God I miss my mom! How I wish I could pick up the phone and call her, especially during these long nights without you.) Back to the movie, rumor has it that when Robert Mitchum was auditioning for the part of the Reverend, the director explained the character as a "diabolical shit." Robert Mitchum raised his hand and said "Present!"

Sunday, September 28, 2008   1:08 p.m.

I fell asleep with the TV on last night and didn't hear Fakhir and Lucia come back from their date. I also didn't hear any of the shenanigans being perpetrated in the dark of night by Rory and Josh, which I found out about at breakfast this morning.

Rory, Josh, Fakhir, and I were sitting at the kitchen table drinking coffee and eating bagels and cream cheese. Fakhir was telling us about

"Tropic Thunder" when Lucia shouted something unintelligible from upstairs.

Rory yells back, "What?! We can't hear you! Come downstairs and talk to us."

Lucia tromps down the stairs and into the kitchen wearing her robe and slippers. "Has anyone seen my hair straightener? I can't find it."

"Did you look in the cabinet under your sink?" I ask.

"Yeah. That's where I usually keep it, but it's not there. I've looked everywhere."

Fakhir says, "Is it under one of the many piles of clothes on your floor?"

"Haha. Very funny. But no — I checked," she replies.

I glance over at Rory and Josh, who've been looking studiously at their bagels ever since Lucia came into the kitchen. Lucia's eyes follow mine and come to rest on the two of them. "Do you guys know where my hair straightener is?" she asks.

They shake their heads vigorously, eyes wide, lips suggesting the slightest hint of a smile. "No," they say in unison.

Lucia tilts her head. "Then what's so funny?"

"Nothing," Rory says. Josh is back to studying his bagel.

"Are you sure you didn't borrow it for some reason?" she asks, folding her arms. "Maybe you guys had a little pube-straightening party during your sleepover last night?"

"Eww, gross!" Josh says, finally taking his eyes off his bagel.

Rory says, "Real funny Lucia. But, no — we didn't borrow your hair straightener."

Fakhir pours more half 'n half in his coffee and says to Lucia, "Well if it makes any difference, I like your hair just the way it is."

Her expression softens. "Thanks."

"Well, it's gotta be around here somewhere," I say. "I'm sure it'll show up soon."

Lucia gives one last look to Rory and Josh, then turns on her heel to go back upstairs and finish getting dressed.

Meanwhile Rory and Josh have both taken gigantic bites of their bagels, appearing to chew with extreme pleasure.

Fakhir and I exchange glances, curious what those two are up to.

We find out soon enough a few minutes later when Lucia comes tromping down the stairs again, this time more loudly. She turns the corner and stops in the middle of the kitchen, hair straightener in hand, and stares directly at Rory. "What was my hair straightener doing in the middle of my bed, underneath the comforter?"

Rory swallows the last of his bagel and leans back in his chair, a mischievous gleam in his eye. "Oh … that's right," he says, as if suddenly remembering something.

Lucia is not amused. "I'm waiting."

Rory looks at Josh, then back to Lucia. "Josh and I put it there last night before you and Fakhir got home from your date."

Lucia figures out where this is going long before Fakhir and I do. "You little shits," she says.

Rory smiles widely, no longer able to contain himself. Josh covers his mouth with his hand, trying not to snicker.

"What's going on?" Fakhir asks, looking from Lucia to the boys, and then to me.

"Don't look at me," I say. "I'm as confused as you are." I turn to Rory and Josh. "Guys. Explain yourselves please. Why in the world would you put Lucia's hair straightener in her bed?"

Rory takes a deep, satisfied breath. With his eyes on Lucia he says, "I'm not saying you didn't sleep in your bed last night. It's just that, if you *did* sleep in your bed, you would've known where your hair straightener was."

It finally dawns on Fakhir and me what's going on. Our eyes meet; he offers me a sheepish look. As for Lucia, she glowers at Rory, her neck mottled with red splotches. "Fuck you, you little jackwagon!" She turns to run back upstairs, but not before flipping Rory the bird.

I rest my chin in my hand, not sure if I should laugh or cry.

Fakhir looks at Josh and Rory, shaking his head. "I should have known you guys were up to something. I can read you two like the back of my book."

Rory pulls the Book of Fakhir and a pencil out of his jeans pocket. "You mean, 'you *know* us like the back of your *hand*,'" he says, jotting down Fakhir's latest fux pux.

"I think he meant he can read you two like a book," I offer.

Fakhir replies, "Either way. I guess the joke's on me and Lucia." He looks at me apologetically. "I'm sorry. That was not good judgment on our part."

"It's all right Fakhir," I say, shaking my head. "I should've seen this coming. It's kind of an old joke around here. Except the original version involves a priest and a maid and a serving spoon." I turn my attention to Rory. "You think you're real funny, doncha?"

Looking immensely pleased with himself, he wisely chooses not to respond.

"Go upstairs and apologize to Lucia," I say.

Rory obediently slides out from the table and heads toward the stairs.

"And no more shenanigans please," I call out after him.

Rory turns to look at me, fingers pointing toward his chest. "*I'm* the one who's being called out for shenanigans?"

Josh slouches further down in his chair, looking at no one in particular.

Once Rory is out of sight, I catch Fakhir's eye, and smile sympathetically. "I bet you feel like next weekend can't get here soon enough," I say, referring to his move-out day.

This makes him smile.

"Hey. I have an idea," I say. "Would you be interested in a roommate?"

Fakhir pulls his head back in surprise. "Emilie, I love Lucia a lot but we're not ready to move in together," he explains.

"No, dumbass. I'm talking about me. I come live with you, and the rest of these jokesters can stay here."

Fakhir laughs.

"You think I'm kidding?"

Monday, September 29, 2008   7:09 p.m.

Did I just see you on CNN? Could it possibly have been your face in the crowd of Marines standing behind Gen. Kelly? I just happened to turn on the TV while folding laundry in the family room after dinner. They were doing a news story about the handover of Anbar Province back to the Iraqis, and they showed Gen. Kelly sitting at a table with the governor of Anbar signing some papers. There was a brief shot of the Marines standing behind the general and I swear one of them was you. I screamed for Rory to come downstairs and he came tearing into the family room but the camera panned away and they didn't show the crowd again. I'm keeping the TV on the rest of the night to see if they rerun the clip, but so far they haven't. (Damn those news stations. They play shit over and over again until you're ready to stab yourself in the neck with a pencil, and then the one time you actually want them to replay something, they don't. Bastards.)

Was it you? If so I can see why you've been so busy lately and we haven't heard from you much. It's a pretty big deal, handing Anbar Province back to the Iraqis, right? I read something in the paper about Iraq's parliament working on their constitution and laws for provincial elections. Won't that be wonderful when Iraqi citizens are able to vote in a real election?

Seeing (what looked like) your face on the TV among a sea of desert cammies reminded me of the time I was driving to the commissary on Quantico and I saw you running along the road in your green silkies. I leaned my head out the window as I drove up behind you and called out "Nice ass!" A buff Marine (who, to my eternal embarrassment, was not you) turned to look at me, a huge smile on his face, and replied, "Thanks Mrs. Mahoney!"

Note to new military spouses: If you're driving on base during lunch hour and you see a muscular guy with a high and tight wearing teeny weeny green running shorts, wait until you can actually see his face before engaging in commentary on his physique.

I miss you so much Liam. You and your green silkies.

p.s. One thing that bothered me about the news clip — none of the Marines were wearing helmets or body armor or carrying weapons. Isn't that unsafe? I mean I know things are supposed to be more peaceful in Anbar these days but Hell's bells. Marines (including a general) walking around outside in the middle of Iraq and nobody has a goddamn gun?

I thought you told me you guys always wore full battle rattle when you were outside the wire?

Tuesday, September 30, 2008   11:10 p.m.

Good news! Fakhir received his appointment notice for his naturalization interview. He's scheduled to go to the immigration office downtown on October 14th. He said he's not nervous — he's more than ready to get the interview over with. If it were me I'd be a wreck! At some point after the interview he'll take the English & Civics test, and hopefully after that he'll get his invitation to a naturalization ceremony. By then I hope Arifah and Farah have made it to the U.S. so they can see him take the oath.

Rory and I went to Woolley's tonight for cheddar burgers. I wanted to talk to him about the prank he and Josh pulled on Lucia and Fakhir the other night.

"You know, Rory, that was kind of an uncouth thing you did with Lucia's hair straightener."

I watch as he intently spreads mustard on his hamburger bun, making sure the mustard covers every last edge. "When did you pick up Fakhir's obsessively neat eating habits?" I ask. "Wasn't it just last week you were talking with a mouthful of potato chips?"

"Thanks Mom." He carefully places the bun back on the burger and slices the burger in half with his knife. That is definitely a Fakhir move.

"So, what drove you to pull that trick on them?" I ask. "I thought everything between you and Lucia was fine?"

"I know Mom. It was stupid. I didn't think it would upset her as much as it did. I apologized to her and we talked it out. I told her it's probably because I'm upset about Dad's deployment getting extended and I must have been taking it out on her and Fakhir." He carefully bites into his burger, chewing with his mouth closed this time.

I finish salting my fries and set the shaker down. "You told me you weren't upset about Dad's deployment getting extended."

He actually swallows his food before answering. "I didn't think I was. And then Finn and I were talking about it on the phone the other night and I realized if Dad isn't coming home until April, he's going to miss my entire hockey season."

"Aww. I hadn't thought of that. I'm sorry Rory."

"It's okay. Finn said he'd come home from Chicago some extra weekends so he can watch me play."

These guys. They're growing up so fast.

I grab Rory's hand across the table and give it a squeeze. "Say, how about if we order vanilla malts for dessert?"

Wednesday, October 1, 2008   9:36 p.m.

Before I left for work this morning I found another anonymous gift on our front porch — a lovely statue of a garden faerie, with a note taped on one of its wings that said, "You are capable." Who would know that's exactly the thing I needed to hear today? You think maybe it was Tammy? I didn't mention anything to her at book club about your deployment getting extended — it didn't seem like the right time since she was telling me about Ken getting deployed to Afghanistan. But do you think she heard about it from Ken and decided to leave a little something to cheer me up? It seems like something she would do. Or do you think Wanda left it, as a sort of apology for cheating at Words With Friends? That would be nice, except even if it was her who left the gift, I'm still not going to accept any more of her game invites. It seems trivial, but like my mom always said, it's the small things that reveal a person's character.

While I was glued to the TV the other night trying to catch another glimpse of you, the news reports were mostly about the stock market crash, which I'm sure you've heard about by now. (Unless you're out on another bivouac you forgot to tell me about.) The Dow fell by more than 700 points Monday which is pretty fuckin' scary if you ask me. Thank God most of your TSP is in the G Fund. (Aren't you glad I talked you out of putting it all in one of the L Funds?) The Labor Department keeps reporting thousands of job losses every month and boy howdy am I glad Wade got locked in with a good company. From what I've read in the paper, Mondo isn't suffering like most companies in the private sector. I've said it before and I'll say it again Liam, it's times like these I'm thankful you're in the Marines. Even if they do act like a bunch of fuckity-fuck McFuckers sometimes.

Semper Gumby.

Thursday, October 2, 2008   6:58 p.m.

So it *was* you on CNN the other night. What an experience that must have been! And I'm glad to know there was security in place; we just couldn't see it on TV. While you were standing behind Gen. Kelly I don't suppose you whispered something in his ear about shaving those extra three months off your deployment? No? Didn't think so.

I had a rather resourceful student in ISS today. The incident report cited Cooper for "engaging in unauthorized business transactions on school property." I was surprised he didn't get an OSS for dealing weed at school but when I asked him about it at lunchtime he laid it all out for me. Turns out he was selling ice cold Dr. Pepper and Mountain Dew out of his locker for a buck a pop. Cooper showed me a photo on his phone of the inside of his locker (this was before he got busted). He had ingeniously outfitted his entire locker with insulated liner (like the kind you would find in a shipping box for perishables). And then he installed wire shelving units he got from the Container Store. He'd buy the 35-packs of soda from Sam's Club for around ten bucks a case (which comes out to less than 30 cents per can), and then turn around and sell them in between class periods for a dollar.

The administration started to get suspicious when they noticed the crowds of kids at Cooper's locker throughout the day. So yesterday Officer Dempsey brought in the drug-sniffing dog and — haha! — the dog finds nothing but a lockerful of cold Mountain Dews and Dr. Peppers. Damn I wish I could've been there and seen their faces when they opened Cooper's locker. So that explains why he got ISS instead of

OSS—he wasn't selling anything illegal per se, but Dr. Gouwens said it's against school rules to turn your locker into a mini-mart, even if it is just pop. Cooper is a junior this year and tells me he'll be applying to Harvard Business School next fall. God I love my job sometimes.

Friday, October 3, 2008   11:10 p.m.

General Lewis' wife Virginia called last night. She was wondering if I'd be interested in heading up a committee in charge of revamping the way the spouse phone tree works. I like Mrs. Lewis but man, you know how much I hate this committee crap.

Does the military brass honestly think spouses don't have enough to do already without asking us to organize phone trees and key spouse networks and shit like that? I mean, if a spouse *enjoys* that sort of thing, by all means have at it. Obviously the spouses who volunteer their time to the unit are much better human beings than I am. Because, we all have the same 24 hours in the day, right? We all have to deal with PCS moves and deployments and raising kids and trying to have careers of our own. And yet, here I am. The spouse who can't even embrace the suck.

Why am I such a dilligaf when it comes to this stuff? Why does the idea of serving on some stupid-ass committee keep me awake half the night, brooding on it until my stomach gets so churned up I have to get out of bed and pop a handful of berry-flavored Chewy Tums before I can finally fall asleep?

I thought I'd gotten myself squared away after I wrote the email of fucks and came to terms with your deployment being extended. Maybe my state of mind is more precarious than I realized. A phone call from Mrs. Lewis should not push me over the edge this way. It's just a phone call. Why am I so stressed about it?

Am I going to get you fired if I say no? Is this one of those situations where I'm being voluntold? If it's important to you that I do it, Liam, just say the word and you know I will.

Saturday, October 4, 2008   4:48 p.m.

Fakhir moved out today. Send potato chips.

Sunday, October 5, 2008   12:09 p.m.

Thanks for your email. I knew you'd tell me it was fine not to do the committee if I didn't want to. And I know you genuinely mean it. But sometimes I worry I'm holding back your career by not being more involved in the unit. I know there are other spouses who are less involved than I am (if that's even possible — Tammy comes to mind; I thank my lucky stars for her). And you've assured me their husbands' careers haven't suffered for it. And yet, I wonder.

Speaking of Tammy, she and I enjoyed some unexpected bonding time last night. Apparently Fakhir noticed how stressed I've been lately and decided I needed a break. After we helped him move yesterday (and without telling me), he called Tammy and suggested she and I have a girls night out.

She and Ken showed up at the house just as I was getting ready to pop a frozen pizza in the oven for Rory and me. Tammy announced she was taking me out for Mexican and Rory could have the pizza all to himself. I protested somewhat because I was still wearing the clothes I had on when we helped Fakhir move. Tammy gave me enough time to run upstairs, brush my teeth, and swap out my grimy sweatshirt for a clean top.

Ken dropped us off at Manuel's, saying he'd be back to pick us up later. I asked if he wanted to join us for dinner but he said it was girls only, and besides, he had to get back home to fix dinner for the kids.

Tammy and I enjoyed a few margaritas — well, more than a few — over chips and salsa. She told me how the family is dealing with Ken's upcoming deployment to Afghanistan. She said the boys have been asking a lot of questions but overall they seem to be taking it pretty well. (Ha. I'll be sure to check in with her a few weeks after Ken leaves. By then the

Deployment Curse will have kicked in to full gear.) On the plus side, this isn't their first rodeo. Ken was in Bosnia for six months before the boys were born. And Tammy says he's also been to Eritrea and Djibouti. Now they can add Afghanistan to the list.

As we split a large order of deluxe nachos and polished off our first pitcher of margaritas, I recounted for Tammy everything that's been going on at our house lately, culminating in the email of fucks. Which she of course found hilarious. She asked to see the email on my phone and, by the time we were halfway through our second pitcher of margaritas, we were taking turns doing dramatic readings of the email as we sat across from one another in the booth. We tried keeping our voices down but—you know how it is—the more you try to be quiet, the funnier everything becomes.

Evidently we caused a small stir, and when the servers brought us our sopapillas, they "accidentally" took our pitcher of margaritas away before we we could finish it. (This is the same Mexican restaurant where I picked up Wade back in February—which seems like eons ago. Nonetheless I got the feeling the staff remembered me.) Tammy and I were laughing so hard she about split her white jeans and I think at one point I might have even peed my pants a little.

Luckily Ken showed up before we caused too much of a ruckus. On the way home Tammy and I flopped around in the backseat, laughing our asses off while Tammy insisted on reading the email aloud to Ken, who tried his best to stay focused on the road with two drunk females rolling around in the back of his vehicle. Tammy and I also decided we are best friends and why didn't we realize that sooner? Before I got out of the car I thanked Ken for being our DD. I also informed him that I did not think he was an asshole, even if everybody else at the unit says he is.

Fakhir happened to be at the house picking up Lucia (Rory had gone to Josh's house, thank goodness) and so they came out to the car to help me in the house and put me to bed. When they were tucking me in I told Lucia I love her even though she's a slob and a bed hog, and I told Fakhir I love him too even if he talks funny sometimes. Be prepared for the rumors to start flying in the likely event Agnes was watching last night's activities unfold from her living room window.

Better get going. I'm meeting Mrs. Lewis for coffee at one o'clock and I need to jump in the shower. I hope it will sober me up some — I'm still feeling a little woozy. Is it possible to be drunk and hungover at the same time?

p.s. While we were at the restaurant I tried my damnedest to get Tammy to fess up that she's the one who's been leaving the anonymous gifts on our doorstep. She swore it isn't her. Not sure if I believe her.

Monday, October 6, 2008   7:47 p.m.

The dinner table felt empty tonight without Fakhir here to eat with us. Thankfully Lucia kept Rory and me distracted with chitchat about her cosmetology classes and what's been going on at the salon lately. She completed her 150 hours of basics (shampooing, sanitation, etc.) and is well on her way through the required hours for haircuts, color, and chemical treatments.

The salon legally can't let her start cutting clients' hair yet, but she is earning some credit hours for the work she does there. She also told us she finished paying for her supplies last month. Now that she's got a little extra income, she said she wanted to give some of it to her parents, but they are adamant she put it in a savings account. Carmen is still looking for work unfortunately, and with the economy the way it is, it might be a while before he finds something.

My coffee with Mrs. Lewis yesterday went extremely well. More on that in a sec. Guess who's working at Fidelia's now? Eugene! He was at the register when I ordered my latte. He seemed embarrassed at first — it wasn't just two months ago he was a bank vice president, and now he's a barista in training (most likely filling Finn's old position). I congratulated him on the new job, and told him he's going to love working at Fidelia's. He said he's enjoying it so far, and that it feels good to be working again. Props to him. If he's working there full-time he'll be able to get on their health insurance plan — better than paying COBRA premiums. I really do need to call and check in on Agnes one of these days.

Mrs. Lewis found me at my usual table in back near the window (the one where Agnes and I like to sit). As she set down her double-chocolate Frappuccino with extra whip (I happened to hear the barista call it out when she picked it up), I stood up to greet her. "Hi Mrs. Lewis."

"Oh please Emilie, sit down. And call me Virginia." She slings her purse over the back of her chair and slides into her seat. "So. I heard you and Tammy had quite a night on the town last night." She smiles at me over her Frappuccino.

"Geez, that sure got around fast," I reply, glancing down at my lap. My face suddenly feels hot.

"You know how the folks on base love to talk," she says, eyeing me with amusement. "They think 'Tell It to the Marines' is a call to action."

I can't help but smile. "So how'd you hear about it?" I ask, more than a little curious.

"Oh — Gerald had to go into the office earlier today and the duty sergeant mentioned it." She swirls her straw through the huge mound of whipped cream, mixing it in with the rest of her drink.

"And the duty sergeant heard about it because … ?"

"Well, according to Gerald, Sgt. James ran into his neighbor, Cpl. Roberts, when they were both outside getting their papers this morning. And Cpl. Roberts told Sgt. James that he had taken his wife to Manuel's last night for her birthday. Cpl. Roberts said they saw you and Tammy there. And that the waiters had to take away your second pitcher of margaritas." Mrs. Lewis leans back in her chair, her smile growing wider.

"Oh great. So I suppose Gen. Lewis thinks Tammy and I are delinquents now."

"Don't be silly. Gerald adores you Emilie."

"Really?" (I notice she doesn't say anything about Tammy here.)

"Of course. He thinks very highly of you and Liam. Ever since we met you two back in Quantico — when Liam was Gerald's Chief of Staff.

"Gosh that seems like ages ago."

"Tell me about it," she replies. "But it was only — what — eight years ago?

"Yeah, I think so ..." I gaze up at the ceiling, doing the calculations in my head. "So for us that would've been after Great Lakes and before Yuma."

"Isn't it funny how we divide our lives into segments, depending on where we were stationed at the time?"

"Oh God — I thought I was the only weirdo who did that." I take a sip of my latte, wondering when she's going to bring up the committee thing.

As if reading my mind, she says, "So. About this phone tree committee. The way it's set up now isn't really working. If one spouse doesn't pick up or get the message, no one else down the chain gets a call. And sometimes even if they do get the message, they forget to call the next person in line, and the whole system breaks down. We need to figure out a foolproof way to get everybody in the loop when there's important intel to be shared among the spouses."

"Would email work?" I ask half-heartedly, not wanting to get sucked in before it's too late.

"I mentioned that to Gerald. He knows that's probably the direction things are going eventually, but right now he's not ready to go that route. Too easy for people to forward sensitive information outside the unit."

"I understand." I nod my head slowly, feigning interest.

"So we've decided to form a committee to brainstorm ideas on the best way to reach as many spouses as possible. And —" Mrs. Lewis pauses, searching my face. She sets down her extra-whip Frappuccino. "Emilie, I hope you don't mind me saying this, but you look like a deer caught in the headlights right now." She picks up her drink and puckers her lips for a nice long sip.

"I do?" I match her sip-for-sip with my half-skim latte.

"Yeah. I kind of figured you wouldn't be thrilled about the idea of serving on a committee. To be honest, Gerald is the one who put me up to this. He's been worried about you, what with Liam's deployment getting extended. He thought you might be bored and need something to do."

Upon hearing this last comment I practically choke on my coffee.

"I know, right?" She leans in toward me as I attempt to compose myself. "These guys, they mean well, but they just don't get it." She continues, her voice softening. "I've been where you are Emilie. I know what it's like. You wake up in the morning and wonder how you can possibly make it through another day. And somehow you do, but that doesn't stop you from waking up the next morning and wondering the same thing all over again. And every morning after that. Until they come home."

She holds my gaze with her hazel eyes, and I will myself not to look away. To be seen so clearly by another human being is both exhilarating and excruciating. I search for something profound to say, yet all I manage to come up with is, "You're good at this."

She laughs. "So I've been told." Turning serious again, she says, "Listen. It's not a problem if you don't want to do this committee thing. Jerri Jablonski has been chomping at the bit to be in charge of it ever since it came up at the last FSG meeting, so it's not like it won't get taken care of."

"I appreciate that Mrs. Lewis."

"Emilie. Will you *puhlease* stop calling me Mrs. Lewis."

"Okay, I'm sorry. Thank you … Virginia. Also, I want to apologize for not coming to any of the FSG meetings lately. What with Finn leaving for college, and Rory's hockey season starting up, and me going back to work and everything—"

"Emilie." She's looking at me rather sternly now. "You've gotta stop apologizing for everything. You don't owe me—or anybody—an explanation. Those meetings are in no way mandatory. Some of the spouses find them helpful, while others find it more useful to focus on other things. I only want you to come if they help ease your stress, not make it worse."

"Thank you for that. It means a lot to me."

"And besides, you think we don't know how much you do for other people? You may not be out front all the time like Jerri Jablonski, but Gerald and I are well aware of the work you do behind the scenes. Like the way you support Maj. Miller and his wife. And how you've befriended Leah Gibson, while her husband's away at sniper school. And that girl from the high school you took in last spring. Not to mention

Mr. al-Azzawi, the interpreter who did so much for our Marines in Iraq. Believe me, Emilie, your good works have not gone unnoticed."

"Oh, they've all helped me, much more than I've helped any of them," I reply, trying to quell the lump in my throat. "I don't know how the boys and I would've made it this far into Liam's deployment without each and every one of them."

"Which reminds me," Virginia says, adopting a more business-like attitude. "Tell me what Gerald and I can do for *you*. What do you need from us, Emilie?"

"Honestly, what you've told me today is all I needed to hear. I feel so much better after talking to you. I admit I was beginning to second guess myself, feeling like a jerk for not wanting to take on the committee when you told me about it on the phone the other night."

"I totally get it," she says before polishing off the rest of her Frappuccino. Then, "Do you think I actually enjoy all those functions I have to attend with Gerald? Especially when the kids were younger — I'd much rather be at home with them than going to yet another 'mandatory fun' event."

I can feel the tension leaving my shoulders. "It's good to know I'm not the only one who hates those things," I reply. "I guess I assumed since Gen. Lewis is the CO that you guys liked that sort of stuff."

She laughs. "We just happen to be better than most at pretending we're having fun. Now seriously Emilie — what can we do to make your life easier until Liam comes home?"

"I can't think of anything right now. But I promise to let you know if something comes up." I take the last sip of my latte. "I do have one question though . . ."

"Of course," she replies. "Ask me anything."

"How the hell can you drink double-chocolate Frappuccinos — with extra whip — and keep that gorgeous figure of yours?"

Tuesday, October 7, 2008   8:39 p.m.

I read that the Polish troops held a ceremony at Camp Echo, marking the end of their mission in Iraq. Did you happen to travel there for that?

It was just a small item in the back of the paper. But you know how I scour the International section every night, searching for hints of what you might be doing and where you may be traveling. Do you think you'll be able to call this weekend? It's been a while. I miss your voice.

Looks like the temperatures in Baghdad are cooling off a bit—with a high of 91 yesterday, getting down to the 60s at night. Funny how 90 degrees is considered moderate over there. Things here have cooled off substantially. No more short-sleeves for me. Of course all the kids are still wearing shorts to school, including Rory. It will probably take a blizzard for the high schoolers to switch over to jeans. And maybe not even then.

On my way home from work tonight I saw hundreds of swallows lining the telephone wires at the intersection by the school. Probably planning their migration route in between stuffing themselves on insects for the journey. Agnes finally pulled out all her sunflower stalks. I already miss the hummingbirds and butterflies. And yet—I look forward to the leaves turning from yellow and orange to red. With fall here, we're one season closer to you coming home.

Wednesday, October 8, 2008   10:06 a.m.

Finn called this morning before I left for work. He already ran out of his allowance that was supposed to last until Friday. He asked if he could have his money a few days early. I said no. He said he doesn't have any money to buy food and he's going to starve. I asked him if he had any of those crackers left from when we went to Trader Joe's and he said yes. I told him to eat those, because he's not getting any more money until Friday.

Did I do the right thing Liam? I feel so mean. I want so bad to call him back and say I'll put the money in the account. But if I do that, he'll never learn to make his money last the full week. I warned him about this before I left Chicago—I specifically said we will not make exceptions to the weekly deposit schedule, and if he runs out of money before that he's SOL.

It would be easier if the school had a meal plan and a cafeteria like a normal college. Then we wouldn't have to worry about a weekly food budget. How I wish I could talk to you about this.

Am I a horrible mother?

11:14 p.m.

Dottie called tonight. I had called her last night to find out how Joey's been doing lately but he was hovering nearby and she couldn't talk. So she called me back tonight while he was at his VFW meeting.

Dottie says she thinks Joey is falling into a depression. In addition to his sleep problems, his tinnitus has come back with a vengeance. She says he had it pretty bad after the war—a constant, high-pitched ringing. After he got his job at the Railroad Administration, it seemed to improve. They say that can happen sometimes.

"Of course back then they just called it 'ringing in the ears,'" Dottie explains. "But that was the least of his worries after he came back from his last tour. That was when he was in the hospital recovering from Post-Vietnam Syndrome or whatever the hell label they were using at the time."

"How long was he in the hospital for?" I ask.

"He told me several months," she replies. "And that was also when he found out his ex-wife left him. He got the divorce papers from Louise while he was lying in his hospital bed."

"Oh my gosh. That's awful Dottie."

"Yeah. Louise was a real horse's petute."

This makes me laugh. "So getting back to Joey's tinnitus ... what's the story with that?" I ask.

"Well in those days it wasn't rated as service-connected. Damn bucket heads. But now they know all these guys' hearing problems are from noise exposure. In Joey's case it was because he spent so much time in the cargo hold of a C-130, which is even louder than most aircraft. And they weren't big on ear protection in those days either. The Air Force supposedly started issuing earplugs at some point but the guys didn't like wearing them. Made it too hard for them to hear each other. Joey said by the time he got out in '77 more people were using them. But by then the war was over and for Joey, the damage was done."

"Has he been back to the doctor since the ringing started up again?"

"As a matter of fact he's been to see his PCM a couple times lately," she replies. "At first it was for his sleep problems. The doc gave him Ambien but Joey refuses to take it. Says it makes him feel groggy the next day."

Upon hearing the word "Ambien" I can't help but recall Finn's senior prom misadventure. Hard to believe that was only five months ago. It seems so far away now.

"And now that he went back in for the tinnitus," Dottie continues, "they're working with the VA on getting him a disability rating. God knows how long that'll take. Not that it matters much. He doesn't care about the money. He just wants the ringing to stop."

"Why do you think it came back all of a sudden after all these years?" I ask.

"They say it can be stress-related, and I certainly think that's part of it," she says. "He just can't seem to find his footing since he retired back in April. It's like he doesn't know what to do with himself Emilie. That's why I'm sending him back to the doctor next week to talk about his depression symptoms. It's all related as far as I'm concerned."

"I'm sure you're right Dottie. I'm sorry you guys have to deal with this. Joey is such a positive, cheerful person. You'd never know he was suffering inside."

"If I didn't live with him I might not even realize it myself," she replies. "But it's the little things, you know? Like I notice he's been having trouble concentrating lately. He and I like to read before bed, and I've seen him stare at the same page for 30 minutes. I don't think his bookmark has moved in two weeks. And his appetite isn't what it used to be. You know what a huge eater he is. He won't let me see the scale but I'd bet he's lost fifteen pounds."

"It must be hard for you, seeing him go through this."

"I hate to complain, Emilie. He's so good to me. But … he's also been kind of irritable lately, which is unusual for Joey. Like the other night he chastised me for sucking on a mint too loudly while we were sitting on the couch together watching 'American Idol.' And by the way, I think the media is being way too hard on that Hernandez boy for having worked as a stripper at a gay night club. He's got a lovely voice and that physique of his, well, I wouldn't kick him out of bed for eating crackers."

"Dottie!"

"I'm just sayin'. No need to get your knickers in a knot."

"Okay. Listen, I gotta go — the dogs are barking like crazy. Must be a raccoon outside. I'll call you again next week to see how Joey's appointment went. I love you Dottie. Joey too."

Thursday, October 9, 2008   10:55 p.m.

I'm glad you have my back on this thing with Finn. (And also that you don't think I'm a horrible mother — thanks for that.) We need to stick together on this. I'm surprised Finn hasn't emailed you. Maybe he knows you can't transfer money from over there so there's no point in communicating with you. Speaking of which, when was the last time you heard from either of the boys? They should be emailing you more often.

I like your idea of switching Finn's allowance day from Friday to Sunday. That way, if we deposit his money on Sunday morning, he can go grocery shopping Sunday afternoon and plan his spending for the week ahead. It might also prevent him from blowing his entire allowance over the weekend since he won't be getting it on Friday. I'll call him tomorrow to explain the new system.

He hasn't called me again since yesterday, but he did text me a photo of his box of crackers next to a half-eaten jar of peanut butter. So at least I know he's not starving. No doubt he was hoping the photo would tug at my heart strings and prompt me to drop a few bucks in his account. To be honest, I was tempted. But I resisted. Instead I had myself a good cry. Damn, that kid drives me crazy sometimes. And yet, I miss him like crazy. You too.

I called Wade tonight to talk about Joey. I never had a chance to follow up with him after Labor Day weekend, when he said he was going to try to catch Joey alone at some point. Wade told me that when he and Fakhir and Joey made that Costco run for Finn's party, they did get into a conversation about post-traumatic stress. Wade shared a bit of the progress he's made with Greg, and Fakhir talked about how his job and Lucia help him keep his mind in the present. Joey confided that he misses the structure of going into the office every day, and how he's felt rudderless since retirement. He added how thankful he is to have Dottie in his life—that she's the center of his universe, the reason he gets out of bed every day. Wade says Joey didn't share anything other than that.

I don't know what Joey would do if something happened to Dottie. Thank God she's healthy as a horse. Did you know she takes zero medication, and that she walks three miles every morning before Joey wakes up? I hope I'm as fit as she is when I'm 75. (I guess that means I need to start exercising more than once a week.)

Wade promised me he'll reach out to Joey in the next week or so. He says he's been super busy with work, and—oh! Guess what? Wade got that promotion! He's now the warehouse supervisor, and his boss, Jenn, has been promoted to site leader. So he's even busier than he was before, but he also mentioned he got a nice little pay raise.

"Wow! So does that mean you guys could maybe sell the house in Buell City and Isabel and Chloe could move to Wakeville?" I ask.

"I wish it were that simple," he replies. "We're still underwater on our mortgage. I don't know if we'll ever be able to sell that ball and chain. Fucking mortgage lenders should've never loaned us that much money in the first place. What the hell were we thinking?"

"You had no idea the economy was going to take a nosedive, Wade. When you guys bought that house, the market was a lot different. Regular people like us didn't know the balloon was about to burst."

I silently give thanks that you and I bought below our means when we moved here. And that my mom taught me how to make a budget and stick to it. Still, we could have just as easily found ourselves in Wade and Isabel's shoes. Who knew real estate prices would start plummeting the way they have?

"Have you guys thought about renting that place?" I ask Wade. "You could put the money toward your mortgage payments, and then you and Isabel could rent a small apartment in Wakeville. Or maybe Mondo would even let the three of you stay in the corporate apartment for a while."

Wade sighs. "I'd like nothing better than that Emilie. I miss Isabel and Chloe so much during the week. It's great seeing them every weekend, but it's not enough. Chloe is growing up so fast. I swear she looks older every Friday when I come home. And I gotta tell ya, it feels like me and Isabel are growing apart lately. She's always so busy with work and her classes and Chloe. I know she's got a lot going on. But then when she does have free time, she's either out doing something with Leah or Leah is over at the house and Isabel says she can't talk very long."

"Aww, I'm sorry Wade. This is a suck-ass situation all around — for you, for Isabel, for Chloe. For Leah too. I can see why she'd want to stay overnight there. What with Cpl. Gibson being gone so long, I know she gets lonely on the nights she's not at work — "

"Wait. Back up a minute," Wade says. "Leah spent the night at our house? When was this?" he asks.

"A couple weeks ago. I texted her because she missed book club and she told me she and Isabel had a few too many mojitos so she decided to spend the night instead of driving home."

"A couple weeks ago, huh? Isabel never said anything to me about that."

"Wade, come on. It's not that big of a big deal."

"If it's not a big deal then why didn't Isabel tell me about it?"

"I'm sure she just forgot. Like you said, she's got more than a full plate right now what with work and classes and taking care of Chloe. I do know that Leah is a big help with Chloe, which I'm sure Isabel appreciates. So that's another reason Leah spends a lot of time over there."

"Like how much time does she spend over there?"

"I don't know Wade. That's something you should talk to Isabel about. You're not jealous of Leah are you?"

"No I'm not jealous. Why would I be jealous? It's just that there's a whole lotta things Isabel 'forgets' to tell me. Like when she decided to sign up for night classes a few months ago. And then a couple weeks ago, Chloe started standing up by herself. I didn't hear one word about it until several days later when I came home for the weekend. And now this thing with Leah spending the night. It's just stupid. It makes me feel like I'm not part of the family anymore."

"You guys really need to sit down and have a talk, Wade. You can't let this fester. You gotta get it out in the open. I'm sure you and Isabel can work through this if you just talk about it with her."

"I know," he says. "It just feels like I'm on deployment all over again. Like last time I was in Iraq and she bought Chesty from a breeder without telling me. I love Chesty but man, she blew three thousand fucking bucks on that dog! I would have been happy with a Heinz 57 from a shelter. But no, she has to go and buy a purebred. And then when I was in Afghanistan she went and bought all that living room furniture using my combat pay. I didn't hear a fucking word about that until I came home and walked in our living room and saw all the new shit she bought. Now I'm stuck in fucking Wakeville and geez I wonder what else she's not telling me."

"I'm sorry Wade. I thought you guys worked out a lot of this stuff in marriage counseling."

"We did!" I hear him take a deep breath and slowly exhale. "I think what is happening," he says in a more controlled voice, "is that we're both under a lot of stress right now. And some of the things that have happened recently are making me feel like the old problems are starting to crop up again."

"I can understand that. How about if I watch Chloe Saturday night when you come home this weekend, and you and Isabel can go out for a nice long dinner and talk things out."

"That would be great Emilie. I'll talk to Isabel and get back to you."

"Hang in there Wade. It's gonna be okay."

"Thanks Emilie. I hope you're right."

Friday, October 10, 2008   10:39 p.m.

Rory's hockey game tonight was so exciting Liam. I wish you could have been there. Rory came away with a goal and two assists. One of those passes was to Riikka, who scored her first goal of the season. Lucia and

Fakhir took them out for pizza to celebrate. They invited me to go but I decided to come home. It's been a long week and besides, "The Best Years of Our Lives" is on TCM at eleven.

I don't know how many times you and I have seen this movie, but every time I watch it I can't get over how on-point it still is. It could just as easily be the story of Iraq or Afghanistan vets coming home from the war as it is about World War II vets.

You know that scene where Al and Milly (played by Fredric March and Myrna Loy) are talking about marriage, and their daughter Peggy thinks her parents never had any trouble in their marriage? That's when the Myrna Loy character sets the daughter straight with a little spiel about all the squabbles she and Fredric March have had over the years. She ends the speech by looking at her husband and asking, "How many times have we had to fall in love all over again?"

It's been more than sixty years since that movie was made. Funny how the story of a military marriage never changes. Every time you leave and come back Liam, we fall in love all over again. It's not that we fall out of love when you go away. In fact sometimes when you're away I feel like I can't love you any more than I already do. Something about being so far apart for so long puts everything into sharper focus.

And you know what? It's not the big things I think about when you're away. It's all the little things that make my heart smile when I think of you. Even the annoying things. *Especially* the annoying things.

Like the way you blink at me when you're irritated. And the way you sometimes fall asleep while I'm trying to talk to you in bed at night. And that thing you do when we're alone in the kitchen together and I'm telling you a story about my day. You start putting dishes away or wiping at a stain on the counter or picking tufts of cat hair off the floor. And I have to follow you around the whole time I'm talking because you have all that nervous energy. Even now, I picture you reading this email at your desk and doing several other things at the same time—like listening in on a VTC, organizing your desk drawer, chewing on the end of a pencil, and jiggling your foot.

Remember that time when we were stationed at Great Lakes and I called you at work to tell you I'd gotten a promotion at my newspaper job, and while we were talking I could hear you typing in the background? (Turns out you were answering a work email while I was sharing my big news and, yeah, I'm still a little mad about that.)

To be fair, I am well aware of the looong list of things I do that annoy the hell out of you. Like when I ask you the same question three times in a row because I'm so deep in thought I don't remember asking the question twice before. So I ask the question a third time—and I still don't pay attention to your response because I'm already off in my own world again.

And then there's the thing that happens when we go see a movie together. I try to whisper something in your ear because I like guessing what's going to happen next and I want someone to know I had the whole movie figured out in the first thirty minutes. You stare straight ahead at the screen, not looking at me. But I can see your eyes start to blink real fast so I know you're super irritated with me. And then, just to make sure I know how annoyed you are, you swat at the air like there's a mosquito buzzing around your ear.

And how about those times I don't do a very good job washing out the blender after I make a smoothie? You come home from work and find all the gronklies in there and get all cranky with me about it and tell me I should take the thing apart when I wash it. But I never do, and you end up giving it a thorough scrub every night before you come to bed, so it's clean for me in the morning.

When you come home Liam, I'm going to try harder to pay attention to my own questions and not whisper to you during movies and maybe I'll even take apart the blender when I wash it ('cuz I'm certainly not doing that now). And in spite of all our flaws, we'll love each other just the same, or maybe even more.

Saturday, October 11, 2008   3:26 p.m.

I ran a few errands on base this morning. The PX had aviator sunglasses on sale so I picked up a couple pairs for the boys. I plan to hide them away until Christmas. Only problem is I can't use your footlocker in the garage anymore since Rory discovered I was hiding my chips in there. So I have to come up with a new hidey-hole. Any ideas? (Come to think of it, I still can't remember where I hid some of last year's Christmas gifts.)

When I came home from the PX I found a piece of paper stuck to the front door. Turns out we got another citation from the city! No, it wasn't for leaving the trash cans out too long like the one we got in February. This citation was for "excessive dog barking." With a $50 fine! What. the actual. fuck?

I called the number listed on the citation and got a recording since it's Saturday and the office is closed. The small print reads, "The city does not investigate or make a determination that a barking dog violation has occurred. Citations are based on a sworn affidavit signed by the complainant."

Well of course they didn't make a determination that excessive barking occurred because it didn't. Brig and Soda do not bark excessively! Okay, they bark at squirrels sometimes. But whenever they start with the crazy barking we immediately bring them in the house. And the other night, when I was on the phone with Dottie and the dogs were barking at what I thought might be a raccoon outside, both Brig and Soda were inside the house. They weren't even outside! So there's no way a neighbor could have heard them barking. Or if they did, it would have been muffled because there wasn't a single window open.

So now the question becomes which of our asshole neighbors went to the trouble of signing a fucking sworn affidavit for something that never even happened? And we're supposed to pay $50 based on nothing?! I am going to fight this, Liam. I'm sure the city won't tell me who the jackass is that filled out the complaint, but I will figure it out. They don't know who they're dealing with.

First person who comes to mind is Agnes. But I thought she and I were on friendly terms, especially since our last coffee together. Could she be mad at me for not getting in touch lately? I know it's been a couple months since we last met for coffee. But her fingers aren't broken — she can pick up the phone and invite me out if she wants to meet up. What about Ethan? Do you think he might be up to his old pranks again? No, I doubt the city would let a minor sign one of those complaints.

Next up would be Wanda. Or Vince. But it just doesn't seem like something either of them would do. And besides, they always say how much they love Soda and Brig ... I know! Do you think it might have been one of the Stevens? Ever since their kids lit off that M-80 in our bushes and Finn went over there and told them to knock it off, the parents pretend like they don't see us when we're out in the yard.

This is so fucking stupid. Why am I spending time even thinking about this? And whoever it was, why didn't they just come talk to us instead of filling out some stupid complaint? People are so mean sometimes.

Sunday, October 12, 2008   10:50 p.m.

Well, I babysat Chloe for Wade and Isabel last night and all I can say is what a weird night. Everything seemed fine when they dropped her off before dinner. Wade and Isabel were smiling and talkative, and they seemed excited about the prospect of a night out alone.

Chloe was shy at first when Isabel handed her over to me. That stung a little but I understand—Chloe hasn't seen me in a while and she's at that age when kids get separation anxiety. At least she didn't cry when they left. And once I got out Finn's old pound-a-peg (remember that?) it was just like old times. I also dug up Rory's Fisher-Price parking garage, and boy did she love that—I'm going to offer to let her keep it since it's bulky and we really don't need to keep moving it around with us every time we PCS. After she and I played on the floor a while, I fed Chloe dinner, gave her a bath, and changed her into her pajamas. We were reading *Hand Hand Fingers Thumb* together when Wade and Isabel came back a couple hours later.

"Oh hey, Chloe and I were just finishing up. How was dinner?" I ask as I get up from the couch and hand Chloe to Isabel.

Wade looks at me, his lips puckered to the side. Isabel smiles brightly, her eyes wide. "It was super fun. We went to Tony's for Italian."

"Fancy," I reply. "I love their chicken spiedini."

"Yeah, that's what Leah had," Isabel says.

"Leah had dinner with you guys?" I look from Isabel to Wade, but Wade is bent down not looking at me, picking up Chloe's things from the floor and putting them in the diaper bag.

"Yeah. She met us there," Isabel says nonchalantly, bouncing Chloe on her hip.

My eyes slide over in Wade's direction but he's still busying himself gathering up Chloe's stuff, avoiding eye contact. "Oh. I thought it was gonna be just the two of you," I reply.

"Well, that was the plan," she explains. "But then at the last minute I called Leah and told her to meet us over there. She hasn't been to a nice restaurant since before Jacob left and I thought it would be good for her to get out. It really lifted her spirits."

"I see."

Wade snaps the diaper bag shut and finally catches my eye. He looks upset.

"Well I'm happy to watch Chloe next weekend if you guys want to go out again," I offer. And before Isabel can reply I add, rather pointedly, "Just the two of you."

Wade says, "We'll take you up on that Emilie. Thanks." He looks at Isabel. "We'd better get going. She looks like she's getting sleepy and I don't want another scene like we had last night."

"What happened last night?" I ask. Normally I wouldn't pursue a comment like that but something in Wade's voice makes me think he brought it up for a reason.

"Oh nothing," Isabel waves her gelled nails in front of her face. "You know how one-year olds are."

"Chloe had a huge meltdown in the car on the way home from Chuck E. Cheese," Wade says. "And then once we got home it took us, like, an hour to get her to calm down, and another two hours to get her to finally fall asleep."

"She was just overtired," Isabel says.

"Right," Wade replies, locking eyes with Isabel. "So I want to get her home tonight before she reaches that point again."

"Hokay then," Isabel replies, raising her eyebrows and rolling her eyes at Wade.

"Don't patronize me Isabel," he says.

She shrugs. "I'm not patronizing you Wade."

"Yes. You are," he insists, glaring at her. "Just because I'm gone during the week doesn't mean I don't know how to anticipate the needs of my own daughter."

I make a motion toward the door. "I'll let you guys get going. Looks like Chloe might be getting fussy." Indeed, Chloe seems wide awake now as she squirms in Isabel's arms.

The two of them continue to stand there, trying to kill each other with their eyeballs, so I walk to the front door and open it.

Wade turns away from Isabel and follows me to the foyer, diaper bag in hand. "Right. Thanks for watching her Emilie. We really appreciate it." He steps through the doorway and pauses to look back at Isabel. "Are you coming?" he asks.

"Yes. I'm coming," she says, switching Chloe from one hip to the other as Chloe struggles against her. Isabel barely glances in my direction as she follows Wade out the door.

Well that was an endearing family vignette. Why the heck do you think Isabel invited Leah to meet them for dinner? She knew it was supposed to be a special night out with just her and Wade. That's why they went to a nice restaurant and the whole reason I watched Chloe for them. I don't blame Wade for being upset. Isabel clearly didn't consult with him before inviting Leah to join them. What the hell is going on with her?

Monday, October 13, 2008   6:38 p.m.

I understand why you couldn't call this weekend. It seems like your emails lately are even more cryptic than usual. Is it because you're going on more secret squirrel missions you can't tell me about? Or maybe you're just busier than you were before, if that's even possible.

I wonder if you have more stuff going on because of all the violence that happened in Baghdad at the end of last month. There were so many reports it's hard to keep them straight. A bomb blast outside a newspaper office in central Baghdad. A roadside bomb in northern Baghdad that struck an Iraqi police patrol. And several car bomb attacks near crowded markets, aimed at Iraqi civilians celebrating the end of Ramadan. And that's not even counting the violence in other parts of Iraq.

I know Baghdad is a big place, and that Camp Victory is just one part of it. But I read about gun attacks in Baghdad too. One report said gunmen with silencers ambushed an Iraqi military officer on his way to work in western Baghdad, wounding the driver. And another Iraqi officer was wounded when gunmen opened fire on his vehicle in eastern Baghdad as he drove to his job at the Interior Ministry office. I saw something that said residents there are afraid the security situation in Baghdad is deteriorating. I thought things were getting better?

Do you guys still use MRAPs or Rhino Runners when you go off base? I'd hate to think you might be driving around in a civilian vehicle. You never do that, right? It's bad enough thinking about car bombs and IEDs and mortar shells. I don't know why, but reading about the gun attacks has me spooked. Maybe it's because a gun attack seems so much more personal than a roadside bomb. It's not random. Like what happened to Wade and Fakhir sitting in their vehicle in Ramadi. Those guys knew who they were going after. I worry something like that could happen to you.

Maybe it's time for me to take a break from reading the news.

Tuesday, October 14, 2008   6:27 p.m.

Today has been a banner day for Fakhir. His Uncle Zareb called this morning to say Arifah and Farah got their visas! Their journey to the U.S. has begun. According to the uncle, they heard a knock at the door in the middle of the night. Although whoever it was had knocked softly, it woke the entire household, including Arifah and Farah, who came out of their rooms. Zareb signaled for them to stand back as he approached the door, armed with his pistol and a Kalashnikov. But when he opened the door, no one was there.

He scanned the courtyard to make sure no one was hiding in the darkness. He listened intently to the sounds of their quiet neighborhood. A car driving off in the distance. A wild dog barking somewhere nearby. It was then that Zareb glanced down and found an envelope at his feet, addressed to Arifah. Inside they found two visas, one for Arifah and one for Farah, along with a handwritten note to get to the U.S. embassy in Amman, Jordan where they would find plane tickets to the U.S.

Fakhir's uncle told him that a "friend of a friend" is driving Arifah and Farah across the border to Jordan at the very moment he and Fakhir were speaking. (This would be the same friend who drove Fawzia and Farida to Amman last month.) Zareb couldn't (or wouldn't) tell Fakhir any more than that — like when his mom and sister will arrive in Amman, what flight they'll be taking, or when and where in the U.S. their flight will arrive. Nonetheless, Fakhir is beyond excited. With Fawzia and Farida safely in Norway, and Arifah and Farah on their way to the U.S., Fakhir will no longer have to worry about the insurgents trying to harm his family.

And on top of all this, Fakhir also had his naturalization interview today. He feels it went very well. The questions the immigration officer asked were mainly things Fakhir already answered on his application, so no big surprises. Fakhir said the officer asked a lot of detailed questions about his service as an interpreter, which Fakhir sees as a good sign. He's hopeful that his work with the military will tip the scales in his favor.

Next step is the citizenship test. The immigration officer said they'll mail Fakhir a notification with the results of his interview. If he passes, they'll follow up with information on when and where to take the test. And after that, if all goes well, we'll get to watch him take his Oath of Allegiance. How wonderful that his mom and sister will be in the U.S. by then.

Since Fakhir had already taken the morning off work to go to the interview, he decided to take the rest of the day off so he could continue cleaning and setting up his apartment for when his mom and sister arrive. I had offered for them to stay here with us, in Fakhir's old room in the basement. But Fakhir said he wants Arifah and Farah to stay with him. His new place has two bedrooms, and he's saving the larger room for them to share. It's one of the reasons he chose that apartment.

I can't wait to meet them! Lucia is excited too. (Although ... this could very well put an end to Fakhir and Lucia's slumber parties, at least for the time being.)

p.s. Do you think Maj. Salazar had something to do with arranging the flights and having their visas delivered to the uncle's house? We know he's been in contact with the State Department and the intel team at Camp Slayer all along. Or ... did *you* have anything to do with making this happen? I know, never mind — if you told me you'd have to kill me.

11:03 p.m.

Isabel called tonight. I can't remember the last time she and I spoke on the phone, so I was surprised to hear from her. She wanted to talk about what happened with Wade after they left our house Saturday night.

Not surprisingly, Chloe had another meltdown in the car on the way home. As I mentioned, she was already getting fussy right before they left. She was fine when they first came to pick her up, but once they started bickering I could see her mood shift as she listened to her parents' voices.

According to Isabel, by the time they had strapped her into her car seat and pulled away from our house, Chloe was in full-on meltdown mode, screaming and crying and pushing her feet against the backseat. Isabel was driving so Wade undid his seatbelt and tried to distract her with her plastic car keys and some juice, to no avail. At one point she was screaming so loudly that Wade gave up, turned back around, put his head down, and covered his ears.

When Isabel pulled the car into the garage, she could see that Wade had begun hyperventilating. She quickly got Chloe out of the car seat, brought her inside the house and put her in her playpen in the family room, where Chloe continued to cry, holding onto the side of the playpen and angrily bouncing up and down.

Isabel ran back out to the garage where she found Wade on the concrete floor next to the car, curled into a ball, still covering his ears. His shirt was wet with perspiration and he was having trouble catching his breath. Isabel asked him if she should call 911 and he shook his head. She ran back inside to check on Chloe, who was still crying but no longer screaming. Isabel grabbed a Zwieback to give to Chloe, who took the cracker and plopped herself down in the playpen to suck on it, whimpering quietly now.

Leaving the door from the house to the garage open in case Chloe started crying again, Isabel ran back out to the garage with a small paper bag and offered it to Wade, telling him to breathe into it. He shook his head again and waved her away. She stood there a moment, not sure what to do as she watched Wade try to regain control of his breathing. Finally she lay down on the concrete beside Wade, spooning him from behind and resting her arm over his body. She concentrated on her own breathing, slowing it down as a way to calm herself as well as Wade. Eventually Wade's breathing matched her own, and she felt his limbs begin to relax.

They lay there for thirty minutes, or maybe more. Isabel thought Wade might have fallen asleep but out of the blue he said, "You're not supposed to tell someone having a panic attack to breathe into a paper bag. That's just what they do on TV. You end up breathing in carbon dioxide and it makes you pass out."

Isabel apologized. Wade didn't reply. After another minute or two she got up off the floor and went inside to check on Chloe, who had mercifully fallen asleep in her playpen.

"So then after that," Isabell tells me, "Wade came inside and said he needed to go out for a walk. He left the house—this was around midnight—and didn't come home until five the next morning."

"Where did he go?" I ask.

"I don't know. He wouldn't tell me," she replies.

"Was he sober when he got home?"

"Totally. He seemed calmer. He took a shower, fed Chloe her breakfast and played with her a while. Then he said he was going back to Wakeville. Packed up his weekend bag and left."

"Doesn't he usually stay until Monday morning?"

"Yeah. This is the first time he's gone back on Sunday since he started the job."

"Have you spoken to him since he left?" I ask. "Do you know if he's okay?"

"No," she says, somewhat defiantly. "I'm not going to call him."

"Why not?"

"I'm sick of trying, Emilie. I just don't think I can deal with this anymore."

"Deal with what?"

"All of Wade's shit. It's just ... too much."

"Are you saying you're going to leave him?"

"No. I don't know. Maybe."

"Well, in that case, you should be talking to Wade, not me."

"I just thought you might have some advice or something."

"I wish I knew what to tell you Isabel. I understand things haven't been easy. Marriage is hard. Military marriage ... there's no way to prepare yourself for that. You're pretty much flying blind. And things don't automatically get better once your spouse gets out. Wade's been through a lot. It could take years — maybe an entire lifetime, for him to get his equilibrium back."

"That's not exactly what I was hoping to hear," she says.

"I know. But look how far Wade has come since earlier this year. He's sober. He has a good job. He goes to counseling. He's doing all the things he needs to be doing to stay healthy. So he had a panic attack. It's not all that unusual. In fact I'd say it's a fairly normal response when you consider what he's had to overcome."

"I suppose," she says reluctantly. Then, "I'm sure it didn't help matters when his oldest sister called from Minnesota last week to tell him off."

"Tell him off for what?"

"The usual. His siblings are like a broken record. He doesn't come home often enough to help out with his mom and dad and sister, yada yada yada."

"Do they have any idea of the things Wade's been struggling with these last few years?"

"No. He would never share that stuff with his family. He says there's no point. The one time he tried to explain PTSD to them they said it's because he's weak and he can't handle it."

"That's ignorant."

"You know one of his sisters is severely disabled right? Wade says his parents measure everybody else's problems against what his sister has to deal with. And of course no one's problems come close. Wade knows more than anybody what a rotten hand his sister was dealt. He was the one who took care of her growing up, all the way through high school. His parents made it clear he was expected to be her primary caregiver — for life. Enlisting in the Marines was his ticket out. You knew he was prior enlisted right?"

"Yep, he's a mustang all right."

"When he left town to join the Marines, his parents said he deserted his sister. And they've never forgiven him."

"Geez. That's a heavy load. You'd think they'd have more compassion for their own son."

"One would think. Wade loves his sister. It tears him apart that he had to make a choice between being there for her and having a life of his own. He carries a lot of guilt about that. And his family never lets him forget it. That's why he stays away."

"I can see why. As if multiple combat deployments weren't enough to deal with ... He's got a lot of healing to do."

"If only Wade's family could see it that way. His wounds are every bit as real as his sister's. And I'm not talking about the scars from the bullets that ripped through his body."

"That's very perceptive of you Isabel. Look. I know this has been rough on you too. But whatever you're thinking, you have to call Wade and talk to him directly about your concerns. Give him a chance to know what's going through your head. He can't respond to something if he doesn't know about it."

"I know." She lets out a long sigh.

"And my offer to watch Chloe Saturday night still stands. You guys can go out to a quiet restaurant and have a heartfelt conversation. Just the two of you."

It's too late tonight but tomorrow night after work I'm going to call Wade to see how he's doing. I won't tell him what Isabel said — I'll leave that up to her. But I'm worried about him.

Wednesday, October 15, 2008

The Midwest Courier Times
Local News, online edition

Active shooter at Buell City High School in custody

BUELL CITY—A former Buell City High School student is being held by the Walker County Sheriff's office for questioning after he entered the school with a semi-automatic weapon earlier this morning. Police received a report of an active shooter in the building at 10:26 a.m. Witnesses said the former student entered via a side door, bypassing the security desk at the front entrance.

Security footage obtained by BCTV News shows the intruder, carrying what is believed to be an AR-15 rifle, walking past a small number of students who were in the hallway at the time. The students are seen quickly scattering, running into classrooms and hiding in doorways. Within seconds a Code Red Lights Out was issued.

Fifteen-year-old Shelley Griffith, a sophomore at BCHS, said she was in Geometry class when another student ran into the room, yelling, "He's got a gun! He's got a gun!" Griffith said their teacher, Mrs. Garner, immediately locked and barricaded the door while instructing one student to buzz the office on the intercom and another student to call 911.

Dr. Amy Gouwens, the school's principal, said, "It was this teacher's quick thinking that caused the school to go into lockdown so soon after the alleged shooter entered the building. I'm certain Mrs. Garner's actions saved many lives today."

According to police, the former student then made his way toward the rear of the building where several of the para-professionals work, until he reached the classroom for students serving In-School Suspension. Due to the Code Red Lights Out having been issued just moments before, the door to the ISS room was already locked and barricaded when the alleged shooter attempted to open it. A police spokesperson said it appears the suspect used his assault rifle to shoot out the door's window, which allowed him to unlock the door and push through the barricade in order to enter the classroom.

Meanwhile, a SWAT team had arrived at the school at 10:38 a.m. They quickly located the alleged shooter using information provided by the assistant principal, who was watching events unfold via live video feed in the security office. When the SWAT team came upon the scene, they found the alleged shooter on the ground, having been subdued by School Resource Officer Sean Dempsey.

According to SRO Dempsey, hearing the initial shots from the AR-15 enabled him to run from his location in the nearby science wing toward the sound of shots fired. As he came upon the incident taking place, he found the former student with his back to the door, attempting to gain entry to a locked janitorial closet located inside the classroom. Dempsey discharged his weapon, striking the suspect in the back of the knee, causing him to fall to the floor.

The SWAT team arrived on scene and quickly handcuffed the alleged shooter, confiscating the assault rifle. Officials stated they have yet to determine how the student obtained the weapon or if it was purchased legally.

Once the suspect was removed by medical personnel, it was discovered that a staff member and three students had been hiding in the janitorial closet. It is not known if any of these individuals were the alleged shooter's intended targets. They were unharmed and no other students or staff were wounded during the incident.

Gouwens told *The Midwest Courier Times*, "Officer Dempsey is a hero. If it weren't for his bravery, this story would have turned out much differently."

Parents began picking up their students around noon at the sports complex across the street, where many emotional reunions were taking place.

Other schools in the district were also dismissed.

This is a developing story and will be updated as new information becomes available.

Update 10:32 p.m.: The alleged shooter has been identified as Marcus Oliver, who had previously attended Buell City High School. Records show he is currently enrolled at Buell Academy as a senior. Oliver was admitted to the county hospital where he is in police custody under round-the-clock guard. A motive is unknown at this time.

Thursday, October 16, 2008   8:58 p.m.

Dear Family and Friends,

Thank you to everyone who reached out to us in the last 36 hours. Instead of responding to each text, email, and phone call individually, I am writing to all of you at once to let you know we are safe. Rory and I are unharmed and thankfully no one else at the school was harmed. The shooter is in police custody at the hospital, and we are told he is in stable condition.

I spoke to Liam yesterday. Unfortunately he heard about the active shooter at our school before we could reach out to him ourselves. It was an emotional phone call.

We owe our lives to Officer Dempsey and Mrs. Garner. Their quick actions saved many lives yesterday. If it weren't for them, I don't even want to think about what might have happened.

Rory and I are taking the rest of this week off, and we hope to return to school / work on Monday. We are shaken up emotionally but feel that after some rest over the next few days, it will be best for us to get back into our routines.

We have spoken to Finn a number of times and he is doing okay. His college in Chicago has already put him in touch with a counselor, and Rory and I have also been in touch with our school psychologist. We will be okay.

Please forgive me for not being able to respond to each of you individually, now and for the foreseeable future. I'll try to send out another update when possible but for now we need to keep our focus inward, so we can take care of ourselves and each other.

On a final note, a lot of speculation has been going around about the identity and motivation of the shooter. We can confirm that the former student is known personally to both Rory and me, but we have been asked by investigators not to share any information beyond that.

Thank you for understanding. And thank you for the many well wishes.

Emilie, Rory, and Finn

Friday, October 17, 2008   10:42 p.m.

Dear Liam,

Finn surprised us and came home this afternoon. But you already know that. I asked him who paid for his train ticket and he said you did, with some logistical help from the Red Cross. Thank you for that.

Rory said he still wanted to play in his game tonight so we all went to the rink to see him play: Fakhir, Lucia, Finn, and me. He didn't score any goals this time but he held his own. I give him credit for getting back out on the ice so soon after what happened this week. He said it felt good to be out there.

We thought it best not to go out to a restaurant after the game so we picked up sub sandwiches and ate them back at the house. A lot of people were coming up to us at Rory's game to talk about the shooting, which is understandable. But we didn't want to repeat that scene at a restaurant.

The phone has been ringing off the hook with reporters and other people wanting to talk but we are letting all calls go to voicemail. I'll pick up if I see "U.S. government" on the caller ID in case you're able to call again this weekend. I did call Dottie last night since she doesn't have email. She and Joey were distraught but I convinced them we're okay.

There've been some reporters hanging out in front of our house the past couple days but Officer Pizza Roll (the one who came by this summer due to a noise complaint—remember her?) has been making sure they stay in the street and don't block our driveway. She says she'll keep coming by regularly as long as they're out there.

I'm in my pajamas in bed with all the pets as I write this. Smedley and Daly are perched on the headboard watching over me, and Brig and Soda are snuggled on each side of my legs, protecting me and comforting me. Lucia has gone to Fakhir's for the night. I can hear Finn and Rory talking quietly in their room.

Tomorrow is my birthday, and I am grateful.

I love you so much.

Yours,

Emilie

Saturday, October 18, 2008   11:48 p.m.

And did you also know about all the other people planning to show up at our house today to surprise me for my birthday? (At least that's what people are telling me—that they've come for my birthday. But I know better. They're worried and they want to be here for us, birthday or no birthday.)

I was still in my pajamas, lying on the family room couch chatting with Finn and Rory when Aunt Dottie and Joey walked in the door just before lunchtime. They didn't even ring the bell—just let themselves in! I was so happy to see them—even Jacques, who wriggled his way out of Dottie's humongous purple tote bag as soon as she set it down in the foyer.

They quickly made themselves at home—Dottie made lunch for us (fried bologna sandwiches—I haven't had one of those in ages) and Joey raked the leaves in the front yard. After lunch Joey recruited Finn and Rory to help him hose off the porch cushions while Dottie did a few loads of laundry for us and I continued lounging on the couch doing crossword puzzles.

I should have known more people were going to show up. Fakhir and Lucia came over around four o'clock carrying a gigantic cheese tray. And do you know who they had with them? Arifah and Farah! I was flabbergasted. And totally embarrassed because I was still in my pajamas. Fakhir had gotten a call this morning to pick them up at the airport. What a whirlwind. They seemed pretty tired (kind of shell-shocked if you ask me) but Fakhir explained they didn't want to miss the chance to come over and meet the boys and me.

They are both adorable. Arifah is short in stature but man does she radiate strength and power. If I didn't know she was Fakhir's mom I might be a little afraid of her. She has a friendly smile and is very pleasant, but her penetrating eyes have a certain look that says "don't even think about fucking with me." (Or whatever the equivalent of that sentiment would be in Arabic. I'll have to ask Fakhir about that sometime.) She doesn't speak much English so Fakhir and Farah translate for her.

And then there's Farah. All I can say is that girl is not the least bit shy. I've never met a teenager who moves with such confidence and grace. She acts much older and wiser than her 17 years, and no wonder—she's been through a lot. Appearance-wise, she looks like a young Arifah except taller, with the same penetrating eyes. Finn and Rory were immediately taken with her. Fakhir plans to bring Farah to the high school Monday morning to get her enrolled as a senior, and Rory offered to eat lunch with her the first couple days if she wants (even though he's just a lowly sophomore — his words, not mine).

A little while after Fakhir et al. arrived, Wade, Isabel, Chloe, and Leah showed up carrying buckets of fried chicken (Wade), containers of cole slaw and mashed potatoes (Isabel) and another gigantic tray piled high with fresh fruit (Leah). And of course they also brought Chesty. So now we had four dogs jostling for attention plus two cats prowling in the background.

Chesty (the big galoot) made himself comfortable on Wade's lap while we sat in the family room visiting. Jacques had previously made a beeline for your chair, which didn't sit well with Soda, but there wasn't much Soda could do about it (besides glare at Jacques from across the room).

Speaking of the dogs, it seemed as if Brig and Soda were actually happy to see Fakhir now that he doesn't live here anymore. In fact it was pretty unbelievable — they were not only tolerating Fakhir, they were vying for his attention! Brig sat in Fakhir's lap, nosing Fakhir's hand whenever he stopped rubbing her ears. And Soda sat on the floor next to Fakhir's feet, sniffing his socks. Wasn't it just eight or nine months ago the dogs were hell-bent on letting Fakhir know he wasn't welcome here?

And then there were Wade and Isabel, who kept their distance from each other. On the surface they acted normal, and if I hadn't spoken to Isabel the other night I might not have caught the tension between them. But they were definitely not acting warm and fuzzy toward one another. They avoided sitting next to each other the entire evening. During the first part of the gathering Wade sat on the couch with Chesty on one knee and Chloe on the other while Isabel and Leah sat on the hearth.

When Isabel was helping me set the table I quietly asked if she had called Wade this week after our little talk and she said no, it turns out she "didn't have a chance" to talk to him before he came home yesterday. I asked if she "had a chance" to talk to him last night and again she said no, Leah had come over to watch a movie with them and there was no time for a private chat. And now they've brought Leah here with them today. I like Leah and I'm glad she's here, but do you get the feeling Isabel is using Leah as a sort of protective shield to keep Wade at arm's length?

Everybody quickly gravitated toward the kitchen as soon as we began putting out the food, so my conversation with Isabel was cut short. I noticed once we sat down that Isabel conveniently seated herself away from Wade, with Leah and Chloe between them.

As we crowded around the table and dug into the fried chicken, I felt warmed by the chaotic scene around me—everybody squished together, smiling and laughing, talking over each other with multiple conversations going on at once. Amidst the chatter I couldn't help but overhear a testy exchange between Wade and Leah. They were speaking quietly, but I was sitting next to Wade and heard everything. Leah scowled at Wade when he cut some chicken off a thigh bone and put it on Chloe's plate. "What?" he asked, looking at Leah, and she said, "Chloe is a vegetarian. We don't let her eat meat at home." Wade looked at Leah in disbelief. "We? Who the fuck is 'we'?" he whispered forcefully. "If I want to give my daughter some fucking chicken I don't need your permission Leah." I looked around the table to see if anyone else was paying attention. Everyone was otherwise engaged, except Dottie, who saw the whole thing and raised her eyebrows at me.

Realizing we might have overheard his little exchange with Leah, Wade quickly deflected our attention by insulting Fakhir. "Dude. What I wanna know," he says, looking from Arifah and Farah to Fakhir, "is how you turned out so damn ugly. You don't look anything like your mom and sister. Have you ever thought maybe you're adopted bro?"

Farah laughs, clearly enchanted by Wade's sense of humor.

Fakhir doesn't skip a beat. "And is your family tree a cactus?" he asks Wade. "Cause you're a prick."

Now Farah is laughing even harder, along with Lucia, Finn, and Rory.

Arifah looks questioningly at Farah, who begins to translate.

"Don't tell her the thing I said about Wade being a prick," Fakhir warns Farah good-naturedly.

Farah finishes her translation and Arifah laughs, then says something in Arabic. Farah turns to Wade. "My mom says Fakhir looks like our dad. He has the same square jaw and big nose as his father."

Fakhir looks at his mom, feigning hurt. "I like to think of it as a strong nose Mama."

Wade says, "See, even your own mama thinks you're ugly." This little tête-à-tête lightens Wade's mood considerably and we spend the rest of the meal picking on Fakhir, which Fakhir pretends not to enjoy but in truth I've never seen him happier.

Raquel and Carmen came by with the boys just in time for dessert, which we ate in the family room. Andy, Arthur, and Angel sat on the floor playing with Chloe's toys while Chloe again found her spot on Wade's lap. Wade and Chloe had an entire conversation which sounded mostly like gibberish. Chloe's new favorite word is "no," which she says now in reply to everything, even when she means yes. Like when we asked her if she wanted some of Dottie's peanut-butter pie she shouted "No!" and then happily let Wade feed her a few bites of his.

As we sat around the family room eating Dottie's pie, Soda finally got revenge on Jacques for his earlier transgression of taking over your chair. Jacques must have been worn out from the morning car ride from St. Louis, because by this time he was snoozing soundly at Dottie's feet. Soda casually sauntered over, mounted Jacques from behind, and humped him enthusiastically for about five seconds before Jacques woke up and figured out what was going on. At which point Jacques wriggled out from under Soda with a snarl. But by then it was too late. Soda had finally succeeded in establishing dominance over Pol Pot!

Jacques was so humiliated he skulked into the laundry room and hung out there the rest of the night, suffering alone in his defeat. We didn't even have to put up the baby gate to contain him. He didn't come out until Joey and Dottie announced they were going to bed. Jacques emerged from the laundry room, ears back. When he saw Soda curled up near Fakhir's feet, he let out a yowl. I didn't think dogs could give each other dirty looks but I swear Jacques looked at Soda like, "Ima gonna kill you next chance I get." He may have lost the battle, but he has not yet lost the war.

Everyone is in bed now and the house is quiet. Honestly, Liam, if someone had asked me if I wanted all these people here today I would have said "Hell no!" But having everybody here, being surrounded by so much love and laughter, is exactly what I needed. I couldn't have asked for a better birthday present. The only thing that would have made it perfect is if you could've been here with us.

Time to log off. Lucia just pulled the comforter *and* the sheet away from me, and on top of that, she's snoring. Since Dottie and Joey have taken over her room, I told Lucia she could go sleep in Fakhir's old room, but she said she'd rather sleep in here with me. I don't know if it's because she feels sorry for me or what. I do know the Fakhir / Lucia slumber parties are definitely on hold now that Arifah and Farah have arrived.

Sunday, October 19, 2008   11:30 p.m.

The best thing about everybody hanging out here this weekend was that no one asked Rory and me about Marcus showing up at the school with a gun. They were here for us, but gave us space to breathe. No pressure to talk about it, or to even think about it. There'll be time enough for that later.

It helped having Arifah and Farah here. Those two were the stars of the weekend. Everybody wanted to hear about their journey to the States, starting with their car ride from Baghdad to Amman with a mysterious stranger. When Fakhir brought them back here this morning, they were well-rested and even more animated than yesterday. I was happy to see them again, especially since I'd showered and gotten dressed this morning.

Wade and Isabel and Chloe (sans Leah) came back for breakfast. Wade said that he and Carmen had a good chat last night and that Wade is going to look into getting Carmen a job at Mondo. Unlike the rest of the private sector, Mondo's business is growing. They're in need of warehouse workers, and Carmen's skill set from working at the Ford plant would translate well. It wouldn't be ideal for Carmen since Wakeville is three hours away. But Wade said that if Carmen gets the job Wade will let him stay in the corporate apartment with him during the week, since no one else is living there at the moment (pointed look at Isabel here).

To save me from having to cook breakfast for everybody, Joey and Dottie drove to the bakery downtown to pick up bagels and cream cheese which we ate along with the leftover fruit from last night. As we busied ourselves around the table spreading cream cheese on our bagels, Dottie jokingly complained that Joey always has to back into parking spaces anytime they go anywhere. "It doesn't matter if we're only going to be in the store five minutes. He can't just pull into a parking space front-first like a normal person. He has to swing the car all the way around, and then everybody else in the parking lot has to wait while he slowly backs the car into the space just right."

Wade says, "Did the Air Farce teach you that in bus driver school Joey?"

"Very funny jarhead," Joey replies. Looking around at everyone else at the table, he explains, "You never know when you're gonna have to make a quick getaway."

"Agreed," Wade says, nodding.

Lucia says, "Fakhir does that too. Backs into the parking space. Every time. He also changes lanes when we go under an overpass."

"Wade does that too," Isabel replies, seeming to forget for a moment she and Wade are not really talking to one another.

"You never know when some fuckleberry is hiding out on the overpass, waiting to drop explosives on your vehicle," Wade says.

(I'm pretty sure these are the most words those two have exchanged the entire weekend, if you can even call it a conversation.)

As if reading my thoughts, Isabel chooses not to acknowledge Wade's comment and instead keeps her eyes on Lucia. "He also swerves when he sees trash or a dead animal on the road."

"Same with Fakhir," Lucia replies.

"IEDs," Fakhir and Wade say simultaneously.

Finn says, "Dad backs into his parking spots too. And when we go to a restaurant, he always has to sit facing the door."

"Same with Joey," Dottie says.

"We need to know where the exits are, Pookums," Joey replies.

"And keep an eye on everyone who walks through the door," Fakhir adds. "You know, to look out for nefarious individuals."

"Ooooh, big word there Einstein," Wade says to Fakhir. "Nefarious. Were you reading the dictionary again last night?"

"Just keep talking assclown and maybe you'll say something intelligent someday," Fakhir shoots back. He quickly looks at Farah, who's been translating the entire conversation for Arifah's benefit. "Don't tell Mama I said assclown."

Lucia says, "Fakhir won't put his shoes on until he shakes them out first."

"Wade does the same thing," Isabel replies.

Wade says, "Scorpions."

Fakhir says, "Camel spiders."

"Does Wade hoard baby wipes too?" Lucia asks Isabel.

"Yep." Isabel answers. "And he always has to have a bottle of water with him, wherever he goes."

"Yeah, same here," Lucia says.

"Baby wipes and water bottles are hot commodities in a combat zone," Fakhir explains.

Wade agrees. "Good items to always have on your person."

Again, Isabel avoids looking at Wade and continues speaking to Lucia. "Wade can't go to sleep without his white noise machine."

Lucia says, "Fakhir has one of those too."

Fakhir says, "You can thank the generators on base for that. Nothing like the sound of heavy machinery to help you fall asleep." He shrugs. "You get used to it."

"Maybe that's something I should look into," Joey says. "A white noise machine. My doctor mentioned something about that. Says it would help drown out the ringing in my ears when I'm trying to sleep."

"You should definitely get one," Wade says. "I personally prefer the summer thunderstorm setting."

"No way man," Fakhir interjects. "The best setting is the one with crickets and a crackling fire."

Rory asks, "Will Dad's hearing be messed up when he comes home?"

I'm surprised Rory was able to tear his eyes away from Farah long enough to join the conversation. He hasn't stopped staring at her since she and Arifah arrived. I'm going to have to talk to him about that. I hope he's not making her uncomfortable. Although — I have to say — she doesn't appear the least bit self-conscious. You'd think she's been here two months already instead of two days.

"He's mentioned the generators outside his CHU on a number of occasions," I reply. "And he did have some slight hearing loss last time he came back from Iraq. Occupational hazard I guess."

Joey says, "The doc says I'm probably going to get a disability rating for my tinnitus. That shit drives me fucking nuts. Makes me feel like ramming a chopstick through my eardrum sometimes." He turns to Farah. "Don't tell your mom I said fucking nuts. Or shit."

With a look of glee Chloe claps her hands and shouts to no one in particular, "Shit!"

Isabel purses her lips and looks disapprovingly at Wade as if it's somehow his fault.

"Sorry," Joey says, looking from Isabel to Wade.

Wade says, "No worries dude." He looks at Chloe and calmly says, "That's a chili pepper word honey. We don't say that."

Dottie pipes up. "Joey won't take a shower without his shower shoes on."

"A habit from Vietnam," Joey confesses. "Can't seem to shake it after all these years. Don't want to catch somebody's foot fungus and end up with jungle rot."

"You could always get a fish pedicure, Lovebuns," Dottie says as she slips off her leopard-print Vans, raises her leg above the table in an amazing display of flexibility. Quickly removing one sock, she presents a dainty-looking foot for all to see, wiggling her purple-painted toenails (the same color purple as her velour Adidas track suit).

"Darling you know how the sight of your pretty little feet drives me wild," Joey admonishes. "Please put them away until later, when we can be alone." He wiggles his eyebrows suggestively at Dottie.

"Dottie, what in God's name is a fish pedicure?" Wade asks.

"It's a thing at my nail salon," Dottie replies. "You put your feet in a tub of water and there's a bunch of little fish in there and the fish eat away at your dead skin and then your feet come out all soft and pretty-looking."

"They're called doctor fish and I strongly recommend you don't get any more fish pedicures Aunt Dottie," Lucia says. "My salon won't do them. You can get toenail infections, and besides it's not very nice to the fish. They're supposed to eat plankton and stuff. Not people's dead skin cells."

Rory sets down his half-eaten bagel. "This is the most disgusting conversation I've ever heard. Aunt Dottie please don't get another fish pedicure."

"Well butter my butt and call me a biscuit," Dottie says. "Who knew those little fish could be so controversial?"

"I still think your feet are the prettiest, Princess," Joey says. "No matter what these wiseguys have to say about it."

"Well on that note," Wade says, pushing away from the table, "I've got to drive back to Wakeville this afternoon so it's time for me to hayaku out of here. Thanks for the breakfast you guys." He nods toward Joey and Dottie.

"You're going back today?" Isabel asks, clearly surprised.

"Yeah. I told you that Friday night when I came home. I have a meeting with my supervisor first thing tomorrow morning so I need to get back today." He turns to me. "I'll call you this week to check on you and Rory, Em. Take care of yourselves." He punches Rory in the arm and messes with Finn's hair. "See you later douchebags."

Isabel follows Wade out the door carrying Chloe and the diaper bag, looking perturbed — and once again forgetting to say even a goodbye or a thank you.

"Well, we should probably hit the road too, Pookums," Joey says. "You've got me thinking about your feet now and I plan to give them a good massage as soon as we get back to St. Louis."

Dottie jumps from her chair. "I'll drive home so we get there faster. You drive too slow."

Fakhir says, "Lucia and I are taking Mama and Farah for a drive downtown. We promised to show them around today."

"And Rory and I have to take Finn to the train station pretty soon," I say as we all get up from the table. I take hold of one of Arifah's hands and one of Farah's. "I hope to see a lot of both of you. We're so happy to finally meet you."

Arifah and Farah each kiss me on the cheek. Farah translates for her mom, who seems to be thanking me profusely for taking care of "her boy." As we all make our way to the foyer to continue our goodbyes, Finn awkwardly shakes Farah's hand as he says, "It was nice meeting you." She smiles and says, "Same." Finn is still shaking her hand, staring at her. "Well, good luck at school," she says, gently extricating her hand from Finn's. "Right," he says, looking rather dreamy as she makes her way down the walkway. "See you next time I come home from Chicago," he calls after her.

"See you tomorrow at school!" Rory shouts, glancing at Finn as he waves goodbye to Farah.

Do I detect a note of triumph in Rory's voice?

Liam, I wish you were able to call this weekend but I understand. Maybe we can talk one night this week? Tell Gen. Kelly your wife needs to speak with you.

Gotta go. Rory just came in our room to ask for a back rub. I can't remember the last time that happened.

Monday, October 20, 2008   9:07 p.m.

Work today was exhausting. Everybody was super nice. In fact too nice. You know how I hate being on the receiving end of that look people do when they feel sorry for you — what Dottie and I call the puppy-dog eyes? It happened a lot after you left for Iraq. Now it's happening again, times a hundred.

I didn't have any students in ISS. I don't know if that was by design or just a coincidence. And they put me in a room down the hall instead of my regular room, which is still a crime scene. Dr. Gouwens said I could stay in the new room if I want but I said no, I want to go back to my old room. The one with the janitorial closet. As soon as they take down the crime scene tape and replace the shot-out window.

An investigator from the police department came to talk to me after lunch. Detective Dunhill. The same guy I spoke with last week. I already gave him an extensive statement but he had a few more questions. I had questions for him too but most of them he couldn't or wouldn't answer. He did tell me Marcus is out of the hospital and in police custody. He's in the regular jail since he's 18 and not considered a juvenile anymore. Detective Dunhill said they'll be prosecuting him as an adult.

I saw his mom on the news the other night. The reporters ambushed her as she was coming out of their apartment building. Sticking microphones and cameras in her face as she was trying to get in her car. As a mother, it made my heart hurt. The reporters are still hanging around outside our house, but at least I can get in the car in the garage and back out the driveway with the windows rolled up.

It was hard saying goodbye to Finn at the train station yesterday but he promised he'll be back soon. Rory seems to be doing okay. I've been watching him carefully, keeping a close eye on him in case it looks like he's struggling with what happened last week. But so far he seems fine. It helps that he's been distracted by Farah. He had lunch with her at school today, which turned him into an instant celebrity with his friends — apparently the mysterious "new girl" has caused quite a stir. After he got home from hockey practice tonight he couldn't stop talking about her. Farah this, Farah that. I just hope he doesn't get his tender heart broken again.

Tuesday, October 21, 2008   10:22 p.m.

Rory and I went to dinner at Manuel's tonight, just the two of us. It turns out he's been going over the entire ordeal in his head, trying to work through some things. He asked a lot of questions while we ate. Mainly he wanted to know if Marcus is going to get out of jail. I said I'm pretty sure that's a no. They haven't set a bond yet, but whenever they do set it I don't think Marcus' mother has the type of money or collateral to get him out. Having typed up the letter that's mailed home anytime a student gets put in ISS, I know the apartment where he and his mom live, and that she's a single parent. The other thing Rory wanted to know is if the police have evidence to show Marcus had specific targets in mind — namely, Rory and me.

"The detective won't say," I answer carefully, stirring my iced tea. "I asked Detective Dunhill about what kind of evidence they have when he came to see me at school yesterday. He said there were certain things he couldn't share with me yet while the investigation is underway. But he promised he'd keep us in the loop as much as he could."

"That's stupid," Rory says, biting into his taco. He swallows his food and takes a swig of his lime Jarritos before continuing. "Come on Mom. You and I both know Marcus was going after you. And me too — after he was done finishing you off."

"Rory!"

"I'm just stating the obvious," he says, waving his bottle in the air. "Why else would he show up at the school with an assault rifle?"

I consider whether or not to tell Rory what I know about Marcus' intentions. I don't want to be dishonest, and yet I'm not sure it would be in Rory's best interest to hear the details of what was said that day. Not now — or maybe not ever. In the moment, it doesn't occur to me that the details of what Marcus said could eventually come out whether I want them to or not, in court or in the news. If physical proof of Marcus' motive is uncovered by investigators, I'll share that information with Rory as soon as Detective Dunhill shares it with me. But for now, I cling to the irrational hope that I still have the power to protect Rory.

"Let's wait to hear what the investigation uncovers," I reply. "But, speaking of the assault rifle. Have you heard anything from your classmates about where he might have gotten his hands on something like that? It's scary to think Marcus had access to an AR-15."

"Yeah, tell me about it," Rory replies, picking up his second taco. "I haven't heard anything about the rifle but I did hear Marcus has been hanging out with Ethan's old buddies."

"Seriously?" I pause, holding a forkful of my chicken enchilada mid-air while I wait for Rory's response.

"For real. A kid in my Chemistry class said he's seen Marcus a bunch of times with those guys, hanging out in the alley behind the library. This kid knows them because they all went to the same church. And he says they're a bunch of troublemakers. The kid in my class volunteers at the library, and he told me they had to install security cameras back there because those jackwagons kept spray-painting graffiti on the bricks."

"Definitely sounds like the kids Ethan used to hang out with. Have you talked to Ethan lately?"

"Yeah. He's in my History class. He says those guys used to call and text him constantly after he came back from rehab. He ended up blocking their numbers and eventually they stopped trying to get in touch with him. Ethan said his family even switched to a different church just to get away from those kids and their parents."

"Lovely. I'm going to see Agnes at book club tomorrow night. If I get the chance I'll ask her if she's heard anything about that group. In the meantime, I don't want you to worry, Rory. Marcus is in jail. We're safe. Nothing bad is going to happen to us." I reach across the table and grab his hand.

"I know. I just want to make sure he stays in jail."

"Me too."

Rory lets go of my hand to squeeze a lime over his remaining steak taco, then changes the subject. "Do you think Fakhir and Lucia will come to my game this weekend?"

"I don't know. You should ask them. I know they like watching you play."

"Yeah. And they can bring Farah and her mom too." He quickly takes a huge bite of his taco.

"Oh. I see. Now the real reason comes out. You don't care about Fakhir and Lucia coming to your game. You just want to know if Farah's gonna be there."

"Well maybe she and her mom have never seen a hockey game before," he says. "It would be, you know, a cultural experience for them."

"Right. So your main concern here is their cultural edification."

He smiles and pops the last half of his taco into his pie-hole.

Wednesday, October 22, 2008   11:23 p.m.

Charlene hosted book club tonight. I gotta hand it to her, she has good taste in books. We discussed Wally Lamb's I *Know This Much Is True*. Thank God I already read it in the '90s when it first came out. It's something of a door-stopper and I had neither the time nor the wherewithal to read it again this month, what with everything going on. But I remember it vividly, because it was such a good book. I loved his first book, *She's Come Undone*, and I thought his second book was even better. There was a lot to unpack, and we had a good discussion. I was especially interested in the relationship Dominick had with his therapist, and how she helped him recognize his PTSD symptoms as a result of everything he's been through.

I have to confess, I did something kinda sneaky. But it was for a good cause — mostly, to save my sanity. After we finished discussing the book, the conversation turned to what everyone *really* wanted to talk about, which was Marcus coming to school with a gun. I answered a few questions, but people were getting more and more probing, and I'm just not ready to go there with this group. Not yet. Maybe not ever. So in an act of self-preservation, I threw out a conversational hand-grenade: the upcoming presidential election. And boy howdy did that do the trick! All I had to do was ask who everybody's voting for, and then sit back and watch the fireworks. Even Patty put down her phone long enough to join the fray.

Patty announced she's voting for McCain because he's a veteran. She looked at me as she said it, maybe expecting me to nod in agreement? Because I'm a military spouse? Not the first time I've run into the assumption that if you're a milspouse you're automatically voting for the veteran.

Agnes said she's voting for Obama because he opposes the war and vows to end it. She glanced at me apologetically, as if I'm going to have a problem with that. She doesn't really think I *want* the war to last longer, does she?

Wanda said she's voting for McCain because Obama isn't even a U.S. citizen. Oh my fucking God. Luckily I didn't have to say a thing because Agnes and Roxanne quickly set her straight.

Genie said she's not sure who she's voting for yet. She likes McCain but thinks his running mate, Sara Palin, is a nutjob. I hate to diss a fellow hockey mom, but I'm afraid Genie's right in this instance.

Normally I despise political discussions at social events but if that's what it took to keep people from asking me about Marcus, so be it. And I didn't even have to join the conversation. All I did was mention "presidential elections" and they were off and running.

Tammy and Leah didn't say much either. As military spouses, we're used to being tactful when it comes to politics. And why bother? Everyone assumes we're all Republicans anyway.

Speaking of Leah, remember when I asked her to wear something crazy to book club this month so we can see if Kim and Charlene copy it next month? Well! Leah did not disappoint. Her basic outfit had the potential to be adorable, but Leah pushed it totally over the edge to the point of ridiculousness.

First, the skinny jeans— totally normal and cute. Then, a tribal-print blouse with bell sleeves—also very cute. And then over the blouse, she wore a brown suede fringe vest. A little much, but still fine. Then came the boots: a pair of brown suede Minnetonka moccasins that went all the way up to her knees, with no less than three layers of fringe. And to take the entire getup to the next level, she wore a brown suede Native American-looking headband with turquoise studs and FEATHERS HANGING DOWN THE BACK. Hahahaha! She might as well have worn a fucking headdress. God love her.

I cannot wait until book club next month to see if Kim and Charlene take the bait.

Thursday, October 23, 2008

The Midwest Courier Times
Local News, page 1

School shooter makes court appearance, charges filed

BUELL CITY—Marcus Oliver, who police said is the suspect in the Buell City High School attempted shooting last Wednesday, appeared in court today. Prosecutors say Oliver, 18, who is being represented by a public defender, is charged with three counts of attempted second-degree murder and two counts of attempted first-degree murder.

Oliver, who smiled at the judge as she read the charges against him, did not enter a plea during the court appearance. No bail amount was set "due to the significant risk of harm to others," according to the judge.

A source from inside the police department, who asked not to be named, said investigators found a note allegedly written by Oliver during their search of the apartment Oliver shares with his mother. The source stated the note contains a possible motive, with the intended targets being a BCHS staff member and her teenage son, both of whom the source refused to name. An investigative team for BCTV news uncovered public court records showing a protection order had been filed against Oliver this past spring, which they believe may be connected to the attempted shooting.

A spokesperson for the Walker County Sherriff's Department confirmed an AR-15 rifle was used in the attempted shooting. The ATF is working to determine where the suspect obtained the weapon. One witness, a sophomore at BCHS who was interviewed by *The Midwest Courier Times*, stated they had knowledge the assault rifle was purchased at a gun show by a known associate of the suspect. *The Times* has not been able to confirm the veracity of this claim and cannot reveal the identity of the source due to the witness being a minor.

Friday, October 24, 2008   11:58 p.m.

Wade called last night. He saw the news about Marcus' court appearance, including the thing about the "intended targets." Liam, you and I both know Marcus intended to kill Rory and me that day. I told you as much in our phone call after it happened. And now everybody else knows it too. They didn't have to publish our names in the paper for people to figure out it was us. And Detective Dunhill finally talked to me this morning about the note they found (*after* I read about it in the paper — nice). He says if it's proven Marcus is the one who wrote it (and who else would it have been?) they should be able to prove the whole thing was premeditated. (Hence the two counts of attempted first-degree murder. The three counts of attempted second-degree murder are for the three students who happened to be with me that day. Marcus clearly said he was going to shoot them too — we all heard him say it.)

Rory got an earful about it at school today. Luckily I saw the article in the paper after work yesterday and was able to talk to Rory as soon as he came home from hockey practice, before he heard about it from someone else. He said he knew Marcus was out to get us but seeing it in print was still kind of a shock. I should have said something to Rory sooner. Like when he brought it up at Manuel's the other night. I could have told him what I knew then. How I wish you were here to help me navigate this, Liam.

Everybody went to Rory's game tonight (Fakhir, Lucia, Arifah, Farah, and me). I felt bad for Rory because he didn't play very well. And I know he was hoping to show off a little for Farah. (She and Arifah seemed impressed anyway, but that was little consolation for Rory, who knows he didn't play his best.) He got a couple offsides which is unusual for him, and he also ended up in the penalty box for unnecessary roughing.

On a brighter note, Riikka had a gift for Rory which she gave him in the lobby after the game. It's a Wayne Gretzky poster for his room, the one with the quote, "I skate to where the puck is going to be, not to where it has been." She also gave him a handwritten note with the poster, which Rory quickly scanned and stowed away in the inside pocket of his jacket. He introduced Riikka to Farah, and they seemed to click. Riikka said something to Farah about hanging out sometime, and they exchanged phone numbers.

On the way home in the car, Farah asked Rory if Riikka is his girlfriend. Rory said no, they're just teammates. Farah then told Rory she thinks Riikka is cute, and that Rory should ask her out. Upon hearing that, Rory choked on the can of Fresca he'd been guzzling. Once he got his wits about him, he explained that he likes to keep his love life separate from his sports. After which he promptly asked Farah if she had any interest in trying out for the track team next spring.

Getting back to my phone call from Wade, he said he'd been meaning to check in with Rory and me all week. Seeing the item in the paper yesterday finally prompted him to pick up the phone. He apologized for not calling sooner, and asked how we're holding up. I told him Rory is a little off his game right now, but I feel like he'll be okay once things die down a bit. It helps that Marcus is in custody and it doesn't look like he'll be getting out anytime soon with no bail being set.

"And what about you Emilie? How are you doing?" he asks.

"Oh. I'm fine. It's fine. Everything is fine," I reply.

"Okaaay," he says. "You do know, it would be fine if you weren't fine, right?"

"Hm-hmm."

"I know you think you're fine Emilie. But don't be surprised if you and Rory end up experiencing some PTSD symptoms because of this. It's always good to have self-knowledge about this stuff. Just in case."

"That's what the school psychologist told us," I reply. "I'm fine, Wade—really. Rory is the one I'm worried about. He's mature for his age but he's too young to have to even think about these kinds of things. He's got enough on his mind already with Liam being gone."

"I understand your focus is on Rory, because that's what moms do. But don't sweep your own feelings under the rug, Em. It's one thing to have a gun pointed at you in a combat zone, when you're expecting that kind of shit to go down. But to go to work one day — at a fucking high school — and have some kid come after you with an AR-15? That's fucking unreal."

"It was kind of scary."

Wade doesn't reply. Just waits in silence at the other end of the line.

After a long pause, I continue. "I knew Marcus was coming for me and Rory because he said so when he was standing outside the closet, jiggling the handle trying to get in. He was talking in a sing-song voice, like you know that scene in The Warriors? 'Mrs. Mahoney … come out and play-ay.'"

"Oh for Chrissakes. Could that fucking dickhead be any more unoriginal?" Wade says.

This makes me laugh. "Oddly enough I had the exact same thought when the kids and I were huddled in the closet together. It's strange, some of the things that cross your mind when you think you're about to die."

"Tell me about it," Wade says.

"My ISS kids were so brave that day, Wade. I don't know what I would've done if it was just me alone in that room. Jerry — he's a kid I had in ISS earlier this year, who got in trouble for bringing a giant pink stuffed poodle to school. This time he was in for throwing a sloppy joe bun at the cafeteria ceiling. Jerry was the one who jumped up and locked the door and barricaded it as soon as the Code Red Lights Out was announced. If he hadn't been so fast on his feet, we'd probably all be dead."

"Or if he hadn't thrown a sloppy joe bun at the cafeteria ceiling," Wade replies.

"Right," I agree, smiling. "Or if the cafeteria monitor wasn't such a kumquat who gives kids ISS when they should've just gotten a detention."

Wade chuckles. "Well, thank God for Jerry. And it's a good thing you had that closet in your room."

"That's another thing that saved us. Luckily the students and I had gotten in there and locked the door from the inside before Marcus shot his way into the classroom. Without that closet, we would've had nowhere to hide."

"I'm surprised he didn't start shooting up the closet door as soon as he got inside the classroom," Wade says.

"You know, that's what I was expecting too. But I've been playing the scene over and over in my head, and I think what Marcus was looking forward to the most was fucking with our minds and seeing the fear on our faces before he killed us. Like when I had him in ISS all those times before — his whole deal was to fuck around with people's heads. He really got off on that. For him the goal was to see how much misery he could inflict on other people. And the day he finally came for me and Rory, it was like he had this whole scenario planned out, down to the exact words he wanted to say to us."

"Well, at least he didn't get very far," Wade says.

"Yeah. I don't think he knew the closet door could be locked from the inside — that messed up his game plan. I'm certain he wanted to see my face before he shot me. That's why he didn't shoot through the door."

"So how'd you know he was planning to go after Rory too?" Wade asks.

"Well, once we were hiding in the closet — wait, lemme back up a minute. Besides Jerry, I also had Sabrina (a first-timer who was in for unserved detentions), and Derek (one of my regulars who was in for licking a popsicle into the shape of a penis)." I hear Wade's soft laughter and resist the urge to elaborate on Derek's now-famous popsicle sculpture.

"We were crouched on the closet floor, pressing ourselves against the cinderblock wall out of the line of fire from the door. I had both my arms around Sabrina because she was crying and shaking, and I was trying to keep her quiet. But Marcus knew we were in there because he's been in that room so many times. And he knew that's precisely where we'd go during a lockdown.

"So I'm holding onto Sabrina, and Jerry's holding onto me, and Derek is on the other side of Sabrina holding onto her. And we're just trembling on the floor of this closet in the dark. And after Marcus jiggled the door handle and did his stupid Warriors voice, he says, 'I know you're in there Mrs. Mahoney. And as soon as I get this door open I'm going to kill you. And I'm also going to kill whoever else is in there with you. And then I'm going to find your stupid little faggot son and shoot him in his stupid fucking face. Because —'

"And that's when we heard a gunshot, which was terrifying because we all thought it was Marcus at first, trying to shoot his way through the door. But it turns out it was Officer Dempsey shooting at Marcus. Everything happened really fast after that. We heard the SWAT team come in, and we could hear Marcus howling up a storm, so we figured he'd been shot. But I signaled for the students to stay quiet, because we couldn't tell through the commotion if Marcus still had his gun in his hands or what. And I didn't want to take any chances as long as he was still in the room. Sabrina was shaking even harder so we all held onto her really tight. Then we heard the EMTs come in and take Marcus away. That's when Officer Dempsey unlocked the closet with his master key and found the four of us huddled together in there."

"Man. That's one helluva story Emilie. Have you told Rory what that shitbird said to you?"

"No. I mean, he knew Marcus was planning to kill the two of us," I reply. "And then after yesterday's story in the paper, that made things even more certain. But I don't think it would serve any purpose right now for Rory to know exactly what Marcus said."

"Good call. But you may have to rethink that before the case goes to trial. Because I'm sure you'll have to testify about it," he says.

"Ugh. I can't think that far ahead Wade. I'm just getting through the day right now. It was hard enough after Liam left. And now with all this other shit, it's just too much. The biggest decision my brain can handle at the moment is what to make for dinner. Which explains why Rory and I have been eating mostly frozen pizzas lately."

"I understand. You guys are still going to counseling, right?"

"Well, we've talked to the school psychologist a few times. Rory and I … we just want things to go back to normal. Whatever that is."

"You know you can call me — anytime, day or night, no matter how late it is?" he says.

"Thanks Wade. That means a lot. You've been a good friend to me."

"Well, since you're already married to that lucky Irishman, I guess I have no choice but to stay in the friend zone."

"I'll pretend I didn't hear that. Speaking of Isabel, has she called you this week?"

"I didn't say anything about Isabel," he laughs. "But no. Why?"

"Oh, no reason. Just wondering how communication is going between the two of you. Seems like there's been some tension."

"Yeah. That's for sure. I don't know what the fuck is going on."

"You guys need to talk. To each other. In private."

"You're right. We do."

"I can watch Chloe Saturday night if you guys want to try going out to dinner again. Minus Leah."

"Oh. Uhhh, I'm not coming home this weekend."

"What? Why not?"

"Isabel is taking Chloe to see her parents in NOLA."

"And she didn't want you to come with?"

"It's complicated. She's taking a four-day weekend and I can't take time off work right now. We're prepping the warehouse for the holiday rush, and things are already getting busy. The good news is I spoke to my boss and Carmen has an interview with Mondo next week."

I notice Wade conveniently pivots the conversation away from Isabel, but I decide to let it go. Instead, I say, "That is fantastic news! Lucia will be so excited when she hears. So how did Carmen get an interview so fast? You had to wait months for an interview?"

"He's not interviewing for a management position. We need warehouse workers real bad. My boss took one look at his resume and said 'Bring him in.'"

"Well. That was nice of you to put a word in for Carmen. He and Raquel have been through a lot this year."

"He's a great guy. And I've been there—I know what it's like to be unemployed for months on end. It starts to wear on a person."

"By the way, have you been able to touch base with Joey, to see how he's doing? I know you guys chatted a lot last weekend at our house, but I was hoping the two of you could talk one-on-one."

"He and I are talking on the phone about every week now," Wade replies. "He calls me on his way home from his VFW meetings. We talk about a lot of heavy stuff, and I don't think he wants Dottie to hear his side of the conversation."

"That's funny. Because Dottie calls me when Joey's at his meetings. She says she doesn't want him hearing her side of the conversation."

Wade laughs. "There's just some things you can only say to your battle buddies. Joey and I may have fought in different conflicts, but some shit never changes, especially when it comes to war."

"So what's your assessment of Joey? Dottie's really worried about him not sleeping and losing weight and not being able to focus …"

"Honestly, I'm worried about him too," Wade replies. "Tinnitus may not seem serious to most people, but for some it can be a motherfucker. Especially for a veteran with PTSD. It's like a chicken-and-egg thing. Tinnitus makes the PTSD worse, and the PTSD makes the tinnitus worse. For someone like Joey it can be debilitating."

"Can't they do anything to stop the ringing in his ears?"

"There's no cure. But there's things he can do to manage it. You know, like masking the sound, doing relaxation exercises, going to therapy, and just in general doing things to take his mind off the ringing."

"Why do you think the tinnitus suddenly got worse after all these years?" I ask.

"We don't know if it actually got worse or if it's always been bad and Joey just started noticing it more after he retired. The mind works in powerful ways Em. Being busy with a rewarding career like Joey had his whole life — you'd be surprised how that can distract a person from stuff like tinnitus or PTSD. And he probably just got desensitized to it after all these years. Plus, hardly any Vietnam vets got treated for tinnitus back then. Everyone in their goddamn platoons had ringing in their ears. A guy's not gonna go to a doctor to complain about something all his buddies have, ya know?"

"So it sounds like a combination of things created a sort of perfect storm, and now all of a sudden his tinnitus comes raging back with a vengeance."

"Yeah — along with his PTSD. Among other things."

I wonder about what those "other things" might be, but decide not to probe.

Wade continues, "Based on the things he's told me, I'd really like to see Joey do some Cognitive Behavioral Therapy. That shit can do wonders for someone like him. But he's resistant to the idea. There's still too much stigma in the military when it comes to mental health. Especially for someone who's old-school like Joey. I'm workin' on him though."

"Thanks Wade. I'm glad Joey has someone like you to talk to. Which reminds me, are you still seeing your guy at the VA?"

"Oh yeah. I love Greg. Wouldn't miss my Friday sessions with him for anything."

"That's good to hear. You know you can call me anytime too, right? No matter how late at night?"

"I know that Emilie. You're a good piece of gear. We need all the friends we can get right now."

Saturday, October 25, 2008   6:59 p.m.

Agnes came over this afternoon. I was still in my yoga clothes when the doorbell rang. Lucia was at work and Rory had gone to Josh's house. Since I was home alone I'd been looking forward to catching up on bills and all the other stuff I've neglected lately. My heart sank a little when I opened the door and saw her standing there with a plate of brownies. I wasn't really in the mood to see anyone — let alone her — but it turned out to be a surprisingly nice visit.

I invited her to come sit in the family room, and she got me up to speed on everything going on at their house. As I've mentioned, Eugene is working at Fidelia's now and Agnes says he really likes it there. Obviously it's a huge paycut from his bank salary so they're having to cut corners. Agnes said she sold a bunch of her jewelry (including that gigantic emerald ring, remember that?) and she put some of her clothes, shoes, and purses on consignment at the local shop. She also stopped getting her nails done and colors her own hair now too. And you know what? She looks great — maybe even better than before. Her hair is more strawberry blonde than red now, and she's using less hair-spray, so it doesn't look like a helmet anymore. And with less makeup, you can see her natural skin tone, which is quite lovely.

She told me she's been getting into minimalism and they're selling a bunch of their furniture on eBay. It's all Ethan Allen stuff and worth a pretty penny, even used. (Or I don't know, maybe in these economic times everyone is trying to sell their Ethan Allen furniture on eBay and it's all going for really cheap. Who knows.)

Agnes also informed me she's looking for a job. Her old insurance office doesn't have any openings so she's in the process of sending out resumes all over town. And Ethan got a job working at Smollett's. They're not quite as busy now since the weather turned cold, but he's still getting a good amount of hours after school and on weekends. We'll have to stop by there for ice cream sometime when he's working. (And if we go through the drive-thru, Rory will not be the one behind the wheel. I don't care how good a driver he's become.)

Agnes said it was hard for Ethan when he first came home from rehab this summer and his former friends were trying to draw him back into their circle. But she says she's really proud of Ethan for staying away from them. He wouldn't have been able to stay sober otherwise. The three of them hang out at home most weekends and play board games as a family. Ethan introduced Eugene and Agnes to Settlers of Catan, which they're all obsessed with. No wonder we never see them outside anymore.

The whole time Agnes talked I braced myself for the moment she would finally ask me about Marcus. Because I feel like that's all anybody wants to talk to me about these days. But she never even brought it up! The closest she came to talking about it was when she asked me if you'd be coming home soon "because of what happened."

"Oh, you mean like emergency leave?" I reply.

She nods and says,"Yeah."

I explain, "Well, apparently it wasn't enough of an emergency for them to allow Liam to come home. Maybe if one or both of us had actually been murdered, then they'd let Liam come home. But at that point it wouldn't really matter now would it? Because we'd be … dead."

She looks at me, horrified.

"That was supposed to be funny Agnes."

"Oh." She looks unsure. "So he'll be home for Thanksgiving then?"

"Ummm, no. His deployment was supposed to end in January. But they've extended it another three months. So it looks like he'll be back home around mid-April now."

"But he'll get to come home for Christmas," she asks. "Right?"

"That's a big fat no. When they're on deployment they don't get the holidays off Agnes," I gently point out. "I mean, it's not like the war stops because someone wants to sit down to Christmas dinner with their family. Or celebrate their 25th wedding anniversary. Or see their first child being born."

Her eyes well with tears. "I had no idea. I'm so sorry Emilie."

I reach for her non-manicured, non-accessorized hand and give it a good squeeze. "It's all right Agnes. I don't expect you to know how this stuff works. Hell, Liam's been in the military 26 years and I'm still trying to figure this shit out."

She smiles uncertainly.

"Let's talk about something more fun," I suggest. "There's this thing going on at book club I've been meaning to tell you about ..."

I lean in and proceed to fill her in on the conspiracy Leah and I have concocted to see if Kim and Charlene will copy the kooky outfit Leah wore to book club the other night. I go on at length, describing each of Leah's previous outfits in detail, along with Kim and Charlene's efforts to copy her outfit the following month. Agnes leans her head back and cackles gleefully, admitting she did think Leah's outfit this month was "a little over the top."

Happily, the old Agnes is back, along with her infamous cackle. (Which you may recall I once described as sounding like a chicken in respiratory distress). I hereby vow not to make fun of Agnes' laugh anymore. Besides, once you get to know her, she's not nearly as annoying as she seems. And her brownies are delicious.

11:47 p.m.

Liam, I've been going back and forth on whether or not I should tell you about what happened when I went to yoga this morning. Maybe I shouldn't even repeat the conversation. I'm sure it's nothing. In fact I'm probably reading too much into things. God knows I've been guilty of that before.

But you're the only person I can talk to about this. And I need you to tell me what — if anything — I should do about it.

The class was fine. It was what transpired after class that threw me for a loop. As I was rolling up my mat, Portia came up to me, put her hand on my elbow, and asked how I'm doing. Which lately I've learned is basically another way for people I don't know very well to say, "Tell me all the juicy gossip about that kid who tried to murder you and your son last week." Also, she was giving me the puppy-dog eyes which did not endear her to me. At all. I smiled, told her I'm doing really well, and left it at that. So as not to be a total jerk, I thanked her for a great class. I had just turned to leave when she says, "Oh — it was good to see Wade a couple weekends ago." Which stopped me in my tracks. I turned back to face her.

"You saw Wade? Did he come to your veterans yoga class?" I ask. I'm trying to figure out in my head how Wade could've managed going to yoga on a Saturday afternoon when normally his weekends at home are earmarked for family time. And besides, he told me he wasn't going to yoga anymore.

She smiles at me coyly. "Well no. That's not where I saw him. He stopped by my place to say hello. It was pretty late — past midnight in fact. But I didn't mind. He needed someone to talk to. And I was just so happy to see him!"

Well I'll be dipped in shit and rolled in cracker crumbs, as Dottie would say. I had just spoken to Wade Thursday night, and he didn't mention anything to me about seeing Portia. I mean, it's not like he has to report back to me on every conversation he has with a mutual acquaintance. And we had a lot of other important stuff to talk about. It's just weird. Weird that he wouldn't mention it to me, and even weirder that he'd go over there in the first place—after midnight no less. How'd he swing that without Isabel knowing? Because there's no way in hell Isabel would be okay with Wade making a late-night visit to Portia's house.

When I got home from yoga I looked through my calendar. If Portia said she saw Wade a couple weekends ago, he must have gone to see her that night Isabel said he had the panic attack. The night he left the house at midnight and didn't come home 'til five in the morning.

What the actual fuck. Should I say something to Wade? Or just stay out of it? It's probably nothing, right? Just a visit to an old friend. He needed someone other than Isabel to vent to. But why didn't he just call me? Or Fakhir?

Sunday, October 26, 2008   11:12 a.m.

It was so good to hear your voice this morning, and thanks for your advice about Wade. Talking to you calms my mind. Except I hate that our conversation got cut short again and you had to hang up on me like that. I heard the mortar sirens this time you know. I'm going to assume you're fine. (Although a quick email to confirm as much would be nice.)

Finn called after I got off the phone with you. Things at school are going well. And he hasn't run out of money again since the one time he asked for his allowance early and I refused. I guess it pays to be a hard-ass sometimes. Even if it kills me.

He says he's coming home again in a couple weeks, for the Birthday Ball. I wish you could be here for the Ball, Liam. I would rather stay home and not go at all if I can't have you by my side. But the boys love going. And Tammy asked if she could be my date since Ken left for Afghanistan yesterday. Fakhir is taking Lucia, and they've decided to get tickets for his mom and Farah as well. Even Wade mentioned the other night that he and Isabel are going. I wonder if I should invite Dottie and Joey? A little military pomp and circumstance might be just the thing to lift Joey's spirits. Maybe I'll call the unit and see if they have any spare tickets we can buy. We could fill our own table. Or two.

Getting back to Finn, he mentioned he and Farah have been texting ever since she got her own phone, which Fakhir bought for her soon after she and Arifah arrived. (He bought one for Arifah too.) I asked Finn if Rory knows he and Farah have been in touch and Finn said I dunno, why? So I explained to Finn that I'm pretty sure Rory has a crush on Farah. Finn replied that he and Farah are just friends anyway — "purely platonic" in his words. (We'll see about that. And I wonder what Fakhir would have to say in the event those two start "hanging out" — or whatever it is they're calling it now.)

Finn assured me that even if he and Farah were to become "more than friends," Rory will be fine, because he basically gets a crush on every girl he meets. Which is pretty much the truth. Nonetheless, I encouraged Finn to let his brother know that he and Farah have kept in touch. Just so Rory isn't caught totally by surprise when and if he discovers the current love of his life has eyes for another. Who happens to be his brother.

Oh, and guess what else? Cpl. Gibson will be home from California by the end of the month. I ran into Leah at the commissary and she said Jacob is graduating from advanced sniper school this week. They don't have the funds for her to fly out there to attend the ceremony, but they do plan to attend the Birthday Ball. Even though Cpl. Gibson works in your shop, I'm pretty sure I've never met him. It will be interesting to finally lay eyes on the mystery husband. (Reminds me of how Uncle Wally used to jokingly accuse me of having an "imaginary husband" because you were always TDY or deployed whenever he and Dottie came to visit.) Leah said she's kind of nervous about Jacob coming home after him being gone for six months. Which is totally understandable. Sometimes reintegration is even harder than being apart.

Monday, October 27, 2008   9:02 p.m.

After I sent yesterday morning's email, Fakhir called and invited us to Sunday dinner at his place. He made his mom's upside-down chicken, and this time when he flipped it over onto the platter, it didn't fall apart. (I think his mom supervising in the kitchen had something do with it, but I didn't want to rain on Fakhir's parade so I refrained from pointing that out.)

Arifah taught Lucia how to make these fried eggplant thingies that were stuffed with spicy meatballs and covered in a tomato-based sauce — absolutely scrumptious. I had to nudge Rory under the table, signaling him to slow down and save some for the rest of us.

Farah made a dessert that reminded me of baklava but was way more delicious. It was dense like a fudge, made with flour, sugar, milk, clarified butter, date syrup, and coconut. She told us they used to buy it by the boxful from the bazaars in Najaf, and that her homemade recipe doesn't compare to the taste of the confectioners' version, which she misses a lot. I thought her recipe was pretty damn good, which makes me wonder what a boxful from an Iraqi market would taste like. I wish you had the freedom to go shopping at a bazaar to try the authentic version for yourself.

When I mentioned this to Farah, she promised to make a batch for you when you come home. Fakhir added that they plan to prepare a feast to celebrate your homecoming, including the dishes we ate tonight, and much more. (Speaking of you coming home, I'm still waiting for an email saying you survived the mortar attack.)

Since Farah and Fakhir have to translate everything for Arifah, and then translate what Arifah says back to everyone else, you might think dinner table conversation would get awkward at times. But it's not a problem at all. In fact — generally speaking — conversation flows freely when we're all together. Except for last night. Everything was fine until we ran into a bit of a snag at the end of the evening, when the subject of Fakhir's father came up. I'll get to that in a minute, but first let me tell you the fun stuff.

Lucia seems to have hit it off nicely with Arifah and Farah, which I'm glad to see since I know she was nervous about meeting them. She and Farah have a plan to get together at our house one night this week to make homemade lip balm to send to the troops. Lucia's been experimenting with a compound made from coconut oil, shea butter, aloe vera, and eucalyptus oil. She says the aloe will help soothe the troops' sunburned lips, and the cooling scent of eucalyptus will promote stress relief. Fakhir agrees the concoction will be a big hit in the desert.

"You never know — this could be the beginning of Lucia's beauty products empire," he says, smiling at Lucia. "And we can say we knew you before you were famous."

Lucia returns Fakhir's smile, then looks at Farah. "Farah can be my spokesperson. Or my operations manager."

"How about both?" Farah says, and everybody laughs.

Somehow I can totally see these two going into business together.

Fakhir waves his arms expansively. "I can see it now: Lucia & Co. Cosmetics. They're gonna sell like pancakes."

Lucia, Rory, and I exchange looks.

"What?" Fakhir asks.

Our smiles grow wider. Rory whips the Book of Fakhir from his back pocket and starts scribbling.

Farah and Arifah study our faces, obviously curious as to what we find so amusing. Farah says, "Hey, let me in on the joke so I can tell Mama. Is there an American saying about pancakes I haven't heard yet?"

Rory looks up from the notebook and says, "Yeah, you haven't heard of it yet because it's not a saying. Nobody says, 'They're selling like pancakes.' Except Fakhir."

"It's supposed to be 'hotcakes,'" Lucia explains to Farah. "As in, 'they're selling like hotcakes.'" She eyes Fakhir affectionately. "Not 'pancakes.'"

Farah, not quite seeing the humor in the situation, politely replies, "Okay. I guess that's *kind of* funny?"

Taking matters into his own hands, Rory describes in detail Fakhir's penchant for mixed metaphors. Paging through the Book of Fakhir, he reads aloud a number of Fakhir's greatest hits, including "going to hell in a handbag," "it's not rocket surgery," and "let's stop eating a dead horse." The more he reads, the more Farah's eyes sparkle with glee.

"Okay. I get it now," she says, nodding enthusiastically. She translates the conversation to Arifah, and the two of them chat excitedly while the rest of us look on. Farah gestures toward the book Rory holds in his hands, and their merriment intensifies as they point and giggle in

Fakhir's direction. It appears Fakhir's family enjoys poking fun at him even more than we do.

Fakhir, looking none too pleased with the situation, says, "I don't see what the big deal is. First of all, what I said is technically not even a mixed metaphor."

"That's true," I feel obliged to confirm.

"And secondly," Fakhir adds, "I'd like to hear one of you explain to me the difference between a pancake and a hotcake." He folds his arms and leans back in his chair, looking satisfied with himself as he waits expectantly.

Lucia says, "It has something to do with baking soda I think. One of them has it and the other one doesn't."

Rory nods vigorously in agreement, as if he knows anything about pancakes versus hotcakes.

Fakhir, looking unconvinced, eyes Lucia suspiciously. "So which is it?"

"You mean which one has baking soda?" she replies, feigning exasperation. "I don't know! Why don't you Google it?"

"Because I think you're MUSADI, that's why," Fakhir says.

"I am not MUSADI!" Lucia argues. "I'm positive there's a difference. I just don't know what it is."

"What's MUSADI?" Farah asks.

Rory answers, "Makin' Up Shit And Defending It. Like when someone is saying something that's total bullshit, and they know it's bullshit, and you know it's bullshit, and they know you know it's bullshit, but they keep talking anyway, like what they're saying isn't bullshit, even though everybody knows it's total bullshit."

Farah slaps the table in delight, then translates the exchange for Arifah, who's now laughing so hard her belly shakes.

Not the least bit amused, Fakhir says, "Can we please get back on tangent?"

That last bit, I'm pretty sure, was intentional. Even if the pancakes comment was an honest mistake, you get the feeling Fakhir knows exactly what he's saying more often than not. He's a smart one.

Having his mom and sister here must be such a relief for him, after all those months of worrying about their safety. Getting to know them has helped me understand why Fakhir is such an extraordinary human being. He comes from an extraordinary family.

As I mentioned, we happened upon an uncomfortable topic near the end of the evening—shortly before Lucia, Rory, and I called it a night and came back home. We had moved on from the subject of Fakhir's mixaphors (much to his relief), and as the evening wound down, we were chatting about things to do in Buell City. Arifah and Farah, eager to familiarize themselves with their new surroundings, had asked us for suggestions on places Fakhir can take them sightseeing on weekends. Rory mentioned the Buell City Zoo, which he described as being on the small side but nice. Farah was excited to learn we had a zoo nearby, saying it sounds like something she'd like to do because she loves animals, and so did their father. She went on to explain to Rory that their dad was an administrator at the Baghdad Zoo, which at one time was one of the finest zoos in the Middle East.

I could see Fakhir's jaw tense as soon as Farah mentioned their dad, and it looked to me like he was trying to catch her eye. But Farah was oblivious, eager to tell Rory how much her dad loved working at the zoo, how smart he was, and what a perfect job it was for him. Meanwhile Fakhir, who was sitting at the opposite end of the table, was looking more and more agitated, still unable to catch Farah's eye.

Lost in her memories of her father, she shook her head sadly, saying that if it weren't for his job at the zoo, their dad would probably be alive today. At which point Fakhir quickly interjected something in Arabic. Which surprised me because Fakhir is always careful to speak English around us. (I assume so we don't feel left out of the conversation.) This got Farah's attention. He hadn't spoken harshly, but whatever it was he said to her, she didn't seem to agree with. She gave Fakhir a defiant look—one I've seen many a time from Finn and Rory—a look that says "You're not the boss of me." Fakhir returned her gaze and said something else in Arabic, his tone careful and gentle. His eyes traveled around the table as if to remind her of our presence. She appeared to reconsider whatever it was she was originally going to argue. Turning to Rory, she asked what other places in Buell City he'd recommend they visit.

Fakhir got up and began clearing the table. Lucia and I followed suit while Rory, Farah, and Arifah remained at the table chatting. Before long the kitchen had been tidied and it was time for us to go home.

What is it about Fakhir's dad he doesn't want us to know?

Tuesday, October 28, 2008   10:37 p.m.

Fakhir got his official letter in the mail today — he passed the interview!!! I'm no expert on the naturalization process but it seems like he's made it through all the biggest hurdles. Now it's just a matter of passing the written test, which I'm sure he's going to ace. He goes in for the civics exam on Friday, November 7th, the day before the Birthday Ball.

Even though we were all just together two nights ago, Fakhir was in the mood to celebrate. He took everybody out to Peroni's for pizza. We had fun, and I'm happy to report all appears to be well between Farah and Fakhir. Whatever it was he said to her the other night, there are no hard feelings — at least none that I could see.

After we got home from Peroni's I got a strange phone call from Tammy. She was pretty upset. Apparently she ran into Jerri Jablonski at the package store, and Jerri said something to Tammy about how noble it was of Ken to volunteer to go to Afghanistan. Tammy replied that Ken hadn't volunteered, he'd been ordered to go. Jerri was insistent, saying she was certain Maj. Jablonski told her Ken had volunteered. Tammy said Jerri must be mistaken, because she knew for sure Ken didn't want to go on the deployment, and that he was only going because he had to.

Now Tammy is beside herself wondering why Jerri would have said something like that. Is it possible Maj. Jablonski somehow got the story mixed up, and innocently passed along the misinformation to Jerri? But what if the story is true, and Ken did volunteer? Why would he lie to Tammy and say he'd been involuntarily deployed when he wasn't?

p.s. Still waiting for that email from you saying all is well after the mortar attack.

Wednesday, October 29, 2008   8:26 p.m.

I've been reading in the paper about some strange goings-on in the Middle East. A few days ago there was an article saying a Syrian government source claimed four U.S. helicopters coming from Iraq had violated Syrian airspace. And then in yesterday's paper, U.S. officials said the helicopter raid into Syria killed a key figure involved in the smuggling of foreign fighters into Iraq. (The White House neither confirms nor denies the incident.) And now today, the Iraqi cabinet is saying they want to reopen negotiations on the Status of Forces Agreement because of the Syria thing. It all sounds rather complicated. Have your communications been blacked out by any chance? I'm just wondering because I still haven't heard from you. I'm not worried really ...

Tammy has been trying to get a hold of Ken but apparently he's still in transit to Afghanistan and therefore unreachable. What should I say to her? Do you know any of the details about Ken's deployment? Or is that outside your purview since you're busy with your own mission in Iraq? Or if you do know something, is it one of those things you can't (or won't) share with me? Tammy says she's planning to call the unit to see what she can find out but I've encouraged her not to do that until she talks to Ken first. Help?

On a completely unrelated note, when I was gathering up the laundry from Rory's room tonight I found one of Lucia's bras under his bed. Just a run-of-the mill black sports bra, but how did it find its way into Rory's room, and then underneath his bed? I'm going to ask him about it when he gets home from hockey practice tonight. I'll ask Lucia about it too after she gets home from class.

Oh! Speaking of Lucia's cosmetology classes, she's very close to getting all her required credits! And there's going to be a graduation ceremony November 15th. It's even possible she could get her license before the end of the year. Isn't that exciting?

I called Dottie tonight to see if she and Joey would like to come to the Birthday Ball. She said she'll have to check with Joey first, but she thinks he'd like to go. And she sounded excited too, saying she hadn't been to a Ball since Wally was alive, adding that the Marine Corps Balls are so much more fun than the Navy Balls. I told Dottie I've never been to a Navy Ball but I agree it's hard to beat the Marine Corps when it comes to balls. That made her laugh.

Joey was at his VFW meeting (I purposely timed my call that way) which gave Dottie and I a chance to catch up unencumbered. She told me that Joey had been having a rough week. Apparently his ex-wife Louise got wind of his retirement from the Railroad Administration and wanted to know when she was going to start receiving her share of his pension. Hell's bells! Joey hasn't heard from her in years — decades! — and she has the gall to track him down and ask for more money?

Joey told Dottie it's no surprise Louise would do something like that. Apparently his ex-wife hounded him for months about his non-existent Air Force pension, convinced Joey was hiding money from her. Joey explained repeatedly to Louise that he would've had to stay in the full 20 years to get a military pension. And since he got out after 16 years, there was no pension for him to share with Louise. But she wasn't having it. She was convinced that since she and Joey were married while he was in the service, she had some money coming to her. She hired a lawyer and Joey had to produce all his service records to get Louise to lay off.

So now she wants a piece of his Railroad retirement. Joey reminded Louise that he started working for the Railroad after they got divorced, and she's not entitled to one cent of that. Louise replied that if he's not going to share his Railroad pension with her, he should share it with their daughter Stephanie. (Who by the way, Joey financially supported until she became an adult, including putting her through college.) Stephanie also continues to cash the birthday and Christmas checks Joey sends her, but never bothers to pick up the phone and call him. Or even send him a thank you note for that matter. What a load of crap.

Dottie was hopping mad and I don't blame her. She said the phone call from Louise sent Joey into a tailspin. He hasn't slept all week, he refuses to take the Ambien his doctor prescribed, and he's running on fumes. Dottie is hoping his night out at the VFW will help get his mind off things.

Will you send an email please? Or if you're under some kind of communications blackout, could you have someone at the unit call and let me know you're okay?

Thursday, October 30, 2008   9:14 p.m.

Work today was pretty crazy. The kids are getting ramped up for Halloween tomorrow so the hallways were extra rowdy between class periods, and lunchtime in the cafeteria was bonkers. Luckily I only had one student in ISS, a junior who apparently considers herself a budding Georgia O'Keeffe — she'd been sent to ISS for making a "flower" painting in art class that looked suspiciously like a vagina.

I think the art teachers should just allow the kids to paint all the penises and vaginas they want — let them get it out of their systems, ya know? Better yet — make it an assignment so they *have* to create artwork based on genitalia. That would surely take the fun out of it for them, don't you think? It might even put me out of a job — once the kids are no longer obsessed with making penis sculptures out of popsicles and pie crusts, miming sexual relations with CPR dummies, and using their watercolors to paint vaginas, my classroom would be empty half the time.

Speaking of which, I'm back in my old room now — though the window in the door Marcus shot out with his AR-15 hasn't been repaired yet. They did clean up all the broken glass and blood however. When I first moved back in, the place smelled nauseatingly like bleach. We're not allowed to burn candles so I bought some of those scented things you plug into the outlets. Now my room smells like sandalwood.

Detective Dunhill has called a few times, but nothing really new on that front — or so he says. Obviously they're working on building their case against Marcus so, according to the detective, there's not much to say at this point, now that I've given my statements. And since there haven't been any earth-shattering developments in the case since Marcus appeared in court, the reporters who were hanging around our house have left. For the time being, anyway.

I'm writing this from upstairs while Lucia, Farah, and Riikka have taken over the kitchen making lip balm for the troops. Farah was the one who suggested inviting Riikka to join them, and they've even roped in Rory to help. Lucia is at the stove melting the shea butter. (I have a feeling a few of our pots and pans are not going to survive past tonight. Or at least not be food-worthy after this.) Farah is designing labels while Riikka is measuring out the essential oils. Rory has been tasked with sterilizing the containers. Did I mentioned they're wearing lab coats and plastic goggles? Rory tells me his Chemistry teacher said it was okay to borrow the lab coats and other supplies. It's a serious operation down there.

I've put away the lightweight summer comforter and now the mink blanket you brought home from Korea is back on the bed. Smedley and Daly are in cat heaven, purring and making biscuits on the faux fur. Next time I switch out the bedding, exchanging the winter blanket for the spring bedspread, you'll be on your way home.

p.s. The anonymous gift-giver struck this morning. I went out to get the paper before work and found a $50 gift certificate for the spa downtown, tucked inside the flower pot on our front porch. Inside the envelope, along with the gift card, was a note that read, "Be kind to yourself." I'm ruling out Tammy, because no way would she have the time right now to drive over here and drop off a gift for me, what with Ken having just left and everything she's got on her mind. I'm back to thinking these anonymous gifts are from Wanda. Not because it seems like something she would do, but because I don't have any other good suspects at the moment, and she does live next door. Next time I see her I'm going to mention it. I'm pretty sure I asked her about it before, when I first started receiving the gifts after you left. And she said it wasn't her. But I'll ask again.

Friday, October 31, 2008   8:41 p.m.

Well, it's Halloween night and I'm in bed getting ready to watch one of our favorites, the original 1959 version of "A Bucket of Blood." The first time I watched this movie was when you and I were dating. I remember we were at your parents' house. Your mom was sitting on the family room couch knitting an afghan, and your dad made popcorn in the fireplace. (Seems like that happened a lot — I have multiple memories involving your parents, old movies, afghans, and popcorn.) We might have watched another movie before or after "A Bucket of Blood," but if so I don't remember. All I remember is being surprised by how goddamn funny a horror movie can be. And if anybody had told me a year prior that I would fall in love with a guy whose family loves a movie about a nerd who accidentally kills his landlady's cat, covers the body in plaster to hide the evidence, and becomes an instant art sensation for his brilliant "sculpture," I would have told them they were out of their minds.

Rory is at Riikka's host family's house for a Halloween party. It's mostly kids on the hockey team, but Riikka also invited Farah. I let Rory take the car and he picked up Farah on the way. Lucia is at Fakhir's apartment giving out candy to trick-or-treaters. Since this is Arifah and Fakhir's first Halloween, they parked their lawn chairs in front of the building so they could see all the kids in their costumes walking around the neighborhood. Lucia texted me a photo — they've got a card table set up with a big bowl of candy and an urn of hot apple cider for the adults.

We had a few trick-or-treaters earlier in the evening, but I confess my heart wasn't in it this year. I turned off the porch light early and came upstairs to put my pajamas on. Normally I love Halloween, and I admit to feeling judgy in the past toward our party-pooper neighbors whose houses go dark at five o'clock (ahem Wanda and Vince, cough cough). Now I'm one of them — I even forgot to buy pumpkins this year. I promise to be back in the spirit next year.

I did have a chance to ask both Rory and Lucia (separately of course) about the sports bra I found under Rory's bed. Rory was nonchalant about it, saying he has no idea how it got there. He went on to remind me that Lucia, being the huge slob that she is, leaves her clothes all over the house (true), so why am I making such a big deal about a bra, since I've already found like, fifty of them in other places? I said because this time it's under your bed which seems odd to me. Rory just shook his head and walked away, looking at me as if I'm paranoid and delusional (a look I've grown accustomed to unfortunately, now that he and Finn are teenagers).

My conversation with Lucia went similarly, except she didn't admit to being a huge slob, naturally. She instead offered her theory that the bra probably got accidentally mixed in with Rory's clothes while someone was folding laundry. And then when he found it in his stack of clean laundry, rather than taking the few steps across the hallway to return it to Lucia's room like he should have, he most likely just threw it under his bed. Because, according to her, Rory is a "lazy ass." (Sorry to say, that does sound an awful lot like something Rory would do.) Even so, how anyone would mistake Lucia's sports bra for something belonging to Rory is beyond me, and I said as much to Lucia. She responded by giving me the same look Rory did. So I let it drop — lest I be permanently labeled by my housemates as paranoid and delusional.

Thinking about the dead cat sculpture in "A Bucket of Blood" got me reminiscing about Button, buried in the backyard. I sure do miss him. When we get our next cat, can we name it Walter Paisley?

Saturday, November 1, 2008   12:27 p.m.

I got a call from Virginia Lewis this morning. She told me that you had messaged Gen. Lewis asking him to let me know you're okay. (Thank you for that.) She didn't say if there's a communications blackout but I assume that's why you haven't been able to call or email. Did someone on base get injured in the mortar attack that happened when you and I were on the phone last weekend? I didn't bother asking Virginia for details, recognizing she either didn't know anything herself or couldn't talk about it if she did. I've been reading and watching the news more closely than usual this week, but there's been nothing about the mortar attack on Camp Victory. If there is a blackout, I hope it ends soon and we can talk again in the near future. I miss you.

I realize it's futile asking you questions about the mortar attack while you're there and I'm here. Someday, when we're together again, I trust you'll tell me all about it. Maybe not right after you get back. Maybe not until a few years have gone by. Or maybe not until after you've retired. It's okay. I can wait.

I figured since I had Virginia on the phone I'd mention the situation with Ken Phillips. I told her about the conversation Tammy had with Jerri Jablonski in the package store, and I asked Virginia if she had any advice about what I should say to Tammy, if anything.

"Hmmm. The package store incident sounds like an honest mistake on Jerri's part," she replies. "And yet—as an experienced military spouse, Jerri should've had the sense to let the matter drop as soon as Tammy corrected her."

"I guess I never realized this was such a sensitive topic," I say.

Virginia sighs. "Unfortunately, this type of thing happens more often than I'd care to admit."

Attempting to inject some humor into the conversation I ask, "You mean spouses having misunderstandings in the aisles of the package store?"

Virginia chuckles. "Well that too. But no—I mean service members telling their spouses they were involuntarily deployed when in fact they weren't." She quickly adds, "No that I'm saying that's what happened with Col. Phillips."

"Why would anyone do that though?" I ask. "I mean, Liam gave me a heads-up before he volunteered to go to Iraq this last time. He even asked for my blessing."

"Probably because he knew you'd do what you did—give him your blessing, one hundred percent," she says.

"Well, I think it was more like ninety-five percent," I reply.

Virginia laughs. "That's better than what a lot of spouses are able to give. Look, I'm not judging Tammy—I mean anybody," she says, correcting herself. "I'm not judging anybody who gives their spouse pushback on these deployments. Especially our younger troops, who've been sent to the Middle East two and three times now. That's rough. I don't blame the spouses who put their foot down and say 'no more.' It's one thing if their service member is forced to deploy, but another thing entirely when they volunteer to go over there. Sometimes the call to serve is so powerful, our Marines can't live with themselves if they don't step forward to serve alongside their peers. I'm not saying it's okay to be dishonest about it with their spouses. In fact it would prevent a helluva lot of problems if they were up front with their families from the get-go. But Marines are human too. They don't always choose the difficult right over the easy wrong."

"I understand. So what should I say to Tammy?"

"You don't have to worry about that," Virginia says. "I already spoke with her before I called you."

"You did? Wow. I guess I assumed I was telling you something you didn't already know. How'd you hear about it?"

"Oh, you know how the Lance Corporal Underground works," she replies. "Except in this case it was Maj. Jablonski who went to Gerald about it. After Jerri and Tammy had that conversation at the package store, Jerri went home and told her husband what happened. Realizing a shitstorm was in the making, Maj. Jablonski briefed Gerald on the 'spousal miscommunication' first thing the following morning. Gerald immediately contacted Col. Phillips on the DSN line to inform him of the 'misunderstanding.' In Gerald's words, he ordered Ken to get himself unfucked a-s-a-p. Told Ken to call his wife and get this shit straightened out the moment he has access to a USO phone. If I know Gerald, he was probably pacing around his office, giving Col. Phillips the knifehand from seven thousand miles away. No doubt Ken could visualize exactly what was happening from the sound of Gerald's voice."

"Man, I'd hate to be Ken Phillips right about now," I say. "Good on Gen. Lewis for encouraging Ken to do the right thing."

"If that's what you wanna call it," Virginia says. "I'd be more inclined to say Gerald ripped Ken a new asshole."

Good thing I hadn't taken a sip of my coffee just then or I would've spit it out. God I love Virginia. "Thanks for the morning chuckle," I tell her. Turning serious again I say, "So, if I may ask, what did you tell Tammy when you spoke with her this morning? Does she know the truth?"

"Not yet. Her husband needs to be the one to tell her that. I just told her that Gerald was in contact with Ken while he's en route, and that Ken's itinerary involves some detours for security reasons. But once Ken gets to his final destination he'll call Tammy as soon as he can. I wanted to let her know that the unit is in contact with Ken, and that he's safe."

"Did she mention anything about what Jerri Jablonski told her?"

"No. I admit I didn't give Tammy much of a chance to bring it up. It was a quick phone call. It's best not to get in the middle of these things," she explains.

"Well that's a soup sandwich if I ever heard of one," I say. "It was nice of you to reach out to Tammy. I'm sure she appreciates it."

"Just doing my part," she says. "It's gotten to the point I kinda know the drill."

9:39 p.m.

Rory and I helped Lucia take the boxes filled with lip balm to the post office this afternoon. Even with the discounted rate for packages sent to FPOs, the bill was hefty so I offered to cover it. Lucia resisted at first, not surprisingly. But I told her we admire what she's doing and want to contribute to her cause. She finally let me pay after a bit of back-and-forth in front of the postal clerk. I know Lucia spent a lot on the ingredients and containers and labels and whatnot. She's super excited and can't wait to hear how the lip balm goes over with the troops in the field. She also sent some to you, Liam — one for you and a few extra to share. I found that touching, especially since she hasn't met you yet. Obviously she feels a connection with you. I can't wait for you to meet her.

On our way home, Lucia told us that her dad got the warehouse job at Mondo! Her parents are ecstatic. Carmen starts a week from tomorrow. He's going to live with Wade in the corporate apartment at first, until the Caputos figure out their financial situation. The hope is that they'll be able to afford their own apartment once Carmen gets a few paychecks under his belt. Living with their friends from church hasn't been easy. Carmen and Raquel are grateful of course. But Andy, Arthur, and Angel need room to spread out and just be kids—especially now that the weather is turning cold and they're playing inside more.

Obviously, Raquel and the boys eventually plan to move to Wakeville so they can be closer to Carmen. But that means the boys will have to switch schools. And—most importantly—Lucia will have to make a decision on whether she wants to move to Wakeville to be with her family or stay here, where her job and Fakhir are. I think I can guess which option she'll choose, but I imagine it won't be an easy decision for her. She has a close relationship with her parents, and her little brothers adore her. It would be hard for all of them to live three hours apart from one another. But Lucia loves her job, and it's clear she loves Fakhir too. I guess that's something she'll have to figure out on her own.

We went to Rory's final hockey game of the season tonight. They didn't make it to the playoffs, but I'm happy to report Rory's mind is back in the game. He played extremely well, and ended the night with two assists (one of them to Riikka for the goal). And no penalties. The kids were in high spirits (considering they didn't make it to the playoffs), and the coach invited everyone back to his house for a team party afterward.

I confess, I was getting a little worried about Rory after the Marcus incident—although he wouldn't admit it, I began to notice he was feeling rattled. (And understandably so—it would be weird if he wasn't.) His anxiety seemed to manifest itself in his hockey game, mostly—not playing as well as usual and landing himself in the penalty box more often. Other than that, his grades have been fine, and his moods have been normal (for a teenager).

But I've also noticed something else that tells me Rory's been feeling off kilter lately: He's been coming into my room for a back rub almost every night since the day Marcus showed up at school. If you remember, it wasn't that long ago Rory decided he was too old for back rubs from his mom. But now—for the time being at least—our son, just shy of six feet tall, saunters into our room late at night, plops himself on the bed and asks me to rub his back, "just for a few minutes" he says. We sit in the dark, not talking much while I lightly run my fingers up and down his spine and across his shoulders, until his eyelids get droopy and he stumbles back to his own bed, his mind empty at last, ready for a night of slumber.

It doesn't take a psychology degree to understand Rory's current sense of disquiet is connected to the Marcus ordeal. It's comforting to know, however, that Rory feels he can come to me to help calm his nerves, in whatever form that may be. He may soon decide once more he's too old for back rubs from his mom. And that's okay, because when that happens, I'll know he's feeling like his old self again.

Seeing him get his mojo back in hockey tonight was a step in the right direction. It's good he wrapped up the season feeling confident. Before he left the rink for the team party, I told Rory I've decided to extend his curfew from 10:30 to 11:00. This made him deliriously happy, which in turn made me happy. He's been dealing with a lot. I guess you could say I'm proud of that kid. And I know you are too.

Sunday, November 2, 2008   5:15 a.m.

After I got home from the game and sent you that email last night, I was just about to turn off the lamp on my nightstand when I got a call from Wade. Which was something of a surprise since it was almost ten o'clock on a Saturday night.

"Hey, what's going on?" I ask.

"Not much. I put Chloe to bed a while ago. Isabel is over at Leah's place, helping her get things ready for Jacob. I was just sitting here doing nothing, so I thought I'd give my favorite person a call," he says.

"What are they doing—baking him a cake?"

"Don't sound so excited to hear from me Emilie. Aren't you going to tell me I'm your favorite person too?"

"You're one of my favorite people Wade. You know that," I reply. "So what is it exactly that Leah needs help with?"

"I don't know. Isabel said something about helping her clean."

"Don't they live in a one-bedroom apartment? It can't be that hard to clean. Besides, she's known he's coming home for over a week now."

"Who knows Emilie. Those two are glued at the hip. They're like Frick and Frack. Pete and Repeat."

"Well, at least you and Isabel will have tomorrow night together before you have to go back to Wakeville," I say.

"Uh, I'm not staying over on Sunday nights anymore," he says. "Work is busy and ... it's just easier for me to drive back on Sunday instead of waiting until Monday morning."

"So let me get this straight. Out of the two nights per week you're home, Isabel decides it's fine to spend one of those nights helping Leah clean her apartment? On a Saturday night?"

"Guess so," he says.

Silence.

"Anyway I don't mind," he adds. "It's nice having some alone time with Chloe."

"If I'd known you were home alone with Chloe tonight I would've invited the two of you to come to Rory's game with us."

"It's okay. We had some daddy-daughter time. She loves that Fisher-Price parking garage you guys gave her."

"Aww, that makes me happy. Finn and Rory used to love that thing."

More silence.

Using one of Wade's tactics, I decide a conversational pivot is in order. "Hey, Lucia told me Carmen got the job at Mondo — thanks to you. That was really nice of you to put Carmen in touch with HR. The whole family is thrilled. You've made a real difference in their lives, Wade."

"Well, it's nice to know I'm making a difference in somebody's life."

"Wade — that's crazy talk. You make a difference in a lot of people's lives. Just look at Chloe. She adores you. And how about Joey — having someone like you to confide in? You're giving him something he really needs right now. And you've made a big difference in our lives too — all of us. Finn and Rory look up to you. When you're around, it's like they have a piece of their dad with them. That means a lot. To me and to Liam. Liam has told me a number of times he's able to rest easier over there knowing you're keeping an eye on us."

"I haven't done as much as I should," he says. "I've been too wrapped up in my own problems. I wish I'd done a better job being a part of your lives like Liam wanted me to."

"That's not true! You've been a huge part of our lives Wade. You've been here for all our important celebrations, and you've been here for the hard times too. You're the one who was there for me when I had to put Button down. And when I was in denial about the thing that happened with Marcus—when I was telling everybody I was fine? You're the one who saw through that, who knew I wasn't fine. And you knew all the right things to say to help me make sense of things. I don't know what I'd do if I didn't have you to talk to."

"You're just sayin' that Em. I've been a shit. To everybody. I'm not as nice a person as you think I am."

"That's bullshit Wade. Don't say that. You're just feeling a little down right now because you and Isabel are going through a rough patch."

"Ha! That's an understatement. This is more than a rough patch Emilie."

Silence. I wait him out.

"I don't know what to do," he continues. "She won't talk to me. I know something's wrong, but she won't say what it is."

"What do you think is wrong?" I ask.

"I think she's thinking about leaving me."

I happen to know that's true, since Isabel told me as much the last time she called. I don't want to break her confidence, yet I don't want to be untruthful with Wade either. I decide the best thing is to just keep him talking. "What makes you say that?" I ask.

"Just a feeling. This isn't my first rodeo. Same shit I went through with Shelley. You can tell when they're about to check out."

"I'm sorry."

"You don't need to apologize. I fucked this up all on my own. As per usual."

"So what are you gonna do?"

"I've been going over my options. I did something stupid a few weeks ago. I won't bore you with the details, but I fucked up. Big time."

"Does Isabel know about … whatever it is?"

"No. She doesn't. At least I don't think she does. She's too busy with her own shit. She's so far off in her own world Emilie, she barely even notices when I'm here anymore. Sometimes I think it would be easier for everybody if I wasn't here."

"Wade! That is not true. Why would you say something like that?"

"Because it's true? Everything I do, I fuck it up. My first marriage to Shelley, fucked that up. That Civil Affairs mission in Ramadi where my poor decisions ended in the deaths of two of my Marines and Fakhir getting seriously injured? Yep—fucked that up. My Marine Corps career? Came close to letting 22 fucking years go down the fuckin' drain 'cuz I couldn't lay off the fucking alcohol. My relationship with my family? Check, fucked that up. My marriage to Isabel? Totally fucked that up. Oh, and let's not forget the Battle of Fallujah in '04 when I—oh hell. What's the fucking point."

"Liam told me you were awarded the Bronze Star after the Battle of Fallujah." It seems like a stupid thing to say, but it's the only thing I can think of.

Wade laughs. "Those fucking medals don't mean shit. What matters is what's in my head—the things I remember. The things I can't forget. That shit is always going to be inside my fucking brain. And it's never gonna go away. Until I die."

"Wade, Do you want me to come over there? I don't think you should be alone right now."

Silence.

"I'm coming over. I'll be there in ten minutes. Will you stay on the phone with me while I grab my keys and drive over?"

"Yeah, sure. Whatever you want."

"What I want is for you to not hang up the phone. Keep talking to me until I get there. Okay?"

"Okay."

Monday, November 3, 2008   7:41 p.m.

I'm sorry I didn't write sooner to let you know what happened. I had planned to tell you the rest of the story yesterday but since I got zero sleep Saturday night I was worthless most of the day. I fell asleep on the couch in the afternoon, slept through dinner and didn't wake up until it was time to go to work this morning.

When I pulled up in front of Wade's house Saturday night, still on the phone with him, I told him to give me a minute before coming to the door to let me in. While still in the car, I quickly tried calling Isabel but she didn't pick up. I tried calling Leah's phone too, but she didn't pick up either.

Standing on Wade's front porch, I knocked softly on the window so as not to wake up Chloe. It reminded me of the last time I came to their house late at night, when Isabel was beside herself with worry because Wade hadn't come home. (That's the night Fakhir and I found him at the American Legion bar — the night before his interview at Mondo. That was almost five months ago and he's been sober ever since.)

I quietly slipped inside when Wade opened the door. Chesty greeted me, tail wagging, but didn't make any noise other than a few happy chuffs. The house was dark — not even a TV flickering in the background. Wade motioned for me to come sit in the living room. We sat on the couch in darkness and talked most of the night. Mostly he talked and I listened.

He told me about his sister in Minnesota and how he feels like he abandoned her. He talked about the ambush on his and Fakhir's vehicle in Ramadi. He told me the reasons he and Shelley split up — some of which I already knew because that was when we were all stationed on Okinawa together. (Hard to believe that was more than twenty years ago now.) He even talked about the Second Battle of Fallujah — his third deployment to the Middle East in as many years, and his second time in Iraq with I MEF. Back when he was still a captain.

"Talk about a fuckin' hellhole," he says. "Four years ago this month. In fact we celebrated the Marine Corps Birthday during that fight. Stuck some matches in a pound cake from an MRE and listened to the Marines' Hymn over the ICOM."

"So is that what the Bronze Star was for—sticking matches in a pound cake?" I ask.

"You think you're real funny huh?" he replies, adding, "That would be 'Bronze Star with a V' by the way."

"And the V stands for ... ?"

"What do you think it stands for?" he asks.

"Vagina?"

"You're a fuckin' nut," he says, tossing a throw pillow at me.

"Okay. So seriously. Tell me about the Bronze Star," I say.

He waves his hand dismissively. "Just your typical war bullshit."

I hug the pillow to my chest and wait.

He lets out a long sigh. "You're not gonna let this drop, are you?"

I shake my head.

"Has anyone ever told you you're like a dog chewing on a fucking bone?" he says.

"I'm waiting."

He starts out speaking in a monotone, as if purposely trying to keep the emotion out of his voice. "We'd been in Fallujah six or seven days. The worst of the fighting had subsided by then. My guys were exhausted. But we were starting to feel like maybe we'd won this thing. We knew there were pockets of resistance out there, and that's what we were focusing on—mopping up the last of the insurgents."

"I had set up a forward headquarters for my company in an abandoned garage, like an auto shop on the first floor with an apartment above it on the second floor. The building had suffered some previous damage—all the windows were blown out—but it was still standing, and by Fallujah standards that was good enough. By zero-dark thirty our squads had spread out across our sector of the city, so they could get their sniper teams positioned on rooftops before daylight.

"I was on the second floor with my first sergeant and our radio operator. We had a sniper and a spotter on the roof. And there were several Marines on the first floor who were in dire need of some shut-eye—they'd been going house to house, fighting almost a week straight without much sleep. So I rotated them in to get some rest before going back out again. They were racked out on the floor, using their helmets as pillows. A couple of the lucky ones took ownership of some ratty-looking seats that had been ripped out of a vehicle and scattered around the chop shop — or whatever this shithole place was."

As Wade becomes more immersed in the story, emotion gradually seeps back into his voice.

"Just before sunrise we could hear the call to prayer from a nearby mosque. The area surrounding us had been secured in the last 24 hours, but at that moment we spotted an enemy position inside the minaret of the mosque. We could see these dickwads through our binos — dudes in black pajamas with RPG launchers strapped to their shoulders. These fuckers were counting on us not to attack the mosque. But once we spotted them we had no choice. We'd just had radio contact with our sniper team about picking these guys off when we started taking small-arms fire from an apartment building across the way.

"Faster than you can say Mike Foxtrot, the grunts on the first floor had grabbed their M-16s and were returning fire from the blown-out windows of the garage. At the same time, our sniper on the roof had gotten off a couple of good shots on the dudes in pajamas. But he didn't get all of them, because that's when an RPG hit the building next door, the blast causing chunks of concrete and debris to rain down onto the street in front of us. Those pajama-wearing assclowns were notorious for their bad aim, but I wasn't about to bet my guys' lives on their next RPG being a miss.

"I directed my Marines to vacate the garage from the rear and exit into the alley, where they could advance to the next corner and continue returning fire on the apartment across the way, using the buildings between us as cover. My first sergeant and radio guy glanced back at me as they headed down the stairs, as if they were expecting me to be right behind them. I told them to get the fuck out of here while I go check on our sniper team. Those two wankers hadn't responded to my order to move out. I wasn't gonna leave until I knew we had everybody.

"I scrambled up to the roof to find they'd both been hit by chunks of falling concrete from the building next door. Sgt. Garnett's legs were covered in dust and rubble but he was still trying to get off another shot at the one guy left in the minaret with the RPG launcher. I started clawing at the pieces of concrete, trying to lift them off my sniper's legs when he waved me away and pointed at his spotter, saying take him, he's the one who needs a medevac. Besides, Garnett said, turning back to his scope, I gotta wait for this fucker with the RPG to show himself so I can take him out. The spotter, Cpl. Cotten, had blood running down his face, a dazed expression in his eyes, his radio nowhere to be seen. From the looks of his helmet it was obvious he'd taken a chunk of concrete to the head. I picked him up and threw him over my shoulder, telling Sgt. Garnett I'd be back ricky-tick, and not to do anything stupid in the meantime.

"I clambered back down the stairs and out of the building with Cpl. Cotten over my shoulder, hauling ass down the alley and around the corner until I reached an alcove where two of my Marines had taken cover. They were returning fire on the few insurgents still alive in the apartment across the way. I dropped Cpl. Cotten at their feet and told them to radio for a medevac.

"I popped smoked back down the alley to retrieve Sgt. Garnett and that's when the second RPG hit the garage, right on target this time. The fucking roof fell in and Sgt. Garnett was buried in the rubble. We found his body not long after the shooting stopped. I don't know why they gave me a fucking Bronze Star over that. I wasn't able to get back there in time to save him."

"But the spotter survived, right?" I ask.

"Yeah. Thank God. He ended up with a concussion and a nasty-ass scar on his grape, along with a medical discharge for TBI. His memory's a little fucked up, but thank God he made it. I wouldn't have been able to live with myself if Cpl. Cotten hadn't survived. But Sgt. Garnett? I mean, we suffered a lot of casualties that month. But that's the one that stays with me. I see his face in my dreams, telling me to take his partner instead of him. I keep wondering if I did the right thing. Did I rescue the right guy? How do you choose who lives and who dies? And what right do I have to play God?"

"Wade, you saved a guy's life. If you hadn't gone up to the roof they both would've died. You saved one of them. That was the best you could do."

He shakes his head. "My best wasn't good enough."

We sit in silence for a while. When Wade gets up to use the bathroom I try calling Isabel and Leah again. Both their phones are off.

In spite of everything we've just talked about, Wade seems unusually calm. I feel confident he's not in any danger of hurting himself, as I thought he might be earlier in the evening. And yet, I'd prefer not to leave him alone until I know Isabel is on her way.

When he returns from the bathroom he says, "You don't have to stay here, Em. I'm fine. You should go home and get some sleep."

"I know. I just—"

"You just wanna make sure I'm okay," he says.

I nod.

"I am—I'm okay. I promise," he assures me.

Still, I'm not ready to leave him alone. "Do you have anything to eat?" I ask. "I'm starved."

"It's three o'clock in the fucking morning," he replies. Then, "You know what? I'm hungry too. You want a grilled cheese?"

"That sounds perfect," I reply.

We go to the kitchen and make two grilled cheese sandwiches with garlic salt and extra butter. While we're sitting at the kitchen table eating, Isabel calls Wade to say she fell asleep at Leah's but she's on her way. Wade and I finish our sandwiches and rinse our plates at the sink.

"I'm gonna get going," I say, turning to face him. "I'm glad you called me tonight Wade."

"I'm glad I did too," he says.

Tuesday, November 4, 2008   11:49 p.m.

I'm sure you've heard the news by now that Obama won the White House. Finn texted a while ago to say he and Mel were on their way to Grant Park to watch Obama's acceptance speech. I'm glad they went. Now Finn can say he was there—live and in person—to see history in the making.

I'm glad, too, that you were able to cast your absentee ballot from Iraq (and that Finn was able to vote from Chicago). I brought Rory with me to our polling place after school today, as I've done since he and Finn were toddlers. Soon Rory will be old enough to cast his own vote. Color me sentimental, but I still get choked up every time I step foot inside a voting booth.

Lucia took Farah and Arifah shopping last weekend, in search of dresses to wear to the Birthday Ball. They're excited, and I'm told all three of their gowns involve a plethora of sequins. I had taken Rory to get a new suit the week before, since he's already outgrown the one he wore to Turnabout. I made sure the sales guy kept Rory's new tie knotted this time before we left the store. Wouldn't want a repeat of what happened back in January, when none of us knew how to properly tie a tie and Rory had to look it up on YouTube at the last minute. (That was the weekend after you left. It feels like ages ago.)

I'm going to wear the same Ball gown I wore last year. I know, I'm committing a major fux pux — wearing the same gown two years in a row. But I don't care. I'll get a new one next year when you and I can go together. Tammy said she's wearing the same gown she wore last year too. When they round up all the repeat offenders, she and I can support each other during the lineup.

Wednesday, November 5, 2008   9:10 p.m.

We had a light dusting of snow this afternoon — the first snow of the season. I took Brig and Soda on the trail after I got home from work and they loved it. Walking through the woods with the dogs pulling me along, I spotted a pair of cardinals in a birch tree. They made me think of you, and how you love watching the cardinals that come to our feeder in the winter. I wonder, do you miss the snow?

Lucia was over at Fakhir's place tonight helping him study for the citizenship test on Friday. Fakhir told me the test has two parts, English and Civics. The Civics portion has 100 questions about the Constitution, branches of government, etc. He's good at memorization and will probably ace that part, especially since he's been studying for months now. He said the English part looks like it shouldn't be too hard either.

I replied I'm sure he'll do fine on that as well, as long as there's nothing about metaphors on there.

Rory and I pulled a couple chicken pot pies from the freezer and warmed those up for dinner. I told him I'm sorry I haven't been cooking much lately, and he said that's okay, he likes frozen pizza and Taquitos.

Tammy called after dinner. She finally heard from Ken, who called her from Kandahar on a USO phone. He admitted to her he had volunteered for the deployment and lied about it. He said there was no excuse for what he did, and asked for her forgiveness.

Tammy told me she's not ready to forgive Ken yet, but she doesn't want to be in a fight with him while he's in a war zone either. She's afraid that if they fought, something might happen to him and he could die before they have a chance to make up. So she told him she forgives him.

The remaining 45 minutes of my phone call with Tammy involved her venting to me about how absolutely pissed off she is with Ken. Which I totally get. She needed to be able to tell someone her true feelings. And I really do understand. Especially the part about not wanting to be in a fight with your spouse when they're in a war zone.

Thursday, November 6, 2008   10:08 p.m.

Fakhir asked me to go to the tux place with him after work tonight to pick up his rental tux for the Ball. Lucia had to work and he wanted me there to help him make sure everything fit properly. The salesgirl in the tux place was totally flirting with him, tugging at the hem of his jacket more than necessary and standing a little too close to adjust his bow tie. He did look handsome, and I was about to tell him so when I noticed his shoes.

"What the fuck are those?" I ask.

"What the fuck are what?" He replies, grinning at the young sales associate, who's practically melting under the glow of Fakhir's radiant smile.

"Those," I say, pointing toward his shoes.

"Those are shoes, Emilie."

"I know they're shoes, Fakhir. But what are they and who's idea was it for you to wear them?"

Fakhir looks indignant. "It was my idea. And they're called …" he glances at Tux Girl for help.

"Spats," she says, nodding and smiling at me helpfully before quickly returning her adoring gaze to Fakhir.

I let out an exasperated sigh. "I know they're spats. I'm just … puzzled as to why you want to wear them? Your tux looks so nice," I explain. "And then there's … this." I wave my hand toward his feet. "They make you look like the Great Gatsby."

"Who's the Great Gatsby?" Fakhir asks.

"I think he's one of the bad guys in the Twilight series," the salesgirl explains, not taking her eyes off Fakhir.

"Uhmmm … no. That's not, umm … no." I reply, shaking my head. I'm suddenly having flashbacks to that time Fakhir and I went to DSW together to pick out work shoes for him. That was when I learned he has the weirdest taste in shoes of anyone I've ever met, male or female. I should've known better than to allow him to make his original trip to the tux store unchaperoned.

"Let me try again," I say, eyeing the extremely shiny black-and-white wingtips. "They make you look like Al Capone."

"Who's —" Fakhir starts to say.

I'm afraid Tux Girl is going to say something about The Hunger Games here so I quickly cut in. "These shoes make you look like a penguin, Fakhir. Do you want to go to the Marine Corps Birthday Ball looking like a penguin?"

He looks at himself in the three-way mirror and then at me. "No," he says uncertainly.

I take a gamble and make a play to recruit our sales associate to join my team. I offer her my most winning smile. "In your professional opinion, do *you* think these shoes truly enhance the ensemble?"

She folds her arms, placing one hand under her chin and circling Fakhir, as if appraising his attire. (In actuality I catch her checking out his ass, which I pretend not to notice.)

"Wellll …" she says, "Some all-black Oxfords might be nice. And I think we have a pair in his size."

"Yes!" I exclaim. "Thank you." Turning to Fakhir, I say, "That's the perfect compromise. Oxfords are kind of like wingtips, but without being too … gangster-ish."

"What's wrong with looking like Al Capone?" he asks.

"So you *do* know who Al Capone is," I say.

Fakhir catches Tux Girl's eye and rolls his eyes in my direction. "Can we just finish up here please?" he says to me. "Unless you want to stand around all night and talk until the cows turn blue in the face?"

Friday, November 7, 2008   5:33 p.m.

I heard from Fakhir after he took the test today; he says he thinks it went well. He was hoping maybe they'd grade it on the spot but no such luck. He said the immigration officer told him he should get his notification in the mail pretty quickly. God I hope so.

I'm heading out soon to pick up Finn at the train station. He asked if he could have "a few people" over to the house tonight. I told him as long as it doesn't turn into a full-blown party like what happened Labor Day weekend. He said it's just going to be him, Crystal, Neil, and Darryl. "Oh — and maybe Farah too," he said, as if it were an afterthought.

Dottie and Joey should be arriving soon after we get back from the train station. I'm happy they decided to come in for the Ball. The only downside here is that Lucia will be sleeping with me this weekend.

p.s. Are they doing anything special on Camp Victory for the Marine Corps birthday? (Something more than sticking matches in a pound cake I hope.)

Saturday, November 8, 2008 11:56 a.m.

Finn's get-together last night was fun. We decided to invite Arifah and Fakhir to join us since Farah was coming anyway. And of course Lucia, Joey, and Dottie were here too. Finn asked Rory if he wanted to invite a few friends, so Josh, Ethan, and Riikka came over — in addition to Crystal, Neil, and Darryl. (I called Wade at the last minute to see if he and Isabel wanted to stop by, but Wade said he was hoping to have some "alone time" with Isabel after they put Chloe to bed. I sure hope those two were able to have a serious conversation this time. It's long overdue.)

Even though it was chilly outside, everybody went out to the garage to hear The Smoking Lamps fire up their instruments and play a few tunes. They weren't as rusty as you might think, having not performed together in a few months. But they sounded pretty good. They even tried out a new song ("I'm Yours" by Jason Mraz), with Finn on lead vocals and keyboard. Seems like our tuition money is paying off — his musicianship skills sound more professional every time I hear him play. Of course, I'm partial, obviously. But I was impressed. (And so was Farah, apparently. I'm pretty sure she and Finn were eyeflirting while Finn was singing the lyrics to "I'm Yours." Rory didn't seem to notice — or he pretended not to. He was having too much fun horsing around with Josh, Ethan, and Riikka.)

I woke up before everyone else this morning. Lucia had her arm over my face most of the night, her forearm resting on my mouth, or my eyes, or my neck. At one point her hand was splayed over my entire face. I'd carefully pick up her wrist and gently place her arm back onto her side of the bed, only to have her fling it back onto me within minutes. And did I mention she snores? Around 5:30 a.m. I gave up and came downstairs to make some coffee and let the dogs out.

Dottie must have smelled the coffee or heard me puttering around in the kitchen, as she came tiptoeing down the stairs with Jacques in her arms about twenty minutes later. It's too cold to sit on the porch now — the air is chilly enough in the evenings and early mornings that you can see your breath. The black ash tree in the Stevens' back yard has lost all its leaves already, and the hawks have begun their southward migration for lack of frogs and snakes to snack on. When we let Jacques out in the yard for his morning constitutional, he interrupted the squirrels in their hunt for acorns, sending them scattering with his crazy yips. (Let's hope no one calls the dog police again.)

Once we let the pets back in and filled our coffee cups, Dottie and I cozied up on the couch together, sharing an afghan spread across our laps. Brig and Soda quickly laid claim to your chair, where they proceeded to have a stare-down with Jacques, who positioned himself on Dottie's lap (a strategic move that provided protection from the threat of being humped again by Soda).

Dottie wore a monogrammed baby-blue fleece robe and matching slippers with baby-blue poufs. I commented that her robe and slippers matched her silvery blue hair, and she replied that she had asked if Lucia would touch up her roots this afternoon before the Ball. Knowing how Dottie loves to dress according to a theme, I asked if her Ball gown was light blue too.

"Of course darling," she replies. "Baby blue is Joey's favorite color, remember?"

"I do remember. Only he calls it Air Force blue, right?" I smile at her over my coffee cup. "And is Joey going to wear blue tonight also?"

"Darn tootin'!" she says. "He bought a powder-blue tux with satin lapels and satin stripes down the sides of the pants. And a powder-blue ruffled shirt with a matching cummerbund. Oh, and a black bow-tie. He looks so damn handsome in it I could just eat him up."

It all sounds very '70s to me — typical Joey. Gotta love that guy. Although I wonder why he bought a tux instead of renting one — it's not like he's going to have a chance to wear it again anytime soon.

Dottie continues, "He was thinking of wearing his Air Force dress uniform — he tried it on and it actually fits, due to all the weight he's lost. But then he remembered he'd have to get his hair cut short if he wanted to wear his blues, and he wasn't willing to chop off his beautiful permed locks. He looked so spiffy in his uniform when he tried it on — it kind of got me all hot and bothered. I won't go into detail about what happened on the living room sofa that day — but let's just say I'm glad he's not getting his hair cut. I love running my fingers through his perm and—"

"I get the idea—no need to elaborate," I reply, holding up my hand. Smiling slyly, I add, "I guess that explains why Joey was in such a chipper mood last night when you guys got here."

Dottie is absolutely glowing. I wish I could look as good as she does at six o'clock in the morning. "Well, it was a bit of a mood-booster if I do say so myself," she says.

"So how's he been doing overall?" I ask.

"Well, he's been to the doctor a couple times since you and I last spoke. They're running some neurological tests."

"Why? What do they think is going on?"

"They said he might have undiagnosed TBI," she replies.

"Like, from the war?"

She nods. "I guess it happens, especially with Vietnam vets. Maybe they were in a collision or too close to a blast, and since they didn't have any obvious injuries, thought they were fine—just a bump to the head and a bad headache or whatever. They knew about TBI back then but the focus was mostly on more obvious injuries, like open head wounds."

"So Joey's been walking around with a brain injury all these years and not even known it?" I ask. "That doesn't seem possible—he's done so well in his career. He obviously doesn't have any cognitive issues."

Dottie shrugs. "Not that we're aware of. That's the reason for the neurological tests. I went with him to his last appointment and the doctor said mild TBI can go undiagnosed for years. And Joey could have been compensating for it all this time without even realizing it. That was the mentality back then you know. You don't seek treatment for things like headaches or noise sensitivity when your buddies are coming back in body bags."

Dottie and I sit silently, each of us lost in our own thoughts.

"Well. That would probably explain the tinnitus then," I say, breaking the silence.

"And the depression," she replies, absentmindedly petting Jacques.

"Does Joey remember a specific incident where he might have gotten a head injury?" I ask.

"I asked him about that on the way home from the doctor," she replies. "He didn't share much. Said something about a C-130 incident and then he clammed up."

"Well, he certainly seems to be taking things in stride."

"It's been a good week for him in spite of everything," Dottie says. "His daughter called the other night."

"Stephanie?! No way. I thought he hasn't heard from her in like, forever."

"That's true. It was quite a shock. But Joey's excited. She said she wants to get together with him, maybe have him meet his grandkids."

"Wow. Doesn't she live out in California?"

"Yeah, Louise moved out west after she left Joey, when Stephanie was just a little girl. It broke Joey's heart not to be able to see his daughter. He even tried flying out there once. Showed up on Louise's doorstep to plead with her to let him see their daughter. Louise called him a war criminal, told him never to come back, and slammed the door in his face."

"God. I remember you telling me about all the awful things Louise accused Joey of when he came back from Vietnam," I say.

"Even though Joey knows in his heart those hateful accusations are total lies," Dottie explains, "he says all that stuff might as well be true as long as his daughter believes it."

"So Joey sees this as his chance to maybe change her mind then."

"Right," Dottie agrees.

"Is Stephanie planning to fly out to St. Louis to see Joey, or ... ?"

"That's the plan," Dottie replies. "She's coming out the week before Thanksgiving. Joey's been walking on air ever since he talked to her. He hasn't seen her since she was twelve."

"Wow. That sure came together quickly. I can see why he's been in such high spirits. This is big news."

"Yes, it is." Dottie stares down into her coffee cup.

"Something tells me you're not all that happy about it," I say.

She hesitates. "I hate to be a Negative Nellie. And I would never say anything to Joey. But I don't have a good feeling about this."

I study Dottie's face. "It does seem awfully coincidental that Joey suddenly hears from his daughter after that call he got from his ex-wife asking about her share of his pension," I say.

"Bingo," Dottie replies.

Sunday, November 9, 2008   9:56 p.m.

Oh. My. Word. That was one wild Birthday Ball. Not quite as wild as the one on Okinawa where we ended up dancing on top of the bar at the O' Club at two o'clock in the morning. (That was the same night the XO spent the evening dancing with a potted plant after a few too many shots.) But this was one for the books. So many things to tell you, I'm not sure where to start. Perhaps a confession is in order: Things got a little out of hand regarding Tammy and me and some rum and Cokes. Nothing serious—just a difference of opinion concerning mine and Tammy's (and Dottie's) definition of hilarious versus Finn and Rory's entirely different interpretation of certain events. I suppose I should start from the beginning.

Everybody looked so spiffy. Sequins were definitely a thing this year—especially when it came to Dottie's outfit. Her powder-blue form-fitting gown had more sequins than Lucia's, Farah's, and Arifah's dresses combined. Lucia wore a black off-the-shoulder gown—the top was velvet with a satin band at the waist, and the full skirt shimmered with metallic studs and sequins. She and Fakhir looked stunning together (thank God we talked him out of the spats). In addition to touching up Dottie's pastel blue hair yesterday afternoon, Lucia gave all of us updos—including a last-minute updo for Tammy before our group got in our cars and drove over to the base, caravan-style.

Isabel and Wade looked marvelous too, even if they spent most of the night ignoring each other. (Either they never had that conversation Wade wanted to have the night before, or they had it and it didn't go well.) The few times they did stand side-by side, Isabel's low-cut crimson gown perfectly matched the blood stripe on Wade's dress blue trousers. If you didn't know about the trouble between them, they looked like the perfect couple.

I finally got to meet Leah's mystery husband, Cpl. Gibson. A little more pocket-sized than I expected. I mean, for someone who made it through advanced sniper school, I thought he'd be more of a hunk, you know? (Thanks to Hollywood stereotypes, I find myself guilty as charged.) Jacob was nice enough — if not a little full of himself. (Was he always that way, or is this a new development since he came back from California? I know he works in your shop but I'm not sure how much interaction you've had with him.) Leah looked gorgeous of course. Her canary-yellow gown absolutely popped against her long dark hair. She's the only woman I know who can pull off wearing yellow. She and Jacob weren't at our table, but from what I observed, they didn't spend a lot of time together either. In fact after the band started up Leah spent more time at our table than she did at her own.

Finn and Rory looked dashing in their suits. You would have been so proud of them, Liam. Everybody at the unit made a big deal about how much they've grown since the last time they saw the boys at Family Day. At just shy of six feet tall, Rory has almost caught up to Finn in the height department — assuming Finn is done growing. And they each towered over me by at least six inches when they asked me to dance. Those boys were so thoughtful — whenever the band played a slow song, Finn and Rory went out of their way to make sure I had someone to dance with. Whether it was one of them, or Joey, or Wade, or Fakhir, I got a chance to dance with everybody at least once. It was no substitute for being able to dance with you, but I was touched knowing how much the boys were looking out for me.

When he wasn't dancing with me, Finn spent most of the night dancing and talking with Farah. I haven't spoken to Fakhir or Arifah about Finn and Farah's budding romance, but from what I could tell last night they didn't seem to mind. It appears Rory has caught on that those two are an item now. Maybe he and Finn talked about it during one of their late-night conversations, and Rory gave Finn his blessing. If so, that would make Farah one of Rory's most short-lived crushes on record.

The night started out somber enough. I mean, how could it not when the first thing you see when you walk inside the community center is The Fallen Comrade table. When Lt.Col. Cromwell talked about it during the ceremony, it was impossible not to get choked up. He spoke with reverence about the empty chair, the inverted place setting, the lighted candle, the blank ID tags, the single red rose ... . I couldn't help but notice both Wade and Joey fighting back tears. Fakhir, stoic as always, stared straight ahead, his expression blank. (Was I the only one who glimpsed his Adam's apple move up and down, as if to swallow the lump in his throat?)

When Lt.Col. Cromwell mentioned the slice of lemon symbolizing the missing man's bitter fate and the salt sprinkled next to it representing the family's tears, the boys and I exchanged glances. Liam, I know The Fallen Comrade table is for those who died and those who are missing in action, but that moment gave us a chance to remember you, too. As we honored those who break bread with us in spirit only, I made a silent plea to the universe that our story will turn out differently. I smiled at the boys with tenderness, hoping to reassure them that everything will be okay. When you come home, the three of us will hug you tight. We'll sit down to share a meal together at the kitchen table, and your empty place setting will be empty no more.

Once dinner and the ceremony and all the pomp and circumstance — the standing and sitting and standing up again — were over, it was time to cut loose. And boy did people let their hair down, Tammy and I included. She kept us both supplied with a steady stream of rum and Cokes from the bar. It brought to mind our night at Manuel's and the pitcher(s) of margaritas. A different night, but same situation: pent-up nerves, and a chance to let off steam among friends. I'm happy we had each other to lean on (quite literally, by the time the evening was over).

When the band played Sade's "By Your Side," Wade asked me to dance, knowing it's one of our special songs. I think I would have cried if I didn't have anyone to dance with during that song and I told Wade so as we danced together.

"Thanks for remembering this is one of mine and Liam's songs," I say.

"Who could forget the sight of you two dancing to this song at the Quantico Ball," he replies, shaking his head. "No way would I let you sit this one out."

"You look nice tonight," I say, admiring his chest full of medals. "That's quite a fruit salad you've got there."

"Thanks." He lets go of my hand briefly to point to one of the medals. "Do you know what this one is for?" he asks.

"No, I have no idea what any of those medals mean," I reply. "Except for the Bronze Star."

"Well this one," he explains (acting rather self-important if I do say so myself), "Is a medal I got for … having the most medals." He holds my gaze, looking extremely serious.

"Wow. I didn't know they gave out a medal for that," I reply. Then, catching a glimmer in his eye, I say, "Wait a minute. You're full of shit, aren't you?"

He laughs and pulls me close again. "Oh Emilie. You are so gullible."

While Tammy and I were enjoying our rum and Cokes, Isabel and Leah were going to town on mojitos. No way Tammy and I could've kept up with them, even if we tried. At one point, when Tammy and I stumbled into the women's restroom together, we came upon Isabel and Leah huddled near the sinks in what appeared to be an intense conversation. Except as soon as they saw us, they abruptly stopped talking.

Meanwhile Jacob spent most of the evening holding court with a few Marines fresh out of boot camp, an unlit cigar in one hand and a glass of whiskey in the other, telling stories about sniper school as they gathered around him. Wade spent a good amount of time in the lobby, chatting with Gunny Lee or talking on the phone with his sponsor. I had asked him when we were dancing if it was hard for him being around alcohol, and he admitted it was. But he also said it was important to him to be at the Ball, and that he wasn't willing to miss out on meaningful events the rest of his life. He feels he needs to learn how to navigate these situations. He said if things got too rough he could always leave, and that Isabel could get a ride from Leah and Jacob if she wasn't willing to leave with him. Which is what ended up happening. Not that Wade left all that early — we were well into our cups when he decided it was time to make his exit. And not surprisingly, Isabel said she wanted to stay.

By the time Gen. and Mrs. Lewis made their usual early exit from the Ball (so the troops could get a little crazy on the dance floor without worrying if the CO was watching), the band had dispensed with the slow songs and things were already getting rowdy. It should come as no surprise that Dottie and Joey were a big hit on the dance floor. The Marines and their dates loved watching those two cut a rug, and Dottie and Joey pretty much owned the night.

It was a good thing Tammy and I had each other to dance with, as this is where Finn and Rory drew the line — they were perfectly willing to slow dance with their mom, but no way did they want to have *anything* to do with me when it came to the faster songs. This is also probably the point at which our perceptions of the evening began to diverge. For example, I saw both Finn and Rory covering their faces, heads down, when Tammy and I attempted to learn the moves to the Soulja Boy dance. (Those two will never again be able to hear "Crank That" without recalling the absolutely mortifying sight of their mother cranking her wrists on a pretend motorcycle followed by a lunge into Superman pose. But I digress.)

While Tammy and I were yukking it up on the dance floor, guess who we ran into? Portia. She was there with a Marine she met in her veterans' yoga class. (Questionable ethics from a teacher / student standpoint, wouldn't you say?) Anyway, I don't know how we didn't spot her earlier in the evening — her dress was hard to miss. It was made of a body-hugging flesh-colored mesh material that basically made her look like she was nude, except for strategically placed sequined appliqués that covered her private parts. Holy cow. I mean, people tend to go all-out on their gowns, and I love that. And she has the figure to pull it off. But if there were a handbook on What Not to Wear to a Marine Corps Birthday Ball, this dress would be Exhibit A.

I don't know if Wade caught sight of her before he left—I didn't see them talking or anything—but I wonder if seeing her is what precipitated his early exit, more so than the alcohol? (Another weird thing is that not long before we left, Tammy and I noticed Portia talking to Isabel and Leah. What I would've given to be a fly on the wall during *that* conversation.)

As the band played the last notes of its final song and the servers waited anxiously along the sidelines to start removing tablecloths and centerpieces, we gathered our belongings and reluctantly called it a night. Wade had taken their car so Isabel hitched a ride with Leah and Jacob. Lucia said she would get a lift with Fakhir, Arifah, and Farah. That left Finn as the designated driver for the rest of us. Tammy and I walked (okay, more like careened) across the parking lot arm-in-arm while I attempted to teach her the lyrics to "I'm a Rambler, I'm a Gambler" (which, as you know, is the song I like to sing after a certain number of drinks).

We piled into the car—Finn behind the wheel, Joey in the passenger seat, Rory all the way in back in the third seat, and Dottie, Tammy, and I happily squeezed together in the middle seat. We had heard a rumor they were doing sobriety checks at the gate, but since Finn was driving we had nothing to worry about. (If you had been with us, Liam, I might have allowed Finn a beer or a glass of wine at the Ball, but since we didn't have you to drive us home, we had decided in advance Finn would be our DD.)

As I mentioned, Finn and Rory were already unhappy with me due to my "Crank That" antics on the dance floor. They rolled their eyes at one another in the parking lot as Tammy and I sang the "Rambler, Gambler" song, and when Dottie, Tammy, and I needed assistance buckling our seatbelts, they were clearly about out of patience. (And I can't say I blame them.) As we waited in the line of cars to exit the base, headlights turned off, we could see the gate guards directing every third vehicle or so to pull off to the shoulder, where they would then have the driver blow into a Breathalyzer. No arrests had been made so far that we could see—whoever gave the weekend safety brief must have done a good job of scaring the bejeebers out of the Marines about drinking and driving.

When the MP gave the go-ahead to the car in front of us, Finn carefully pulled our car forward, and upon reaching the guardhouse he stepped on the brake, put the car in park, rolled down the window, and handed the gate guard his ID. Breathalyzer in hand, the MP studied Finn's ID, then leaned over to stick his head in our vehicle and get a good look at all of us crammed inside. Elbows resting on the driver-side door, he smiled and asked us if we had a good time at the Ball. Everyone cheerfully replied in the affirmative. The guard continued smiling at us, doing a visual check of everyone in the car. Maybe it felt like an awkward silence that needed to be filled, or maybe I thought I was being helpful, but it was at this very moment that I blurted —

"Officer, would you like me to blow you?"

As an MP no doubt he'd seen a lot in his career, and yet my question apparently catches him off guard. His smile falters and he looks at me as if maybe he hasn't quite heard me correctly. Sticking his head a little further inside the car, he says, "Ma'am?"

Tammy and Dottie dissolve into hysterics, rolling around helplessly beside me.

Realizing my mistake, I hurriedly correct myself. "I mean, do you want me to blow into your thing?" I wave theatrically toward the Breathalyzer in his hand.

Which sends Tammy and Dottie into another round of hysterics. I look at them gyrating on each side of me and, registering their laughter, I attempt to correct myself once again. "What I mean to say is, do you want me to do the blowie thing to you?"

Rory shouts from the third seat, "Oh my God Mom!!!" while Finn sits silently in the driver's seat, staring straight ahead, and Joey, in the passenger seat, holds his head in his hand, belly laughing.

Officer Friendly pulls his head out of the car and stands up, rocking back on his heels as he clearly struggles not to laugh. He looks at Finn sympathetically. "Dad is deployed, huh?"

"Yes, officer," Finn replies.

Smiling widely now, the MP hands Finn back his ID and says, "Take care of your mom tomorrow, son. She's gonna need it."

Monday, November 10, 2008   11:26 a.m.

Happy 233rd Birthday, Marine. And thank God tomorrow is Veterans Day and therefore no school today — I would've had to call in sick. Pretty sure I'm still hungover.

Finn and Rory didn't stay mad at me for long. They were on the grumpy side when they woke up yesterday morning — giving me that look teenagers tend to give when they're convinced no one else's parents are as embarrassing as their own — but once we all gathered around the kitchen table for a late breakfast, they were laughing and making fun of me along with everybody else.

Dottie and Joey (and Jacques) left for St. Louis at the same time Rory and I left to take Finn to the train station. Saying goodbye to Finn is never easy, but knowing he'll be back soon for Thanksgiving made our goodbye a little less tearful.

After we returned from dropping off Finn, Rory and I watched old movies the rest of the day, sharing a big bowl of popcorn for dinner. TCM was hosting a retrospective on Sidney Poitier so we got to see a bunch of our favorites including "The Defiant Ones," "A Raisin in the Sun," "In the Heat of the Night," and my number-one pick, "A Patch of Blue."

Dottie and I were talking about movies over the weekend and she told me I should start a film blog. I said I was surprised she knows what a blog is since she doesn't even have email, and she replied she read an article about blogs in the latest issue of *Wired*. Dottie is a walking enigma. She doesn't have a computer, and yet she reads *Wired*. When I told her that, she smiled mysteriously and said there are a lot of things I don't know about her.

I miss you. Will you be able to call soon?

Tuesday, November 11, 2008   7:10 p.m.

Happy Veterans Day my love. I don't suppose you got the day off. (Still wondering if you got to do anything special for the Marine Corps Birthday.) Besides Agnes and Eugene, we're the only other house in the neighborhood flying our flag today. It makes me sad to see so many of our neighbors not flying flags on a day meant to remember our veterans. Even if they don't have a flagpole, they could spend five bucks on a mini flag from Walmart and stick it in the grass on their front lawn. I guess for most people it's just another day off work.

Carmen started his new job at Mondo yesterday (no three-day weekend for them). Lucia said her mom and brothers helped him move into Wade's apartment Sunday night. Not that there was a lot to move — mostly just work clothes, toiletries, loungewear, and a few books. While Lucia was telling me about her dad last night, she brought up the likelihood that her mom and brothers will move to Wakeville at the end of the year. (That will give them time to save up for a deposit and rent money, and it will also allow the boys to finish out the semester here before enrolling in a new school in Wakeville.) She said that her parents invited her to come live with them again once they get their own place, but that they also understood if she wanted to stay here in Buell City where her job and Fakhir are. Lucia told me she's been thinking about it a lot. And then she hesitantly asked me if I'd mind if she kept living here with us for a while. I told her that we'd love for her to stick around and that there's always room for her in our house — even after you come home from Iraq. She said that was a big load off her mind and helps solidify her decision to stick around.

With her cosmetology classes coming to an end (her graduation ceremony is this weekend), Lucia says the salon is offering her more hours and that they'd like to keep her on as a stylist once she gets her license. It's one of the most popular salons in town, and it's a good thing she got her foot in the door by working for them as a shampooer while she was still in high school. They must realize what a catch Lucia is if they're already asking her to stay.

Rory went over to Isabel's yesterday afternoon to do some fall clean-up for them. Last time he was there, over a month ago, it was still warm out and the leaves had just started to turn. Now most of them have fallen. Rory mentioned to Isabel at the Ball Saturday night that he'd come over to rake leaves and get the lawn ready for winter.

When he got there, Isabel was still at work and Chloe was over at Mrs. Nardi's. The key to the shed was in the flower pot where it was last time, but Rory said when he went inside the shed to grab their rake, he noticed the gun safe was open and Wade's pistol wasn't in there. That concerned me because my first thought was that the gun had been stolen, but if the shed was locked then whoever took the gun knew where to find the key to the shed. And they also had to have known the combo to the safe. I texted Isabel to see if she knew the gun was missing and she replied yes, Wade had taken it back to Wakeville with him. I find that weird, don't you? Why would Wade need his pistol in his apartment in Wakeville? It's not like it's a high crime area or anything. I was planning to call Wade this week to check in anyway so I'll ask him about it when we talk.

Wednesday, November 12, 2008

The Midwest Courier Times
Local News, page 1

Accused school shooter pleads not guilty, trial date set

BUELL CITY—The suspect accused of attempting to carry out the shooting of multiple individuals at Buell City High School last month made his second court appearance today.

Marcus Oliver, his wrists handcuffed and wearing the orange inmate uniform issued by the Buell City detention center, pleaded not guilty to two counts of attempted first-degree murder and three counts of attempted second-degree murder, in addition to weapons charges including illegal possession of a firearm. Accompanied by his public defender, Oliver, 18, smiled and looked around the courtroom as the judge directed the defendant not to contact the individuals named in a criminal protection order issued at the request of law enforcement. The criminal protection order supersedes the previous civil restraining order filed against the defendant last spring.

The Midwest Courier Times has reached out to the individuals named in the protection order for comment but received no response in time for this article. A spokesperson for the family asked the media to respect the family's privacy.

After consulting with prosecutors and Oliver's public defender, the judge set a trial date for March. According to the judge's orders, pretrial motions will be heard in Walker County beginning March 9, 2009 through March 20, 2009. Jury selection will then commence on Monday, March 23, 2009. At one point during the hearing Oliver could be seen holding his handcuffed wrists in front of him while signing a court document.

Oliver, a former student at BCHS, is accused of planning and attempting the murders of a BCHS staff member and her son, also a student at the school, along with threatening the lives of several other students. The suspect entered the school with an AR-15 that authorities say was purchased illegally at a gun show by one of the defendant's associates. Weapons charges for that individual are pending, according to law enforcement.

School Resource Officer to be honored

School Resource Officer Sean Dempsey of the Buell City Police Department will be honored in a ceremony to take place next week at City Hall. Dempsey, a Gulf War veteran, is credited with saving multiple lives the day accused shooter Marcus Oliver entered the high school carrying a semi-automatic rifle. Oliver had written a letter which he left in his bedroom stating his intention to kill a paraprofessional at the school and her son. Oliver had also allegedly threatened to kill several students that were with the staff member at the time of the attempted shooting. A SWAT team had already entered the school when SRO Dempsey located the alleged shooter in a classroom as the suspect was attempting to gain entrance to a custodial closet where the staff member and her students were hiding. Dempsey quickly discharged his service revolver, striking the suspect in the back of the knee and incapacitating him. As an Army veteran, Dempsey stated his military training was beneficial in his response to the incident. "When I came upon the suspect and saw that he was armed with an AR-15 my training instincts kicked in," Dempsey stated. "I'm not a hero. I just did what any law enforcement officer would do in that situation." Dempsey's citation will be read by the mayor next Tuesday, November 18 at 3 p.m.

Thursday, November 13, 2008   6:43 p.m.

Rory and I decided not to go to school today after we saw the article in the paper last night. It seems like every time there's a news story about the Marcus incident, we get bombarded with questions the next day from students and staff alike. I understand everyone is still trying to process what happened, especially because it took place right here in our own school. It's healthy to want to talk about it. (In fact Rory and I are still touching base with the school psychologist, and she's been very helpful.) It's just hard for Rory and me when we're trying to have a regular day, and people keep bringing up the shooting. It's not something we can chat about peripherally, as if it happened to someone else. I called Dr. Gouwens this morning to explain why Rory and I wouldn't be in school. She was completely understanding, and encouraged us to take as much time as we needed. I told her we just needed the one day. We might need to take a day here and there in the coming months, but for now we feel like one day is enough to refill our wells.

So the trial is set to begin March 9th. I did the math. You left on January 13th. You were supposed to come home one year from that date. But with your deployment extended three months, you're not slated to come home until the middle of April. I was hoping the trial wouldn't start until after you came home. I know this is a long shot — or a total impossibility — but is there any chance you could come home just one month earlier? The trial is going to be hard enough, and without you here, well, I don't know how we'll be able to handle it on our own.

Were you able to open the link to the article I sent you? If the security firewalls over there won't allow you to access the newspaper website, let me know and I'll copy and paste the text into an email. One of the things that puzzled me about the item in the paper was the mention of the "family spokesperson" who requested that the media "respect the family's privacy." I have no idea who this so-called spokesperson is, because I didn't designate anyone to speak on our behalf. Our strategy so far has been to just not pick up any phone calls from numbers we don't recognize, and to avoid talking to reporters.

There were a few reporters hanging around out front last night and this morning, but Officer Clemmons managed to convince them to maintain a respectful distance. (By the way, I was finally able to get Officer Pizza Roll's real name, which is Officer Clemmons. Once the reporters got their location shots this morning and packed up and left, I brought her a cup of coffee and one of the breakfast burritos Rory and I had made earlier. I thanked her for looking out for us, and she greatly appreciated the gesture. I told her to swing by anytime she was in the area and we'd rustle up a snack or a cup of coffee for her if she needed sustenance.)

After the reporters cleared out Rory and I took a bike ride on the trail to enjoy the beautiful fall weather. It was unseasonably warm this afternoon — hard to believe just last week we had a dusting of snow. Rory and I stopped at our special spot where we like to skip stones in the creek. (He's still an ace stone skipper — me, not so much.) We saw some wild pumpkins growing on the other side of the creek, which again reminded me we forgot to carve pumpkins this year. We also forgot to harvest some of the wild blackberries that grow on the edge of the forest, in that spot where the creek bends. When we came upon the brambles today, the deer and raccoons and birds had already stripped them of their fruits. (These are the things I'm looking forward to doing with you next fall, when all of us are together again.) Near the end of the trail Rory and I saw a pair of cardinals perched on that exact birch tree where I saw them last week. I swear it's the same couple I encountered when I was walking Soda and Brig. I wonder how long they've been together, and if they have any young cardinals back in the nest, waiting for them to come home.

Friday, November 14, 2008   7:22 p.m.

I read an article in the International section this morning that an Iraqi soldier armed with an AK-47 opened fire on U.S. troops in Mosul, killing two and wounding six. Apparently the American troops were at an Iraqi outpost, waiting for their colonel to wrap up a meeting with an Iraqi Army officer. The Americans returned fire and killed the Iraqi soldier. But still. I thought the Iraqi military were our friends? More importantly, have you made any trips outside the wire recently — like, to Mosul for example?

I called Wade last night. I'd been meaning to touch base with him on a number of things — how Carmen's first week on the job went, if Wade had a chance to talk with Joey, what's the latest with him and Isabel, and why he brought his gun back to Wakeville.

He said Carmen's first week on the job has been stellar. The other supervisors are thrilled with Carmen's performance so far, and Wade said people are thanking him for bringing an experienced worker on board just in time for the holidays. Wade also said Carmen is an outstanding roommate. Last night he made mostaccioli with homemade meatballs after they got home from work, and he promised Wade he'd make his legendary tiramisu one night next week.

I mentioned to Wade that Rory had been by the house earlier in the week to do some fall cleanup and that he noticed the gun safe in the shed was empty. I told Wade I texted Isabel about it and that she said Wade took the gun back to Wakeville with him. I didn't want Wade to feel like I was interrogating him about it, but I admitted I was curious as to why he suddenly decided he needed to have his pistol at the apartment with him. Wade acted like it was no big deal. He said there's a shooting range nearby and he's thinking of going there sometime after work to practice his target skills and blow off some steam. The job is pretty stressful right now and he's looking for another hobby besides running. Which all makes perfect sense. Right?

Wade said he saw the item in the paper about Marcus' court appearance, and he asked how Rory and I were holding up. I told him we were kind of stressed about the prospect of a trial — as well as facing the inevitable questions about it at school — so we decided to call in sick and go on a bike ride instead. And it was the right decision, because being outside enjoying nature and the beautiful fall weather was the perfect antidote to our uneasiness. (Speaking of the weather, I noticed temperatures in Baghdad have cooled off considerably, with highs in the 70s and getting down to the 50s and 60s at night. Are you back to running at lunchtime now that it's cooled off during the day?)

Getting back to my phone call with Wade, I asked him if he'd had a chance to talk with Joey lately. Wade said Joey had called Wednesday night but Wade was still at work and didn't pick up. But they did have a chance to chat for a few minutes at the Ball, and Joey told Wade about his daughter flying out next week, and how excited he is about it. Wade and I filled each other in on what we each know about Joey's history with his ex-wife and daughter — like putting the pieces of a puzzle together. Turns out Wade and I have the same concerns as Dottie. One has to wonder about Stephanie's motives — why would she suddenly pop up in Joey's life after all these years of radio silence? Wade and I agreed that all we can do at this point is wait and see what happens. And to be there for Joey when the fallout begins.

I never got around to asking Wade about him and Isabel. We had already been on the phone a long time, and we both had to get up for work in the morning. I decided I'd ask him about it next time we talk.

Saturday, November 15, 2008   11:48 p.m.

I was so happy to hear your voice this morning. It's been so long since we last spoke. I admit I'd begun feeling more worried than usual after reading that article about the incident in Mosul. (And I knew you couldn't say anything about it on the phone, which is why I didn't bring it up. Hearing your voice was all the reassurance I needed.) I was also beginning to feel like I've been talking into a vacuum. It's good to know you've been receiving my emails, and that they help you feel more connected to all of us back home. I understand why you can't ask to come home early for the trial. It's not really an emergency by wartime standards. We'll be okay. I know I said that Rory and I won't be able to handle it, but we will. Or maybe Marcus will change his plea to guilty and we can avoid a trial altogether. Wouldn't that be nice.

After I got off the phone with you I told Lucia what you said about the troops loving her lip balm, and that it's become a hot commodity in the desert. She was super pumped to hear the Marines are already asking for more, and she immediately got on the phone with Farah and Riikka to discuss the recipe for their next batch.

Her graduation ceremony was tonight. I'd never been to a cosmetology school graduation before and I have to say it was a wonderful event. It was a lot like any other graduation except all of the graduates — guys and girls alike — were particularly glam. No surprise there. Lucia looked so beautiful. She truly was the most gorgeous person out of all the graduates. And I'm not just saying that because I love her.

When we saw her slowly walking in as they played pomp and circumstance, my heart swelled and my eyes got teary. Fakhir was sitting next to me, and when I opened my purse to grab a tissue, he held out his hand for one too. I assumed he was gesturing for a tissue for his mom, but when I glanced up to hand it to him, I saw tears spill over onto his cheeks. I could hardly believe my eyes. I've never seen Fakhir cry. He dabbed at his eyes and cheeks, then loudly blew his nose. As if to explain himself, he turned to me and whispered, "I'm just so proud of her." I put my arm around him and squeezed his shoulder. "Me too," I said.

After the ceremony I offered to treat everyone to a celebratory meal at Tony's. I had called earlier to ask them to reserve the large table in back since there were eleven us, including Lucia's parents and brothers as well as Fakhir's mom and sister and of course Rory and me. I had even called Wade this morning to see if he and Isabel wanted to come, knowing how fond they are of Lucia. Wade told me that he had opted not to come home this weekend. Then he said he had to go and that he'd tell me more next time we talk.

When we got home Rory went upstairs to read in bed while Lucia and I stayed up late chatting in the kitchen. We were having a really nice conversation when she received a text. She looked down at her phone, and I could see her eyes widen in disbelief. "You are not going to believe this," she said, showing me her phone. Without my reading glasses, I squinted at the screen. It was a text from Brian, pleading with Lucia to take him back because he decided he can't live without her. When I finished reading Lucia took the phone back and explained, "Crystal told me his latest girlfriend broke up with him, like, two days ago — for cheating on her." "Geez," I said. "What are you gonna say to him?" Instead of answering me, she looked down at her phone and quickly typed something, then without speaking showed me her screen. Squinting, I slowly read her text aloud: "If you can't live without me then why aren't you dead yet?"

God I love that girl.

Sunday, November 16, 2008   11:38 p.m.

I had quite the enlightening conversation with Wanda this afternoon. I was coming back from a walk with Brig and Soda when I saw her raking leaves on their front lawn.

"Hey," I call out, waving as I approach their property.

She looks up and says, "Oh. Hey Emilie," then continues raking. Her tone is decidedly not friendly. What's up with that, I wonder.

"Haven't seen you since book club last month," I say, smiling. I stop at the curb with Brig and Soda at my feet.

"I was just going to say the same thing," she says, still raking and not smiling. Then, as if suddenly remembering something of interest, she says, "Vince and I saw the article in the paper. So I guess there's going to be a trial?"

"Guess so," I reply. Scrambling for a different topic, I say, "Hey, there was something I wanted to ask you about."

Wanda stops raking and her body becomes still. "Okaaay," she says warily. "What did you want to ask?"

This conversation is way too weird. "I might have asked you this before," I say, "but I was just wondering if you're the one who—"

"It wasn't us," she interrupts, her hand still on the rake, her body frozen in place.

"Okay," I reply. "Well then maybe you can tell me if you know who—"

"I don't know who did it," she interrupts again. She looks like she's holding her breath.

Now I'm really confused. What is her deal? "Wanda, what are you talking about?"

She regards me carefully. "What are *you* talking about?" she replies.

"The gifts," I say. "The anonymous gifts I've been getting since Liam left. I'm asking you if you're the one who's been leaving them on our porch. Because they're really thoughtful. And I just want to thank who-ever's been doing it. I can't begin to explain how much those gifts and notes have cheered me up these last ten months."

"Ohhh," she says, smiling now, her body becoming unfrozen. "I thought you were going to ask if we were the ones who filed the complaint about the dogs barking."

"No," I reply, slowly shaking my head. "That's not what I was ask-ing about."

She's very animated now. "Whew. Well that's a huge relief." She starts raking again.

"Wanda, how did you know about the dog complaint?" I ask.

"You told me about it," she says, looking at me like I'm looney-tunes.

"I never told you about that."

She stops raking again. "Yes you did."

I'm one-hundred percent certain I never mentioned this to Wanda, or to anyone at book club. "No. I did not," I say, more forcefully this time. "I never told anyone about it. Except for Liam."

She looks behind her, as if searching for an escape route, and says nothing.

"Wanda — there's no way you could've known about that complaint," I say. "Unless you were the one who filed it."

She shakes her head, still not speaking.

"Why didn't you just come knock on our door and talk to me if there was a problem with the dogs?" I ask.

She exhales loudly through her nose. "Vince and I are just tired of dealing with all the infractions," she says.

"All the infractions? What are you talking about?" I ask. Then, a light bulb goes off. "Wait. Are you the ones who filed the complaint about the trash cans too?"

She looks at me defiantly. "Like I said, Emilie. There've been a lot of infractions."

My eyes travel downward to Brig and Soda, sitting patiently by my feet, waiting to go in the house. My mind searches back in time, over the last several months. I lift my eyes again to look at Wanda. "And I suppose you're also the ones who called in the noise complaint on The Smoking Lamps?"

She rolls her eyes in disgust. "Don't even get me started on those kids and that band," she says. "Every. Friday. Night. Vince and I had to listen to that nonsense."

"I thought we were friends Wanda? You and Vince came to Finn's graduation party. You even invited me to go to Bunco with you after Liam left —"

"Oh!" she exclaims. "Don't remind me. One of the most *embarrassing* nights of my life. I brought you to Bunco with me because I felt sorry for you, Emilie. And then you have the nerve to go and get salty with someone because they make an innocent remark about Muslims and the ninja outfits those people wear?"

I swallow hard, trying not to cry. "I didn't know you felt that way."

"And then that night I fixed all those healthy foods for book club and you just brazenly go and order a pizza as soon as you get home? Do you think I didn't notice the pizza delivery guy pulling up in front of your house 30 minutes after you left?" She's really on a roll.

I look toward our house, my thoughts jumbled. How could I have been so wrong about someone? I feel like such a dumbass. Pausing to consider Wanda one last time, I say, "So I take it you're not the one who's been leaving the anonymous gifts on my porch." It's more of a statement than a question.

Her puzzled expression tells me she fails to grasp the irony of this last comment

I gently tug on the dogs' leashes, and they follow me across the lawn, tails wagging. Once I'm safely inside the house I close the front door and lean against it, letting out a long sigh. I drop the leashes to the floor but Brig and Soda remain close by, watching me with concern. I search my coat pockets for a tissue. I find a crumpled but clean one — from last fall, probably — and use it to wipe my tears away. The second time in as many nights.

Monday, November 17, 2008   9:59 p.m.

I'll be okay. Don't worry about me. It's not like Wanda and I were best friends or anything. I was just so taken aback by the whole thing. And I guess she caught me at a vulnerable moment. I'm fine, Liam — really. It's good to know, after all this time, who was behind those stupid complaints. When I told Rory everything Wanda said, he called her "the Picasso of Pettiness." Ha! That made me laugh.

Speaking of Rory, he just came in our room asking for a back rub. Gotta go.

I love you.

Tuesday, November 18, 2008   6:26 p.m.

Lots of news coming out of Iraq lately. I read something that said Iraqi authorities have taken over responsibility for the security of Wasit province from U.S. military forces. Which would make it the 13th province to be transferred back to the Iraqis, out of a total of 18. So that sounds like a good thing.

And in even bigger news, the Iraqi cabinet approved the Status of Forces Agreement between the U.S. and Iraq, which calls for the complete withdrawal of U.S. forces from Iraq by the end of 2011. It still needs to be approved by the Iraqi Parliament, but this is also good news, with the end of the war now in sight. I only wish they included a stipulation to leave more of a U.S. peacekeeping presence in Iraq, to ensure stability after the war is officially over. Like we've done in Japan, and Korea, and Germany. I don't understand why that's not happening in Iraq. No doubt those in power have their reasons. Does it feel to you like you're making progress over there? You're doing hard work Liam, and I hope that once in a while you feel like you're accomplishing things.

Rory and I went to Officer Dempsey's ceremony at City Hall this afternoon. We got to leave school early which was nice. Several of us from the school were there, plus Officer Dempsey's family, some local press, and the mayor of course. Mayor Gunderson gave a speech about everything Officer Dempsey did the day of the shooting, then read the citation aloud and presented him with a plaque. Officer Dempsey said a few words, mostly the same thing he's been saying all along, which is that he was just doing his job. Rory and I had already sent him handwritten letters expressing our gratitude for saving our lives and those of the other students. Today we brought him a bouquet of red roses and a gift card to Target, which we presented to him after the ceremony ended. The mayor spoke to Rory and me, shook our hands and said how happy he was that we could make it. When the reporters started circling, snapping photos and asking questions, Mayor Gunderson's bodyguard escorted us through a door labeled "staff only," then down the hall to a rear exit, making sure we made it to our car without being bothered.

Wednesday, November 19, 2008   9:22 p.m.

I almost didn't go to book club tonight. Although I had read the book, I just didn't feel ready to see Wanda again so soon after our encounter the other day. I called Tammy last night to talk it over, and she convinced me to go. Besides, she said, Leah is hosting and wasn't I curious to see if Kim and Charlene will try to recreate Leah's outfit from last month? (They did not disappoint.)

It was the first time I'd been to Leah's apartment. It's small, but super cute. Jacob stayed in the bedroom most of the night, except to come out and say a brief hello while we were having appetizers and drinks. Leah made plant-based finger foods with ingredients from Alfalfa's that were unexpectedly delicious: cucumber and avocado crunch rolls, buffalo cauliflower bites, and the cutest little quesadillas stuffed with peppers and carmelized onions and some sort of vegan cheese that I surprisingly did not hate.

While a few of us were standing around the punch bowl filled with Sangria (and loaded with fresh fruit like blueberries, strawberries, and pineapple), Wanda came up to pour herself a cup. When I said hello, she promptly turned her back and began talking to someone else. Geez. Obviously I was mistaken if I thought she might act like a grown-up. She pulled pretty much the same shit the rest of the evening, turning her back to me whenever I was in the vicinity (which was most of the night due to the close quarters), leaving me out of conversations, and basically trying to pretend I wasn't there. Whatever. I won't say her behavior didn't hurt my feelings and make me feel uncomfortable. It did. But it also clarified for me what a childish jerk she is. How I never realized this before is what puzzles me. I thought I was a better judge of character than that.

Knowing what had transpired between Wanda and me (because I had filled her in the night before), Tammy made sure to include me in her conversations, pulling me around by the hand most of the night. Even Agnes seemed to sense the discord, and was especially warm and friendly to me the entire time, making a lot of eye contact, and drawing me back into the book discussion whenever Wanda talked over me.

We discussed a crime thriller called *Sharp Objects* by a new author named Gillian Flynn. It was a change of pace from the classics and literary fiction we tend to read for book club, and most of us enjoyed it. It was pretty dark, which I didn't mind, although some of the others did. Overall a good pick on Leah's part. I'm interested to see what this author comes up with next.

Now, for the exciting part of the evening: Kim and Charlene's outfits. It appears they went all-out on their attempts to replicate Leah's outrageous getup from last month. Both of them wore skinny jeans and tribal print blouses — that was the easy part. They must've had a hard time locating fringe vests unfortunately — Leah said she got hers in a thrift store. So no fringe vests. But they did have on moccasins. Not the knee-high moccasins Leah had on (again, another thrift-store find on her part). But definitely Minnetonkas (or at least Minnetonka knock-offs). And the best part? The headbands. Including the feathers down the back. I admit, these outfits may have been cute in the '70s. But in 2008? Kim and Charlene looked like they were a month late for Halloween.

So far Leah, Tammy, Agnes, and I are the only ones in on the joke. (Although we did notice some of the other members giving Kim and Charlene's apparel the side-eye.) It's been an interesting social experiment. And yet, I think the next time I talk to Leah I'll suggest the prank has run its course. Maybe my latest interaction with Wanda has made me a little more sensitive to these matters. The last thing I want is to hurt someone's feelings. Let Kim and Charlene wear whatever they want, if it makes them happy.

Thursday, November 20, 2008   7:14 p.m.

After I got home from book club last night, I had a voicemail from Dottie. She said Joey's meet-up with Stephanie on Tuesday did not go well. At all. Even though it was late, I called Dottie back. Joey had gotten home from his VFW meeting by that time, so Dottie told Joey she was going to fill the tub and take a bath while she talked on the phone with me. Which allowed her enough privacy to speak freely.

So Joey met Stephanie at a nearby coffee shop Tuesday afternoon. Stephanie had flown in from California and taken a cab to the coffee place. Joey said it was very emotional seeing her. They both cried, and she let him give her one of his famous bear hugs. (She said she remembered those hugs from when she was a kid.) Everything seemed to be going okay in the beginning. Stephanie showed Joey pictures of his grandkids — two girls and a boy, ages nine, eleven, and thirteen. Grandkids which he never even knew he had. Joey asked Stephanie a lot of questions about the children — what hobbies they're into, what foods they like, what are their favorite subjects in school, and so on.

After they discussed the kids at length, Joey asked Stephanie about her career (she's "in between" jobs at the moment) and he also inquired about her husband (there were two husbands, both of them out of the picture now). When Joey asked Stephanie about her life in the years between his estrangement with her mother and now, she was vague on details, repeatedly returning to the subject of "Joey's grandkids," as she kept referring to them. Joey took that to mean maybe she'd had a hard life and didn't want to talk about it, which was fine with him. Strangely, Stephanie didn't seem all that interested in Joey's life, except to ask how many years he worked at the Railroad Administration. Joey had thought maybe he'd tell Stephanie about Dottie, but the longer they spoke the more he realized Stephanie didn't want to hear about Joey's personal life, most especially not his girlfriend.

They talked for about two hours. It seemed they had covered all they could, and the conversation began to wane. Stephanie said she needed to return to the airport soon — she was taking the red-eye back to California. Joey offered to give her a ride but she said she'd call a cab. Joey was hoping he would have a chance during the course of the conversation to clear up any "misunderstandings" there might be about his time in Vietnam, but the moment to bring it up just never seemed right. He told himself he would try to talk about it with his daughter next time they met.

As they stood up to leave, Joey asked Stephanie if he could meet his grandkids sometime in the near future — he understood that Thanksgiving might be too soon, but how about Christmas? He offered to fly out to California to meet them, and he would bring them Christmas presents — anything they wanted, just send him a list. At that, Stephanie acted like Joey had just reminded her of something she had forgotten to mention these past two hours. She said that she'd *love* for Joey to meet the grandkids, but she needed a favor from him. Joey said of course, anything, just ask. She smiled and said, "Great, that's what I was hoping to hear." And then she asked Joey if he could add her as a beneficiary to his Railroad pension. And his life insurance too, if he had any. She was a little tight on funds at the moment, and if he could expedite the paperwork, she'd be happy to set up a meeting between him and his grandkids as soon as she started receiving the checks.

"Oh my fucking God," I say to Dottie. "What did Joey tell her?"

"Well," Dottie says, "he told me he was so gobsmacked he could only reply that he'd look into it. And in response to that, Stephanie asked if she was at least included in his will, since she is his biological daughter."

"And what did Joey say to that?"

"He told Stephanie that he loves her very much, that he'll never stop loving her, and that he wishes things had turned out differently."

"And then?" I ask.

"And then he left the coffee shop and came home," Dottie replies.

"He's not really going to give her any of his money, is he?" I ask, incredulous.

"I don't know Emilie. To be honest I didn't ask Joey about that. I feel that's his decision to make, and if he wants my input he'll ask me for it. Besides, I get along just fine on Wally's pension from the Navy. So it doesn't matter to me what Joey does with his money."

"I understand. I just hope for Joey's sake he doesn't get taken by that con artist daughter of his."

"Me too," Dottie says. "It's not the money I'm worried about. I just feel terrible for Joey."

"So how is he? I mean emotionally?"

"He came home yesterday and told me the whole story. Then he went straight to bed. Didn't even put his pajamas on. Just laid down in his clothes, on top of the spread, staring at the ceiling. Stayed like that, awake, the rest of the night, until it was time to go to his doctor appointment this morning."

"Oh man. That breaks my heart. How did the appointment go?" I ask.

"Not real well. The doctor said the CT scan they took last week shows signs of mild TBI. An old injury, from what they can gather. They want to admit Joey to the hospital after Thanksgiving to do more tests and keep him there for observation."

"I am so sorry Dottie. What can I do? Do you want me to come to St. Louis? I can take off work. Just say the word."

"That's sweet of you darling. But no, that's not necessary. I was just glad to see Joey go to his VFW meeting tonight. To me that was a good sign. I was afraid he was going to stay in bed all day again after his doctor appointment. I'm relieved he went out. Those meetings are important to him."

"Well, at least tell me you guys are coming here for Thanksgiving then?" I ask.

Dottie replies, "Is the Pope Catholic? We wouldn't miss it for the world."

Friday, November 21, 2008   7:39 p.m.

Fakhir passed the written test! And they gave him a date for his swearing-in ceremony: Monday, December 22nd. He's going to be a U.S. citizen. This is such good news. It's been a long haul for Fakhir. He was absolutely glowing when he stopped by tonight to pick up Lucia for their date. He said his mom and Farah are thrilled, too. And of course Lucia is delighted. They were on their way to Woolley's to celebrate.

In other good news, Fakhir said they heard from his two older sisters, Fawzia and Farida, and things are progressing for them in Norway. It took them a while to find jobs, but they finally got hired as housekeepers at a high-end hotel in Oslo. Even though both of them speak English quite well, it's hard to get a job outside the tourist industry if you don't speak Norwegian. So the uncle has helped them sign up for online classes to learn the language. They say it hasn't been easy getting acclimated, and they miss Arifah and Farah and Fakhir, but they feel safe in Norway — and that's all that matters.

When I got home from work today I realized I hadn't done laundry in a while. I threw in a load from my hamper and went into Rory's room to gather up his dirty clothes. (Amazingly, Lucia has been doing her own laundry, and last week I saw her actually fold her clothes and put them back into her dresser drawers instead of tossing them on the bed. There are still several piles of clothes on her floor, but progress is progress.) Getting back to Rory's room, it was quite a mess. I found a half-eaten PBJ on his dresser that looked like it might have been there all week. When I was picking up the clothes from his floor, I spotted a piece of clothing sticking out from underneath the bed. I knelt down to grab it. Imagine my surprise when I discovered a peach-colored camisole. I looked under the bed again and pulled out a matching pair of peach-colored underwear.

I went down to the basement where Rory was playing Mario Kart, the camisole and underwear in my hand.

"Rory, what were these doing under your bed?" I ask, one hand on my hip and the other holding forth the undergarments.

He glances impatiently at me, irritated that I'm interrupting his video game. "I don't know." He goes back to playing his game.

"Listen up. First I find one of Lucia's bras under your bed. Now I find a camisole and a pair of underwear. How in the world is this stuff getting under your bed?"

He rolls his eyes but doesn't look away from the game. "I don't know Mom. Ask Lucia."

I stand there a minute, the lingerie in my hand, going over the possibilities. "Rory, turn off the video game please." I walk to the couch and sit down next to him. "I want to talk to you."

He lets out an exaggerated sigh and pauses the game, eyes still on the screen.

"Son, will you look at me please?"

He folds his arms and reluctantly turns his head my way, his body still facing the TV set.

"Rory, you know you can talk to me about anything, right?"

He nods, still acting extremely put-out.

"Even embarrassing stuff. You know I'm always here for you, right?"

"Hmm hmm." He steals a glance at the paused screen.

I shift my weight on the couch. "So, you know, if you ever have any … questions … like about sex or anything—"

"Mom. We've already had that talk. Like a million times," he says.

"Well I just want to make sure you know you can always come to me. And Dad too."

He nods impatiently. "Yeah. I know."

I glance down at the lingerie in my hand. "So is there anything you'd like to talk to me about right now?"

"I'm kind of busy here Mom. I was just about to get to the next level." He glances at the screen again.

"Okay. But you know Dad and I will always love you no matter what, right?"

"I *know* Mom," he says, his irritation bubbling over.

"What I mean to say, Rory, is that if you ever have any inclinations … or urges … that you don't feel comfortable talking to anyone else about …"

His expression changes from annoyed to appalled. "Mom! What are you talking about?"

I make my voice as normal as possible. "Well, for example, let's say if you ever wanted to wear women's clothing— "

He looks at me, absolutely horrified.

I rush to finish my sentence. "That would be totally fine with me and Dad. I just want you to know our love for you is unconditional. We're a very accepting family you know."

"You know what Mom?" he says.

"Yes?" I nod encouragingly.

"I pretty much hate you right now."

"I'm just trying to be a good parent Rory."

"I would like you to leave the room please." Rory turns his attention back to his video game, unpausing it.

I get up from the couch but remain standing there, watching him.

Rory pauses the game again and shoots me a threatening look. "Am I going to have to call Dad and tell him you've finally lost your mind? Because I will. If you do not leave here in the next five seconds."

I slowly back out of the room as Rory glares at me. When I reach the stairs I hear him restart the game. I also hear him muttering to himself. Something about living in a fucking nuthouse.

Saturday, November 22, 2008   4:44 p.m.

Leah called last night. I was up in my room watching "Dial M for Murder." Rory had Josh over. They were in the kitchen making bagel bites and laughing hysterically. I'm guessing Rory told him about our conversation earlier.

I can't remember the last time Leah and I chatted on the phone, so it was something of a surprise to hear from her. We made small talk at first, about the Ball and book club and whatnot. I shared my thoughts about calling off our fashion prank on Kim and Charlene, and Leah agreed the caper had run its course. When I asked her how it's been going with Jacob back home, she said, "Well … that's what I was calling about. It hasn't been going great."

"I'm sorry to hear that," I say. "But it's only been — what — less than three weeks? These things take time."

"Yeah. Three weeks this Sunday," she replies. "I feel dumb for even calling you about this Emilie. It's not like he was deployed overseas or anything."

"There's going to be an adjustment period no matter where he was," I say. "He was gone a long time."

"He left in April," she says. "It feels like forever ago."

I think back to when I first met Leah and feel a twinge of regret. It was at the FSG meeting in May when she shared how lonely she was, and told us the thing about shaving only one leg. I was a jerk for laughing in response to her heartfelt confession. (And yet that doesn't stop me from wondering if she's back to shaving both legs now.)

"So what's been going on?" I ask, trying to shake off my guilt over the FSG debacle. I silently remind myself that I did in fact reach out to Leah after that, inviting her to join us for Father's Day. I hope I've more than made up for my initial transgression by now. If anything I think we've done a lot these last several months to help her feel less lonely. Come to think of it, that cookout is where Leah and Isabel first met … .

"… And so I told him he just seems different since he got back and he said I seem different too," she says.

Catching the tail end of what Leah has just told me, I chastise myself for letting my mind wander. I vow to give her my undivided attention. "You know that's pretty common though, right?" I ask.

"Feeling like strangers to one another?" she says. "I had no idea this would happen. I thought him being gone for seven months was the hard part, and that coming home would be the easy part."

"Thanks to all those homecoming videos they show on YouTube nowadays," I say.

"Tell me about it," she says. "I guess I never thought about what happens after the cameras are off."

"Now you know."

"You knew we got married a week before he left, right?" she asks.

"Now that you mention it, I do remember you telling us that," I reply. "Which makes things even more complicated. You guys are still figuring things out."

"We did live together for six months before we got married," she says. "And we had a nice little routine going. Now, it's all messed up."

"How so?" I ask.

"Like …" There's silence on the line as she gathers her thoughts. "Before he left, we used to make dinner together as soon as we both got home from work. But when he was gone, I got into the habit of decompressing for a while before starting the meal prep. I'd sit on the balcony and read a magazine, or go over to Isabel's to sit in the sun and have a cocktail before dinner. Now Jacob comes home starving and gets mad at me because I don't want to eat as soon as I get off my shift at Alfalfa's."

"You guys developed different routines while you were apart. It's going to take a while to get back into a rhythm again," I say.

"Like how long?" she asks.

"Well, you were apart for seven months. It could take at least that amount of time to get used to each other again," I reply.

"That's not what I was hoping to hear," she says. "He just seems more rigid than he used to be. And when I told him that, he said I've become too 'laid back' about stuff. I don't know how we're ever going to get back to the way we were."

"You're not ever going to get back to the way you were, Leah," I say. "People grow and change during deployments and TDYs. Jacob got used to the strict rules and structured routine at sniper school. He's going to have to unlearn some of that. And you became more independent while he was away. You got to know yourself a little better, your likes and dislikes. The trick is to find a way to meet each other in the middle."

"I don't think I can last through another seven months of this," she says. "How did you and Liam ever do it? You guys probably didn't fight over stupid stuff the way Jacob and I do."

This makes me laugh. "I wish you could have seen us when Liam came back from his first deployment, Leah. It was pretty much a clusterfuck."

She laughs. "I don't believe you Emilie. But feel free to convince me by sharing the details. And I mean *all* the details."

"We were newlyweds — just like you guys," I begin. "Well, maybe we'd been married six months or so. Liam had gone on his first deployment — to South Korea. He was only gone three months but when he came back I barely recognized him."

"What do you mean?" she prods.

"Well, first off, he'd started smoking while he was in Korea. Something he'd never done back home. I put an end to that ricky-tick. And then — well, you'd have to know how fastidious Liam is about his belongings and personal hygiene to fully appreciate this one — but when he came back from Korea, his footlocker stunk up the entire house! I'm talking cigarette smoke, sweat, and garlic. Oh my God. The garlic. He had developed a liking for kimchi over there. He'd been eating so much of it his skin literally reeked of garlic. For days." I can hear Leah chuckling on the other end of the phone. Turning serious, I continue, "But those were minor things. What bothered me the most was the way his personality changed. He had become gruff. Not as considerate as he typically is. And the worst thing? He started ordering me around, like I was one of his troops or something. That was when I blew. I told him to cut that shit out right this minute or I was going to walk out of there quicker than he could say fuck a rubber duck."

"Wow. How did you guys work through that?" she asks.

"First thing I learned from that deployment was not to let them bring their footlocker in the house. Ever. That sucker stays in the garage. Second thing is not to be afraid to push back when they start acting like assholes. Because they will. And third thing is to give each other space. Like, a *lot* of space. That first deployment after Liam came back, we fought like cats and dogs. Over every little thing. He didn't like the way I loaded the dishwasher. I didn't like the way he folded the laundry. After his second deployment, we realized it was better to let that shit go. Give each other a wide berth, physically and emotionally. Be kind to each other. And eventually everything will be okay again."

"I wish I had your optimism," Leah says. "Jacob says he feels like a stranger in his own house. And that I'll never understand what it was like for him at sniper school—the constant pressure, the stress and worry that he'd be the next one to drop out. I admit, Emilie, it's weird having him around after being on my own for so long. And I feel like he doesn't appreciate how much I held things together while he was away. A lot has happened since he left."

I wonder what she means by that last thing. Does she mean "a lot has happened" in an abstract way, like she's grown and become more independent? Or does she mean it in a literal way, as in *oh boy, if you only knew the shit that has gone down these last seven months*. And if it's the latter, what exactly was it that happened?

I realize I've let my mind wander again. Somehow, I feel as if probing for details on what Leah means by that last statement isn't the right response here. I decide a dose of reality mixed with encouragement is in order. "It's true you'll probably never fully understand what it was like for him," I say. "And he'll never fully appreciate all that you did to take care of things back home. But you can't hold that against each other.

You're both just doing the best you can right now. Give each other some space."

"That's another thing," Leah says. "Jacob doesn't like it when I spend time with Isabel after work some nights. He says he's used to having me all to himself. But I'm not going to stop hanging out with Isabel. And he can't make me." There's a fierceness in her voice when she says this last thing, more so than at any other point in our conversation.

"It's important to be close with people other than our spouses," I say. "And not just during deployments. Is Jacob actually trying to say you can't hang out with Isabel?"

"Not exactly," she replies. "But he pouts on the nights I go out with her."

"Would it help if he got to know Isabel?" I ask. "Maybe the four of you should go out on a double date one of these weekends. I could watch Chloe and you guys could do something fun together. You never know — it might be good for you and Jacob to get out and do something with another couple."

Leah grows quiet. After an awkward pause she says, "I don't think that's gonna happen."

I'm just about to ask her why not when she quickly adds, "It's getting late. I'll let you get back to your movie Emilie. Thanks for talking to me. You're a good friend."

Something about Leah's tone during that last part of our conversation leaves me wondering. I grab the remote and turn the TV back on. "Dial M for Murder" has ended so I decide to call it a night. I switch off the lamp on my nightstand and scooch myself under the covers, lying awake in the darkness. The pets are already snoozing as they lay alongside me. There's something niggling at me about my conversation with Leah. I run through everything we talked about, hoping whatever it is that's on the fringes of my brain will come to the forefront. Something about Isabel. My mind meanders and I'm starting to feel sleepy when it hits me: Why did Leah call *me* for advice? Why not Isabel? From what I gather, those two are much closer than Leah and I are. And Isabel has lots of experience with deployments and TDYs. Maybe not as many as I've been through, but enough to have learned a thing or two about reintegration. Why would Leah call me when she's got Isabel to confide in? Or is there something about her marriage to Jacob that Leah doesn't want Isabel to know about?

Sunday, November 23, 2008 5:18 a.m.

Finn texted me yesterday to say he ran out of his allowance a day early, and could I please spot him an advance so he could go out to eat with his friends? He must have caught me at a weak moment because I went ahead and transferred the money into his account, no questions asked. I don't know what's gotten into me. Maybe I just didn't have the energy to say no this time. I'm turning into a soft touch, Liam. You'd better get back here soon, before I go completely soft on these boys.

I also meant to tell you that yesterday afternoon Lucia, Farah, Riikka, and Rory had taken over our kitchen again, cooking up a new batch of lip balm for the troops. This time Lucia made two recipes: the soothing eucalyptus with aloe that she made before, and a new citrus-flavored balm with lemon and lime oils. She says she might try a coconut-almond mix next time. She also appropriated my milk frother (without asking) to blend the oils before mixing them into the shea butter. (Bottom line is, I'm gonna need a new milk frother.)

Later in the evening, after they finished making their lip balm and had eaten the pizzas I ordered for dinner, Fakhir picked up Lucia for a date while Farah and Riikka hung out in the basement with Rory and Josh watching reruns of "The Office." I was in the family room brushing Smedley and Daly (they, along with Brig and Soda, are shedding like mad now that the weather's changing) when there was a soft knock on the door. It was Wade, standing on our front porch, hands in his jeans pockets, looking sheepish.

"Hey, come on in," I say, holding the door open for him.

He ambles inside, not saying anything, and follows me into the family room, where he plops himself on the couch.

"You want some water or juice or something?" I offer, standing halfway between the couch and the kitchen.

"I'll take some water," he says.

I fill two cups with ice water, then set them down on the coffee table in front of us as I take a seat beside him.

Wade takes a packet of Nescafé instant coffee from his jeans pocket, tears it open, tilts his head back, and proceeds to pour the contents of the packet onto his tongue. He then takes a swig of water, swishes it around in his mouth, and swallows, releasing a satisfied sigh as he sets his glass back on the coffee table.

"What the fuck did you just do?" I ask.

"Made myself a cup of coffee," he says, smiling.

"I could've made you a cup of coffee," I say. "All you had to do was ask."

He shrugs. "Sometimes I like to drink it the way we did out in the field. Just for old times' sake."

"That's disgusting," I say. "More importantly, it's eight o'clock on a Saturday night. Why the caffeine? You're not normally a nighttime coffee drinker, are you?"

"No. But I'm driving back to Wakeville tonight. I need to be alert for the drive."

"Why are you going back tonight?" I ask. "And — before I forget — why did you not come home last weekend?"

"Last weekend I stayed back in Wakeville to look at apartments. It's time for me to move out of the corporate apartment and get my own place," he says.

"I thought you liked having Carmen as a roommate?" I say.

"Oh — he's a great roommate. I was only supposed to have that apartment a few months, and it's been almost five months now. Carmen's next in line anyway — he should have the place to himself," Wade explains.

"Makes sense," I say, nodding.

"Also ..." he continues, "I was hoping that if I snagged a decent place in Wakeville, I'd be able to convince Isabel and Chloe to come live with me."

"And what's the verdict on that?" I ask.

"That's a no-go," he replies.

"How come?"

"Well, at first she told me she wants to continue taking classes here in Buell City so she can finish her paralegal degree. She said she's already signed up for classes for next semester."

"She can't do that in Wakeville?"

He shakes his head. "There's not a community college there. We had a big fight about it. She said I asked her to quit school the first time she tried to get her degree — when she was at UNO and I got orders here. She says I was the one who suggested she quit her classes when I asked her to marry me."

"And did you?" I ask.

"Hell no," he replies. "I may be an asshole about a lot of things Emilie but I would never ask her to quit her classes. In fact I specifically remember her bringing up the idea of quitting school when we got engaged, and I tried talking her into finishing. I said we could live apart another year and get married after she gets her degree. But she didn't want me coming up here without her, so she went ahead and quit school anyway. Now she's blaming it on me."

"That's not good," I say.

"She's mad as hell at me. Remember that night before the Ball, when I told you I was hoping to have a talk with Isabel? We had a talk all right. Out on the patio, so we wouldn't wake up Chloe. We yelled at each other for two hours straight. Finally Mrs. Nardi came over and told us to go inside."

"I thought you guys seemed pretty pissed at each other the night of the Ball."

"And it hasn't gotten any better since then. Tonight she told me she wants a divorce." He'd been leaning forward on the couch, elbows resting on his knees, but at this he drops his head.

I reach out and put my hand on his forearm. "I'm sorry."

He raises his head to look at me. "I asked her if we could go back to marriage counseling and she said no. She said we're no better off than we were before we went to counseling so why bother going through all that again. She's made up her mind, Em. I think we're screwed."

I wonder if this is why Leah got so quiet when I suggested she and Jacob go on a double date with Wade and Isabel. She must have already known Isabel was going to ask Wade for a divorce this weekend. I don't know why I'm surprised — Isabel told me she was thinking of leaving Wade when she called me over a month ago. I guess I was hoping she wouldn't go through with it.

Wade continues, "She said she's not going to give me any problems over shared custody of Chloe. She said I can have her every other weekend and during school vacations — when Chloe gets to be school age." Wade stares off into space. "Chloe is only thirteen months, Em. I can't believe we're doing this to her." He turns back to look at me. "I feel like I let her down. Like I let everybody down."

"It takes two people to make a marriage work, Wade."

"Well, it's not like I don't deserve it," he says. "I don't blame Isabel for wanting to leave me."

"Why do you say that?" I ask.

"I've got a lot of baggage Em. I've already been married and divorced once before. I have PTSD. Panic attacks. Nightmares. Depression. Hell, I'm a recovering alcoholic. And ..." he hesitates, searching my face. "I ... haven't been one-hundred percent faithful to Isabel," he blurts.

"What do you mean you haven't been one-hundred percent faithful?" I ask. "Isn't being unfaithful kind of like being pregnant — you're either pregnant or you're not Wade."

"Well no, I disagree," he argues. "I mean, I've been like ninety percent faithful to Isabel."

"That makes no sense whatsoever," I reply. "You can't be just partially unfaithful."

"Well I mean, in comparison."

"In comparison to what?"

"To when I was married to Shelley. With her I was only like fifty percent faithful."

"Oh my God Wade. Are you forgetting we were all stationed on Okinawa together? You were zero percent faithful to Shelley."

"You're right. What I'm trying to say is I was doing really well with my marriage to Isabel. Until I met Portia."

We stare into each other's eyes a long time, saying nothing.

"Are you still involved with her?" I ask.

"No. I broke it off a long time ago — all the way back in June. It was a short-lived thing. But then I ... had a relapse. That night you babysat Chloe, and Isabel and I went out to dinner, supposedly to talk about our relationship. That was when Leah showed up at the restaurant. And then Chloe had a meltdown in the car on the way home. I ended up having a panic attack. A bad one. When I was finally able to breathe again, I said I needed to go for a walk. And, well ... I fucked up. Big time. I went to see Portia."

"I thought you said you weren't involved with her anymore?"

"I'm not. After it happened I called her to apologize for showing up at her place like that in the middle of the night. I admitted it was totally unsat. And I promised her it would never happen again."

"And how did that go over?" I ask.

"Not well," he says.

"From what she said to me, it sounded like she was pretty happy to see you that night."

He leans forward slightly. "She told you I went over there?"

"Wade, even if Portia hadn't told me, I had a feeling there might have been something between the two of you. It's not rocket surgery, as Fakhir would say."

"Fuck. Why didn't you tell me you knew?" he asks. Then, "Wait — did you tell Isabel? Is that why she's divorcing me?"

"No I did not tell Isabel. Because I didn't know for sure what exactly was going on between the two of you. Yeah, I knew you went over there and yeah, I had my suspicions. But I wasn't about to go running to Isabel as if it were a foregone conclusion. Anyway, I would've talked to you first."

"So why didn't you say something?" he asks.

"Well, if I remember correctly, I did try talking to you about it once after we went to yoga together. That time you and Portia were flirting like mad during partner pose. And when I brought it up, you accused me of being jealous."

Wade tries to hide his grin by closing his mouth and thrusting his tongue against the inside of his cheek but it doesn't work. He breaks out into a full-on grin and says, "That's because you were."

I let out an exasperated sigh and tilt my head back to stare at the ceiling. Lowering my head again, I look Wade in the eye. "You know what Wade? You're an ass. And as Rory would say, I pretty much hate you right now."

He shrugs. "I can't help it if women find me irresistible."

I open my mouth, intending to expound further on why I think he's an asshole, but think better of it. He's trying to distract me from the matter at hand.

"Other than that one time," I explain, "I didn't bring it up with you because—like I said—I didn't know for sure what was going on. And I guess I decided it really wasn't any of my business. Besides, you're an adult. If you want to replace one addiction with another that's your prerogative."

"What the fuck are you talking about?" he asks, turning serious now.

We stare at each other in silence. I watch Wade's face and can practically see the gears in his brain turning.

"Oh," he says, nodding. "I see what you did there. You're saying I've replaced my alcohol addiction with a sex addiction. Or vice versa."

"Darn tootin'. As Dottie would say," I reply.

"Well aren't you Mrs. Smarty-pants."

"You're still seeing Greg, right?" I ask.

"Yeah, why?" he replies.

"I guess you guys have a lot to talk about at your next session."

At that moment Rory, Josh, Farah, and Riikka come barreling up the stairs from the basement.

"Hey Wade," Rory says, as the rest of the group chimes in with various hellos. "Mom, we're going out on the driveway to shoot some hoops."

"It's freezing out there," I reply. "In fact they say we might get snow tonight."

"It's not that cold," he says, waving me off. "We'll be outside if you need us."

"Wear your coats!" I call after them, but they ignore me.

Once the kids have disappeared through the garage, Wade stands up and says, "I guess I'd better get going. I have a long drive ahead of me."

"No you don't," I say, getting up from the couch. "You're staying here tonight. You can sleep in Fakhir's old room. There's clean sheets on the bed. And you can drive back to Wakeville tomorrow."

He smiles. "I was kind of hoping you'd say that."

"You knew I wouldn't let you get on the road this late at night," I say, making my way toward the stairs. "I'm going upstairs to read. There's all kinds of snacks in the cupboard if you get hungry. And help yourself to the juice and Fresca in the fridge. Or some more water, in case you've got another packet of instant coffee you wanna pour on your tongue."

"Funny girl," he says. "Emilie — thanks for being my friend. I'm sorry I was giving you shit. I don't know why you put up with me."

I pause at the bottom of the stairway. "We're all flawed in one way or another, Wade."

"Some of us have more flaws than others," he replies.

"And some of us have flaws that not everyone sees," I say.

"Well in my case, my flaws are pretty damn obvious," he says. "Hell — even my flaws have flaws."

This makes me smile. "We all need to do better. Goodnight Wade."

"Goodnight Emilie."

Monday, November 24, 2008   6:11 p.m.

I read another article in the paper about the burn pits in Iraq and Afghanistan. The *Military Times* ran a feature on it this summer, and the story seems to be gaining traction lately with non-military news outlets. This most recent news item talked about the burn pit at Joint Base Balad, where they dump everything from dining hall trash to unexploded ordnance to medical waste from the hospital (as in, used needles and amputated limbs). And then they throw jet fuel on everything as an accelerant. Service members at JBB are reporting respiratory issues, skin irritations, and headaches after being anywhere near the gigantic plumes of black smoke. Of course the Pentagon is saying any harmful health effects from the smoke are temporary. It makes you wonder though. Could this be the next Agent Orange? I looked up the Balad Air Base on the map, to make sure it's not too close to where you are. But then it occurred to me, is there a burn pit on Camp Victory?

Wade hung around a while yesterday morning before driving back to Wakeville. It had snowed overnight — just a few inches, but enough for me to suggest he wait to get on the road until the streets had been cleared. We had coffee in the kitchen while Rory and Josh slept in. (Wade allowed me to serve him a regular cup of coffee — out of the coffee-maker — this time.) We talked about the latest with Joey — what happened with Stephanie, and his CT scan suggesting an old brain injury. Wade said he was looking forward to seeing Joey over the long holiday weekend. Talking on the phone is one thing, but you can get so much more out of an in-person conversation.

Speaking of Thanksgiving, Wade said Isabel and Chloe are going to her parents' house in New Orleans. (That's when I invited him to stay with us over the weekend.) He told me he had toyed with the idea of going home to Minnesota, but now that Isabel has asked for a divorce he doesn't want to have to deal with explaining all that to his family. They'd probably take her side anyway, he says. I mentioned to Wade that I had invited Leah and Jacob for Thanksgiving dinner, but they're going back to North Carolina to be with their families.

"I'm surprised Leah's not going to New Orleans with Isabel and Chloe," he says.

"Why is that?" I ask.

"Well, Leah went to NOLA with Isabel and Chloe last time Isabel drove down there," he replies.

"She did?"

"Yeah. I thought I told you Isabel had taken a four-day weekend to visit her parents. That was about a month ago."

"Okay. I remember now. But you didn't say anything about Leah going with."

"That's because I didn't know. I only found out after the fact that Leah went too," he says.

"Why would Isabel not tell you Leah was going?" I ask.

"Hell if I know," he replies, shaking his head.

"What do you think is going on?"

"With those two?" He takes a sip of his coffee. "It could be any number of things."

"Such as ... ?"

He takes a deep breath and exhales. "I've been going over it in my mind a while now. And I don't know what to think Em. So maybe you can tell me if I'm missing something."

"Okay."

"Let's start with option 'A.' My first thought was that Isabel has been using Leah as some kind of emotional shield. Like, to keep me from getting too close. I noticed it after I moved to Wakeville. As long as she's busy with Leah, or Leah is hanging out with us, there's no time for me and Isabel to talk about anything serious, like our relationship."

"Go on." I get up to grab the coffee carafe and refill both of our cups.

"Then we have option 'B,' which is the one that makes the most sense. Isabel and Leah are best friends. They were both in desperate need of a friend and they came along at just the right moment in each other's lives. They fill that need extremely well for each other, and voilà, best friends for life. The problem — for me at least — is that they've come to rely on one another for everything. To the exclusion of everyone else. Including me. And Jacob."

"Do you think that might change now that Jacob's back home?"

"I have to admit, I was kind of hoping that once Jacob came back from sniper school, Leah wouldn't be over at our house as much," Wade confesses. "It's not that I don't like her — she's a good person. Even if she is a vegetarian. Or vegan. Or whatever she calls herself." He smiles, looking charming as ever. "Seriously though. She helped Isabel a lot after I started the job at Mondo — taking care of Chloe, helping with errands, and just being a good friend. Isabel really needed someone like her. Especially with me gone during the week." His smile fades, and I can tell he's blaming himself for their marriage not working.

"So maybe you should wait it out a few more weeks," I suggest. "Once Leah and Jacob settle back into a routine, maybe you and Isabel can get more quality time together."

Wade shakes his head. "I don't think so. Leah is still over at our house a lot. And even when the two of them aren't together, they're talking on the phone or texting each other." He eyes me carefully. "Also, there's another option we haven't talked about yet."

"And that is ... ?"

With very little emotion in his voice, Wade stares directly into my eyes and says, "Option 'C.' Isabel and Leah are lovers. That's why she wants to leave me."

I hold Wade's gaze and slowly set down my coffee cup without looking away from him, considering this last option. Am I really that surprised? The more I think about it, no. It's certainly not out of the question, and yet I wouldn't call it a fait accompli either. I'm surprised, and yet not surprised.

"Hello? Anybody in there?" Wade says, waving a hand in front of my eyes.

"I'm here."

"So ... ?"

"So I think you've covered all the options pretty well," I reply.

"Well, in light of what we talked about last night, it's not like I don't deserve it," he says.

"Deserve what? Isabel having an affair?" I ask.

"Yeah." He looks away, fiddling with the handle of his coffee mug.

"Well ... whatever's going on," I say, "do you think Isabel might change her mind about the divorce? For example, if Leah and Jacob are able to work things out—do you think there's a chance Isabel would want to give your marriage another shot?"

"No. Not a chance. There's too much other shit. I mean, yeah, that would be a neat and tidy explanation, if she wanted to leave me for Leah. But that doesn't explain all the other stuff she's mad at me about. And it doesn't make me any less of an asshole either."

"Wade, don't say that."

"I'm serious Em. I don't deserve Isabel. I don't deserve anybody really."

"That's not true." I reach across the table, holding my hand out, palm up, waiting for him to take it.

Silently, he looks at my hand, then places his hand in mine.

I give his hand a squeeze. "You still love her, don't you?"

He nods. "Yeah. I do."

I'm worried about him, Liam. He seemed really down when he left our house after breakfast. I told him to call me when he made it back to Wakeville. Instead of calling, he texted me later in the afternoon. Just two words: "Made it."

Tuesday, November 25, 2008   9:51 p.m.

Rough day at work. I didn't have anyone in ISS, so it was a chance to catch up on entering incident reports into the school database. I thought that would be a good thing, but I ended up feeling spooked. Sitting in my room by myself, I kept glancing at the custodial closet where the kids and I hid from Marcus. I couldn't stop replaying the scene in my head, hearing the things he said to us over and over again in my mind. I dropped by the school psychologist's office after lunch and she was kind enough to set aside her paperwork to chat with me. She suggested I request a room change for next semester so I don't have to keep seeing that closet as a reminder of what happened. On the one hand that sounds like a good idea but on the other hand, that closet saved our lives. I don't think I'd feel safe in a room with nowhere to hide from another school shooter.

After I finished entering the last of the incident reports about an hour before the final bell, I stopped by Dr. Gouwens' office and asked if she'd mind if I left early for the day. Something about the look on my face must have given her pause. She asked me if I was okay, and I said not really. But nothing a Party Size bag of Lay's couldn't fix, I told her, mentioning my plan to stop at the commissary on my way home. She laughed and said I was dismissed.

When Rory got home from school I was parked on the family room couch, bag of Lay's in my lap, reading Michael Herr's *Dispatches*. I read it back in college for an American Lit class. I'm not sure why I picked it up again, but it's even better than I remembered. Rory dropped his book bag on the kitchen floor and came over to sit next to me on the couch, asking if he could have some of my Lay's. I told him there's no "we" in chips, and directed him to the cupboard, where he'd find a second bag I had bought just for him. We sat on the couch together eating our chips and reading (Rory's current read is your old copy of *The Martian Chronicles*). The house was silent except for the sounds of crunching and the crinkle of our chip bags.

After we stuffed ourselves on chips (foregoing the need to think about dinner), Rory told me Josh is planning to ask Riikka to be his date to the Winter Dance. Apparently Josh has developed quite a crush on Riikka since they all started hanging out together. I asked Rory who he's going to ask to the dance and he said he's not going to ask anybody. There's no one special he has his eye on and he doesn't want to ask someone just to go to the dance and have an awkward time making small talk with somebody he doesn't care about.

When Lucia got home from work I told her there was a third bag of chips in the cupboard for her. Rory went upstairs to study for a test while I sat at the kitchen table working on the meal planning for the weekend. Lucia sat across from me eating her chips and paging through the latest issue of *Entrepreneur* magazine. She's researching the idea of forming an LLC for her own line of organic grooming products created especially for men. When I asked her what she's going to name her company, she told me she's thinking about calling it Bravo Zulu. It was either that or Asses & Elbows, which I find fitting but which she ultimately eliminated after some research. Apparently swear words in company names can be problematic when it comes to trademarks and marketing and whatnot.

I miss you and hope you'll be able to call this weekend. As much as you've been away throughout our marriage, I think this will be the first Thanksgiving we've ever been apart. I try not to dwell on the number of holidays we've celebrated without you. (Not that I'm counting or anything.) Then there's the holidays we've spent with you here at home, but far away from our extended families. The lost opportunities for Finn and Rory to hang out with their aunts and uncles and cousins. If the four of us could be together on a holiday, that was always enough for me—a reason to be grateful. But sometimes I wonder what life would have been like if we lived closer to family. How nice it would have been to have grandparents as backup babysitters, like a lot of young families. I never thought much about it when Finn and Rory were little, but looking back now, I'm amazed how we got through it. I don't regret those years. They made us stronger—and closer—as a family. Nobody can take that away from us.

Your mom invited us to come spend the holiday weekend with them, which was thoughtful of her, but I just couldn't muster the energy to travel. It would be nice if once in a while, our families offered to come see us for a holiday, instead of expecting us to always be the ones to travel. Maybe next year, when my brother moves back to Milwaukee after his stint in Germany, we can invite John and his family to come here for Thanksgiving. Thank God for Dottie, who's always been willing to come see us, no matter where we're stationed.

She and Joey (and Jacques) are scheduled to arrive tomorrow after I get home from work. I'm curious to see what Joey's mood will be like what with everything he has going on right now—his various health issues, and the thing that happened with Stephanie. I wouldn't blame him for feeling depressed. We'll do our best to distract him and wrap our arms around him even more tightly than usual.

I've invited Tammy and the boys to join us for Thanksgiving dinner since Ken isn't here. She said their families invited them to come home for the weekend but she wasn't up for traveling either. She told me she's at that deployment stage where getting out of bed and putting on a pair of sweats is a major accomplishment. She's trying to hold it together for Kenny and Kevin but it hasn't been easy, especially now that the holidays are upon us. I told her not to cook anything, just show up. And if she wants to show up wearing sweats, that would be fine too. She laughed and said she was planning on wearing sweats before I even mentioned it. And she'll bring a bottle of Chardonnay and a Riesling to go with the meal. I told her to bring as many bottles of wine as she has on hand. I have a feeling we're going to need them.

Finn's train gets in tomorrow night. Mel's family invited Finn to spend the holiday weekend at their house, but I told Finn we need him here at home. I don't think I could handle having both you and Finn absent from the Thanksgiving dinner table. We'll set a place for you, Liam. And next year I'll make an extra batch of green bean casserole just for you.

p.s. The anonymous gift giver struck again. When I got home from the commissary I found a beautiful arrangement of flowers in fall colors on the front porch. Mums, marigolds, orange daisies, and sunflowers arranged in a pumpkin-shaped vase. The attached note read, "For your Thanksgiving table. Remember you are loved." I still don't know who's leaving this stuff. But I can tell you one thing: the list of potential Good Samaritans has one less name on it than it did ten days ago.

Wednesday, November 26, 2008   11:01 p.m.

Dottie and Joey picked up Finn at the train station on their way over here. Which helped a lot since I'd been scrambling to clean the house and do some meal prep for tomorrow. (I've already got the turkey in the oven for a slow roast overnight.) Joey was in a surprisingly upbeat mood. He gave Rory and Lucia and me his traditional bear hugs, then rolled up his sleeves and asked me what he could do in the kitchen to help get ready for tomorrow. I set him to chopping the onion and celery for the stuffing while Dottie made the cranberry sauce and Finn and Rory ran interference between Jacques, Soda, and Brig. Lucia had already made the green bean casserole for me, and promised to peel the potatoes in the morning. And Dottie and Joey didn't arrive empty handed — when they walked in the door Dottie handed me a homemade apple pie. Carmen's bringing his tiramisu, so we'll have plenty for dessert. (And no one but you likes pumpkin pie anyway.)

Wade had to stay late at the warehouse tonight getting ready for Black Friday, but he promised he'd get in the car tomorrow morning and be here by noon, with Carmen in tow. Wade's boss, Jenn, knows Wade's been going through a rough time personally, and she gave him the rest of the weekend off. She said he's gotten the warehouse teams running so smoothly and they are so well-prepared for the holidays that he deserves some time off, especially after working his ass off these past five months. Unfortunately Carmen will need to head back to Wakeville after dinner tomorrow night since he's the FNG. He has to be at work by zero-dark-thirty on Friday, and is scheduled to work the rest of the weekend. But he says he doesn't mind, he's just happy to have a job. And Raquel agrees. It's a small price to pay for the peace of mind of being financially stable again.

Wade will go to the VA Hospital Friday afternoon for his appointment with Greg, but other than that he'll be hanging out with us for the weekend. No sense knocking around in an empty house by himself with Isabel and Chloe gone. At least that's what I said when I invited him to stay here. In reality, I confess to having an ulterior motive: The more time Wade spends here with us, the easier it will be for me to keep a close eye on him. He's just not acting like himself lately, and I'm concerned he might be falling into an even deeper depression. At least he's keeping his appointments with Greg.

So counting us, Lucia and her family, Fakhir and his mom and sister, Wade, Dottie, Joey, Tammy and the boys, we'll have a total of 18 for dinner. That's quite a crowd but I don't mind. It will be good to have a houseful of people to distract us from the fact of your absence. We might not have room for your place setting after all. But you'll be in our hearts, as always.

I love you.

Friday, November 28, 2008   1:18 a.m.

Today was a wonderfully busy, hectic, noisy, crazy day. Exactly what we needed. Tammy's boys, Kenny and Kevin, kept Lucia's little brothers (Andy, Arthur, and Angel) occupied in the basement playing with Finn and Rory's old Fisher-Price toys. (Finn asked what happened to the parking garage, and was somewhat perturbed with me when I told him we gave it to Chloe. Oops.)

Dottie and Arifah have become quite friendly. Dottie has taken it upon herself to teach Arifah some phrases in English — phrases Dottie considers essential. For example, "Yes I want fries with that," "Please add extra chocolate sauce," and — my personal favorite — "I'd like to start a bar tab." Then Raquel got in on the action and decided she wanted to teach Arifah some phrases in Spanish, including, "Make that a triple espresso" and "Is the salsa made fresh or from a jar?"

Tammy was good on her word and showed up wearing sweats, a hoodie, and house slippers, her hair in a messy bun. I told her I was proud of her for showing up at all. And she came through on the wine too, every drop of which was gone by the end of the night.

Joey was in an even more cheerful mood today than he was last night, giving everyone bear hugs as they came in the door, lifting the younger kids way high in the air and making them giggle with delight. When Andy, Arthur, and Angel weren't in the basement playing with Finn and Rory's old toys, they were climbing on Joey, asking him if they could stand on his feet while he took giant steps across the room, making them laugh their heads off. He sure has a way with kids. I wonder if he's ever going to get the chance to meet his grandkids.

Wade helped Arifah serve the appetizer she brought (browned eggplant slices with mint yogurt — they disappeared in five minutes). He also filled your place as my sous-chef, helping with last-minute meal prep, keeping the sink free of dirty dishes, and carving the turkey once it came out of the oven. He was helpful and cordial throughout the day, but not fully engaged like he normally is. It must have felt weird for him to be celebrating the holiday without Chloe. And Isabel. At one point he stepped outside to give them a call and wish them a Happy Thanksgiving. He wasn't gone very long, and when he came back inside he looked deflated.

After dinner, Lucia, Farah, Finn and Rory ended up watching "A Christmas Story" in the basement while Fakhir, Wade, and Joey stayed in the kitchen doing the dishes, and everyone else hung out in the family room. I floated among the various groups, handing out coffee and dessert and catching snippets of conversation here and there. I heard Joey ask Wade about Isabel and Chloe. Wade explained that he and Isabel are getting a divorce, adding, "I guess if the Marine Corps wanted me to have a wife they would've issued me one." He smiled when he said this last comment, but the sadness in his eyes was unmistakable. Later, after they had finished all the dishes and wiped down the countertops (the kitchen was cleaner than I'd ever seen it), the three of them went out on the back porch to have a beer (or in Wade's case, a Fresca). It was chilly outside but they didn't seem to mind. At one point Carmen joined them and we could hear their muffled banter even with the windows closed.

Did I mention Wade brought Chesty here for the weekend? So now we've got Brig, Soda, Jacques, Chesty, and the two cats, holding their own version of WWIII. Normally Jacques is facing off with our dogs, but with Chesty here, Jacques has been distracted from his usual warfare plan. So it was mostly Pol Pot and Chesty going at it, growling and circling one another while Brig and Soda commandeered your chair for a front row seat to the hostilities (with Smedley and Daly staying above the fray — literally — by perching on top of the refrigerator for a bird's-eye view of the battlefield). Also, major news on the Fakhir front: Before dinner, Brig and Soda not only allowed Fakhir to sit in your chair, they both jumped on his lap and let him scratch their ears while he chatted with Tammy. I'll never forget how different things were the first time Fakhir came over, with Soda lunging at his kneecaps as we stood in the foyer making small talk, trying to pretend there wasn't a psychotic Chihuahua hanging off Fakhir's pants leg.

I'm wondering how your day was — if you're traveling outside the wire or if you were able to stay on base. And wherever you are, I wonder if you were able to get a turkey dinner? We raised our glasses to you before the meal. There wasn't room for an empty placing setting at either the adults' or kids' table, but I lit a candle for you and we poured you an IPA, both of which we set on the mantel in your honor.

(Finn was annoyed with me when he found out he'd have to sit at the kids' table, but once Farah volunteered to sit next to Finn he shut his pie-hole. Rory was also none too happy about sitting at the kids' table, but I got him to be quiet about it by promising to hide an extra piece of Carmen's tiramisu for him in the back of the fridge for later.)

With Dottie and Joey staying in Lucia's room, and Wade staying in the basement in Fakhir's old room, Lucia is back to sleeping in my bed for the weekend. (Which is where I'm currently sitting, upright and awake at 1:00 a.m., my laptop propped on a pillow.) Why is it that the person who snores always falls asleep first? We'd only been in bed a few minutes when Lucia fell into a deep slumber, keeping me awake with her steady snoring. I soon gave up and that's when I grabbed my laptop to write you this email. But she was snoring so loudly I could hardly concentrate. I reached out and gently shook her shoulder until she rolled over and looked at me groggily. "Did you know you snore?" I asked her. She peered at me, one eye open, and said "Yeah." I asked, "Does Fakhir know how loud you snore?" And she said, "Yeah. He snores too." I said, "Don't you guys keep each other awake?" And she replied "No, not at all." Within seconds she was snoring again, but not before plopping one of her legs over both of mine, effectively pinning me to the mattress.

To make life even more interesting, shortly after my exchange with Lucia, Finn and Rory walked into our room carrying their blankets and pillows, asking if they could sleep on the floor next to our bed. "Why?" I asked. "Are you guys having nightmares or something?" And Rory said, "Yeah, it's kind of like having a nightmare." I wriggled my legs out from under Lucia's leg so I could sit up straighter. "What's going on?" I asked. That's when Finn explained Dottie and Joey were having a late-night shower together in their shared bathroom. And that he and Rory could hear everything. "And we mean *everything*," Rory added.

So that's my current situation. Finn and Rory sprawled on the floor beside the bed, Lucia on the other side of me, snoring herself into a blissful slumber while slowly but surely pulling the covers away from me. Dottie and Joey in the shower doing heaven knows what, Jacques probably perched on their bed waiting for them to come out of the bathroom. Brig and Soda standing guard outside Dottie and Joey's closed bedroom door, making sure Jacques doesn't escape before sunrise. The cats downstairs prowling around on the countertops, knocking over the salt and pepper shakers, on the hunt for an errant morsel of turkey or spot of gravy that may have been overlooked during cleanup. Wade downstairs in Fakhir's old room, most likely lying in bed awake, thinking about Isabel and Chloe, Chesty snoozing beside him. And me, sitting in bed with my laptop, missing you.

12:49 p.m.

Hearing your voice this morning made our holiday complete. It was comforting to know they served a nice Thanksgiving dinner at Camp Victory yesterday. I'm sorry I cried when you mentioned you got a hug from a USO volunteer while waiting in line at the DFAC. To think a hug from a stranger on Thanksgiving Day could mean so much made my heart hurt. It's not like I wasn't aware you haven't been hugged in almost a year — I think about our last hug at the airport all the time. It was the image of a volunteer going down the line of Marines offering hugs — someone who probably reminded everyone of their grandma back home — that broke me. Such a basic act of humanity, yet so powerful. I hope that volunteer knows how important her hugs are, not just to the Marines, but to their families back home.

As per usual Dottie and I had a nice chat over coffee this morning before everyone else woke up. (By the way, I was eventually able to fall asleep last night after I finished writing my email. Lucia continued to pull the covers away from me until I finally gave up and moved to the floor where Finn and Rory were sleeping. Letting Lucia have the entire queen-size bed to herself was a small price to pay for a few hours of uninterrupted sleep.)

Dottie looked extra cozy in her bright yellow plush robe and orange slippers. (Her theme this weekend is fall colors, in case you haven't already figured that out.) Also, Dottie's fascination with all things outer space is alive and well. She was describing an article she read in Science magazine, about NASA's Phoenix lander exploring the North Pole on Mars. Dottie says her goal in life is to live long enough to see the first humans land on Mars (somewhere around the year 2030, according to her). That would make Dottie 97 if and when it happens. Somehow, it wouldn't surprise me if she lives well beyond 100. I hope we do send humans to Mars by then, if only for Dottie's sake.

"Enough about me," Dottie says, changing the subject. "Joey told me about Wade and Isabel getting a divorce. It's so sad. But you know, we never really liked Isabel anyway. Wade can do much better."

"I think he's still in love with her," I say. "I'm worried about him. Did you notice how quiet he was during the meal yesterday?"

"I did notice," she replies. "It's so unlike him. He's usually so lively. Joey says Wade didn't share very much about the divorce when they were out on the porch with Fakhir."

"Did he say what they talked about?" I ask.

"Nothing you probably don't already know," she says. "Wade told them he's moving into a new apartment, but instead of moving in with him, Isabel is staying in Buell City to finish her degree. He did admit he's having a hard time accepting the divorce. But other than that, Joey said Wade kept trying to flip the conversation back to him, asking Joey about his latest CT scan and whatnot."

"And what is the latest with Joey? Is he still scheduled to go in the hospital for observation next week?"

"Yes, and he's very unhappy about it," Dottie says. "They want him to report to the VA first thing Tuesday morning. They're going to do some special kind of MRI, to find out more about his brain injury. And they're talking about enrolling him in a clinical trial. Some sort of brand new treatment called TMS — Transcranial Magnetic Stimulation, or something like that. They say Joey is a perfect candidate, since he has almost every condition that this TMS is supposed to help."

"Like tinnitus?" I ask. "I heard Tammy asking Joey about it before dinner yesterday. She asked him when the ringing in his ears bothers him the most, and you know what he said? 'When he's awake.' He said it with a smile but I wonder if he was just being honest.

"That's Joey. Always making light of his situation," Dottie says. "He's very good at downplaying his health issues."

"He does put up a good front," I reply. "So this TMS — what else is it supposed to help with besides tinnitus?"

"Well, the doctor told Joey the people in the trial are veterans with mild to moderate TBI. People with a history of concussions."

"So did Joey ever decide to tell you more about how he got the brain injury?" I ask.

"Not yet," she replies. "He said he'll tell me about it someday soon, when the time is right. After all those years being married to Wally, I know better than to rush these things. When Joey and I first started dating, he told me about what happened *after* he came home from Vietnam — like when he was hospitalized for his mental health issues. I guess he felt like he needed to be up-front with me about all that. Anyway, when he started going to the VA this last time, they dug up his medical records from back then and a corpsman had written something in there about Joey being diagnosed with 'acute combat reaction.' I guess in those days that was the latest euphemism for 'shell shock.' But as far as what he experienced while he was over there, Joey doesn't say much other than telling people he was a loadmaster on a C-130."

"Well, you and I know that's not unusual," I say. "Liam always told me it's the quiet ones who often carry the heaviest burdens. The guys constantly yammering about what tough guys they were probably didn't see nearly as much action as the ones who'd rather not talk about it."

Dottie says, "Wally used to say the same thing."

"So what's the latest with the Stephanie situation?" I ask, switching gears. "I know Joey puts up a good front when he's around us, but how is he at home? Is he still depressed about it?"

"Hard to tell," she says. "He's still not sleeping much, but that's nothing new. I have noticed he's been acting a little secretive lately, which is odd. He went to see his lawyer last week, and when I asked him about it, he said he was updating his will. And he's had a few other errands and appointments he hasn't said much about."

"Hmmm ... I hope to God he's not changing his will because of Stephanie holding his grandkids hostage," I reply. "I know you don't care about the money Dottie. I just hate to see him getting taken advantage of like that."

"Like I said, darling, it's his money. If he decides to share his pension with her or make her a beneficiary in his will, I'm not going to think twice about it."

"Well, maybe these appointments have nothing to do with Stephanie," I say, trying to find a more positive explanation. "In fact ... maybe he's getting ready to propose to you." I smile and watch her face expectantly to see how she reacts.

"Oh, we're already married," she says nonchalantly.

"What?!" Soda had been snoozing quietly on my lap but the sharpness of my voice startles him awake. His ears perk up and he looks questioningly from me to Dottie, trying to discern what's going on.

"We got secretly married the week before the Birthday Ball. At the courthouse. Joey wore his blue tux and I wore my blue sequined gown."

"So that's why Joey bought his tux instead of renting it. I thought it was strange when you told me he bought a tux for the Ball. I guess he had more than one special occasion in mind," I say. "So why didn't you tell me you guys got married?"

Dottie shrugs. "Oh Emilie. You're so traditional. It was kind of a spur of the moment thing. And nothing's really changed between us. We're still crazy in love." She leans forward and lowers her voice. "In fact ... I hope we didn't keep you and the boys awake last night. Joey and I had a rendezvous in the shower and well, things may have gotten a little out of hand."

Instead of telling her that yes, as a matter of fact, Finn and Rory ended up sleeping on my bedroom floor due to her and Joey's late-night antics, I merely smile and sip my coffee. And it's a good thing, because at that moment Wade comes upstairs from the basement, asking if there's any coffee left.

Saturday, November 29, 2008   4:47 p.m.

Rory had told me that Josh called Riikka the night before Thanksgiving to ask her to the Winter Dance and she told Josh she already had a date. Which Rory found confusing, because Riikka hadn't mentioned anything about getting asked to the dance. Rory figured maybe one of the guys on their hockey team invited her, and word just hadn't gotten around yet. And then, yesterday afternoon, after we were done having a late lunch, Rory's phone rang. And it was Riikka. Wanting to know if Rory would be her date to the dance. Can you believe it?! I haven't seen Rory grinning that much since the day we brought home Ozzy. He's been walking around in a daze ever since.

After he got off the phone and told me what happened (as if I couldn't already tell just by watching his face), I asked, "I thought you said there wasn't anyone special you wanted to go to the dance with?" He explained he had automatically ruled out Riikka since he knew Josh had a thing for her. And he hadn't given it much thought after that. But now that he knows Riikka likes him, he realizes he likes her too. So I asked him if this means he and Riikka are "hanging out" now. At which point Rory put his palm in my face and said, "Mom. Stop. You ask too many questions."

Riikka came over last night to listen to The Smoking Lamps perform and it was just the cutest thing how she and Rory kept glancing at one another the entire night. Isn't it funny how things turn out sometimes? Rory did share with me that he called Josh later in the afternoon to tell him about he and Riikka, and Josh said he's cool with it.

Another interesting thing that happened last night when The Smoking Lamps were playing in the garage is that Maggie and her friends showed up. In between sets Finn went over to say hi to them. And it was abundantly obvious that Maggie was being super flirty with Finn. (I wonder if her parents know she was hanging out with "the riff-raff" again?) About a minute into Finn's conversation with Maggie and her friends, Farah appeared by Finn's side, taking his hand in hers. This did not go unnoticed by Maggie, who then told Finn that she and her friends were just stopping by on their way to another party.

The weather was chilly last night but not so cold that we couldn't sit outside to listen to the band, and since we were all bundled up it was actually quite comfortable. Joey, Dottie, Wade, Fakhir, Lucia, and I sat on lawn chairs, our laps covered in stadium blankets, while Farah, Rory, Riikka, and Josh sat in front of us on the ground, seemingly immune to the cold. Finn announced over the mic they had a surprise for Fakhir. When The Smoking Lamps started playing "Call Me The Breeze," dedicating it to Fakhir, it made him so happy I thought he might start to cry. (If you remember, the first time I saw him cry was at Lucia's graduation.) Country rock is not part of the band's usual repertoire, but Neil did a decent job on guitar and vocals, so they almost sounded like Lynyrd Skynyrd. Almost.

I had planned to have the band shut down by ten, so as not to upset the neighbors (i.e. Wanda and Vince). But around nine-thirty Officer Clemmons pulled up in her cruiser. She parked on the street in front of our house and walked up the driveway, adjusting her belt as she greeted us. I said hello and offered her a hot chocolate. (We had two batches going: regular hot chocolate, and hot chocolate laced with Peppermint Schnapps.) Officer Clemmons replied that the Schnapps version sounded pretty good to her, so maybe she'd come back at eleven when she was off-duty. She said she was sorry to bother us but they had received a noise complaint from one of the neighbors — that the band was playing too loud — and she had no choice but to pay us a visit.

"Is that so?" I say. "Ummm, lemme guess. The Reszels?" I tilt my head in the direction of Vince and Wanda's house.

Officer Clemmons says nothing, but nods almost imperceptibly.

"That's funny," I say, "because those are the same neighbors that called in the last noise complaint. And the only reason I know that is because Wanda herself told me. They're also the ones who filed the complaint about our dogs barking. And the one about leaving our trash cans out on the curb too long."

Officer Clemmons takes this in. "And all these complaints were filed this year, while your husband's serving overseas in Iraq?" she asks.

"That's correct officer."

She looks thoughtfully toward Vince and Wanda's house. "You know," she says, "I'm pretty sure that vehicle over there has been parked on the street longer than 24 hours. Does it happen to belong to the Reszels?"

"As a matter of fact it does," I reply.

Officer Clemmons shakes her head sadly. "That's too bad. I'm gonna have to write them up a citation for that."

I exchange glances with Dottie, Joey, Wade, Fakhir, and Lucia, all of whom are trying — unsuccessfully — to hide their grins in one way or another by covering their mouths or coughing. Even the band is quiet, listening intently to our conversation.

"Huh," Officer Clemmons continues. "And that storage shed over there — " she says, raising her chin toward the Reszels' house, "is that on their property?"

"Yes officer, that's their back yard," I reply.

"Darn shame," she says. "I'm sure there's a code violation there. I'll have to write them up for that too." She points to the utility trailer on their driveway. "You know if they got a permit for that thing?"

I shake my head. "I'm not sure. But it certainly seems like something worth looking into. It's been parked on their driveway ever since we've lived here, right boys?" I turn to look at Finn and Rory, who nod vigorously in the officer's direction.

"Hmmm. Alrighty then. I have some citations to write up so I best be on my way." She looks at the band. "Turn it down a few decibels and you can keep playing as long as you want." She then looks at me. "And I'll be back after I'm off duty for that spiked hot chocolate you promised me. You got any of those pizza rolls on hand?"

"An entire box in the freezer. We'll have them nice and hot for you by the time you get here."

It turned out Officer Clemmons never made it back to our house last night. I got a text from her saying she had to work a double shift and wouldn't be coming by after all. I told her we'd love to have her over another time, and thanked her for looking out for us earlier in the evening. She replied a little while later with a text that simply said, "I got your six." Which makes me think — she has to be former military. I'll ask her about that next time we see her.

After the band stopped playing and everyone else had made their way back into the house, Fakhir pulled me aside on the driveway. He wanted to know if I knew anything more about what's going on with Isabel, if there was any chance she might want to call off the divorce.

I shook my head. "I don't think she's going to change her mind Fakhir. And Wade doesn't think so either."

"That's what I thought," he said. "I was hoping they could work things out."

"I know," I replied, thinking about the others waiting for us to come back inside. "How about if you and I touch base after work one night this week? We can make up a game plan on how we're going to help Wade get through this."

"That sounds good," he said. "I'm worried about him, Em."

"Me too," I replied.

Sunday, November 30, 2008   9:07 a.m.

We had quite a late night last night, staying up past midnight listening to Joey's stories. And man did he have stories to tell. Rory was spending the night at Josh's house; Finn was over at Darryl's hanging out with Farah, Crystal, and Neil. Lucia had been studying for her cosmetology licensing exam all day (she takes the exam tomorrow) and went to bed early. Arifah stayed back at the apartment, enjoying a quiet night to herself. So that left me, Wade, Fakhir, Dottie, and Joey to our own devices. We were feeling pretty mellow after all the weekend festivities, so we made ourselves comfy in the family room, curling up in our stocking feet with afghans and throw pillows scattered about. Dottie snuggled next to Joey on the loveseat, her feet neatly tucked beneath her, his arm wrapped around her shoulders. Wade, Fakhir, and I shared the couch, our feet propped on the coffee table.

Wade had started a fire in the fireplace and we were on our second round of hot toddies. I had made a giant batch in my soup pot on the stove, leaving the whiskey bottle and a shot glass on the counter so people could add as much or as little whiskey as they wanted (or in Wade's case, none at all). The aroma of the honey, lemon, and clove swirling around in the hot water filled the house. I remember your dad making hot toddies on cold winter nights, or anytime someone was feeling under the weather. Or around the holidays. Or just because. The steaming liquid comforted us, and went down easily.

Dottie had asked Wade about his family in Minnesota, wondering why he didn't go home for Thanksgiving. Wade explained he wasn't close with his family, and now with the divorce, he especially didn't feel like going back home and dealing with all their questions. "Besides," he said, looking around the room, "you guys are my family now." Sensing Wade didn't feel like saying any more than that, Dottie switched her attention to Fakhir, asking how his mom and sister are acclimating to life in the U.S.

"They love it here," he replies. "Farah is doing really well in school. And she's made some good friends already." At this he raises an eyebrow at me, as if to acknowledge the budding romance between Farah and Finn. "And my mom is finally able to relax. For so many years she lived in fear. She misses Iraq—the old Iraq, before Saddam was in power. But she feels safe now."

"So I take it your parents weren't members of the Ba'ath Party," Joey says.

Fakhir shakes his head. "No, they weren't. Which made life difficult for them. They had to be careful. Especially my dad. His job made him a somewhat visible figure in the Baghdad cultural and political scene. But he wasn't aligned with Saddam's regime, which put him at risk. He had friends who were taken away by Saddam's security services, tortured and killed for no reason other than they were perceived as not loyal enough to Saddam. It was hard on my parents. But you know what? They protected us kids from all that as best they could. I'm just happy my family is safe now."

That's the most I've heard Fakhir talk about his dad in a while. But after sharing these tidbits with us, he goes silent, sipping his hot toddy. He leans his head back to empty his cup, and says, "Anyone else want a refill?" We all answer in the affirmative, so Fakhir and Wade collect everyone's mugs to refill them in the kitchen.

Joey turns to me and says, "Well, since we're talking about parents, I remember you saying your dad died in a parachuting accident. Was he in the military?"

"Oh, no. He was never in the military," I reply. "He was in the advertising business. An account executive. In fact he was on the job when he had the accident. They were filming a commercial for one of his accounts. He didn't need to jump that day, but he was an experienced jumper so they let him go up with the film crew. He was used to jumping with his skydiving club. I don't really know what happened. I was pretty young. My mom said his chute malfunctioned, and he was too close to the ground by the time his reserve chute opened."

Wade returns with Dottie and Joey's hot toddies, and as he hands them their mugs, he says, "I put a full shot in each of yours. Fakhir's making a new batch. We're going through this stuff pretty quick." He returns to the kitchen to grab his mug and mine before rejoining me on the couch. "So. What'd I miss?"

"Joey was asking about my dad's skydiving accident," I reply. "Old news — you already knew about that."

Maybe it was the hot toddies or the talk of parachutes, but whatever it was, Joey got to reminiscing about his C-130 exploits.

"We dropped some loads over Khe Sanh using chutes," he says. "That was in early '68, when road access to the base had been cut off by the NVA. The Marines needed their beans and bullets, and for a while, aerial resupply was the only way to go."

"Like those airdrops you see in old movies?" I ask. "Where a bunch of crates attached to parachutes come floating down from the sky?

"You're talking about high-altitude drops," Joey replies. "We did a lot of those during my time in Vietnam. But not during the Siege. The drop zone at Khe Sanh was too small. No way could we hit our target from that high up."

By this time Fakhir has returned with his mug, rejoining Wade and me on the couch. "So how'd you do it back then?" Fakhir asks. "We saw some pretty crazy C-130 drops in Iraq. Those planes would come in real low and drop the heaviest shit I ever saw. Even tanks."

"We dropped a few Sheridans out the hatch in my day," Joey says. "LAPES was a good system for that." Joey looks around the room, registering our blank expressions. "Low Altitude Parachute Extraction System," he explains. "The pilot slows the aircraft to 130 knots and flies super low over the runway—we're talking five or ten feet off the ground. The loadmaster—that's me—opens the cargo door and lowers the ramp. Basically we used two types of chutes, a small chute that goes out the hatch first, and it pulls out a bunch of larger chutes attached to the pallets. The pilot pulls the nose up, the floor locks holding down the pallets are released, and the force of the larger chutes pulls the load down the ramp, out of the aircraft and onto the extraction zone. And then off we go. Never even had to land. The GIs on the ground got their ammo or fuel or C-rats—whatever they needed to keep them going during the fight."

Fakhir says, "That is fuckin' insane man."

"We eventually had to stop the LAPES deliveries," Joey says. "They became too risky. One of the C-130s—not ours—released its load too soon, and the runaway cargo pallets crashed into a bunker, killing the Marines inside. Damn shame." Joey takes a gulp of his hot toddy, a faraway look in his eyes.

"So what'd you guys do?" Fakhir asks. "After you stopped the LAPES deliveries?"

"Well, for the C-130 transports it was literally touch and go. Dropping loads at Khe Sanh was a real sonofabitch. You gotta remember, those Marines were less than fifteen miles from the DMZ. The North Vietnamese Army had the base surrounded, hiding in the hills and ridges with their machine guns and rockets and mortars. They had howitzers hidden in mountain caves just across the border in Laos. If we landed, more often than not the NVA would pound the airstrip with mortars while the planes were being unloaded. There's a reason they called the C-130s mortar magnets."

Joey pauses, looking suspiciously around the room at each of us. "Do you guys even care about this stuff? Or are you just being polite?"

"No, no—we want to hear this," Fakhir says. Wade and I chime in with similar encouragement.

Dottie snuggles closer to Joey. "Keep talking Lovebuns. I've never heard these stories."

"Okay then. So where was I?" he continues. "We did different types of drops depending on the weather and cloud cover and if the NVA were active or not. After they stopped the LAPES deliveries, we'd do speed offloads. It got so we could offload fifteen tons of supplies in under a minute. The pilot would touch down and continue taxiing. While the plane was still rolling, we'd let down the ramp just a foot or two off the ground and unlock the pallets. The pilot would prepare for take-off, increasing speed until gravity pulled the cargo down the ramp and out onto the airstrip, leaving behind a cloud of red dust. That solved the problem of runaway pallets, but it also made us more vulnerable to enemy fire while we were taxiing.

Joey takes a long sip of his hot toddy before continuing. "And when we were carrying troops, we had no choice but to come to a full stop. The incoming GIs would scramble out of the aircraft and run like hell toward the bunker closest to the airstrip. At the same time, the outgoing GIs clambered out of the bunker, running like hell in the opposite direction, hoping to make it up the ramp before they caught a .30-caliber bullet in the back of the neck on one of their last days in country. We'd only be on the ground a couple minutes, but it felt like forever. And a second was all it took for a stopped C-130 to get destroyed by a mortar coming out of those hills."

Wade quietly lifts himself off the couch to tend to the fire, adding a log with his bare hands and using the poker to stir the embers. He carefully places a piece of crumpled newspaper below the grate for good measure, and the fire is once again crackling by the time he returns to the couch.

Joey continues, "Then there were the times we had to take on a load of wounded GIs, either carried onboard on litters or walking with the help of a medic. The pilot always tried to maneuver the plane as gently as possible when we were carrying wounded troops. Those were some of the softest touchdowns of my entire career. But the worst? Were the body bags. It was hard on everybody when those came on the plane. The loaders just laid the bags on pallets, sometimes they had no choice but to be half-assed about it if they were getting shot at. No time to arrange the bodybags neatly in a row or anything like that. Sometimes I'd straighten them out once we reached a safe altitude."

The room goes quiet. Joey stares off into space as the rest of us look down at our laps or anywhere but at him, giving him a sort of privacy to take whatever time he needs to remember.

Holding up his empty mug, Joey breaks the stillness. "Anybody up for another round?"

Fakhir jumps up from the couch to collect our empty mugs. "I'll be right back," he says. We listen to him clanging around in the kitchen as he refills the mugs, bringing them back to us two at a time.

Once everyone is settled in again, the steam from our now-full mugs warming our faces, Joey resumes. "This one time, we were getting ready to drop 30,000 pounds of ammo into the drop zone at Khe Sanh. We weren't even planning to land or taxi or any of that. Just drop and go. It was an overcast morning — our first run of the day — and we had decent cloud cover. Or so we thought. We were approaching the airstrip from the east, flying on instruments. Whenever there was a break in the clouds our copilot, Capt. Hite, looked for tracers in the jungle below, calling them out to the pilot, Capt. Wilson. But those breaks in the clouds also meant the NVA could see us on approach. We took some intense enemy fire in spite of Capt. Wilson's best efforts to avoid the incoming rounds. Last thing we wanted was one of those .50-caliber bullets hitting a fuel tank, what with all the explosives we were carrying. If that happened we were toast. At one point a round tore through one of our engines, but the engineer, TechSgt. Vestine, shut it down before it caught fire.

"The aircraft got sluggish but that didn't phase the pilot. He kept us on track, continuing our descent. Then a 37mm shell exploded beneath us, damaging our hydraulics. And still Capt. Wilson pressed on, managing to maneuver the plane toward the drop zone. We knew how badly the Marines needed the ammo. Their main ammo dump had been hit by a massive artillery bombardment just a few days before, causing it to go up in flames and depleting almost their entire ammo supply. No way could our guys hold the perimeter against the NVA without this desperately needed ammo drop. So Capt. Wilson stayed the course, even though the aircraft was failing."

Listening to Joey reminisce, I detect a hint of urgency in his voice, as if an unknown force is driving him to release these stories into the universe. The loadmaster needs to unload, I think to myself.

"Then another one of our engines started losing power," Joey goes on. "Luckily by that point we were close enough to the target that we could drop the load. Thank God I had made the decision to open the hatch and lower the cargo ramp a few seconds earlier than planned — we had just enough power left in the aircraft to pull up and start releasing the pallets of ammo. This whole time we're still taking fire from the hills, and now with the hatch open it left the crew in back exposed to all the firepower the NVA had in their arsenal, which was a helluva lot. The navigator — 1st Lt. Mandel — and I pressed ourselves against opposite sides of the cargo hold, trying to stay out of the line of fire as we waited for the last pallet to drop. My hand was on the ramp switch, ready to toggle that sucker the moment we had jettisoned the entire load.

"TechSgt. Vestine, the engineer who'd shut down our damaged engine before it caught fire, stood a few feet away from me on the same side of the cargo hold, ready to help us secure the area as soon as the load cleared. He gave me a reassuring look, as if to say 'we got this.' As the last pallet rolled off the ramp and I activated the ramp switch — in the instant before the ramp began to raise — Vestine stepped forward. He immediately took a hit in the chest from machine gun fire, knocking him backward into the empty cargo hold. He was wearing his flak jacket — as we all were — but those things aren't as bulletproof as you might think, especially when it comes to a .50-caliber round.

"Everything happened in a matter of seconds. Mandel rushed from his spot against the opposite wall, scrambling toward Vestine to pull him to safety, while I kept the ramp switch engaged, praying for that sucker to hurry up and close. That's when incoming fire struck Lt. Mandel in the bicep as he reached for Vestine. He didn't seem to know he'd been hit at that point, because he finished pulling Vestine off to the side of the cargo hold, then helped me reattach the struts once the ramp was up. When I pointed to the lieutenant's arm and told him he'd been hit, he looked at me in a daze, and said 'It doesn't even hurt.' 'Just wait 'til tomorrow,' I replied. 'It'll hurt all right.'

"At that moment Capt. Wilson took a sudden, hard bank to the right, an evasive maneuver to avoid anti-aircraft fire. Lt. Mandel had already been hanging on with his good arm to one of the ramp struts, but I went flying across the cargo hold, landing headfirst on the dual rail system, smacking my head so hard it cracked my flight helmet. The plane had banked so severely I found myself laying against the wall of the aircraft instead of on the floor. TechSgt. Vestine, who'd taken fire in the chest only moments before, merely rolled from one side of the cargo hold to the other, like just another piece of equipment. Mandel and I locked eyes; realizing then that Vestine was probably dead. The aircraft tilted again to right itself, but by then I had grabbed onto a ratchet strap so I didn't go flying across the hold again. Mandel was still hugging the strut with his good arm. Vestine rolled back to the other side of the aircraft where Mandel had originally lain him."

At some point during Joey's story I had removed my feet from the coffee table and planted them on the floor. I leaned forward on the edge of the couch, my hands over my mouth, my hot toddy forgotten. Wade sat beside me, his feet still propped on the coffee table, his mug resting on his lap with both hands wrapped around it. I could hear him taking slow, deep breaths, as if to calm himself. On the other side of me, Fakhir had also taken his feet off the coffee table to sit forward on the couch, elbows resting on his knees, engrossed in Joey's story. Dottie had placed her hand on Joey's chest in a protective gesture, resting her head in the crook of his arm as she listened to him talk, entranced by the steady cadence of his voice.

After taking a moment to sip his hot toddy and gather himself, Joey continues. "My flight helmet probably saved me from cracking my head open. But apparently it wasn't enough to keep me from getting a concussion. I didn't lose consciousness, because I remember hearing Capt. Wilson on the intercom telling us to get strapped in. The aircraft was badly damaged, but we were going to try to make it to Da Nang in what would most likely be a crash landing. I could feel the aircraft gaining altitude at that point, which meant we'd soon be out of the range of

ground fire — if we weren't already. My ears were ringing and I was seeing stars and I felt like I was going to puke. But before I strapped myself
in I grabbed a strip of cloth from the first aid kit, using it as a tourniquet
on Mandel's arm to stanch the bleeding. He'd already lost quite a bit of
blood. Looking at his ashen face, I reminded him he needed to stay the
fuck awake during the thirty minutes it would take us to get to Da Nang.
I helped him get strapped in before returning to my own flight seat,
where I peppered him with questions about his family back home to
help him stay focused.

"By the time we made it to Da Nang our right wing had caught on
fire — thank God we were no longer carrying 30,000 pounds of ammo.
With our hydraulics damaged and one engine out of commission and
God knows what else not working, we made a bone-crunching landing on the airstrip. Parts of the aircraft flew in every direction as we
skidded to a stop, where fire crews and medics awaited us. My vision
was blurry and my head hurt like hell, but I wasn't bleeding as far as I
could tell — unlike Lt. Mandel, who had a pretty good-size piece of his
bicep missing. He and I helped each other out the rear troop door while
Capt. Wilson and Capt. Hite exited through their swing windows.

"The four of us watched in silence as two corpsmen put TechSgt.
Vestine's body on a litter and carried him off the C-130. Later, when they
brought us inside one of the quonset huts to be examined in the receiving ward, I told the doc I was fine. He looked skeptically at the cracked
flight helmet I held in my hands. 'No dizziness? No ringing in the ears?
No nausea? Blurred vision? Headache?' he asked. All I could think about
was TechSgt. Vestine — his reassuring smile, his eagerness to help. No
way was I gonna say anything to that doc about a goddamned headache."

Monday, December 1, 2008   5:33 p.m.

The house is quiet again. Everybody slept in yesterday morning, our
last day of Thanksgiving break. It had been a busy weekend. Finn over-
slept and almost missed his train for Chicago. Rory drove him to the
train station while I stayed back at the house with everyone else. I know

we're going to see Finn again in a few weeks, but I always hate to see him go.

Dottie and Joey brought their bags downstairs, dressed and ready to go, looking refreshed. They were eager to get on the road so they could get back to St. Louis in time to watch their Sunday night programs. I was probably imagining it, but I detected a lightness in Joey's step. He'd been in a consistently good mood the entire weekend, and yesterday morning was no different. I had felt somewhat apprehensive about how Joey's frame of mind might be after Saturday night's heavy storytelling. But he seemed fine. Maybe even better.

I packed up a bunch of leftovers for them and followed them outside. As we stood next to their car on the driveway, Dottie gave me a peck on the cheek, told me she loved me, and went around to the passenger side to sit in the car with Jacques on her lap. Before getting in the driver's seat, Joey wrapped his arms around me in his usual bear hug, picking me up off my feet and squeezing me tight. But this time his hug was a little different, because after setting me down he didn't let go. With his arms still encircling me, he held me close and looked into my eyes.

"You're really special, you know that?" he says.

"Yeah, people tell me that all the time," I joke. "Although I don't think they mean it as a compliment."

"Seriously now. You're always there for me and Dottie," he replies. He loosens his arms and puts his hands on my shoulders, stepping back slightly. "Will you promise me something?"

"Of course," I reply, holding his gaze.

"Promise me that if … anything ever happens to me, you'll take care of Dottie for me. Okay?"

"Joey, nothing's going to happen to you. But yes. I'll always take care of Dottie. And you."

This seems to comfort him. "Thank you, Emilie. For everything."

When I went back in the house, I found Wade pouring himself a cup of coffee in his travel mug. He planned to drop off Chesty at the house before heading back to Wakeville. He seemed preoccupied.

"Will Isabel and Chloe be there when you drop Chesty off?" I ask.

"No. They're not getting home from New Orleans 'til later. Chesty will be fine on his own for a few hours. I need to get back while it's still light out — I'm moving into my new place today."

"Well that's kind of exciting."

Wade shrugs and looks down at the floor. "I guess so."

I put my hand on his arm. "Are you okay?

He takes a deep breath and exhales. "Honestly, I don't know."

"You were awfully quiet last night when Joey was telling his stories. Was it hard for you to hear that stuff? I'm sure it brought back some memories of your own." I'm thinking of the story Wade told me about the Battle of Fallujah. I don't doubt there's a lot more where that came from.

"No, that's not it," he says, shaking his head. "I was glad Joey told us those stories. He needed to get that stuff out there."

I study Wade's face. He looks like he hasn't slept much this weekend, in spite of his break from work. "Wade, it probably doesn't feel like it right now," I say, "but things will get better. Maybe not right away. I know this situation with Isabel has got you feeling pretty raw. But it won't always feel this way. I promise you."

His eyes fill with tears. "I wish I could believe you Em."

"Look. Fakhir and I are committed to seeing you through this. We love you Wade. We're not gonna leave you."

"Okay. Thanks." He kneels to put Chesty's leash on, quickly wiping away a tear with the palm of his hand before standing up again. I hug him and tell him I'll call him soon to check on him. Maybe getting back into his work routine will be a good thing for him, I think. His job helped him get through hard times before. There's no reason to believe it won't again.

I watch Wade walk out the door holding Chesty's leash in one hand and his weekend bag in the other. He looks like a man whose heart has been broken.

Tuesday, December 2, 2008   6:09 p.m.

Dear Liam,

Again, I'm so sorry I had to have the Red Cross reach out to you with such terrible news. Thank God you were able to call me back. We are all in a state of shock. I wish you and I could have talked longer. Fakhir is on his way over here now. As soon as he gets here we're leaving for Wakeville. We hope to reach Wade's apartment before ten. I'm enclosing a copy of the note. I'll write again as soon as I can. I love you.

My Love,

I've been fighting my entire life and I can't fight any longer. I know this feeling and I know it's not going to get better this time. You did your best to understand my struggles but there's no way for you to know the depth of the hole I've been in. I don't think I can claw my way out this time. I am done. Done with fighting, done with blaming myself, done with regret. If anyone could have saved me it would have been you. Until I met you I was living my life on autopilot. You are strong and beautiful. You awakened in me all that is good. I am stubborn and realistic. I refuse to put you through what I've put others through. I'm doing what's best for both of us. I owe every happiness in my life to you. Please forgive me, and remember only the good.

It's time to pull chocks.

Wednesday, December 3, 2008   5:25 p.m.

We made it to Wade's apartment before ten last night. Fakhir knocked softly on the door and it opened immediately. It was as if Wade knew we were coming, though we hadn't warned him. We wanted to tell him about Joey in person, not over the phone. We were worried how he might react when he heard the news. We didn't want him to be alone. Wade took one look at our faces and he knew something terrible had happened.

"Aw Jesus." He stands aside to let us in. Fakhir and I step inside and Wade gestures toward the living room. The only furniture he has are some folding chairs and a moving box turned upside down for a table. Fakhir and I each take a seat but Wade remains standing. "It's Liam, isn't it?" he says. "Something happened to Liam."

"No," I rush to assure him. "Liam is fine. I spoke to him a few hours ago." Wade looks uncomprehendingly from me to Fakhir.

Fakhir says, "It's Joey, Wade."

Wade's entire body sinks in on itself. "Ah Jesus."

"They found him parked outside the VA Hospital this morning," I explain. "He hadn't checked in for his appointment so when the hospital called wondering where he was, Dottie knew right away something was wrong. A security guard found him in his car."

Wade runs his hands through his hair. "Don't tell me he shot himself."

Fakhir says, "No. They found two empty bottles of Ambien on the front seat. He must have taken both of them."

Wade says, "Joey told me he tried the Ambien but hated the way it made him feel the next day. Said he wasn't gonna take it anymore. He must have been stockpiling it. Jesus Christ. How long has he been planning this? How did we not know? How did I not know?" Wade sits on a folding chair and drops his head in his hands. Without looking up he says, "Joey and I talked almost every week. I should have recognized the signs."

"Wade, there were no signs," I say. "Or none that any of us could see. Not even Dottie."

"Jesus," Wade says, looking up at me. "Poor Dottie. My God."

"I spoke to her several times today. Fakhir and I are driving to St. Louis on Thursday," I say.

"I'm coming with you," Wade says. He drops his head in his hands again, shaking it from side to side. "No no no no no. Why didn't Joey reach out to me? I told him I'd always be there for him. I've been too wrapped up in my own problems. I should have known." His shoulders heave up and down as he sobs quietly into his hands.

Fakhir and I get up from our chairs to sit on the floor in front of Wade. We wait in silence as we listen to him berate himself. Finally

Fakhir raises up onto his knees and grabs Wade by the shoulders, turning Wade toward him, but Wade refuses to raise his head. Fakhir gives him a gentle shake. "This is not on you brother. You don't have to keep carrying all these loads. It's time to put down your pack."

At that Wade leans into Fakhir, and Fakhir wraps his arms around Wade, holding him tight. I look away, feeling like maybe I should leave the two of them alone. I quietly get up and look for the bathrooom. When I find it, I close the door, put the toilet lid down, and sit.

After about fifteen minutes I come back out of the bathroom and find Wade and Fakhir sitting in their folding chairs, each drinking a glass of water and looking slightly more composed. Fakhir points to a third glass on the makeshift table and says, "That's for you."

"Thanks." I take the glass and sit back down in my folding chair.

We talk about our plans to drive to St. Louis together on Thursday. Wade says he'll leave Wakeville tomorrow night after work and come to my house. At that Wade glances at his watch and says, "Shit. It's late. I gotta get up for work in the morning. You guys wanna sleep here tonight?"

Fakhir and I glance around the barren apartment. "Dude, do you even have a bed?" he asks.

"I got an air mattress," Wade replies.

"You can have your air mattress," Fakhir says. "We're driving back to Buell City tonight. I'm done sleeping on the ground if I don't have to."

Before we get up to go there's something on my mind that's been gnawing at me. I don't know how to bring it up so I decide to just come out with it. "Wade," I say. "Do you still have your pistol here in Wakeville with you?"

He looks at me strangely. "Yeah. Why?"

"I'd like you to give it to me please."

The room goes still. After a few seconds Wade stands up. "All right. It's in the bedroom closet. I'll go get it."

Fakhir and I look at each other. "We'll go with you," we say, standing up simultaneously.

"You motherfuckers," Wade says. "You really think I'm gonna off myself with you two here?"

Fakhir and I say nothing, waiting for Wade to lead us to his closet.

"Jesus fucking Christ," Wade says as he leads us into his bedroom. He opens his closet and grabs a green steel ammo can from the shelf, opens it, and hands me the 9-mil inside.

I take it, making sure the safety is on, and put it in my coat pocket. "So tell me," I say. "When I asked you why you took your pistol from home and brought it here to Wakeville with you ... ."

Wade folds his arms and says, "Uh-huh."

"And you said it was because you were planning to go to the shooting range after work to practice your target skills ..."

Wade continues staring me down, arms folded. "Uh-huh."

"That was a bunch of bullshit, wasn't it?" I ask.

He lets out a subdued sigh. "Yeah. It was."

Thursday, December 4, 2008   9:19 p.m.

We made it to St. Louis by dinnertime. Dottie is a tower of strength. She is powering through everything that needs to be done like a boss. Fakhir, Wade, and I will go with her to meet the funeral director tomorrow to finalize arrangements. Joey's obituary appeared in the papers today, and the funeral is set for Saturday. Finn is taking the train from Chicago to St. Louis tomorrow. Lucia will be driving in with Rory, Arifah, and Farah — also arriving tomorrow.

Ethan is taking care of the pets for us. Agnes told me not to worry about a thing — they'll keep an eye on the house, bring in the mail and newspaper, and Ethan will make sure the pets get lots of attention. I felt bad calling Agnes on such notice but she seemed genuinely happy to help. I also spoke to Dr. Gouwens. She told me to take as much time off work as I needed. I told her I'd try to make it back on Monday for the last two weeks of school before Christmas break. Rory will go back to school on Monday too, so I might as well drive in with him.

I'm staying in Dottie and Joey's spare bedroom, which Dottie uses as her exercise studio. She's got a yoga mat, one of those giant exercise balls, an elliptical, and a boom box that looks like it's from the 1980s.

There's also a futon in here, which is what I'll be sleeping on. Fakhir and Wade are sleeping on the two couches in the living room, though I don't know how long that's going to last. They talked about renting a hotel room but Dottie says she likes having them here, so they're staying. At least for now.

I'm exhausted. The next few days are going to be rough. Maybe you and I can plan a phone call for Sunday night, after we're back in Buell City. Speaking of going back to Buell City, I was thinking about something in the car on the way here. What would you think if I asked Dottie to come live with us?

Friday, December 5, 2008   10:29 p.m.

The meeting with the funeral director was tough. But Joey made it a little easier because he left written instructions for everything. He wants to be buried in his blue tux—which makes me wonder, had he been planning for this even then, when he bought that tux before the Ball last month? And his courthouse wedding with Dottie—was that all part of his plan too? No time for that now. He specified he didn't want to be buried in his Air Force uniform, because it wouldn't look right with his long, permed locks, and he definitely didn't want a mortician botching up his hair in an attempt at a regulation haircut. (He wrote that he needed all his hair so he could be as good-looking in heaven as he was on earth. That guy.)

Joey wrote that his military medals could be displayed in a shadow box near the casket. The medals had been hidden away in a dresser drawer, stowed in a small brown paper bag underneath some t-shirts. Dottie had never seen them before. When we went through them in the funeral director's office, Wade told us what each one signified. The Vietnam Service Medal, awarded to those who served in Vietnam. The Vietnam Presidential Unit Citation, awarded to certain units for exceptional service to Vietnam. The Air Medal, for acts of merit or gallantry during aerial flight in a combat zone. And the Silver Star, awarded for singular acts of valor in combat. Wade said it's possible

Joey received the Silver Star for his actions during the supply mission to Khe Sanh — the one he told us about last weekend. But we also wondered if it could have been for something else, something entirely separate from the Khe Sanh mission. He did pull three tours in Vietnam after all. Wade said we could look for the citations among Joey's papers to find out more.

After we returned from the morning meeting at the funeral home, Joey's attorney paid Dottie a visit after lunch. Wade, Fakhir, and I said we could go out for a walk if Dottie wanted some privacy to talk with the lawyer, but she insisted we stick around. So the five of us sat at the kitchen table listening to the attorney go through Joey's documents and explain to Dottie what was in them. In a nutshell, Joey left everything to Dottie — with the exception of a $1,000 donation to the Railroad Museum (one of his favorite places to hang out), and another $1,000 donation to his local VFW post. Everything else was to go to Dottie — a sizeable savings account, an even more sizable retirement fund, and she's also the designated beneficiary of his pension. Not to mention two life insurance policies. The attorney, who's known Joey for twenty years, said that Joey lived frugally his entire life, and had therefore socked away considerable sums in his savings and retirement accounts. There was also a nice chunk of change sitting in his checking account, to which he had recently added Dottie's name. Dottie said she did know about that one, because he had asked her to sign the signature card after they got married.

Joey has no other living family members (that we know of), other than his ex-wife Louise, their daughter Stephanie, and Stephanie's kids. Interestingly, Joey had recently removed Stephanie from his will. (She had previously been set to inherit fifty percent of Joey's estate, split equally with Dottie.) In fact, the attorney said Joey had him write up a codicil to the will just before Thanksgiving, disowning Stephanie and explicitly excluding both his daughter and his ex-wife from any portion of his assets.

After the lawyer left, Fakhir and Wade said they needed to take a snooze on their respective couches. Dottie and I decided to take Jacques for a walk. I broached the subject of her coming to live with us (since I had received your brief email this morning enthusiastically endorsing the idea). She said she appreciated the offer, but she needed time to think about it. I told her there was no rush. She could take all the time she needed and if at any point in the future she decided she wanted to come live with us, we'd be waiting with open arms. Besides, I said, I'd been thinking about her suggestion that I start a movie review blog, and I might need an on-site partner to provide moral support if I decide to take the plunge.

Following our walk, I made the short trip to the train station to pick up Finn. By the time Finn and I returned to Dottie's, Lucia had arrived with Rory, Arifah, and Farah in tow. We ordered sub sandwiches and salads for take-out, sitting around the living room eating and telling stories about Joey, sharing our favorite memories of him and making Dottie laugh. She seemed comforted to be surrounded by all of us.

With Finn and Rory here, Fakhir and Wade said they'd reserve a hotel room nearby so the boys could take over their spots on Dottie's couches. Lucia, Arifah, and Farah got a room at the same hotel. Wade had asked Isabel if she and Chloe were coming in for the funeral, and Isabel said "they wouldn't be able to make the trip." I could see that Wade was disappointed, and I don't blame him. It would have been a nice gesture on Isabel's part to show up, even if they are getting a divorce.

I wish you could be here Liam. The boys and I miss you terribly.

Saturday, December 6, 2008   11:43 p.m.

Joey's service this afternoon was incredible. So many people. I'm ashamed to admit I didn't expect a big showing, aside from us. Dottie was blown away by the number of people who came to pay their respects to Joey. There were at least thirty people from the Railroad Administration. When they came through the receiving line at the funeral parlor, every single one of them told us what a kind boss Joey had been, how he treated everybody like family. And then there were his friends from the VFW—a couple dozen veterans if not more. They helped coordinate the service, performing military honors for Joey. It was so moving. And they all talked about how generously Joey gave of himself to his fellow veterans, listening to their stories and being there for them when they needed support from someone who understood. They talked about how fun he was too — how his liveliness lifted everybody's spirits. They said that when he walked into the VFW meetings on Wednesday nights, he lit up the room with his presence. There were even a few guys from his Air Force unit in Vietnam, who drove several hours just to attend the service.

Wade gave the eulogy — per Joey's instructions. I could see he was nervous before going up to the lectern to speak, the piece of notebook paper containing his handwritten notes visibly shaking in his hand. But once he started talking, it was magic. Wade was the perfect choice, and Joey must have known it.

Wade started out by sharing some anecdotes about Joey, which made everybody laugh. Then he touched on Joey's service in the Air Force, how he enlisted when he was 18, his tours in Vietnam, his work as a loadmaster, and that he rose to the rank of Master Sergeant by the time he got out after 16 years. Then Wade relayed a few things Joey's coworkers at the Railroad Administration had said about Joey in the receiving line — including Joey's 30 years of dedication to the job, and how beloved he was by everyone who came in contact with him. Wade then spoke about Joey's relationship with Dottie and how happy they made each other — their mutual zest for life, their positive attitudes, their fun-loving ways, and their deep and abiding love for one another. Wade finished by reading a passage from Tim O'Brien's *The Things They Carried* — the same passage I had underlined months ago, but a slightly longer version. Wade talked about the redemptive power of storytelling, and how this particular paragraph — depicting life and death on the battlefield — explains a lot about what kind of person Joey was:

> *"After a firefight, there is always the immense pleasure of aliveness. The trees are alive. The grass, the soil — everything. All around you things are purely living, and you among them, and the aliveness makes you tremble. You feel an intense, out-of-the-skin awareness of your living self — your truest self, the*

human being you want to be and then become by the force of
wanting it. In the midst of evil you want to be a good man.
You want decency. You want justice and courtesy and human
concord, things you never knew you wanted. There is a kind of
largeness to it, a kind of godliness. Though it's odd, you're never
more alive than when you're almost dead. You recognize what's
valuable. Freshly, as if for the first time, you love what's best in
yourself and in the world, all that might be lost."

Wade continued, in his own words: "Joey was a good man. The kind of person we all strive to be. Decent. Kind. Generous. Just. Whatever awful things Joey experienced as a young Vietnam vet, he took those experiences and turned them into something positive. A life of service, not just in the military but as a civil servant. Not everyone is able to do what Joey did—take their worst experiences and turn them into a life of good. Joey was his truest self—the human being he wanted to be. And he was one of the most alive human beings I ever met. He exuded a sense of aliveness. He embraced life like one of his bear hugs. He would wrap his arms around you and hold you tight and lift you up. Even if he didn't know you very well, Joey would give you one of his bear hugs. Because that's how he treated everybody. He embraced everybody the way he embraced life. Full-on, without judgment, without hesitation. May we all embrace life the way Joey did."

After the service there was a dinner buffet at the VFW hall. The spouses of all the vets had arranged quite a spread—large chafing dishes of mostaccioli, fried chicken, mashed potatoes, and a medley of steamed carrots, peas, and corn. They also made a giant chocolate sheet cake with sour cream frosting—Joey's favorite.

Most of the people who were at the funeral home made the short trip to the VFW post (there was no graveside service, per Joey's request). Thank goodness they had prepared a ton of food, because we had a good-size crowd mingling about. Dottie, Wade, Fakhir, and I were standing off to the side in a small circle, enjoying the sheet cake, when Dottie noticed a woman in her mid-60s enter the hall, pausing to scan the crowd as if looking for someone. The woman was petite, like Dottie, dressed in a black sheath dress, black stockings, black heels, holding a black patent leather purse with hands gloved in black lace. Oh, and a little pillbox hat with a black veil. I was trying to decide if the outfit was more along the lines of "Jackie Kennedy at JFK's Funeral" or "1960s Vintage Barbie Doll" when Dottie nudged me with her elbow.

"Well paint me green and call me a cucumber," Dottie says in a low voice.

"What?" I ask.

"That's her," Dottie replies, tilting her head toward the woman standing near the door.

"That's who?"

"Louise," Dottie whispers. "Joey's ex-wife. I recognize her from the photos."

Wade and Fakhir notice our urgent exchange and lean in closer to hear. "What's going on?" Wade whispers.

I move my eyes in the direction of the door. "That's Joey's ex-wife," I say without moving my lips. (You never know who might be a lip reader.)

"No fucking way," he whispers back.

Dottie straightens her shoulders and raises her head, softly patting her perfectly coiffed pastel blue hair (which Lucia had touched up just that morning). Unlike Louise, who obviously intended to play the bereaved widow, Dottie had chosen a bright and colorful outfit to celebrate Joey, just as he would've wanted. She had on crushed velvet bell-bottom pants (light blue) with a crushed velvet blazer (also light blue) and a multi-color silk blouse, with splashes of pink, orange, turquoise, and indigo. And of course, Old-Skool Vans in a mod floral pattern.

As if sensing our eyes on her, Louise's searching gaze eventually comes to rest on Dottie. The two women stare at each other from across the room. Louise clutches her purse and walks purposefully toward our small group, not the least bit hesitant.

When she comes to stand before us, Dottie says, "You must be Louise." (And not in a friendly way, I might add.)

"And you must be Joey's ... girlfriend," Louise replies with distaste, matching Dottie's cold tone of voice, ice cube for ice cube.

"His wife, actually," Dottie replies. Checkmate. And we're off.

A look of disappointment flashes across Louise's face but she quickly recovers. "How sweet," she says (not at all sweetly). "Joey always did prefer older women."

Wade, Fakhir, and I exchange glances, as if to say buckle up, buttercup.

"You're quite right," Dottie agrees, offering an enigmatic smile. "Especially in the bedroom."

Dottie's comeback achieves its intended effect, putting Louise at a loss for words. Before Louise can muster a reply, Dottie cuts to the chase. "So I suppose you're here to ask about the will."

Louise doesn't bat an eyelash. "I came to pay my respects," she says, as if the will was the furthest thing from her mind. "He *was* the father of my child after all."

"Well, you're late," Wade says. "You missed the service."

Louise looks Wade up and down, taking in his impressive physique. "And who are you?" she says coyly, holding out a gloved hand.

Wade ignores Louise's hand. "I'm Dottie's son," he says with a totally straight face.

Fakhir had just taken a bite of his cake and practically chokes on his fork.

Louise looks admiringly from Wade to Dottie. "I didn't know you had a son."

"I have two sons," Dottie replies, gesturing grandly toward Fakhir. "And this is my younger son."

Louise's eyes widen as she takes in Fakhir's imposing presence, unable to mask her confusion at the fact that Fakhir is obviously Not Caucasian. Once again at a loss for words, Louise can only look at Dottie inquisitively.

Dottie says matter-of-factly, "I traveled a lot when I was younger."

Wade coughs into his hand, attempting to muffle his laughter. Fakhir busies himself by taking a humongous bite of cake, his chewing motions barely disguising a huge grin. I simply turn my head away, pretending to look for someone or something behind me.

Once I've gotten a hold of myself I turn back to Louise. Wanting in on the charade, I say, "And I'm Dottie's daughter." Dottie signals her approval of our antics with a proud, maternal smile.

"Nice to meet all of you," Louise says, nodding slowly at each of us, clearly unsure what to make of this unexpected development.

"So how'd you find out about the funeral?" Wade asks.

"My daughter Stephanie," Louise replies. "She had a Google Alert set up for Joey's name. She got an email when his obituary came online."

"Why would Stephanie set up a Google Alert for Joey?" I ask. Then, before Louise can answer, I hold up my hand. "Wait. There's only one reason she would do that. So she would know right away when he died. There's no other reason Joey's name would suddenly pop up online. He doesn't even own a computer."

Louise sputters, "This is none of your concern. Joey was her father. Of course she'd want to know when he died."

"So if she cared so much about Joey then why isn't she here?" Dottie asks.

Louise appears to be prepared for this question. "She was too devastated to travel. She prefers to mourn her father in private."

Fakhir folds his arms and looks menacingly at Louise. "Let's dispense with the bullshit, okay?" He looks at Louise with his trademark Thousand Yard Stare, the look he gave Marcus and his friends on the track field all those months ago. Thank God I know Fakhir personally. If I met him on the street and he stared at me like that I think I'd pee my pants.

Wade jumps in on the act, looking equally threatening, with his own interpretation of the Thousand Yard Stare. (Why am I not surprised Wade has also perfected this look?) He leans in close to Louise, assuming an expression that suggests he's about to eat her alive. "Yeah. Dottie — I mean, our *mom* — was right. You didn't come here to 'pay your respects.' You came here to find out about the will. Didn't you?"

Her cage successfully rattled, Louise quickly dispenses with the bereaved widow act. "Okay. Fine. Whatever. So — did my husband mention me in his will?"

"You mean your *ex*-husband," Dottie says. "As a matter of fact, he did mention you in his will."

Louise looks pleasantly surprised, her eyebrows raised in a question mark.

Dottie continues. "He added a codicil that specifically states you are not to receive any portion of his assets. As in, Big. Fat. Goose egg."

Louise quickly replies, "Well surely he left something for Stephanie — his own *daughter*?"

"Oh. You mean the daughter who ignored Joey her entire life, until she decided to blackmail her own father by holding his grandkids hostage?" Wade says.

"What are you talking about?" Louise asks, looking genuinely surprised.

Dottie answers, "When she flew out here three weeks ago. And tried to get Joey to put her name on his pension. And his retirement account. Stephanie basically told Joey he wouldn't be allowed to meet his grandkids until she started receiving the checks."

"Back up a minute here," Louise says, holding up an index finger. "Stephanie did what?"

Dottie says, "You mean you didn't know Stephanie flew out here?"

Louise waves her hand impatiently. "Yes. I did know about that. But … what was the thing you said about holding the grandkids hostage?"

Dottie says, "Oh. So you weren't in on the plan to blackmail Joey?"

"No," Louise replies. "I mean, I knew she was probably going to ask Joey for money. But that's not what I'm asking about. What's this you're saying about grandkids?"

Dottie repeats herself, more slowly this time, as if talking to a child. "Stephanie told Joey he couldn't see his grandkids until —"

Louise interrupts Dottie. "Whose grandkids?"

Dottie replies, "Joey's grandkids. You know, Stephanie's children?"

Louise looks at each of our faces, as if we're playing some sort of joke on her. "Stephanie doesn't have kids," she says.

Dottie replies. "She showed pictures of them to Joey."

A look of realization crosses Louise's face. "Were they photos of three kids? Two girls and a boy? Like around 9, 11, and 13?"

"Yes," Dottie replies.

"Those aren't Stephanie's kids," Louise says. "Stephanie doesn't have children. Those are the kids she nannies."

Sunday, December 7, 2008   11:08 p.m.

We made it back to Buell City. It was hard to leave Dottie. But honestly, I think she was looking forward to some time alone. She said she was going to hang out at the apartment with Jacques for a few days and just think. She needs time to wrap her mind around everything that happened.

Before we left her apartment, I told Dottie I didn't want to rush her into a decision about coming to live with us, but would she at least consider staying for a couple weeks over Christmas? She said of course, she'll definitely come stay with us for the holidays. She put her palm on my cheek and told me not to worry about her.

I wish you could have called tonight but I understand. I had the TV on while I was unpacking my suitcase earlier, and I saw something on the news about the U.S. troop drawdown. I didn't catch all of it, but I could swear the news anchor said the official drawdown will begin next month, January 2009. If that's true, is it possible you could come home earlier than April? I mean, if they're drawing down troops, wouldn't they follow a "first in, first out" policy? (Or would that be too logical?) I know there's no way you could come home in January like we originally expected, but I'm wondering if maybe you could come home in March instead of April? Or maybe even February? I'd be happy with anything sooner than April. And I know the boys would be too.

Monday, December 8, 2008   10:29 p.m.

Rory and I went back to school today. We were both exhausted, but there's something to be said for getting back into a routine. The weather as we drove in together this morning matched our mood — gray and gloomy.

With everything going on, I forgot to mention Lucia took her cosmetology licensing exam last Monday. They're supposed to send the results before Christmas. And then, assuming she passes — which I know she will — she'll be a licensed cosmetologist.

Also on that front, when they were sharing a hotel room in St. Louis together, Lucia suggested to Farah that she put in an application for the shampoo station at her salon. (Yes, Lucia is that confident she'll be a stylist before the end of the year.) Farah thought that was a great idea, and filled out an application after school today. Lucia said she'd put in a good word for her. And speaking of Lucia and Farah sharing a hotel room (along with Arifah), we were treated to a number of funny stories about Lucia's snoring and what a bedhog she is. Farah commented that Lucia snores even louder than her brother. So I guess that makes them a perfect match.

I called Wade tonight. It's only been a day since we last saw him, but I want him to know we are sticking to him like glue in the coming months. (Or for the rest of his life — if that's what it takes.)

"Emilie, I just saw you yesterday," Wade says, feigning exasperation when he hears my voice. "You're not going to call me every night now, are you?"

"Probably," I reply. "You'd better get used to it Wade. You're gonna get real tired of me."

"I already am tired of you."

"Glad to see you're still as obnoxious as always."

"Ditto," he replies.

"So I was thinking …" I say.

"Uh-oh," Wade interrupts. "Did it hurt?"

"Come on now. Seriously. I was wondering, have you been in touch with Gunny Lee since the Birthday Ball? I noticed you guys talking that night. He seems like someone you'd want to have on standby as part of your support network."

"First of all," Wade replies, "I'm fine Emilie. I understand you're worried about me, and I appreciate that. But I'm going to be okay."

"I just thought—if he knew what you've been through these last few weeks—Gunny Lee would like to be on call for you."

"Well ... I hate to admit it, but you do have a point," he says. "I've been reaching out to people—Greg added a weekly teletherapy session to our in-person appointments. And I've been talking to my sponsor. A lot. I'm also thinking about starting a vets-in-recovery chapter here in Wakeville. But I hadn't thought about reaching out to Gunny Lee. I'll do that. Thanks."

"You're welcome. And you know you can call me or Fakhir any time, day or night?"

"Only because you've told me that about a million times," he says.

"All right," I say, changing the subject. "There was something else I wanted to ask you about. I was thinking about that bizarre conversation we had with Louise. Do you think Joey wouldn't have ... do you think things would've turned out differently if Joey knew he didn't actually have grandkids? That it was all a scam?"

"Do I think Joey wouldn't have taken his own life if he knew Stephanie was lying?" Wade says. "Maybe he did know. Or he suspected her story didn't add up. Either way, it was obvious Stephanie had only flown out to see Joey because she wanted money from him. So no, I don't think that would have changed anything."

"Okay. That makes sense. It's about the only thing that does make sense right now."

"I don't claim to know what was going through Joey's mind," Wade says, "but there were other factors besides the thing with Stephanie. Like his health issues. That all seems to us like it came on suddenly, but now we know Joey's been dealing with all that—the tinnitus, the headaches, the PTS, the depression—pretty much his whole life. And the way he dealt with it all those years was by throwing himself into his career. Once he retired, everything bubbled to the surface again."

"I know. But he had Dottie. They were so happy together. That's what I don't understand."

"She brought a lot of joy to his life, that's for sure," Wade says. "But the forces of depression are powerful. And on top of all that, the guy couldn't even get a good night's sleep — that shit can really fuck with a person's mind."

"So what you're saying is we'll never really know why he did it," I say.

"Well, there was the note," Wade replies. "I think the best thing for us to do is to take Joey at his word. And then try living our lives the way he would've wanted us to."

Tuesday, December 9, 2008   9:59 p.m.

Some crazy news coming out of Iraq. On the way home from work I heard on the radio that a suicide bomber walked into a packed restaurant in Kirkuk, killing 48 people and wounding 100 more. And last week there was a bomb attack in Baghdad aimed at Iraqi security forces, and another attack in Mosul targeting a U.S. patrol. With Iraq's provincial elections coming up, do you think the violence is only going to get worse?

Instead of things calming down over there it seems like they're heating up again. Forget what I wrote about you coming home earlier than April. That's just wishful thinking. I've got to stop getting my hopes up every time I read something about the drawdown or progress being made. I need to lower my expectations. That way, when the inevitable delays happen, I won't be so disappointed. I will keep reminding myself that the important thing is for you to come home, period. No matter when that is.

Leah called a while ago. She wanted to say how sorry she was to hear about Joey. I asked how their trip to North Carolina for Thanksgiving went, and she said it was good to see their families. She also said things between her and Jacob have gotten a little better. A change of scenery, a break from work, being around family — all of that helped to ease the tension between them. But she also acknowledged they still have a long way to go. Then she shared some big news: Jacob got orders to Camp Lejeune. He's due to report by the end of January.

"Wow! That's happening pretty quick," I reply, "but at least you'll be closer to your families now. So when do you guys leave?"

"Well, Jacob's planning to go out there mid-January to look for an apartment and all that," she says.

"And when do you plan to go?" I ask. "You probably need time to give notice at Alfalfa's and wrap up things here."

"See, that's the thing. I'm not sure I'm going."

"I thought you said things with you and Jacob were getting a little better?" I ask.

"They are. I'm just ... torn."

"Okay." I'm not sure what I'm supposed to say here. I feel like if I ask a question it would seem nosy. On the other hand, I don't want to make any assumptions. (And yes, I realize I'm overthinking this.) Maybe it would be best if I just shut my pie-hole and listen.

"What do you think I should do?" she asks.

"Oh Leah. I don't have an opinion one way or another. This is something you're gonna have to figure out on your own. Have you told Jacob you're thinking about staying here?"

"No. But I did talk to Isabel."

"And what did she say?"

"She wants me to stay, for obvious reasons," Leah replies.

I guess Leah assumes I know more than I actually do. Other than my conversation with Wade, Leah and Isabel's relationship is a mystery to me. If Isabel is urging Leah not to follow Jacob to Lejeune, that does point to something serious, romantic or not. Maybe Isabel knows more about Leah and Jacob's marriage than what Leah shared with me, and that's why she wants Leah to leave him. Or, Isabel and Leah are in love and Isabel simply wants Leah to be with her. Right now I'm leaning toward this last option. If I were closer with Leah — like I am with Dottie or Fakhir or Wade or even Tammy — I'd just ask her directly what's going on. I am not good with all this insinuendo (as my mom used to call it).

"Hello? Emilie? Are you there?" Leah asks.

"Yeah, I'm here. Sorry," I reply. I make a snap decision to focus on what Leah needs, aside from the nature of her relationships with Jacob and Isabel. "Leah, the important thing here is, what do *you* want?"

"That's the problem, Emilie. I don't *know* what I want."

"I wish I knew how to make this easier for you," I say. "You're young. You're still figuring out who you are. Hell, a lot of us are still trying to figure that out. So my only advice to you is to listen to what your gut is telling you. Because, as Elvis used to say, your gut doesn't know how to lie."

"I like that," she says.

"Well, I stole it from Wade," I reply. "He gave me that advice when we were trying to make a decision about putting Button to sleep."

"So basically what you're saying," she says, "is that I need to tune out what everybody else is saying they want from me. And just sit in a room, by myself, think this through, and figure out what I want."

"Right. And at some point, you gotta let Jacob in on the situation, especially since you've already talked it over with Isabel. You can't keep him in the dark on this much longer."

Silence on her end of the line, and a small sigh. "I know," she says. Then, "I feel bad we even got into all this Emilie. I wasn't planning to open up so much when I called you. I did want you to know about Jacob's orders. I guess one thing led to another."

"It's okay, really," I reply. "It sounds like you needed to bounce this around with someone — someone not vested in the outcome. I'm sorry for assuming you'd automatically follow Jacob to Lejeune. That's what started us off on that tangent."

"No, you just asked the same type of questions all of us ask when we hear somebody got orders," she says. "Anyway, the main reason I picked up the phone was to tell you how sorry I was to hear about Joey. He was a nice person."

"Thanks Leah. He was. Keep me posted on your plans, okay?"

"Sure. I'll do that. Thanks Emilie."

Wednesday, December 10, 2008   10:11 p.m.

Fakhir called and asked me if I'd go Christmas shopping with him on Saturday to look for a gift for Lucia while she's at work. I said that sounds like fun. I've been avoiding going anywhere except the commissary. Just not in the mood for all the Christmas music and holiday decorations. Maybe going shopping with Fakhir will help me get in the spirit.

I called Wade to check in with him tonight. And he told me I'm being a pain in the ass, and to stop calling him so much. I said I don't care if he thinks I'm a pain in the ass and also I'm not going to stop calling. I asked him if he was coming back to Buell City this weekend and he said he's not sure yet, he's trying to work out a schedule with Isabel on when he gets to see Chloe. I reminded him that he always has a place to stay at our our house anytime he comes back, including over the holidays.

I also called Dottie to see how's she's doing. She said she and Jacques took it easy the first couple days after we left, but today she started tackling all the paperwork that needs to get done. She hopes to complete the most pressing tasks before the holidays. I asked her when she wanted to come here for Christmas. She's thinking maybe a week from Friday, the 19th. I told her anytime she wants to come is fine, and that there's always a room for her here.

So then after I got off the phone with her I realized I had just offered the spare bedroom in the basement to both Wade and Dottie. If they both end up coming here I'll give Dottie the room in the basement and Wade can sleep on the couch, just like old times.

Thursday, December 11, 2008   11:12 p.m.

I walked over to Agnes's house after work today to give Ethan some money for petsitting and to get our house keys back. When Agnes answered the door, she asked if I wanted to come in for a cup of coffee. I told her I don't drink coffee late in the day but I'd love a cup of non-caffeinated tea if she had one.

I hadn't been in Agnes's house since she hosted book club back in July. She really has taken that minimalism thing seriously. All of the

Ethan Allen furniture was gone (sold) and so were the garish paintings she had everywhere (like the reproductions of cottages and churches they used to sell in shopping malls — I think one of hers even had actual twinkling lights shining through little cutouts). But I digress. The house looked great, all clean lines and simplicity. Maybe something I'd like to try someday. (As it is now, our style of decor is, in the kindest possible terms, what you might call "eclectic." Realistically it's more like a hodge-podge of everywhere we've lived. The rosewood dining room set from Okinawa. The wrought-iron gate from the French Quarter hanging in our foyer. The rattan patio furniture we bought in Pensacola. The big comfy southwestern style sofas in our family room from when we were stationed in Yuma. Now that I'm thinking about it, I kind of love our style. It's "us.")

As we sat at the kitchen table drinking orange herbal tea, Agnes got me up to speed on what's been going on with them. Eugene's job at Fidelia's is going great; he's already been promoted to assistant manager. Ethan has been volunteering at the animal shelter as a dog walker. Agnes says he really likes it because she and Eugene are both allergic to pet hair, so volunteering at the shelter lets Ethan get his pet fix, which he finds therapeutic.

At that moment Ethan came into the kitchen to get a pop out of the refrigerator. I thanked him for taking care of our pets while we were away and he said he'd be happy to do it anytime. When I tried to pass him the envelope of cash, he refused to take it at first, saying he didn't do it for the money. But I insisted, and he finally acquiesced.

After Ethan went back upstairs, Agnes told me she's still looking for a job but hasn't had any luck yet. That's when I got an idea.

"Would you ever consider working as the ISS supervisor at the high school?" I ask.

"I don't know," she says. "Why?"

"Well, I'm thinking about putting in my notice," I tell her. "I've always loved my job, but things are … different now."

"Because of the Marcus incident?" she asks.

"That's part of it. Also, with Joey gone, it's causing me to reevaluate a lot of things."

"I know what you mean," she says. "Although the school shooter thing isn't exactly a great recruiting incentive." She raises her eyebrows and offers a sideways smile.

"You have a point there," I say, returning her smile. "But what are the chances something like that would happen again at the same school? You know, the ol' 'lightning never strikes twice'?"

She chuckles. "Perhaps. But, I don't know if I'd even be good at something like that."

I look at her thoughtfully. "You know, after all you've been through this year, I think you'd be really good at the job. It takes compassion. People think ISS is all about being punitive toward the kids. Yeah, they did something wrong to put themselves there in the first place, and they need to accept the consequences. But you can do that with kindness. Most of those kids just need an adult in their lives who can help them find the best in themselves."

"You think I could do that?" she asks.

"Yeah. I do," I reply. "How about if when I give my notice to Dr. Gouwens I mention your name?"

"Sure. Go ahead," she says, nodding. "Do you realize you've just pivoted from 'if' you leave your job to 'when' you leave your job?"

I laugh. "No, I hadn't realized that. I guess talking it over with you has helped me decide."

"So what will you do next?" she asks.

"I'm not sure. Dottie says I should start a movie review blog. Everybody and their uncle seems to be launching a blog these days. And she says since I'm such a movie buff it could be fun. If anything, it would be more fun than writing obituaries. That was the absolute shittiest job I ever had."

Agnes says, "You should go for it. And I'm not just saying that to be nice. You always have something interesting to contribute at book club. I could totally see you writing movie reviews."

"Thanks Agnes. Well, I guess I'd better get back home. I've got laundry to do and bills to pay. Thanks for the tea."

"Oh! Before you go," Agnes says, "I have a little something for you. Hold on a sec." She disappears into the dining room and comes back holding a large Christmas basket, which she places on the table in front of me. "This is for you guys. I was going to leave it on your porch but since you're here ..." She sits in her chair and folds her hands in her lap, waiting for me to inspect the basket.

"Wow. This is really nice. I'm afraid I don't have anything for you yet—I'm a little behind on my Christmas shopping." I look at all the items in the basket—a bottle of wine, some blocks of gourmet cheese, a box of fancy crackers, a jar of pepper-stuffed olives, some homemade Christmas cookies, and an ornament. The ornament is a small figure of a Marine in dress blues. I press the tiny button in back and it plays the Marine Corps Hymn. "Oh Agnes. This is so thoughtful." My eyes fill with tears.

"Oh dear. I didn't mean to make you cry," she says. "Do you want a hug?"

"Sure."

She gets up from her chair and leans down to give me an awkward hug, gently patting me on the back. When she pulls away and sits down again she says, "There's a card in there too."

I open the envelope. It's a blank notecard, and the handwritten note inside simply reads, 'Merry Christmas to the Mahoney Family. We pray for Liam every day and look forward to his return.' "Aww. That's really nice. Thanks Agnes." I glance back down at the note. I've seen that hand-writing before. I stare at it a few seconds, then raise my eyes again. "So you're the one who's been leaving the gifts on our porch this whole time."

She pulls her head back in surprise, her eyes wide. "I have no idea what you're talking about."

My smile grows wider. "Yes you do. You know exactly what I'm talking about. I recognize your handwriting Agnes. The gig is up."

Her shoulders sag. "That was a dumb move on my part," she says. "I should've just left the basket on your porch like I had planned."

"You know this has been driving me crazy all year?" I say, pretending to be annoyed with her.

She smiles and says, "Sorry about that."

"But you know what else?" I continue, "Those gifts got me though some dark days. And they always seemed to appear at just the right time ... as if you knew exactly when to send them."

"Well, there were times I knew you were feeling down," she says.

I think back, trying to remember all the gifts from the beginning. "So let's see ... the first one was the single red rose back in February. That was obviously for Valentine's Day. You probably felt sorry for me, spending it all alone."

"Yeah. Valentine's Day was part of it," she says. "That was also shortly after you caught Ethan and Rory drinking, when Ethan was staying at your house for the weekend. I knew I was being a jerk about that whole thing, Emilie. I just couldn't help myself. The rose was a sort of apology, even if I couldn't admit it to your face."

"Oh Agnes. That's 'water over the bridge' as Fakhir would say. I haven't thought about that in a long time. And you shouldn't either."

"Okay," she says. "So. Do you remember what came after that?"

I get the feeling she's excited to discuss the gifts, now that the cat is out of the bag. "Hmmm. Let me think ... I know — it was the box of gourmet cupcakes. That would've been in March. But I don't remember anything in particular going on around then."

Agnes's expression turns remorseful. "That was for the thing that happened at book club, when I was questioning you about Finn going to music school. I realized after I got home that night I wasn't being very supportive."

"Gosh Agnes. I wish I would've known you were the one behind these gifts. We could have cleared the air on this stuff a lot sooner. But I get it. And I'm really thankful for these gestures from you. They mean a lot to me."

"Thanks Emilie. So, go on — what came after the cupcakes?" She's back to smiling proudly again.

"Oh man ..." I tap my fingers on the table, trying to think. "The votive candle holder. Back in May. That was obviously for Mother's Day."

"Well yes ..." Agnes replies, looking guilty again.

"Ohhh. I remember now. That was after we had that painful phone conversation when you were like a dog chewing on a bone about wanting us to join you for the Mother's Day brunch." I say this with a smile so Agnes knows I'm teasing her.

"That's correct," she says, her expression softening. "That was also the phone call when you first said we should meet for coffee sometime."

I nod. "I remember that. And I'm glad I suggested it."

"Me too," she says.

"So then after that ..." I scratch my head. "I can't remember what came next."

Agnes is eager to help jog my memory. "That would've been the succulent garden. In July."

"Okay. I remember now. So that was for ... ?"

"I sent that one after the first time we met for coffee. I was so looking forward to getting together with you, and I was worried I blew it, because I brought up some things I shouldn't have. Things about Finn and Rory getting in trouble that were really none of my business. So the succulents were partly an apology. But they were also a thank you. Because that was the same get-together when I told you about Ethan going into rehab, and you were such a good listener that day. I really needed a friend. And you were there for me."

Agnes and I look at one another across the table, not saying anything, except with our eyes. Thanks for seeing past my flaws. Thanks for giving me a chance. Thanks for being a friend.

"All right," I break the silence. "So after the succulents came the garden faerie. In October."

"Oh that was just a belated thank you. For that time Rory invited Ethan to his sleepover with the other boys. I figured you probably had something to do with that."

"No — that was totally Rory's idea," I reply.

At this Agnes looks like she might start to cry, and she quickly looks down at her lap.

I go on. "Then after the garden faerie came the gift certificate to the spa. That was way too generous of you, Agnes. I'm guessing that one was because of the school shooter? If you were trying to cheer me up, it worked. It was a nice distraction."

"Yeah, that was a big part of it," she replies. "And it was also after I found out Liam's deployment had been extended. I felt so bad for you. For all of you. I still do."

I'm so blown away by Agnes' thoughtfulness I almost forget about the last gift — the one in November, a few days before Thanksgiving. "And then there was that vase of beautiful fall flowers you left on our porch," I remind her. "That was obviously for Thanksgiving."

"Well, yes," she says. "But it was also a few days after book club. I noticed Wanda was being kind of a jerk that night. I don't know what her deal was, but she wasn't being very nice to you."

Agnes is so much more perceptive than I've given her credit for. "I owe you an apology Agnes."

"For what?"

"Well, first of all, for shutting you out when Liam first left. You tried reaching out to me a number of times and I kept pushing you away. I'm sorry."

"You were just doing what you needed to do to survive, Emilie. I understand that now."

"Thanks. That is what I was doing—what I *have* been doing this entire year. But maybe I could've done a better job of explaining that to people."

"You did try explaining it to me once," she says. "During that phone call about the Mother's Day brunch. I should've tried harder to see things from your perspective."

"You know what Agnes? I underestimated you. I was wrong. And I'm sorry for that."

"There's nothing you need to apologize for, Emilie. I'm the one who kept messing up."

"No. Not at all. I mean, okay, you do come out with some ... offbeat remarks sometimes. But you try. And you care. And you do good things. A lot of people only do good things when other people are watching. But you do good things when nobody's watching. And that's when it counts the most."

Friday, December 12, 2008 10:44 p.m.

I gave my notice to Dr. Gouwens today. She took it well. In fact, I wouldn't be surprised if she was expecting me to put in my resignation. I apologized to her for not doing it sooner, explaining that I had only just last night made a final decision. (And Liam, thank you for always being supportive of my choices. I knew you'd have my back on this no matter what I decided.)

I mentioned Agnes's name to Dr. Gouwens, saying that she was looking for work and I thought she'd be a good fit for the job. Dr. Gouwens is familiar with Agnes, due to all her work on the various school committees. She said to tell Agnes to put in her resume early next week, and maybe they can bring her in for an interview before Christmas.

Rory and Riikka went to the Winter Dance tonight. They looked adorable. Rory wore the same suit he wore to the Ball, with a black dress shirt and a red tie. Riikka had on a tux-like outfit with slim-fitting black satin pants, a tailored black blazer, a ruffled white blouse, and open-toe red satin heels. They gave each other matching red boutonnières. I've attached a few photos. So cute.

We also got to meet Riikka's parents and brother, who traveled all the way from Finland to spend the holidays here with Riikka and her host family. Rory was nervous about meeting them but they warmed up to him right away. There were several other hockey parents here too, snapping photos of the teammates and their dates in front of our fireplace. The group photo shoot only lasted thirty minutes or so, but it was fun seeing all the kids so excited. Before they left for the dance, I whispered in Rory's ear that he could stay out until midnight. It's a special occasion after all, and he's earned it, don't you think?

Tammy called just when I was settling in to watch "Christmas in Connecticut" on TCM. She proudly announced she has graduated from wearing sweatpants and a hoodie every day to her next "deployment uniform," jeans and a sweater. That bodes well for her chances of making it through Ken's deployment as a functioning adult. (A lot of us never even make it past the pajamas stage.) She even went to the PX today to do some Christmas shopping, which is a lot more than I've accomplished this month.

More importantly, Tammy was wired for sound over the latest rumor she picked up at the PX. She ran into Cpl. Roberts' wife, who told Tammy that she and her husband had gone to Tony's last night for a romantic dinner to celebrate their anniversary. Sitting in a booth in a dark corner at the back of the restaurant they spotted Leah and Isabel, who were, according to Cpl. Roberts' wife, "canoodling."

I've never heard Tammy as worked up about something as she was tonight. "So could this possibly be TRUE?" she asks. "Are Leah and Isabel AN ITEM?" (Tammy is literally shouting into the phone at me, hence the all-caps.)

"Well, if they were in fact 'canoodling' in a booth at Tony's, one might safely assume that," I say.

"Oh come on, Emilie. Stop it with the secret squirrel stuff. Just give me the lowdown."

"I suppose it's all over the base by now if Cpl. Roberts' wife is sharing it with random people in the toy aisle at the PX," I reply.

"I am not a random person Emilie. In fact I saw Cpl. Roberts' wife at the clinic a few weeks ago and I'm pretty sure she said hi to me."

"Tammy, you don't even know her first name. That's why you keep calling her 'Cpl. Roberts' wife.'"

"Well. Do *you* know her first name?" she asks.

"No. I don't. But I'm not the one who's claiming to be friends with her."

"Okay. Fine," she replies. "The point is, everybody except me seems to know what's going on. So it's not like you'd be telling me something people don't already know. Come on Emilie. I wanna be on the gouge train too."

I let out a long sigh. I love Tammy, but my loyalty lies with Wade. "In all fairness to Wade," I tell her, "I feel like I'm not at liberty to say."

"You know you sound like a fucking PAO right now — 'I'm not at liberty to say,'" she repeats, mocking me. "Also, you're being an extremely boring friend. Trustworthy, yes. Fun, no."

"I know," I admit. "I will say this much. This is not something Wade would find terribly surprising. Okay? Now. Having said that, I hope this doesn't get back to him. He's got enough on his mind right now."

Tammy sounds deflated. "You're right. But can I just say one thing? I always knew those two had a thing for each other."

"What made you think that?"

"Well, they did spend an excessive amount of time together after Wade moved to Wakeville. Whenever we saw Leah at book club she was always talking about Isabel. Isabel and I did this and Isabel and I went here. And did you see them at the Ball? They were joined at the hip. Oh, and how about when we walked in on them in the bathroom? I'm pretty sure we interrupted a make-out session."

"I thought they were just having an intense conversation," I reply.

Tammy bursts out laughing. "Oh Emilie. You are such a goob sometimes."

"Whatever. Look, I don't want to reveal any confidential conversations I may or may not have had with the parties involved."

"Whatever you say Agent 99," she says.

"Can we just move on to the next topic please?"

"All right," she replies. "But before we do that, can you answer just one last question?"

"Ask me the question and I'll tell you if I can answer it or not."

"Remember how when we first met Leah at the FSG meeting back in the spring, and she told everybody she only shaves one leg when Jacob is away, so that when she goes to bed at night and rubs her legs together it feels like she's sleeping with him?"

I can't help but smile at the memory. "Yes, I do remember. And I also remember you saying in the car on the way home that you always shave both legs when Ken is deployed so you can pretend you're sleeping with two dolphins."

Tammy laughs. "Right. So my question for you is, do you think that Leah and Isabel go a couple days without shaving before they see each other, so that when they go to bed at night they can rub their legs together and pretend they're grasshoppers?"

"You are such a jerk, Tammy."

"I know. But I'm a funny jerk, aren't I?"

Saturday, December 13, 2008 11:19 p.m.

We received the box you sent today. I set it aside so the boys and I can open your gifts on Christmas morning. We sent you a package too — have you received it yet? Your emails have been awfully short lately (well, even shorter than usual). You must be busy over there in the sandbox. I wonder what's going on. I hope you don't have to be outside the wire over the holidays.

Fakhir and I went Christmas shopping today. I'm really glad he invited me — I was able to help him choose a number of gifts for his mom, his sister, and Lucia. And he helped me get into the Christmas spirit (finally). We went in every store downtown from gift shops to clothing, jewelry, stationery, gourmet food, housewares, toys, music, and book-stores. I bought presents for everybody, including Finn, Rory, Lucia, Fakhir (when he wasn't paying attention), Arifah, Farah, Wade, Tammy and her boys — even Agnes, Eugene, and Ethan. It was fun. And I didn't even cry when we were in the gift shop looking at ornaments and Elvis' "I'll Be Home for Christmas" came over the speakers. Okay well I did cry a little. But not a lot. And then Fakhir grabbed my hands and started waltzing with me in the middle of the store, and that made me laugh in spite of my tears.

We stopped at Woolley's Tavern for a cheddar burger on our way home since we had shopped until the stores closed and hadn't eaten all day (except for two peppermint mochas from Fidelia's). Sitting in the back of the tavern with Christmas lights twinkling and two ice cold beers before us, it felt good to get off our feet. After we ordered our burgers, we talked excitedly about the various gifts we had found.

Fakhir's main purchase was a beautiful gold bracelet for Lucia, which I helped him pick out. He confided in me that he originally wanted to buy Lucia an engagement ring, hoping to propose to her on Christmas Eve. Luckily he "casually" (or so he says) brought up the topic of mar-riage one night when they were out to dinner recently. Lucia responded by telling Fakhir he is the man she wants to marry. So that was good. But then she added that she can see them getting engaged "possibly" in a year or so. (There went Fakhir's Christmas plans out the window.) Her priority right now is getting her cosmetology career on track, while also taking the first steps toward starting her own company. She'd like to try living on her own too, once she saves up enough money. When

Fakhir heard that, he decided to keep his original plans to himself. He intends to fully support Lucia's dreams, no matter how long it takes. And besides, he said, she's worth waiting for.

"Lucia is unlike any woman I've ever met," Fakhir explains, pausing to sip his beer. "I love how independent she is. It's really important to her to be her own person. And she's got so many talents. She can do anything she sets her mind to — style hair, make lip balm, start her own company. I love how passionate she is about things. And, well, what can I say? She's the most beautiful woman in the world."

Fakhir is smiling dreamily when the server arrives with our food. We set about arranging the pickles and onions just so on top of our burgers, spreading mustard all the way to the edges of each bun, and then, after making sure all the ingredients are in place, neatly cutting our burgers in half with our knives.

"You know," I say, picking up half my burger. "You're the one who got us started on cutting our burgers in half."

Fakhir's first half of his burger has already mostly disappeared, his mouth full. Instead of answering he offers an amiable shrug.

While he chews, I return to the topic of Lucia. "I wanted to say, I'm really glad you and Lucia found each other."

He dabs at the corners of his mouth with his napkin and, before taking another bite says, "Me too."

"Also," I continue, "I would like to point out that, if it weren't for me, you guys probably would've never crossed paths." I take a bite of my burger and wash it down with a sip of beer.

"I think about that a lot," Fakhir replies. "Fate is funny that way sometimes." He sets down the remainder of his burger and looks away, momentarily deep in thought.

"What are you thinking about?" I ask, taking another bite of my food.

Fakhir has already inhaled the last portion of his burger so I wait for him to finish chewing. When he's done, he says, "Why do you ask?"

"You just had kind of a funny expression on your face when you said the thing about fate," I say, starting in on the second half of my burger — not even close to keeping up with Fakhir.

He pops a fry into his mouth and considers me for a moment before answering. "Thinking about fate reminded me of someone I used to know. Someone I was in a serious relationship with before I met Lucia."

"Is that so?" I say, taking a sip of my beer. You could say my interest has been piqued — to put it mildly.

The server comes to our table, asking us if we want another round. Fakhir and I look at each other. We both want a second beer, but one of us has to drive home.

Fakhir says, "We could call Rory to come get us."

I quickly agree and we signal to the waiter that yes, we would like another round.

Fakhir empties his beer glass and continues. "She and I went to the same university in Baghdad. We were very much in love. Our plan was to get married after graduation. But ..." His voice trails off.

I sit quietly, a French fry in my hand, afraid to break the spell. I don't want to do anything that would cause Fakhir to stop talking.

The server returns with our beers, placing them in front of us and leaving with our two empty glasses.

"But then we broke up," he says simply, polishing off a few more fries.

I shake more salt over my fries (as if they weren't already salty enough). "I thought you said the plan was to get married."

"It was," he replies, starting on his second beer.

"So ... ?"

"You ask a lot of questions," he says.

"That was technically not a question," I reply.

He smiles but doesn't say anything, taking a long pull on his beer instead.

"Besides," I argue. "You can't just bring up the fact that you had a serious girlfriend in Iraq and then not tell me what happened."

"You're right. I was thinking about telling you the whole story and then I had second thoughts," he says.

I slowly twirl my beer glass in the ring of condensation on the table. "If you'd rather not talk about it that's totally fine. We can talk about something else."

"No, it's not that I don't want to tell you," he replies. "I just started thinking maybe you don't want to hear it."

"Why would I not want to hear it?" I ask.

The server comes to the table to remove our plates.

"You want another beer?" Fakhir asks.

I'm having a hard time keeping up with him but I say "sure" anyway.

The server nods in acknowledgment before turning away.

"It's … it's a tough story to hear," Fakhir says.

"I can handle it," I assure him, having no idea of the magnitude of what I've just committed myself to.

Fakhir takes a deep breath. "I had no choice but to break up with her," he begins. "It turns out she caught the eye of someone very important."

The server reappears and, sensing our conversation has turned serious, quietly slips our beers in front of us before disappearing again.

Fakhir continues, "This person saw her on campus and he was so enamored by her beauty he had his people find out who she was. And in the process of learning who she was, they found out that she and I were dating. So they sent me a message telling me to break up with her. I refused. That's when Uday had one of my schoolmates kidnapped— to teach me a lesson."

"Wait," I interject. "Did you just say Uday?"

"Hm-hmm."

"As in, Uday Hussein?"

"Right."

"As in, Saddam Hussein's son?"

"Correct."

"Fuuuck."

Fakhir and I stare at each other across the table.

"Wow," I say. "That is some heavy shit."

"And that's not the worst of it," Fakhir says, searching my face. "You sure you wanna hear this?"

"Of course," I say, without hesitation. Something in Fakhir's demeanor tells me we've reached an important juncture. He's here, I'm here, and he's ready to talk. "So what happened to your schoolmate?" I ask.

"Uday fed him to the lions at my father's zoo," Fakhir replies.

I was just about to take a sip of my beer but I promptly set it back down, afraid I might drop it. "You're joking, right?"

"No, I'm not. Actually it was Uday's chief executioner, Yasin. He made my father watch. And afterward Uday's people said to my dad, 'Tell your son to break up with his girlfriend or this will be his fate.'"

I reach across the table to grab Fakhir's hand. His face is calm, showing little emotion.

He resumes, "Yasin and two guards brought my schoolmate to my father's office at the zoo just after closing time. Yasin said, 'Uday has ordered you to feed this man to the lions.' My father refused, saying that boy is innocent, he didn't do anything, he has nothing to do with the situation. Meanwhile my friend frantically looked around the room for a way to escape, but there was nowhere to go. He looked pleadingly into my father's eyes. Yasin held a pistol to my dad's head and said 'If you don't do it I'll shoot you in the head and feed your body to the lions along with his.' My father thought of my mother and us kids. He told the zookeeper to get the keys to the lion cage. Yasin made them walk over to the cage together, the guards dragging my friend as he struggled to get away, shouting for help. But no one was there to hear him. Or if they did hear him, they knew better than to get involved. When they arrived in front of the cage, my friend collapsed, screaming in terror. The lions were waiting behind a gate. The guards pushed my friend into the cage and quickly stepped back out. Yasin ordered the zookeeper to release the lions, holding his pistol to my father's head to make sure he watched. The lions pounced. My father and the zookeeper were forced to witness the whole thing, until there was nothing left of my friend but bones and a few pieces of flesh."

I'd been holding onto Fakhir's hand the entire time, squeezing harder and harder as the story progressed. I realize I'd been digging my fingernails into his palm, but he seemed not to notice. I loosen my grip but don't let go.

Fakhir continues, "My father went home that night and told my mother what happened. My mom said she'll never forget the look in my dad's eyes. He died in his sleep that night. They said he had a stroke. We were devastated. But my mom said Allah had shown my father His mercy by taking him that night. Because now he wouldn't have to live another day with the memory of what he had seen. I don't argue with my mom when she says that. But I lost my faith the day my father died. A year later the Allies invaded Iraq. I knew before they even reached Baghdad I was going to help them."

I squeeze Fakhir's hand once more before letting go. We sit back in our chairs to sip our beers.

"I'm sorry your family had to go through that," I say.

He offers me a weak, but reassuring smile. "Thanks. I don't tell that story to very many people."

I raise my eyebrows in mock surprise. "I would certainly hope not. That's not the kind of story you wanna share on a first date."

The familiar twinkle in his eye returns. "No? You mean I shouldn't have put it on my Match.com profile?"

We sip our beers in silence. After a while I say to Fakhir, "I was just thinking how I wish this never happened to you. To any of you. How different your life would be if your dad were still alive. If your friend never got kidnapped. If Uday never laid eyes on your girlfriend. If you and she ended up getting married. But then the thought crosses my mind that if all that never happened, you would've never come into our lives. And I realize how incredibly selfish it is of me to even think that kind of thought. Is it wrong to wish things had turned out differently for you, while at the same time feeling thankful you ended up here, with us?

"That's what I mean about fate," Fakhir says. "I wish my dad was still alive. I think of him every day. I think of my friend. And my first love. All of that. I wish it never happened. But it did happen. And it's one of the reasons I became a combat interpreter. Which led me to Wade. And to Liam. And Maj. Salazar. And meeting them led me to you, and the boys, and Lucia."

The server appears at our table, asking if we want another round. Fakhir and I shake our heads, and I ask for the check. He and I argue over who's going to pay for the meal, and I win.

After I give the server my credit card, Fakhir says, "Thanks Emilie."

I wave him away. "Buying you dinner is the least I could do."

"I'm not talking about that," he says. "I'm thanking you for listening. For not turning away. You listened to my story about the attack on our vehicle in Ramadi. After that, I knew I would tell you this story too. It was just a matter of finding the right moment. I know I've put some terrible images in your head tonight. I'm sorry for that. But I also know how strong you are, and that you can handle it. Lucia too. She knows the story. And telling her helped me a lot. The last piece of the puzzle was for me to tell you. You understand it's a part of me. It's a part of you now too. Just like Joey's stories are a part of all of us. And Wade's stories too. And when Liam comes home, his stories will become our stories."

"You don't have to thank me Fakhir," I say. "We shouldn't have to carry our stories alone. I'm glad you trusted me enough to tell me about this. I wish Joey had someone to share his stories with when he came home from Vietnam all those years ago. They only get heavier the longer you carry them."

"I wish we could've helped Joey more," Fakhir says.

"I think we did help him," I reply. "The last time I saw Joey — the morning he and Dottie left — he looked like a huge burden had been lifted from his shoulders. I wish with all my heart we could have some-how changed the outcome of what happened. But, barring that, I think we gave him some measure of peace."

The server returns with my credit card, and I sign the receipt, mak-ing sure to give him a generous tip.

After he thanks me and leaves I make an attempt to lighten the mood. "You know," I say, "I was gonna thank you for helping me get into the Christmas spirit. But that was before dinner. Now I'm not so sure."

He laughs. "How about if we come over tomorrow and help you put up Christmas decorations? That should get all of us back in the spirit. Plus, this is my mom and sister's first Christmas in the States. They're totally excited. We'd love to help you decorate the tree."

Sunday, December 14, 2008   10:28 p.m.

It's been a good day. Fakhir and his mom and sister came over this after-noon to help Rory and Lucia and me put up the Christmas tree. After resisting buying a fake tree the first twenty years of our marriage, I have

217

to admit I'm glad you finally wore me down. I do love a real tree, but an artificial tree is so much easier. Fakhir put it together and it's up in its usual spot in the family room. I did the lights while Rory and Lucia wrapped the tree in beads. Farah and Arifah hung the ornaments, and I must say they did a beautiful job. Before they left, Fakhir put all the empty storage boxes back in the attic.

It's dark out now, and there's nothing like a twinkling Christmas tree when you're inside on a cold winter night. We got some snow today, and everything outside is fluffy and beautiful. I wish Finn could've been here to help us decorate, but he'll be home from school soon. You were on my mind today more than ever. With every ornament that went on the tree, I thought about where we were when we got it—especially the ones we bought on family vacations. My heart ached with missing you, but I put up a good front. I didn't want to be a downer when everyone else was feeling festive.

But between you and me, I can't deny how much I missed you today—how much I miss you this very moment. I miss you so much I even miss how cranky you get every year over the cats' inevitable attempts to decimate the Christmas tree—kicking off a war of wills between you and them that lasts until the tree comes down, one way or another. The cats' relentless campaign to exterminate every ornament, sabotage every string of beads, and snuff out every twinkling light won't be the same this year without you here to cuss them out.

Remember the year in Great Lakes when we bought that beautiful Balsam Fir? It was the first and only time we lived in base housing where the ceilings were high enough to get a decent-size tree. We had just spent the entire afternoon decorating it, and had retreated to the kitchen to enjoy some hot cocoa with mini-marshmallows on top. That's when we heard the thundering crash coming from the living room. We arrived at the scene of the crime just in time to see the three cats scatter, each in different directions. The tree, which had been vertical just moments before, was now horizontal, lying sadly on its side across the length of the hardwood floor. The angel we had placed so carefully at the top of the tree had been catapulted to the other side of the room, her halo nowhere to be seen. The beads we had painstakingly draped across the tree's branches in perfect symmetry were now piled beneath the tree in a glimmering, twisted heap. The precious ornaments, meticulously hung from thoughtfully chosen branches to create the most pleasing aesthetic, had been propelled from their places of honor — some of them shattered, some of them miraculously whole, and still others hanging precariously from their original spots. The effect was a shroud of shimmering fragments surrounding the fallen tree as if in tribute to its former greatness.

At the first crunch of broken glass beneath our feet, everybody froze. The room went silent. The boys and I stared at one another, our eyes wide. We knew exactly what was coming next. And sure enough, as if on cue, you turned into the dad from "A Christmas Story." Spinning into action as if possessed by an unseen force, you stomped around the living room, hurling nonsensical obscenities in the spirit of Ralphie's Old Man — the very same character who made us laugh with delight when he swore at the malfunctioning furnace, threw a hissy fit over the broken leg lamp, and had a monumental meltdown after the neighbor's dogs ate the turkey. Except in this case you stormed the perimeter of the plundered Christmas tree, condemning the cats to eternal damnation, pausing only to pick up pieces of broken ornaments and gesticulate wildly upon the discovery of each new casualty.

The boys fixed their gazes on me in an attempt to gauge the seriousness of the situation. If I reflected anything beyond mild displeasure, they knew we were on a trajectory toward DEFCON 1, nuclear war being imminent. While Finn and Rory attempted to ascertain our state of alert, you marched to the corner of the room to retrieve the fallen angel, still muttering mumbo jumbo that sounded eerily similar to Ralphie's Old Man ("*You blonker frattle feet sturckle frat! You wart mundane noodle! You shotten shifter paskabah!*") When you realized the angel's condition was inoperable — her halo never to be reattached — your tantrum came to an abrupt halt, as if you'd suddenly run out of epithets. A hush fell over the room as you slowly lowered yourself onto one knee to quietly mourn the recently departed angel.

Trying my best not to draw attention to myself, I discreetly raised my hand to my mouth, pinching my lips with my fingers in an attempt to squeeze away the grin that had suddenly made its appearance, as if of its own volition. When the boys saw that I was literally trying to wipe the smile off my face, they began smiling too. We quietly lowered ourselves onto the nearby loveseat, hoping to remain inconspicuous until the calamity had run its course. Unfortunately, one of us — I won't say who — allowed a tiny giggle to escape her lips. Upon hearing that, you swung your head around to identify the perpetrator, eyes bulging. Seeing that all three of us were not only smiling but trying not to laugh — having failed to grasp the gravity of the situation — you issued forth an exaggerated harrumph. Rising to your feet, head high, you strode past us in a huff. The boys and I remained on the couch, no longer bothering to conceal our amusement as we listened to you banging around in the kitchen, slamming drawers and cupboards. At one point we heard the liquor cabinet being opened and the sound of tinkling glass, a sure sign you were pouring at least two shots of Peppermint Schnapps — one for your hot chocolate and the other taken straight.

Monday, December 15, 2008   11:53 p.m.

I had a logjam of kids in ISS today. The students will be taking finals the rest of the week, so today was the last day they could serve before the holiday break. A couple of the kids had racked up a number of unserved detentions. Several others had excessive tardies, and a few more had multiple unexcused absences. Then there was the sophomore who told another girl in Algebra class that her yellow banana pencil case looked like a dildo. And the senior who nibbled his chocolate Santa into the shape of a penis during their Spanish class holiday party. And then there was the freshman who faked a note from his parents saying he had missed school the other day because he had a vasectomy. (Do you think he meant appendectomy? Or tonsillectomy? Nah. I'm guessing his dad had a vasectomy recently and, not having any idea what was involved, the student figured it would make a nifty excuse for cutting school.) Color me crazy, I'm gonna miss these kids.

After dinner I hid out in our bedroom wrapping gifts and watching "Remember the Night" on TCM. I love that movie so much. It's like slipping into an old pair of shoes every time I watch it. The plot is so weird—Barbara Stanwyck as the shoplifter who steals a bracelet just before Christmas and Fred MacMurray as the prosecuting attorney who ends up taking her home to spend Christmas with his family after the trial is postponed. The scene where they stop at Barbara Stanwyck's jackhole mother's house breaks my heart, but then they go on to Fred MacMurray's house where everyone is all warm and fuzzy. And you think everything is going to be hunky dory but then—bam!—all these complications arise. It's just so twisty and wonderful. What an underrated Christmas movie.

p.s. When I went to get the wrapping paper out of the basement storage room, guess what I found hidden behind a stack of empty moving boxes? Some of last year's Christmas gifts—you know, the ones I couldn't remember where I'd hidden them, because we were so distracted getting ready for you to leave on your deployment? So the boys will receive a few extra gifts this year. I also found a gift I'd hidden away for you. I'll give it to you when you come home, whenever that is.

Do they have a tree for the troops in Al Faw Palace? Or at least in the DFAC? In the box we sent you, there's a string of Christmas lights. The boys and I thought you could hang them in your CHU. We sure do miss you.

Tuesday, December 16, 2008   11:46 p.m.

I couldn't fall asleep earlier after I set my book on the nightstand and turned off the lamp. I could see the light from Rory's room shining in the hallway, so I got out of bed and padded down to his room in my robe and slippers to see if he wanted a back rub. He was in bed studying for his Chemistry final. When I asked him if he wanted me to rub his back, he looked at me as if I had snakes coming out of my head—just like old times. (As if the past two months of him asking me for a back rub almost every night never even happened.)

I knew this phase would end sooner or later—that Rory's renewed interest in back rubs would gradually fade away along with the mental images from the day Marcus showed up at the school with an AR-15. Not that we'll ever forget that. None of us will. But, at least for now, Rory has happier, more important things to think about. (That could change again once the trial starts in March. Nevertheless, we can burn that bridge when we come to it, as Fakhir would say.)

From a parent's perspective, this latest development is a good thing. After all, the whole idea behind raising children is to teach them not to need you anymore, right? And still, I can't help feeling wistful.

As I said goodnight to Rory and wished him luck on his finals tomorrow, Lucia called out from her room that I could give her a back rub if I wanted. So I went in and sat on the edge of her bed and rubbed her back while she lay on her stomach, head turned to the side. Before long she was snoring (loudly, of course). I pulled the comforter over her shoulders, tucked her in tight, kissed her on the forehead, and whispered goodnight.

Wednesday, December 17, 2008   11:59 p.m.

We had our book club Christmas party tonight. Genie hosted. Everybody brought an appetizer so she didn't have to do all the cooking. (I brought my trusty artichoke dip from Costco which I enhanced with green chiles, chopped jalapeño, extra artichoke hearts, and my secret ingredient, cumin.) We played a fun game involving a giant stack of paperbacks Genie had put out on her coffee table. Someone picks a book and reads aloud the blurb from the back cover. Then everybody writes down what they think the first line of the novel is. And the person who read the blurb writes down the actual first line. Then that person reads all the first lines aloud to the group, and we have to guess which one is the real first sentence. And guess who won? Yours Truly. Not only did I guess several of the correct first lines,

I got extra points for writing fake first lines that everybody thought were the real ones.

Wanda came in second place, which totally pissed her off. I'm not usually the competitive type but I couldn't helping gloating a little when Genie handed out the prizes and my 1st place bag of chocolates was noticeably larger than Wanda's 2nd place bag of chocolates. Even before we played the game, Wanda was acting like a jerk — repeating her childish behavior from last month, like turning her back to me and trying to cut me out of conversations. You'd think with Christmas right around the corner she could at least try to get into the holiday spirit. But she couldn't even bring herself to say Merry Christmas to me when I said it to her first. Maybe on Christmas Eve she'll be visited by the Ghost of Christmas Yet to Come, who shows Wanda that five years from now she's not gonna have any friends left if she doesn't stop being such an asshole.

Tammy was wearing her deployment uniform of jeans and a sweater, but she actually had make-up on and her hair was not in a ponytail — a major accomplishment on her part. I asked her if she and the boys would like to come to our house on Christmas Day for beef tenderloin and a charades tournament. She said she thought I was never going to ask.

Kim and Charlene had on matching sexy Mrs. Claus outfits and I have to admit they looked adorable. Everybody else had on either Ugly Christmas Sweaters or other types of holiday attire like Santa hats and necklaces made from mini-Christmas lights. As for myself the best I could manage was a red sweater which I had hastily thrown in the cart at Costco when I went to get the dip.

As I walked out to my car carrying my prize bag of chocolates and some leftovers, Leah called out to me, asking me to wait up. I put the food in the back seat and paused by the driver's side, wondering if she'd made a decision yet about going to Lejeune with Jacob or staying here with Isabel. If I were a betting woman I'd place my wager on the latter option, if only because of the recent sighting of her and Isabel having dinner at Tony's. Leah had been acting pretty cheerful during the party, and I sensed from her carefree mood that she had probably made a decision. If she were still grappling with the issue I don't think she would've been nearly as lighthearted. When she caught up to me at the car, she wasted no time getting to the point.

"I thought you'd want to know I've made a decision about what I'm going to do," she says.

We could see our breath in the cold night air. The stars twinkled overhead, the waning moon faintly illuminating our faces.

"Of course," I reply. "I've been thinking about you."

"Well. I've decided I'm going to Lejeune with Jacob," she announces.

I'm genuinely surprised but I try to act natural. "Good for you, Leah." I give her a hug, then take a step back, keeping my hands on her shoulders. "This is totally your decision, right? Not based on anything anybody else wants?"

"Absolutely," she says, nodding confidently. "Your advice was spot-on Emilie. I tuned out all the voices in my head and listened to my gut. And to my heart. I realized that I want to make my marriage to Jacob work. And he says he wants to make it work too. We talked a lot about what we need from each other. He understands I need him to be more considerate of me and my feelings — that's it's not always all about him just because he's the one in the military."

"I'm glad to hear that," I say. "It's way too easy for spouses to get brushed aside in the effort to 'stay focused on the mission.' I mean of course big things are gonna come up and we have no choice but to take a back seat. But at some point you have to draw a line between real emergencies and things that can be negotiated. We have to resist our natural tendency to assume that whatever the service member is working on at the moment is more important than what anybody else in the family needs."

"Yeah, that's exactly what Jacob and I talked about," Leah says.

A memory pops into my head that makes me smile.

"What are you smiling about?" Leah asks.

"Well, I was just thinking about this one night several years ago when Liam called to tell me he needed to work late. He had missed dinner several nights in a row that week. I was working up a head of steam about it. So when I gave him some pushback on missing dinner again, he responded with some claptrap about whatever the latest 'emergency' was. And I remember saying to him, 'You know what Liam? I don't give a rat's ass if this involves 'matters of national security.' And yes I know 'there's a war on.' But you don't get to play the 'national crisis' card with me for the fourth time in a week. Because if you don't get your ass home in time to have dinner with me and the boys tonight, there's gonna be a shitstorm so bad you'll wish you were married to Osama bin Laden instead of me.'"

"So did he come home in time for dinner?" she asks, smiling.

"Hell yeah."

Leah laughs. "I'm gonna have to remember that little speech. It might come in handy someday."

"Well anyway, I'm happy for you Leah. I know this was really weighing on you."

"I can't thank you enough Emilie," she replies. "You've helped me in more ways than you know. I'll never forget how you reached out to me after the FSG meeting last spring. I was really struggling when Jacob first went away to sniper school. I felt so alone. I was beginning to think he didn't need me anymore. You welcomed me into your home, and made me feel like part of your family."

"We were happy to have you," I reply. "Besides, you were always a big help — there were a few nights when I was watching Chloe I couldn't have survived without you."

"That's another thing," she says. "When I started helping Isabel take care of Chloe after Wade left, I felt like someone needed me again."

"I can understand that," I say.

Leah pauses to scan my face. I don't know for sure but it feels like she's weighing how much to tell me. Before I can say anything else, she presses ahead. "Isabel and I got to be really close. She came to depend on me to help her with Chloe. And I loved spending time with them. I didn't realize I was becoming attracted to Isabel until she made the first move. But from then on it was like we couldn't be without each other. By the end of the summer I was staying there almost every night during the week. Isabel liked having me there in the mornings to take care of Chloe while she got ready for work. And I didn't have to be at Alfalfa's until ten, so I didn't mind. It felt like we were a family."

Leah folds her arms across her chest as if to warm herself. She leans against the car, looking up at the sky. I wonder if I should invite her to sit in the car to warm up, but I'm unsure how much longer she wants to talk. It turns out she had quite a bit more she wanted to tell me.

She picks up where she left off. "But then every weekend when Wade came home, Isabel and I had to go back to pretending we were just friends. It became harder and harder to hide our feelings. Isabel was pretty sure Wade was beginning to suspect something. She told me she didn't care. She said Wade was the one who moved away and left her behind to take care of Chloe all by herself, so it served him right."

That's not exactly the way I remember it, I think to myself. Wade and Isabel were in dire financial straits. Wade really needed the job at Mondo. It was either that or move halfway around the world for the job in Qatar. Both Wade and Isabel agreed that the job in Wakeville was their best option. Isabel also led Wade to believe she'd be willing to move to Wakeville with Chloe as soon as it was financially feasible.

Nonetheless, I decide it wouldn't do anybody any good for me to argue with Leah how things went down between Wade and Isabel — even though I know better. I'm disappointed, but not surprised, Isabel misrepresented the situation to Leah. Besides, Isabel is the one who asked for the divorce. How does Leah square that with Isabel playing the victim? Maybe Isabel lied to her about that, too.

Sure enough, that's exactly what happened.

Leah continues, "One Sunday night after Wade had gone back to Wakeville, Isabel called to tell me he had asked her for a divorce. I figured it was because he found out about us, but —" At this point Leah pauses to look at me uncertainly before plunging ahead. "But Isabel said he wanted to leave her because he was having an affair. With you."

"Whoa. Stop right there," I say. "You know that's not true, right?"

Leah shrugs. "Why would Isabel say something like that if it wasn't true?"

I am pissed. Mostly at Isabel, but I'm also pissed at Leah for believing this shit. I lock my eyes onto hers. "There is absolutely no reason for Isabel — or anyone for that matter — to think Wade and I are romantically involved. He's been a friend of our family for like, twenty years."

Leah looks unsure of herself, like maybe she wants to believe me but is still unconvinced. "Well," she says, "there was this one night Isabel had been at my apartment—I remember it because it was the night before Jacob came home from California. It was a Saturday night, and Wade had come home from Wakeville for the weekend. But it was the last chance for me and Isabel to be together before Jacob came back. So Isabel told Wade she needed to come over to my place for something or other. And he said fine, go ahead. Like he wanted her out of the house for some reason. Anyway, Isabel ended up staying at my place pretty late, like three or four in the morning. She called Wade from the car to say she was on her way. He must not have known she was as close to home as she was. Because when Isabel pulled into the driveway, she saw you pulling away in your car. She said the only logical explanation was that you had spent the night there."

My jaw has dropped in disbelief. "Yeah. That's the night I drove to Wade's in the middle of the night because I thought he might *take his own life*. I spent several hours there that night listening to him talk. Because his own wife was too wrapped up in herself to even notice that her husband was struggling with suicidal thoughts. What the actual fuck Leah?"

Leah's lower lip is quivering and she looks like she might start to cry.

"I'm sorry," I say. I close my eyes and tilt my face to the night sky, trying to pull myself together. After a second or two I return my gaze to Leah, looking her directly in the eye. "I'm not mad at you. I'm just really mad at Isabel right now. What she said is total bullshit. And anyway, she could have just asked Wade about it and he would've told her the truth."

A thought occurs to me. Maybe Isabel didn't talk to Wade about it because she knows it's not true. Maybe Isabel knew all along there was nothing going on between Wade and me. Maybe she made up the whole thing to get Leah to feel sorry for her. And when she saw my car there that night, she couldn't resist twisting it around to fit the stupid scenario she'd concocted.

Leah's lip is still quivering and a tear rolls down her cheek. Maybe she's putting the pieces together too—that if Isabel wasn't honest with her about this, maybe she wasn't honest about other things too. "I'm sorry," Leah says. "I feel so dumb for believing that about you."

"It's okay. You had no way of knowing it was a lie. Except you could've asked me about it."

"I didn't think of that," she says. "I wish I did. My mind was more concerned with other things. Isabel said she wanted me to leave Jacob and move in with her. She said I could quit my job at Alfalfa's and take care of Chloe during the day while she went to work. That way we could be more like a real family. And also Isabel could stop bringing Chloe over to Mrs. Nardi's."

Hmm. Interesting. I can't help but think this arrangement sounds awfully convenient for Isabel — at the expense of Leah's career.

Leah lets out a long sigh. "At least ... that was the plan." She turns her head to the side, staring at some unknown point in the distance.

I'd been holding my car keys in my hand this whole time but I quietly drop them back into my coat pocket. Leah seems like she needs to talk and I don't want to give the impression I'm in a rush to get home. Once again I debate whether or not I should invite her to sit in the car to warm up, but now I'm afraid to interrupt the flow of conversation. I'll just stand out here freezing my ass off for as long as she needs me to listen.

"Then Jacob came back from sniper school," she continues. "I was so mixed up. Even though I was involved with Isabel, a part of me still envisioned this big romantic reunion between me and Jacob. I know — it makes no sense whatsoever. I guess I was secretly hoping things between me and him would go back to the way they were before he left. When that didn't happen it was such a letdown. I started thinking maybe I was meant to be with Isabel.

"And then Jacob and I went home for Thanksgiving. Being in the town where he and I met helped us remember why we fell in love in the first place. I started feeling hopeful about our marriage again. And then Jacob got orders. That threw a wrench into everything. Isabel told me flat-out she needed me to stay here, with her and Chloe. I was more confused than ever. That's when I talked to you, and you told me to listen to my gut."

My curiosity gets the best of me. "If you don't mind me asking ... Was there anything in particular your gut was telling you that helped you decide to stay with Jacob? Or was it just more of a general feeling?"

"It was mostly just a general feeling," she replies. "But ... now that you ask, I think there were a few things I couldn't stop thinking about. Like when Isabel said I should quit Alfalfa's. That kind of didn't make sense to me, because one of the things she said she was mad at Wade about was that he had asked her to quit school when he proposed to her."

Another thing that's not true, I think to myself.

Leah goes on. "And, because of that, she always said it was Wade's fault she's not a full paralegal at the law office yet. So then I had to ask myself, why would Isabel turn around and ask me to quit my job — a job that she knows I love?"

I'm just about to reply when Leah says, "And then another thing that kind of bothered me. When Jacob got the orders to Lejeune and I called Isabel to tell her about it, she kind of laid this big guilt trip on me about how much she and Chloe needed me to stay here to help out with things. She never said she wanted me to stay because she loves me and she can't live without me. It was more like, I need you to stay here and help me with Chloe. And then she really poured it on, and went into how much Chloe wants me to stay. Which, I mean, I love Chloe, and I know she likes me a lot too. But she's fourteen months old. A few weeks from now she's probably not even going to notice I'm not there anymore."

"I'm really sorry Leah," I say. "What a mess. But after listening to your story, it sounds like you made the right choice."

Leah offers a wry smile. "Honestly none of this was that clear to me until tonight. My gut told me to stay with Jacob, and I'm glad I trusted my gut like you said I should. But my thoughts hadn't really clarified until just now, when I'm standing here talking to you."

"So I take it you've told Isabel about your decision?" I ask.

"Yeah." Leah grimaces, as if in pain. "That didn't go the way I planned. I had invited her out for a special dinner at Tony's. I was going to tell her in the restaurant that I'd decided to stay with Jacob. I thought it would be best that way. But ... I lost my nerve. We were having such a nice time. I didn't to want to ruin it. Isabel can be hard to resist some-times. We finished off a bottle of red wine with our dinner and ended up back at her place like we always do. Later that night I finally worked up the courage to tell her I was going to Lejeune with Jacob. She didn't take it well. She threw me out of the house. Chased me down the driveway, throwing my shoes at me and shouting some not very nice things. Even Mrs. Nardi came out of her house to see what was going on. That's when I got in my car and drove away."

That explains the sighting of Leah and Isabel "canoodling" at Tony's. I'd been wondering about that after she told me she'd chosen to stay with Jacob. Now it all makes sense.

"I called Isabel the next day," she says. "To apologize for leading her on at dinner when I had already made up my mind to stay in my marriage. I told her I messed up and I wish I'd handled it better than I did. I thought she might use the opportunity to apologize to me for the mean things she shouted at me. But she didn't. I told her it would be best if we didn't talk for a while. That I needed to focus on my marriage to Jacob. She said fine, she needed to focus on school and her career anyway and it would be easier for her to do that without me hanging around distracting her."

Assuming Leah hasn't left anything out, I notice Isabel hadn't said something here about working on her marriage to Wade. Again, I keep that thought to myself.

Leah straightens her shoulders, as if shaking off the memory of her final conversation with Isabel. "I know I made the right decision," she says. "But I also lost a best friend. Isabel and I could tell each other anything. We had fun together. I'm gonna miss her."

I kinda wanna take Leah by the shoulders here and tell her that no, in fact Isabel was not a good friend. Instead, I put my hand on her arm. "I'm always a phone call away if you need someone to talk to. Even after you move to North Carolina. Don't lose my number, okay?" I have a feeling this might be the last time I see Leah. And, having said enough goodbyes to last a lifetime, I dread the thought of yet another emotional farewell.

Leah's expression suddenly lights up. "Oh! I meant to tell you— I already have a job lined up at the Alfalfa's in Jacksonville. My manager gave them a call when she found out we were moving. And they said they have an opening. It might even lead to an assistant manager position in a few months."

"That is great news. I'm really happy to hear that." I give her a quick hug.

"Well, goodnight Emilie. See ya soon," she says.

"See ya soon," I reply.

Leah walks away into the darkness. I get into my car and let the engine warm up while I sit and think a minute. I'm still angry about Isabel accusing me and Wade of having an affair. How low can a person go? Apparently Isabel can go lower than low. By my count, she has tried to mess with five people's lives — Wade's, Leah's, Jacob's, mine, and yours. We're all better off without her. Who knows what other kind of fuckery she's tried to stir up around here? I make a decision on the spot that I am never going to tell Wade about what Isabel said. As far as I'm concerned that shit is dead on arrival.

I put the car in drive and carefully turn around in Genie's cul-de-sac. As I pull out onto the deserted street, a happier thought occurs to me. Leah might be new at being a military spouse, but she already knows how to say goodbye, military-style. It's true we may never see each other again. And no amount of tears is going to change that. Might as well keep it light. Even better if you can say it with a smile. "See ya soon," seems simple enough. But it means so much more.

Liam, I know this is a bigger clusterfuck than you and I could've imagined, but now that Leah and Isabel have broken up, do you think Isabel might call off the divorce, and try to get back together with Wade?

Thursday, December 18, 2008   9:08 p.m.

Speaking of people getting shoes thrown at them, I saw on the news the other night that President Bush and Prime Minister al-Maliki signed the security pact at the presidential palace in the Green Zone. The news report said the president's trip to Iraq was kept secret until the last minute. Bush also made a surprise visit to the troops. Were you there at either of those events? You've mentioned stuff before about escorting VIPs around Baghdad. Did you get to see the president at some point? I wonder if that's why you haven't emailed or called lately. Maybe there was a communications blackout.

Either you've been too busy to write because of dealing with the logistics of the president's visit, or something else is going on. Maybe you're on a mission outside the wire, and you weren't anywhere near Baghdad during the president's stopover. So many questions. I just wonder why you haven't been able to call. It seems like it's been a long time since we last spoke. I miss your voice. I hope we get a chance to talk before Christmas. I imagine the phone lines at the USO will be jammed on Christmas Eve and Christmas Day with all the Marines calling home.

On a brighter note, we have lots of exciting news to share. First and foremost, Lucia passed her cosmetology exam!!! The letter came in the mail today. It said her test score has already been sent to the state and that she should receive her license in the mail in two weeks. Maybe she'll even get it before the end of the year. Wouldn't that be a great way for her to kick off 2009? She called her mom and dad with the news while she and I were standing in the kitchen. They were so happy I could hear them screaming and crying through Lucia's phone.

And speaking of Lucia's family, Raquel and the kids are moving to Wakeville at the end of the month. Guess where Carmen found an apartment? In Wade's building! So Wade and the Caputos are going to be neighbors. I love this so much. I love the idea of Carmen and Raquel and the three boys living so close to Wade. He needs to be wrapped in as many loving arms as possible right now.

In other exciting news, Farah got the job to replace Lucia at the shampoo station. She starts right after Christmas. Lucia will train her, and Farah will be up and running in the position by the time Lucia's license arrives in the mail. The manager at the salon already told Lucia which chair they plan to give her. Lucia says it's a good one, not too close to the reception area. And Farah is beside herself with excitement about working at the salon.

As I write this, Lucia, Farah, Riikka, and Rory are downstairs in the kitchen making more lip balm. I can hear them laughing and talking and banging pots and pans on the stove. In other words, they're making a racket. But it's a happy kind of noise, and it makes me happy listening to it. They're experimenting with two new concoctions: a peppermint oil lip balm for the holidays (which they plan to set aside as Christmas gifts, to be given out locally); and another batch, which is for the troops and smells like sandalwood. (Lucia calls it a "woodsy" scent.) I told her sandalwood is one of your favorite scents, and she said to let you know she'll make an extra special batch just for you.

Finn has one more final tomorrow, his studio performance review. He's pretty nervous about it. He and Mel are going to perform together. They've composed their own piece, a duet for piano and cello. Finn says they'll record it and send you a copy on CD.

Rory has only one final left also, a vocabulary test for P.E., which he says he already studied for. And Farah was exempted from her Calculus exam tomorrow, having made straight "A"s in all her classes — despite the fact that she arrived here, at a new school, in a new country, in the middle of the semester.

I guess you're well into the rainy / muddy season in Baghdad by now. Probably similar weather conditions to when you first arrived almost a year ago now. Dealing with all the mud must have its own set of problems, but at least there's not as much sand in the air with all the rain you're getting. I still worry about you inhaling dust and other particles. Are you running much? Have you noticed any changes in your breathing from when you first got there?

They're saying we might get a big snowstorm next week. I hope it doesn't interfere with our Christmas plans. It would be more than depressing if we go through all the prep for a party on Christmas Day and no one shows up.

Friday, December 19, 2008   4:53 p.m.

Today was my last day of work. I thought I might be sad but I'm not. I feel excited about the future, whatever it may hold. Whether I end up starting the film blog or doing something else, it was time for me to move on to something new. (And now Rory can enjoy the rest of his high school years without the embarrassment of his own mother being "the ISS lady.")

Dr. Gouwens and Mrs. Nelson gave me a poinsettia and a plaque with the BCHS mascot to commemorate my years at the school. I've only worked there a few years but Dr. Gouwens said it feels like we've known each other longer than that. Probably because of all we've been through together — especially this semester. Officer Dempsey stopped in to say goodbye, and he told me he plans to retire at the end of the year. We exchanged contact info and promised to keep in touch. A lot of the kids I've had in ISS over the years came by to give me cards and notes, thanking me for helping them through some rough times. The best visit was from Derek, Sabrina, and Jerry — the ones who were hiding in the closet with me during the Marcus ordeal. I don't normally give out my personal phone number to students (except that one time I gave my number to Lucia back when she was a senior and thinking about quitting school — gosh that seems like a lifetime ago), but I made another exception for these three. I had them enter my number in their phones and made them promise to pick up the phone and call me anytime they felt like chatting. They had also each written me a letter, which I've stowed away along with the other notes in a special box in our closet. I can't wait to show them to you when you come home.

Agnes stopped by my room after the final bell, when I was loading my personal belongings in a box. She'd been called in for an interview this afternoon, and then came looking for me as soon as it was over. She said she thought the interview went well. Dr. Gouwens told her they'll let her know before Christmas if she got the job. As far as I know, they haven't interviewed anyone else. Wouldn't it be great if Agnes gets the job? It's not like she'll make a ton of money working there (I can vouch for that), but it's a decent job with good benefits. And combined with Eugene's salary from Fidelia's and Ethan's job at Smollett's, they should be able to get by without having to foreclose on their house. (Agnes had mentioned that possibility last time I saw her.)

As Agnes helped me carry my stuff out to the parking lot, I invited her, Eugene, and Ethan to join us on Christmas Day. She said they would love to come, and offered to cook something to go with the main course. If I don't stop inviting people, we may end up with half the town at our house.

Finn is due at the train station tomorrow afternoon. When Rory came home from school today he was giddy with excitement—no school for two and a half weeks! He and Riikka are planning to go to open skate at the ice rink tonight. When he mentioned it, I assumed he meant stick and puck. He said no, tonight's open skate is for figure skating. He then informed me that the last few times the two of them went to open skate, it was for figure skating, not stick and puck. According to Rory, he and Riikka are the two best skaters on the ice. And they've been talking about coming up with their own pairs routine over winter break. Do you think we may have the next Tai Babilonia and Randy Gardner on our hands?

11:27 p.m.

Guess who showed up on our doorstep tonight? Dottie! (With Jacques in her arms, of course.) I thought she was coming tomorrow but either I got my days mixed up or she decided to come a day early. Who cares! I was so happy to see her. I was even happier to see the small U-Haul hitched to the back of her Subaru. She's moving in with us!

The sight of Dottie standing on our porch tonight was exactly the thing I didn't know I needed. I ushered her inside, helping her off with her parka as Jacques ran off to sniff at the Christmas tree (which is still standing in spite of Smedley and Daly's best efforts). Not surprisingly, Dottie was totally decked out for the holidays. She wore a green velour track suit with bright green Vans, a jingle bell necklace, large jingle bell earrings—and a headband with reindeer antlers. She slung her humongous metallic gold leather purse over her shoulder and proceeded to the kitchen, hoping I had some Nutcracker Ale in the fridge. (I did.)

As we sat at the kitchen table drinking our beers, Dottie told me that when she heard I was quitting my job at the school, she knew I would need her to move in so she could give me a "good kick in the ass" every morning to putt my butt to chair and get to work on the "dagnabbit

," I don't recall telling Dottie I had made a final decision about the ↄg, but according to her, it's a done deal. She pulled a stack of magazines out of her bag and handed them to me: a number of technology journals she wants me to read, including a recent issue of *Wired* with a feature article on bloggers — which is where Dottie got the idea for me to start a movie review site in the first place. (The irony has not escaped me that Dottie reads technology journals and yet she doesn't even own a computer. She doesn't own a rocket either, yet she also reads *Air & Space* magazine.) She furthermore announced that she has decided to accept my offer to be my Chief of Staff — another thing I don't recall discussing with Dottie. But, far be it from me to argue with her. As far as I'm concerned, what Dottie wants, Dottie gets.

When I brought her down to Fakhir's old room to show her where she'll be staying from now on, she appeared pleased with her new living quarters, especially the discovery of her very own full bathroom. Dottie then sat me down on the bed to lay out her expectations for the holidays, which she instructed me to pass along to the rest of the family, friends, and neighbors who'll be coming in contact with her.

Her expectations are as follows: 1.) Yes she is aware that she is a widow whose husband recently died. However, that does *not* mean she's going to be a party pooper. Do not expect her to wear black and do not expect her to cry when Joey's name comes up in conversation — in fact she would very much like people to mention his name as frequently as possible. 2.) Do not give her unsolicited advice. Do not ask her if she needs help figuring out any of that "complicated" paperwork (she's got it under control, thank you very much). And definitely do not ask her when she's going to start dating again. And finally, 3.) Do not feel sorry for her. This is her second time being widowed and she knows the drill. Under no circumstances is anyone to look at her with those "clodhopping puppy-dog eyes." Because if anybody so much as even thinks about gazing at her with an expression that remotely resembles pity, she'll have no choice but to give those ninnyhammers "what Paddy gave the drum." (I assume here she means she'll give them a beating — in other words, they'll find themselves in a hurt locker.) Dottie concluded her presentation by telling me she intends to have a Merry Christmas. Because that's the way Joey would have wanted it.

Saturday, December 20, 2008   10:33 p.m.

Finn is home. After we picked him up from the train station this afternoon, he made a beeline for his bed. He's been sleeping ever since. I imagine he'll wake up in an hour or two to root around in the fridge for something to eat. He survived his first semester of music school. And he's got almost an entire month off until he goes back. He said the studio final with Mel went well, but his other finals were killer—hinting that he hopes we're not upset if he gets a couple of "C"s. I told him not to worry. As long as he passes, we're not gonna sweat the small stuff.

Wade called tonight to let me know he's planning to come in tomorrow for Fakhir's citizenship ceremony on Monday. He asked if the offer still stood for him to stay here over Christmas. I said of course. (Isabel's fuckery be damned.) He then asked if it would be okay for Chloe (and Chesty) to stay with us Tuesday through Friday. Apparently Isabel had informed Wade she's going to spend Christmas in New Orleans with her parents, and that she's willing to leave Chloe here with him. She explained that since she had Chloe for Thanksgiving, Wade can have her for Christmas. I'm surprised Isabel is being so high-minded about sharing Chloe, especially after the things Leah told me. But if Isabel does one thing right in this soup sandwich of a situation, I hope it involves being a good parent to Chloe. And sharing co-parenting responsibilities with Wade as equitably as possible.

The plan is for Isabel to drop off Chloe and Chesty on Tuesday on her way to the airport. And then Wade will bring them back to Isabel's after she returns on Friday. He'll then continue on his way to Wakeville that afternoon. He's been working seven days a week since Thanksgiving (except for the days he took off for Joey's funeral). His boss gave him a nice end-of-year bonus, and told Wade to take some time off for Christmas. She said he can make up the time by working on New Year's

Eve and New Year's Day, when several of the other managers will be out. Wade told me he doesn't care about working on New Year's Eve since he doesn't have anyone to kiss at midnight anyway.

"Well," I say, "I heard Carmen and Raquel and the boys are going to be your nextdoor neighbors soon. Maybe you can kiss all of them at midnight."

"I'll be working at midnight," he replies. "But they did invite me to come over for dinner that night since I don't have to be at work until nine. Carmen said they're moving into the new place earlier that day. Raquel already made a ton of homemade tamales—they're in the freezer, waiting to be thawed and eaten on New Year's Eve."

"Yum. I've had Raquel's tamales. They're out of this world. Any chance she made extra for when they come over on Christmas Day?"

"I thought you said we're having beef tenderloin."

"I did. Is there a law against having tamales too?"

"I'll ask Carmen about it next time we talk," he replies.

"Anyway, I'm excited about having Chloe here for Christmas. Do you mind if I run out and get her a few gifts?" I ask.

"Of course not," he says. "Just don't go overboard. We don't want to spoil her."

"So did Isabel have anything else to say when she called you about Chloe?"

"Not really," he replies. "If I try making conversation about anything other than Chloe she shuts me down—changes the subject or says she has to go. Why do you ask?"

"I was just wondering if the divorce is still on track."

"As far as I know, yeah. Why wouldn't it be?" he asks.

"No reason," I reply.

"Right. Come on Emilie. I can see right through your little schtick. What's on your mind?"

"Okay fine. I saw Leah at book club the other night. Did you hear Jacob got orders to Lejeune?"

"Yeah, I heard about that through the LCU," he says. "Lejeune will be a good duty station for him, especially since he has family there. So what does that have to do with me and Isabel getting a divorce?"

"Well, Leah told me she's moving to North Carolina with Jacob."

Silence. Then Wade says, "So what you're saying is Leah and Isabel are no longer a thing."

"Correct."

More silence on Wade's end of the line.

When he doesn't reply, I plunge ahead. "So I was just wondering if you think Isabel might change her mind about the divorce, now that she and Leah are no longer involved."

"Even if she did change her mind, you're assuming I'd wanna get back with her," he says.

"No I'm not. I didn't say anything about that," I reply. "I was just curious if you think she's going to try to back out of the divorce now."

"I seriously doubt it. Even if she did want to get back together, I am not interested. It's over, Emilie."

"I get it. I just remember at one point you thought maybe you and Isabel could work things out."

"Too much has happened since then," he says. "And I'm not just talking about Leah. Or Portia. It was never about that, really. Things between me and Isabel were wrong from the beginning. In one of the last fights we had, Isabel was crying about how hard it was being married to me. And I'm not gonna argue with that. I know I'm a hard person to live with. I've got more baggage than the cargo hold of a C-5 for Chrissakes. But, getting back to my point that she and I were doomed from the start. During this fight we were having, she was giving me this laundry list of all the reasons she hated being married to me. And at one point I shouted at her, 'Then why the fuck did you even marry me in the first place?' And you know what she said? She said she married me because she thought being married to a Marine would be glamorous and fun."

A small choking sound escapes my throat.

"I know, right?" Wade says. "What she got instead was a fucking shitshow."

"Wade, stop it. You're putting all the blame on yourself again. I would say her expectations were … not in line with reality."

"That's putting it mildly," he replies.

ou're right. Her expectations were full-blown ripshit bonkers.
not your fault if she fancied herself as Debra Winger and you as
chard Gere."

Wade laughs. "Exactly. She was totally wrong about that. I am way
more handsome than Richard Gere."

Sunday, December 21, 2008 4:30 p.m.

Dottie and I were both up early this morning. She's settling in just fine.
And despite all her bravado, I can see she really misses Joey. We talk
about him a lot, usually by way of a funny story. And Dottie appreciates
that. I'm glad she's letting us help her get through this.

Jacques has not only staked his claim to Dottie's bedroom downstairs,
he's basically set up a perimeter around the entire basement — including
the TV room — which he now believes to be his domain. Luckily our animals never cared much about being in the basement, so they have no
problem letting Pol Pot think he's won over a big chunk of their territory. Dottie has beds for Jacques everywhere — one in her bedroom (even
though he sleeps in her bed), one in her bathroom (he likes to nap in
there while she's taking a shower), one in the family room (next to Brig
and Soda's beds), and another one in the kitchen (so he can watch Dottie
make sandwiches — one for her and one for him).

Jacques ignored all his beds this morning however while Dottie and
I cozied up on the couch together to drink our coffee and chat. The
cats had already claimed your chair so Jacques snuggled on Dottie's lap
while Brig and Soda dozed on the floor by our feet. Dottie was wearing
a ruby red plush robe with white fleece lapels and cuffs, a robe I've seen
her wear every Christmas as far back as I can remember. Her slippers
were new though — fluffy white polar bear paws with black claws coming out of the toe area.

While we sipped our steaming mugs of coffee, I filled Dottie in on
the latest with Wade and Isabel and Leah. Dottie has been pretty much
aware of the entire situation from the start — even if I tried to keep mum
about what I knew, nothing gets past Dottie's eagle eyes. She notices

everything. And—along the lines of what Tammy told me—Dottie said she always suspected there was something going on between Leah and Isabel. She also made it abundantly clear, once again, that she believes Wade is better off without Isabel.

"You know he's always been in love with you anyway," she says, watching me over the edge of her coffee cup.

I roll my eyes at her and laugh. "Don't be silly Dottie. That's ridiculous. Wade genuinely loved Isabel. It broke his heart when the marriage didn't work out."

"That may be true," she says. "I'm sure he did love Isabel. But what I'm saying is, he's *in love* with you."

I shake my head. "I disagree. You're very perceptive about a lot of things Dottie, but this is one area where I think you've misinterpreted the situation. Yes, Wade and I are very close. We've supported each other through some tough times this year. But I think your imagination has gotten the best of you on this one."

She lowers her cup and offers me an irritatingly smug smile. "Oh Emilie. You are such a ... what is it your friend Tammy calls you? A goob? You are such a goob."

I raise my eyes to the ceiling before looking at her again. "Honestly Dottie. We all love Wade. And he loves all of us—including Liam. Wade would never do anything to jeopardize that."

"So you're basically admitting he's in love with you," she says. "Because what you just said is that he would never *act* on his feelings."

"That's not what I said," I reply.

"But it's what you meant." She still has that smug smile plastered on her face.

I set my cup on the table and turn to face Dottie. "As long as I've known Wade, he has never done one thing that would make me think what you're saying could possibly be true. I'm not denying he's a player when it comes to other women. And he and I do joke around sometimes. But if you're talking about how he behaves toward me, he has always been nothing but a complete gentleman."

"And you've just proven my point," Dottie raises her coffee cup, as if to offer a toast. "He hasn't made a play for you Emilie, because that's much he loves you. He knows you and Liam are totally devoted one another, and he would never do anything to come between the two of you."

I close my eyes and quickly count to ten, like I used to do when the boys were little. When I'm done counting I open my eyes and look at Dottie as sternly as possible. "I don't know where you're coming up with this stuff, but can we just pretend this conversation never happened?"

She raises her eyebrows, eyes wide. "What conversation?"

Monday, December 22, 2008   7:57 p.m.

Fakhir's oath ceremony today was one of the most beautiful things I've ever witnessed. I expected it to be moving, but we were all crying our eyes out — Lucia and her family, the boys and me, Dottie, Wade, Arifa, and Farah. Several of Fakhir's coworkers showed up, and even they were crying.

Our group arrived at the courthouse downtown about 30 minutes before the ceremony was to begin. It was a good thing we allowed extra time because several of us had to run back to our cars and leave our cell phones, since they weren't allowed in the building. Fakhir was a nervous wreck. He kept checking and re-checking his folder containing all his documents. (It reminded me of you before you left on your deployment, checking and re-checking your seabag.)

Fakhir looked so spiffy in his suit and tie. Once they checked all his documents and he was seated with the other applicants, he began to relax, looking around the courtroom, soaking up every detail. The place was packed. The thirty or so people waiting to take their oath sat facing the judge in the front of the courtroom, while the rest of us — families, friends, and coworkers — were seated behind the soon-to-be-citizens.

The ceremony itself was straightforward and fairly brief. The judge said a few words about what it means to be a U.S. citizen, and then she went down the list, naming the twenty different countries each of the immigrants had come from. There was a short video with patriotic music, and then the judge told the applicants to stand and raise

their right hands while she led them through the Oath Of Allegianc
Although Fakhir had his back to us, we had no doubt he was smilin
from ear to ear—even if his hand shook a little as he said the oath.
And then it ended as quickly as it had begun. The judge congratulated
everyone. They passed out the Certificates of Naturalization, and it was
basically a roomful of people hugging and crying—the newly sworn-in
U.S. citizens pausing to stare at their certificates, as if to make sure
what they held in their hands was no longer just a dream.

I invited everybody back to our house for cake and coffee. We had
ordered a sheet cake for Fakhir with the American flag on it. I also had
a small gift for him—a pocket version of the U.S. Constitution, like the
one I gave you before you left for Iraq. After a while people started adding whiskey to their coffee, which prompted me to put out the whipped
cream, sugar, and Créme de Menthe, so people could make themselves
a proper Irish coffee. I finally came upstairs to change clothes and put
my feet up. The celebration downstairs is still going strong.

Such a happy day. We missed you, Liam.

Tuesday, December 23, 2008   4:42 p.m.

I called Agnes this morning to ask if she would mind if I passed along the
Christmas basket she gave me to someone else. I told her we'd eaten all
of her homemade cookies (which were delicious), and that we had hung
the Marine ornament she gave us in a place of honor on the Christmas
tree. But we hadn't opened any of the other items in the basket yet. I
explained that I had woken up feeling like I wanted to recognize her
kindness to me by paying it forward to another person—someone who
needed it a lot more than I did. Agnes said of course, she thought that
was a lovely idea.

I added a few extra things to the basket like a fresh batch of homemade Christmas cookies that Finn and Rory had made, along with
some Target gift cards and a sampling of the various lip balms from
Lucia. I added a Christmas card (unsigned of course), with a handwritten note that said, "I know this is a difficult Christmas for you. You are

er than you think." Then I put the basket in the car and drove to
apartment where Marcus' mother lives. I quietly set the basket on
doorstep, knocked softly on the door, and darted back to my car
before she could answer.

Wednesday, December 24, 2008 8:32 p.m.

Everybody is in the kitchen making more Christmas cookies — Finn,
Rory, Lucia, Dottie, Wade, and Chloe. They gave Chloe her own
small bowl of cookie dough to play with and she's having a blast. I'm
upstairs in our room, listening to the laughter and merriment as it
wafts throughout the house. Mitch Miller's "Sing Along With Mitch"
is playing on the stereo in the family room. The grocery shopping is
done and I've completed most of the meal prep for tomorrow. All the
gifts are under the tree. Outside the night is black — the moon hardly
visible, the air pregnant with precipitation. They're still predicting a
huge snowstorm for tomorrow. I'm praying the snow doesn't hit hard
until after our party is over and everyone has safely come and gone.

We still haven't heard anything from you. I'm not worried. I know
you're okay. I just wish we could talk to you.

I'm wearing your bathrobe and sitting in your rocking chair, looking
at the photo album from our honeymoon. There's the photo of you on
one of the bikes we rented, and the one you took of me after I beat
you at mini-golf. Several of the photos we took of each other at the
beach — you in your green silkies (did you not have a bathing suit back
then?) and me in my crocheted bikini (how I'd love to be able to fit
into that again). There's only one picture with both of us in it, when we
asked a stranger to snap a photo of us having breakfast at the outdoor
restaurant on our last day there. We thought we were so grown-up
back then, having been married all of six days. Of course we knew we
had the rest of our lives ahead of us. But I don't think we could even
begin to fathom the adventure we were about to embark on.

I had to get up to close the bedroom door just now. I didn't want the
others to see me crying. I put a CD in the little player you keep on your

dresser, The Blind Boys of Alabama's "Go Tell It On The Mountain." It fits my mood better than what they're playing downstairs.

I page through each of the books you've left in a stack on your nightstand, some of which you stopped reading halfway through, others you haven't started yet. I wonder which one you'll pick up first when you come home. My favorite track comes on, "In the Bleak Midwinter" featuring Chrissie Hynde. It's such a melancholy song and tonight it makes me cry even harder. I pick up the coaster you like to set your water glass on every night and turn it over in my hand — a ceramic tile with a painting of Old Faithful on it you bought when we went to Yellowstone. You got a coaster for me too on that same trip — mine has a painting of Grand Prismatic Spring. But instead of placing it on my nightstand like you did yours, I stashed mine away in the drawer. I thought the picture on it was too pretty to mess up by getting it wet. Instead I ruined the top of my nightstand, setting my water glass down on the bare wood every night and causing it to warp. You always loved giving me grief about that.

I get up out of your chair and walk into our bathroom to check your side of the vanity — still barren with all your toiletries cleared away. Do you remember the morning you left, you draped your wet bath towel across the back of my vanity chair like you always do (a habit you know drives me crazy). In all the months you've been gone, I still haven't moved your towel from the back of my chair. I've left it there, hanging, where I can see it every morning when I wake up and every night when I brush my teeth before bed. I've begun to see it as a promise. A promise you didn't actually make — but one I know you'll keep — that you'll pick it up and put it in the hamper when you come home. For tonight though, I sit on my vanity chair, gathering up your towel in my hands and burying my face in it so I can pretend it's your shoulder I'm crying on. I'll be happier tomorrow, I promise.

Thursday, December 25, 2008   9:23 p.m.

What a fun Christmas morning it was having Chloe here. I don't think she really understands Christmas yet, but she does understand the ɔf presents. She looked so adorable in her white footie pajamas ρing the paper off her gifts. And I have a confession to make— κind of ignored Wade's request to not spoil her. When I went to the toy store, I had intended to get her a few small items to go with the parking garage we gave her back in October, like some extra cars and more people. But then I spotted the Fisher-Price airport which I felt would go perfectly with the parking garage. So I got that. And some extra airplanes to go with it. And some more people to put inside the planes. And then—sticking with the transportation theme of course—I saw a super cute Fisher-Price boat that actually floats, which she can play with in the tub. Wade raised an eyebrow at me when he saw how much I'd gotten for her. But when he watched how excited she was as she tore away the wrapping paper, his face softened. I might have even seen him shed a tear or two.

The snow was coming down pretty hard this morning and I was getting more and more worried it wouldn't be safe for Fakhir and his mom and sister, Tammy and her boys, and Lucia's family to drive here if the roads weren't plowed. Of course Agnes and Eugene and Ethan could just walk across the street, even if they'd have to shovel a path for themselves. Dottie said I should quit worrying about the weather and just proceed as if everybody was going to make it. We set the table, I put the beef tenderloin in the oven, made the horseradish cream sauce, and started up a giant pot of Gløgg on the stove. I figured if everybody did make it through the snow, they'd want to warm themselves with a nice toasty drink. I also made a non-alcoholic version for Wade and the kids and the designated drivers, substituting the red wine and aquavit with cranberry juice.

The snow kept coming but everybody made it, thank God. Agnes brought a rather fancy spinach and gruyere potato casserole that went perfectly with the beef. Raquel brought her tamales, some filled with pork and red sauce, others filled with chicken and verde sauce. Dottie made a romaine salad with a lemon and pecorino vinaigrette. Tammy brought a cranberry cheesecake (store-bought, but nobody except me knew because we put it in a glass dish as soon as she arrived and threw away the box). Fakhir made blasted Brussels sprouts and his mom brought her yummy eggplant appetizers. Wade was busy keeping track of Chloe but he had a lot of help from Finn, Rory, Lucia, and Farah — even Tammy's boys loved playing with her. And the meal turned out beautifully.

After dinner we retreated to the family room for the charades tournament. But before we got started on the game, we had a few more gifts to exchange. I gave Fakhir the latest edition of *Joy of Cooking*, in recognition of how much he's improved his cooking skills this year. In the inscription I reminded him that when he first came to live at our house, he didn't even know how to boil water. He smiled when he read that, and proudly announced it's been six months since he last burned the toast.

Arifah and Farah gave me a beautiful black silk scarf they had brought from Iraq. When I thought about how few things they were allowed to bring with them to the U.S. — just two suitcases each — I could hardly believe their generosity. The scarf must be something very special to them if it was one of the things they selected from an entire household — an entire lifetime — of possessions to carry across the globe with them. Farah translated my thanks to her mother. Arifah took both my hands in hers, and looked into my eyes. She didn't say anything, but I think I know what she was communicating to me. Gratitude, from one mother to another.

Wade gave Fakhir a gorgeous cowboy hat, saying Fakhir can wear it when he's lip syncing "Call Me the Breeze" and pretending to be Ronnie Van Zant. Finn and Rory had wrapped The Book of Fakhir in fancy paper, presenting it to Fakhir while saying he can keep it now since they're no longer planning to keep track of his mixed metaphors. Fakhir was touched, telling Finn and Rory he's glad to hear they're not going to make fun of him anymore, because "people in glass houses sink ships."

Dottie gave a set of Joey's dog tags to Wade and Fakhir each, which made everybody cry, including Dottie. She gave me Joey's wedding band, saying Joey always thought of me as a daughter and would've wanted me to have it. I promised Dottie I'd buy a gold chain for the ring and wear it around my neck for the rest of my life.

(Before I forget, I want to thank you for the gift you gave me — I opened it this morning. How in the world were you able to find a pair of women's ɔrown suede ankle boots almost exactly like the ones the movers , during our last PCS? Did you have someone in the States search ʒry roadside stand between White Sands and Yuma to find them for ,ou? I can't wait to hear the story of how you managed such a thoughtful gift. The boots fit perfectly — and they're even cuter than the ones I had before. You are hereby forgiven for your perceived lack of sympathy when I discovered the boots had been stolen. Henceforth, I shall never bring up the topic of the stolen boots ever again.)

After we cleaned up the wrapping paper we got serious about the charades tournament. Kenny Jr., Kevin, and Lucia's brothers kept Chloe occupied while the rest of us split up into two teams — "girls" against the "boys." The matchup was uneven — eight of us girls against just seven of them. The guys said we probably needed the extra person to make up for their superior IQs, a comment which they later regretted. And I must say, Arifah was a surprising asset to our team. Farah proved herself adept at translating her mom's guesses while shouting out her own. And Dottie's ability to recall film titles is absolutely uncanny. (I guess that means she'll make a good Chief of Staff for my new endeavor.) With you here next Christmas, Liam, the teams will be more evenly matched. But don't get your hopes up — the guys will most likely get their asses handed to them again next year, just like they did this year.

After we settled on a movie theme but before we began the first round, Dottie declared we needed to choose a "safe word."

"What's a 'safe word'?" Fakhir asks.

For some reason everyone in the room looks at me, as if I'm the Explainer-in-Chief. "Umm. It's a word you say when ..." I look around the room at everyone's faces. It's obvious which of us knows what it means because those are the people watching me with extreme glee — including our very own sons. I rest my eyes on Lucia and say, "I believe this would fall under your field of operations."

Instead of explaining it to Fakhir in front of the entire universe, Lucia deftly turns the conversation back to Dottie. "Why do we need a safe word Dottie? We're just playing charades," she asks.

Dottie replies, "Well, don't they always say the worst time to have a heart attack is when you're playing charades? So I think it would be wise for us to come up with a safe word in case someone is actua[lly] having a heart attack. That way, we won't mistakenly think they're ju[st] trying to act out the name of a movie when they're clutching at the[ir] chest. Right?" She looks at all of us as if we're being obtuse.

The room is silent for a split second before everyone starts laughing and talking at once. (Everyone except Fakhir, that is, because he's still stuck on trying to figure out what a safe word is.)

"All right everybody," I say once the laughter dies down. "How about if our safe word is 'Shirley Temple.' So if you suddenly start having a heart attack in the middle of the game, just say 'Shirley Temple.' And then we'll know you're not just pretending to be Don Corlione in 'The Godfather.'"

I can only say that the hijinks continued in this manner as the game got underway. At one point Fakhir was trying to act out "Rear Window." He's standing in the middle of the family room, gesturing emphatically toward his butt in an effort to get somebody—anybody—to say the word "rear." In spite of his best efforts, however, Fakhir's cohorts manage to shout out every imaginable synonym for "butt"—except for the one he wants them to say. A sampling:

"Ass!" (Carmen)

Fakhir shakes his head.

"Derrière!" (Eugene)

Fakhir shakes his head.

"Hiney!" (Ethan)

"Booty!" (Wade)

"Poop shoot!" (Finn)

"Fart machine!" (Rory).

And on it went, like that.

So while the clock is running out and Fakhir continues pointing to his ass in an exercise of unmitigated futility, guess who saunters into the room amidst the chaos? Soda. And guess what Soda had in his mouth? One of Lucia's bras. Everybody immediately stops talking, the game on pause, as Soda casually strolls past us, dragging Lucia's lacy pastel pink brassiere behind him. We watch silently as he moseys across the room, stopping only when he reaches the bookcase in the corner. He then squeezes behind the bookcase, still dragging the bra, into the

ngular space formed by the back of the shelf and the corner
he walls meet — the corner nobody bothers to vacuum because,
t's blocked off by a bookcase filled with books. But not blocked off
ugh that a certain small, determined Chihuahua couldn't squeeze
rough the space between the bookcase and the wall to create his own
personal hideaway.

As we watch the bra disappear behind the shelf, Rory, Lucia, and I lock eyes. What we just witnessed might be considered merely amusing to the others, but to the three of us, it's so much more. A revelation. And a victory of sorts, for Lucia and Rory, who'd been the objects of my suspicion since Lucia moved in and the bras began showing up in strange places throughout the house.

The three of us walk over to the bookcase to investigate, the rest of the room watching with curiosity. Lucia sticks her head behind the bookcase first, her face reappearing with a grin. Rory sticks his head back there next, his face likewise reappearing with an even wider grin. Finally I step forward to have my turn to peer behind the bookcase. There lies a plethora of Lucia's bras (and a few pairs of underwear), which Soda has absconded with in order to build himself a lair of sorts. And lying in the center of his ill-gotten gains is Soda, looking supremely annoyed that humans have discovered his private sanctuary. The bras are covered in a thick layer of Soda's white fur, signifying that the den of iniquity had been created for the sole purpose of Soda's covert napping sessions.

"So I guess that explains why we kept finding Lucia's bras all over the house," I say, looking sheepishly from Rory to Lucia. "Soda obviously didn't make it all the way to his hidey-hole with several pieces of the pilfered lingerie."

Rory folds his arms and looks at me expectantly.

"And I guess I owe you an apology," I say.

He nods, looking triumphant. "Uh, yeah."

Meanwhile everyone else has gotten up from their places to have a look-see.

"What do you need to apologize to Rory for?" Dottie asks. "As far as I can tell this is all Lucia's lingerie."

Rory quickly replies, "Oh, it's nothing," he says, glancing nervously around the room.

I press my lips together in an effort to suppress a smile.

After taking a look for himself, Finn says, "So why do you think Soda only walked off with Lucia's stuff?"

"Because I'm his favorite person, obviously," Lucia replies. "I mean, it's pretty clear he likes me better than the rest of you derps."

Fakhir steps in to gently chide Lucia. "Uh, no. I think it's because you're the one who doesn't put your clothes in the hamper like everybody else does."

Lucia shakes her head. "No. Rory doesn't put his clothes in the hamper either. Soda could just as easily swipe his stuff," she argues. "But he chooses mine instead."

Finn says, "Uh, if I were Soda I wouldn't touch Rory's dirty underwear either. That stuff is a biohazard."

"So is your underwear, dorkus," Rory says.

"You're a plonker," Finn replies.

"You're a jork."

"All right. Knock it off guys," I warn them. I'm pretending to be annoyed with our sons, but in my heart I'm secretly pleased to see the two of them squabbling just like they used to do before Finn went away to college.

Dottie says, "I don't know about the rest of you but I'm ready for another cup of that Gløgg. What do you say we break for refreshments?"

"And I could use a few more of those Christmas cookies we made the other night," Wade chimes in, heading toward the kitchen.

Carmen signals to his teammates. "This is our chance to regroup guys. Let's strategize our comeback."

As the partygoers pile into the kitchen to dole out beverages and divvy up the cookies, I take the opportunity to go into the front room to sneak a peek outside. In the time since everyone arrived earlier that afternoon, we've gotten at least another six inches of snow. With the accumulation from this morning, I calculate at least three feet of total snowfall. I linger a few minutes longer, my fingers on the cold glass, my breath fogging up the window. Listening to the lighthearted back and

ͻming from the kitchen, I think about how much you'd love it if
ͻuld see our front yard right now, blanketed by drifts of sparkling
ν. I search the street for signs of an approaching vehicle, but the
ιy cars I see are the ones parked in front, silently encased in cloaks
ͻf crystalline powder.

When I finally tear myself away from the window, I realize the group has already returned to the family room—still laughing and talking as they finish the last of their cookies, waiting patiently for me to rejoin them.

"I have an announcement to make," I say, softly clapping my hands to get everyone's attention. "Whoever doesn't feel like driving home in the snow tonight can stay here. We've got plenty of extra blankets and pillows in the linen closet. Just grab a couch or a comfy spot on the floor and make yourselves at home."

Upon hearing that, Kenny, Kevin, Arthur, Andy, and Angel immediately start bouncing up and down with excitement, begging their parents to let them stay. Among the replies of "Maybe," and "We'll see," the teams reassemble on each side of the room as they prepare to resume the second half of the tournament.

Chloe is getting sleepy so I offer to take her from Wade and put her to bed in her crib upstairs. He gratefully transfers her to my arms and gives me a quick hug before taking his place among his teammates. Holding Chloe, I pause at the edge of the family room to look around at the faces of so many of the people I love.

Once everybody has settled in and quieted down again, I say, "I just want to say thank you guys for making this a wonderful Christmas. Even though Liam—and Joey—couldn't be with us, I could feel both of them here tonight."

Dottie smiles at me as the others murmur in agreement.

"And I hope you won't be mad at me," I say, "but I'm going to call it a night. You guys continue the game without me, okay?"

Tammy and Agnes and a few of the others try talking me into coming back downstairs after I put Chloe to bed, but I resist. "I'm ready for some quiet time," I explain. "And besides, I want to check my email. I'm still hoping to hear from Liam tonight."

11:33 p.m.

From: Liam Mahoney
To: Emilie Mahoney
Subj: I'm coming home

Itinerary
Liam Mahoney, Col., U.S. Marine Corps
Reservation code: PBCILYG
Comments

Transportation expenses on this itinerary are billed to a central billed account owned by the U.S. government and these expenses are not reimbursable to the traveler.

BAGHDAD > KUWAIT > RAMSTEIN > BANGOR
CLASSIFIED

BANGOR > SANDIEGO TUE 26DEC08 1100 STATUS:
CONFIRMED TERMINAL 2

SANDIEGO > DENVER SUN 27DEC08 1435 STATUS:
CONFIRMED TERMINAL 1

DENVER > BUELLCITY SUN 27DEC08 2153 STATUS:
CONFIRMED TERMINAL A

PLEASE VERIFY FLIGHT TIMES PRIOR TO DEPARTURE

Glossary

I MEF: 1st Marine Expeditionary Force, or "One Mef." A Marine Air Ground Task Force (MAGTF) based out of Marine Corps Base Camp Pendleton and the largest of the three MEFs in the Fleet Marine Force.

3rd MAW: 3rd Marine Aircraft Wing. Provides the aviation combat element for I MEF (see above), based out of Marine Corps Air Station Miramar.

AAR: After Action Report. A tool used by all military branches for either formally or informally evaluating a particular event after it occurs.

ABC party: Anything But Clothes party in which attendees wear non-traditional, non-fabric materials.

active duty: a service member who works in the military full-time (vs. a reservist, who is available to be activated for military duty in time of war but is not a full-time warrior).

and a wake-up: used when counting down the days to an anticipated event. For example, "four days and a wake-up" equals five days.

asses and elbows: a state in which everyone is busy.

AWOL: Absent Without Official Leave.

Basic School (TBS): The Basic School, in Quantico Virginia, a six-month program in which all newly commissioned U.S. Marine Corps officers further develop their leadership skills.

battalion: In the Marine Corps, a unit composed of a headquarters and two or more companies with a total of 500 to 1,200 Marines.

BCGs: Boot Camp Glasses, issued to Marines at boot camp. Also known as Birth Control Glasses because, well, take a look at someone who's wearing a pair.

BGen: Brigadier General (0-7).

bivouac: (noun) a temporary military encampment. (verb) the act of assembling an improvised shelter. (Think camping trip but with a military theme.)

blood stripe: A vertical scarlet stripe on the outside trouser seams of the Marine Corps dress blue uniform worn by NCOs, Staff NCOs, and officers. The legend that the blood stripe honors the Marines who died in the Battle of Chapultepec in 1847 is false according to the National Museum of the Marine Corps. The blood stripe predates the Mexican-American War.

blue falcon: Buddy Fucker. Someone who puts himself (or herself) first at the expense of his (or her) fellow service members.

blue star: Traditionally, a blue star on a service flag indicates an active-duty family member has deployed to a combat zone during a time of war or hostilities. More recently (in the years following the time period depicted in this novel), the meaning of the blue star has been widened to include those serving during a time of war (not necessarily deployed to a combat zone). The service flag is typically hung facing out from the inside of a front window of the home where the service member normally resides.

Bravo Zulu: well done.

brig: a jail on a naval vessel. Usage later expanded to mean any jail or prison on a military installation.

brigade: In the Marine Corps, a formation that consists of a minimum of three regimental-equivalent sized units.

Bronze Star: Medal awarded to members of the U.S. Armed Forces (as well as civilians serving with military forces in combat) for heroic achievement, heroic service, meritorious achievement, or meritorious service in a combat zone. A "V" device denotes acts of valor.

BTW: by the way.

butthurt: annoyed, upset, or angry about something others perceive as trivial.

C-rats: short for C-rations. Prepared food in a can for troops in the field, first used in WWI. Later known as MREs.

CACO: Casualty Assistance Calls Officer. A member of a two- or three-person team consisting of a notifications officer, casualty assistance officer, and chaplain whose job is to provide in-person notification and support to next of kin when a service member has died.

cammies: camouflage utility uniform.

Camp Slayer: a former Iraqi government palace complex located on the southeastern corner of the Baghdad International Airport, used as a U.S. military base during the Iraq war.

casualty officer: see CACO.

CD: compact disc.

CHAOS: Colonel Has Another Outstanding Suggestion.

Charlies: Marine Corps service uniform consisting of green trousers (or skirt) and khaki shirt. Variations of this uniform are known as Alpha (Service "A" uniform worn with green coat), Bravo (Service "B" uniform with no coat and long-sleeve shirt), and Charlie (Service "C" uniform with no coat and short-sleeve shirt).

Chesty: the English bulldog mascot of the Marine Corps, named after Lt.Gen. Lewis B. "Chesty" Puller Jr., one of the most decorated Marines in history.

chow hall: cafeteria in a military installation, also known as a mess hall or DFAC.

CHU: Containerized Housing Unit, a pre-fabricated shipping container used as temporary living quarters on military installations.

civvies: civilian clothing (vs. military uniform).

CO: Commanding Officer.

COBRA: Consolidated Omnibus Budget Reconciliation Act. A federal law that allows people who have left a company to maintain their current health insurance at their own expense.

Col.: Colonel.

combat pay: all service members assigned to a combat zone receive combat pay, officially known as Imminent Danger Pay (IDP).

command: a body of troops or a station, ship, etc. under the leadership of an officer.

commissary: grocery store on a military base.

Cpl.: Corporal.

CTU: Counter Terrorism Unit (as referred to in the TV show "24").

DD: Designated Driver.

DEFCON: Defense Readiness Condition. An alert system used by the armed forces to signify various levels of readiness in response to a threat, with DEFCON 5 being the least severe and DEFCON 1 being the most severe.

deployment: the temporary relocation of armed forces and materiel within operational areas.

Deployment Curse: Murphy's Law for military spouses. Things tend to go wrong (appliances break, kids get sick, car battery dies) with greater frequency as soon as the service member leaves on a deployment.

Deployment Perk: informal privileges or benefits given to military family members in an effort to lighten the load when their service member is deployed. Can include discounts on goods and services, free babysitting, meals, transportation, etc. proffered by friends and neighbors.

DFAC: (pronounced dee-fack) Dining Facility.

DFAS: Defense Finance and Accounting Service.

DHARMA Initiative: Department of Heuristics and Research on Material Applications, a fictional research project featured on the television series "Lost."

dilliclapper: Do I Look Like I Could Lead A Platoon? A person who does not make good decisions.

dilligaf: Do I Look Like I Give A Fuck? or Does It Look Like I Give A Fuck? A person who is indifferent to the plight of others.

DMZ: Demilitarized Zone. A geographic area that lies between two military powers limiting military activity, personnel, and installations and is often considered neutral territory.

DoD: Department of Defense

dog tags: Identification tags worn on a chain around a service member's neck to aid in identifying someone who is wounded or killed in action. The tags commonly contain the service member's name, ID number, blood type, and religious preference if applicable.

DSN: Defense Switched Network. Department of Defense telecommunications system used for official business.

ducks in a row: to organize and take care of details before beginning a project. Origin uncertain. Could be a Navy shipbuilding term wherein the heaviest parts of the ship are lined up before being lifted by a crane. Or a reference to the energy-efficient V-formation of ducks in flight. Or the way baby ducks line up behind their mother. Or the line of mechanical ducks at a shooting arcade. Take your pick.

duty station: military base where a service member has been assigned to work as a result of a PCS order.

embrace the suck: to adopt an attitude of not letting unpleasant circumstances determine your attitude. In other words, "The situation is bad, deal with it."

FAFSA: Free Application for Federal Student Aid. The form college students must fill out to be considered for financial aid, student loans, work-study programs, grants, and some scholarships.

FEN: Far East Network. The American military network of radio and television stations that operated primarily in mainland Japan, Okinawa, the Philippines, and Guam until 1997. Now known as AFN (American Forces Network).

flash-blast: the act of being chewed out by the senior non-commissioned officer (NCO).

FNG: Fucking New Guy.

FOB: Forward Operating Base.

Fobbit: a perjorative used by troops in the field to describe military personnel who spend the majority of their time within the relative safety of the Forwarding Operating Base (FOB).

FPO: Fleet Post Office. Used when sending mail to military installations.

FRG: Family Readiness Group.

fruit salad: the display of ribbons and medals on a service member's dress uniform.

FSG: Family Support Group.

FUBAR: Fucked Up Beyond All Recognition.

FUBB: Fucked Up Beyond Belief.

Fuckin' A: indicates emphatic agreement. The exact origin of this phrase is unknown, but the earliest written records suggest it was used in the 1940s by U.S. service members during WWII. The "A" possibly stands for the aviation term "affirmative" or the first letter in the military radio alphabet.

full as a bingo bus: Irish slang for drunk.

full battle rattle: protective gear worn by military personnel to include flak jacket, Kevlar helmet, weapon(s), and ammo.

full bird colonel: an officer with the full rank of colonel (O-6) who wears the eagle insignia, as distinct from a lieutenant colonel (O-5) who wears the silver oak leaf.

fux pux: Liam's way of saying faux pas.

FYSA: For Your Situational Awareness (military version of FYI).

G Fund: A government securities fund offered only to service members and civil service employees via the Thrift Savings Plan (see TSP) with no risk of loss of principal.

geedunk: snack bar on a ship that sells candy & other junk food, also used to refer to such snacks.

geo-bachelor: geographic bachelor. A common practice for military families in which the service member lives alone at a duty station while the rest of the family remains in place at another location.

G.I.: a slang term for a service member. Originally an initialism for galvanized iron; later came into widespread use around WWII as an acronym for Government Issue or General Issue.

gold star: a gold star on a service flag indicates a member of one's family was killed while serving in the armed forces during a time of war or hostilities. The service flag is typically hung facing out from the inside of a front window of the home where the service member lived.

got your six: "I've got your six" means "I've got your back." The phrase comes from aviation terminology used to denote the position of an object in reference to a person (or aircraft). So something at someone's "twelve o'clock" is in front of them while someone's "six o'clock" signifies what's behind them, "three o'clock" signifies to their right, and so on.

gouge: informal but essential information, the facts behind the rumors. Originally a Navy term used in reference to test answers (aka cheat sheet).

gouge train: information channel, grapevine.

grab some bench: a phrase used by coaches directing a player to go to the bench, it can also be a non-sports-related directive to sit down.

grape: a person's head.

green weenie: (or big green weenie) used in reference to the Marine Corps when a Marine is negatively impacted by military decisions such as canceled leave, holiday duty, extended deployment, last-minute change in orders, etc. Also used by the Army.

Green Zone: heavily fortified headquarters of the coalition forces during the Iraq War, now known as the International Zone.

GTFO: Get The Fuck Out. Used to express disbelief or displeasure.

Gunny (GySgt.): Gunnery sergeant (E-7).

gyrene: slang for a U.S. Marine. Origin unknown, though some sources say it's a combination of G.I. and Marine. Commonly used by members of the U.S. Navy during WWI to insult Marines, it instead became a popular way for Marines to refer to one another.

Haji: an honorific title given to a Muslim who has completed the Haji to Mecca; when used by non-Muslims (including American military personnel) it's often a derogatory way of referring to anyone who appears to be a Muslim.

hayaku: Japanese for "faster," frequently used to encourage someone to hurry up, but also used by American military personnel to mean leave in a hurry.

HAZMAT: Hazardous Materials. A HAZMAT team is specially trained to dispose of toxic substances.

head: restroom.

heads-up: an alert or warning.

helot: a member of a class of serfs in ancient Sparta, someone whose social status is between a slave and a citizen. In the movie "Meet John Doe," Walter Brennan's character (the Colonel) uses the term helots to describe people who only want something from you ("a lotta heels").

high and tight: a military regulation haircut favored by Marines in which the sides and back are closely shaved (0 inches), with a very gradual and slight increase in length toward the top, usually no more than 1-2 inches (and the shorter the better).

HMFIC: Head Mother Fucker In Charge

Holy Mike Foxtrot: Holy Mother Fucker.

hurt locker: to be in trouble, at a disadvantage, or in bad shape. The term is from the Vietnam era and refers to a situation or mental state, similar to being "in a world of hurt."

HQ: Headquarters.

ICAO: (pronounced eye-kay-oh). International Civil Aviation Organization. The ICAO alphabet is a series of acrophonic codewords assigned to the 26 letters of the English alphabet for use in radio communications. A = Alpha, B = Bravo, C = Charlie, and so on.

ICOM: a field radio used by infantry units and manufactured by Icom America.

IDP: Imminent Danger Pay, also known as combat pay for service members assigned to a combat zone.

IED: Improvised Explosive Device.

IM: Instant Message. A type of Internet-based communication that allows two people to exchange private text-based messages in real-time. Also used as a verb to describe the act of exchanging instant messages.

in-country: being in a country for the purpose of military operations.

Insha'Allah: Arabic for "God willing."

intel: intelligence. Information or the process of collecting information from a range of sources in support of a military command.

International Zone (IZ): formerly known as the Green Zone, the heavily fortified headquarters for the Iraqi Reconstruction Ministries.

invi-told: an invitation to a military event in which attendance is said to be voluntary yet implicitly required in order to remain in good standing.

ISS: In-School Suspension.

IUD: Intrauterine Device. A method of birth control.

jarhead: slang for U.S. Marine. Ostensibly derived from the similarity in appearance of a Marine in dress blue uniform (with its stiff, high collar) and a Mason jar. Commonly used by members of the U.S. Navy during WWII to insult Marines, it instead became a popular way for Marines to refer to one another.

JJ DID TIE BUCKLE: The 14 Marine Corps leadership traits: Justice, Judgment, Decisiveness, Initiative, Dependability, Tact, Integrity, Enthusiasm, Bearing, Unselfishness, Courage, Knowledge, Loyalty, Endurance.

Ka-Bar: combat (or fighting utility) knife, first used by the Marine Corps in November 1942 during WWII.

knife-hand: a hand gesture frequently employed by Marines in which the hand is flat & perpendicular to the ground, used for emphasis or to point, usually in the context of vigorously correcting a subordinate.

L Fund: Lifecycle Fund. A target-date fund offered only to service members and civil service employees via the Thrift Savings Plan (see TSP) which allows for reallocation of assets from more risky stock funds to less risky income funds as the employee gets closer to retirement age.

LAPES: Low-Altitude Parachute Extraction System. A method of releasing heavy loads from an aircraft for the purpose of resupplying ground troops.

latrinegram: wild, unfounded rumor.

Lima Charlie: loud and clear.

LCpl: Lance Corporal.

LCpl. Schmuckatelli: a generic term used to describe any hapless Marine who is frequently in trouble and therefore used as an example of what not to do.

Maine Troop Greeters: a volunteer group of veterans and other citizens who greet the troops every time a military flight stops at Bangor International Airport on its way to or from a war zone.

Maj.: Major.

Maj. Bagadonuts: the officer version of LCpl. Schmuckatelli. A fictional Marine often used as an example of what not to do. A derogatory nickname for an officer on weight control or who has an otherwise sub-par appearance.

make a hole: get out of the way.

mandatory fun: a family-oriented military event intended to raise morale but which feels more like an obligation.

MCSF: Marine Corps Support Facility, a Marine Corps base located in New Orleans, LA.

military brat: a term of affection and respect when used by military families. Not recommended for use by people outside the military, as it can be interpreted as being derogatory.

milspouse: military spouse. Other abbreviations include milspo and milso (military significant other).

Mike Foxtrot: Mother Fucker, as in motherfucker.

MIP: Minor In Possession (of alcohol or other illegal substance).

missing man table: Also knows as The Fallen Comrade Table. A small empty table with a place setting for one, set up at formal military events as a reminder of those who died or are still missing in action.

MNC: Multi-National Corps. A multi-national command charged with directing the tactical battle in Iraq under the parent command of Multi-National Force (MNF) which handles strategic level issues.

MNC-I: Multi-National Corps—Iraq. The tactical unit responsible for command and control of operations in Iraq (see MNC above).

MNF: Multi-National Force. The parent command of MNC that handles strategic-level issues.

MNF-I: Multi-National Force—Iraq (see MNF above).

moonbeam: flashlight.

mortar: a short-range, short-barrel, muzzle-loading cannon for firing low-speed, high-arcing projectiles at (often unseen) targets.

most ricky-tick: as quickly as possible (see ricky-tick).

MP: Military Police.

MRAP: Mine Resistant Ambush Protected. A tactical vehicle designed to resist IEDs.

MRE: Meal Ready to Eat. Individual meals used in the field, formerly known as C-Rations or C-Rats.

Mukhabarat: Saddam Hussein's secret police.

MUSADI: Makin' Up Shit And Defending It. This is not a documented military acronym but a McCarthy family favorite thanks to Lt.Col. Rich Haddad (USMC Ret.).

mustang: a warrant officer or commissioned officer who started his or her military career as an enlisted service member. Also known as prior enlisted.

MWR: Morale, Welfare & Recreation. A program / facility on military bases that offers recreational activities, discounts, and other services for military members and their families aimed at improving morale.

NCO: Non-Commissioned Officer.

NLT: No Later Than.

no go: not going to happen.

NOLA: New Orleans.

nonner: Short for non-sortie generating motherfucker; Air Force slang for personnel in jobs other than aircrew or air maintenance.

NV: North Vietnamese.

NVA: North Vietnamese Army.

O' Club: Officers' Club. A facility for dining and socializing limited to military officers, their families, and guests.

OCS: Officer Candidate School, a training and screening program for potential Marine Officers.

oddy-knocky: on one's own, alone. A term used by the characters in A Clockwork Orange by Anthony Burgess.

OEF: Operation Enduring Freedom (Afghanistan).

OFP: Own Fucking Program. A Marine not following orders or adhering to Marine Corps standards.

oh-dark-thirty: an unspecified time in the early hours before dawn. Same as zero-dark-thirty.

OIC: Officer In Charge.

OIF: Operation Iraqi Freedom.

One Mef: phonetic pronunciation of I MEF (1st Marine Expeditionary Force).

Oorah: an expression of enthusiasm specific to the Marine Corps. (Hooah is used by the Army while hooyah is used by the Navy and Coast Guard.)

OPSEC: Operations Security. The practice of controlling the release of unclassified information that, when pieced together with other data, could provide details of military operations to potential adversaries.

Ops O: Operations Officer.

order(s): In the military, an authoritative directive, instruction, or notice issued by a commander or commanding organization.

Oscar Kilo: OK.

OSS: Out-of-School Suspension.

outside the wire (going outside the wire): to leave the defensive perimeter of an established military base; doing so denotes the end of relative safety.

OWC: Officers' Wives' Club.

P-38: a small can opener used to open canned field rations, also known as a "John Wayne" by Marines.

PAO: Public Affairs Officer. A military officer whose job involves interfacing with reporters and other media representatives.

paracord bracelet: a survival bracelet made using 550-lb.-strength parachute cord (aka 550 cord) that can be unraveled and used for various purposes in an emergency.

PBJ: If you're an English speaker who had to look this up in the glossary you do not belong on this planet.

PCM: Primary Care Manager.

PCS: Permanent Change of Station. Frequently used as a verb among military people to describe moving from one duty station to another (as in "we're PCSing next month").

PERSEC: Personal Security. The practice of controlling personal information in order to protect the safety of service members and their families.

PFC: Private First Class (E-2).

PFT: Physical Fitness Test.

pie-hole: mouth.

POG: Persons Other than Grunt. Any non-infantry military personnel. Depending on speaker and context, can be interpreted as either endearing or derogatory.

pop-flare: a hand-held, hand-launched aerial illumination projectile.

pop smoke: to leave in a hurry. Derived from the military practice of either 1.) igniting a smoke grenade to make an exit without being detected by the enemy or 2.) marking your landing zone for an aircraft coming to extract you from a bad situation.

pound sand: when used in the imperative, a vehement dismissal (as in "go pound sand").

POV: Privately Owned Vehicle. The military's way of saying "car." (It also stands for Point of View when used in a literary context.)

prior enlisted: a warrant officer or commissioned officer who started his or her military career as an enlisted service member. Also known as a mustang.

PsyOps: Psychological Operations. Planned military activity intended to influence the mindsets and decision-making of adversarial target audiences (usually involving cultural considerations) to achieve tactical and operational objectives.

PT: Physical Training.

PTS: Post-Traumatic Stress. A preferred, more up-to-date terminology for PTSD that intentionally drops the "Disorder" label. Not yet common usage during the time period in which this story is set.

PTSD: Post-Traumatic Stress Disorder.

pull chocks: When a plane prepares for take-off and the blocks placed in front of the wheels (chocks) are removed (pulled). Also used figuratively to mean "let's go" or "time to leave."

put down your pack: A metaphor for releasing one's self from warfighting and its accompanying psychological burdens. A useful phrase for veterans and / or those dealing with Post-Traumatic Stress.

PX: Post Exchange. The shopping center on a military base.

qadi: Muslim judge.

rack: bed, short for barrack.

rank-dropping: akin to name-dropping, mentioning someone's rank for the sole purpose of impressing others.

recon: short for reconnaissance—to surreptitiously patrol in an effort to gain information.

Ret.: Retired.

Rhino Runner: an armored bus used extensively in Iraq, especially on Route Irish (between Baghdad International Airport and the International Zone).

ricky-tick (also "most ricky-tick"): as soon as possible, quickly. Used by Marines when an order needs to be carried out expeditiously. The origin of this phrase is disputed as either being derived from an unknown Japanese phrase or from the children's tale Rikki Tikki Tavi, in which the title character is a mongoose (known to be extremely fast).

RPG: Ruchnoy Protivotankovy Granatomyot, aka Rocket Propelled Grenade, a hand-held anti-tank grenade launcher.

SACO: Substance Abuse Control Officer.

sandbox: Iraq.

Schmuckatelli: aka LCpl. Schmuckatelli. A generic term used to describe any hapless Marine who is frequently in trouble and therefore used as an example of what not to do.

screw the pooch: to mess up badly.

seabag: cylindrical canvas bag used by sailors and Marines to carry personal items such as uniforms.

secret squirrel: all things classified: intelligence personnel, communications, or top-secret operations. Also a derogatory term for someone who is sneaky or withholds information.

Semper Fi: short for Semper Fidelis, the Marine Corps motto (Always Faithful).

Semper Gumby: a play on the Marine Corps motto "Semper Fidelis" ("Always Faithful"), to mean "Always Flexible."

sent to the brig: confined to jail on a military installation.

separate: (verb) in the military, when the required term of service has been completed and a service member is released from active duty.

shitbird: a Marine (or anyone) who is not squared away in appearance or discipline.

shithot: a Marine who is tactically skilled, hardcore, way above average. Also applies to an operation that is particularly well carried-out.

shit on a shingle (SOS): creamed chipped beef on toast, traditionally served in military mess halls.

shitstorm: an extremely unpleasant culmination of unfortunate events.

shut up and color: quit complaining.

Sierra Bravo: Shit Bird, as in shitbird.

Sierra Tango Foxtrot Uniform: Shut The Fuck Up.

silkies: Marine Corps PT gear often used for running and / or as underwear. These extremely short, green "silk" shorts were phased out in 2011 in spite of a cult following among Marines (and their admirers).

Silver Star: Medal awarded to members of the U.S. Armed Forces for gallantry in action involving singular acts of valor or heroism over a brief period. The third highest military combat decoration after the Medal of Honor and Service Cross.

sitrep: situational report.

Skype: a software application that allows people to talk in real-time using their computers and an Internet connection, usually via video. Also used as a verb to describe the act of video chatting.

smoking lamp: a nautical term used to signify when smoking is allowed on a ship; when the smoking lamp is lighted, smoking is allowed; when the smoking lamp is out, smoking is not allowed.

SNL: Saturday Night Live.

SOFA: Status of Forces Agreement. An agreement between a host country and foreign military forces outlining the framework by which the military personnel operate in the host country.

SOL: Shit Outta Luck.

SOS: Shit On a Shingle (chipped beef on toast).

soup sandwich: messy situation.

spousal unit: military wife or husband, suggesting she / he was issued to the service member similar to other military gear. Can be used affectionately or not.

squared away: a nautical term meaning to align the sails at right angles to the mast and keel of a ship for optimal wind direction. In general military terms, to be organized and ready.

SRO: School Resource Officer. A police officer responsible for providing law enforcement and crime prevention in the public school environment.

SSgt.: Staff Sergeant (E-6).

stay frosty: be alert and on guard.

stealth wife (or husband): a military spouse whose efforts are often invisible but who supports the mission by working behind the scenes to keep the family and household running smoothly, especially during deployments.

T-minus: in aeronautical terms, the time before rocket launch. In military circles, commonly used to refer to the time until a service member returns home after a deployment, used for countdown purposes.

T-wall: a 12-ft. high blast wall made of concrete and shaped like an inverted "T" commonly used by U.S. forces in Iraq and Afghanistan.

TAD: Temporary Additional Duty. A Navy and Marine Corps term for a service member's travel assignment to a location other than one's permanent duty station. Also known as TDY (Temporary Duty) among other service branches as well as the general military population.

Tango Yankee: Thank You.

TARFU: Things Are Really Fucked Up.

tasker: an official DoD document that contains a direction to perform specific tasks. Informally, another thing to do in addition to all the other things a person has to do.

TBI: Traumatic Brain Injury.

TBS: The Basic School, in Quantico Virginia, a six-month program in which all newly commissioned U.S. Marine Corps officers further develop their leadership skills.

TDY: Temporary Duty. Also known as TAD (Temporary Additional Duty) in the Navy and Marine Corps. Refers to a service member's travel assignment to a location other than one's permanent duty station.

terp: interpreter.

thousand-yard stare: a vacant or unfocused gaze into the distance exhibited by war-weary service members.

TK: a publishing reference used as a placeholder for an item yet to be inserted (to come).

TMI: Too Much Information.

TMO: Transportation Management Office. Coordinates packing and shipping for PCS moves. Now called PPSO (Personal Property Shipping Office).

TMS: Transcranial Magnetic Stimulation. A noninvasive procedure that uses magnetic fields to stimulate nerve cells in the brain to improve symptoms related to depression, PTS (Post-Traumatic Stress), and mild to moderate TBI (Traumatic Brain Injury).

tour: period of military service in one location.

TSP: Thrift Savings Plan. A retirement plan for service members and civil service employees similar to a private-sector 401(k).

un-ass: to leave the area, remove one's butt from wherever it happens to be resting.

un-fuck: to correct a deficiency, usually on a person, to bring something or someone into proper order.

unsat: unsatisfactory. A behavior that is well below the required standards.

USMC: United States Marine Corps. Also: Uncle Sam's Misguided Children, U Suckers Missed Christmas, U Signed the Motherfucking Contract.

USO: United Service Organizations, a non-profit group that provides programs and services to military members and their families.

VA: Veterans Affairs.

VBC: Victory Base Complex (Iraq). A cluster of military installations to include Camp Victory, where Al-Faw Palace was located and which housed the headquarters of the Multi-National Corps—Iraq (MNC-I).

VC: Viet Cong.

visual contact: sighting of an aircraft / ground position.

voluntold: when a service member (or family member) is encouraged to participate in an activity that appears voluntary but in reality is not voluntary at all.

VTC: Video Teleconference.

War Department: a service member's spouse. Can be used affection-ately or not.

wheels up: ready for departure.

Whiskey Delta: Weak Dick.

Whiskey Tango Foxtrot: What The fuck.

Wilco: Will comply, meaning "I understand and will do as instructed."

woobie: A nickname given to military poncho liners. A popular piece of military gear often used as a blanket in the field.

XO: Executive Officer. The second in command of a unit, under the CO (Commanding Officer).

zero-dark-thirty: an unspecified time in the early hours before dawn. Same as oh-dark-thirty.

Author's Note

Although this is a work of fiction, real-world historic and cultural events appear throughout the story. While I've tried as much as possible to incorporate these events accurately and in the correct timeframe in which they occurred, some events have been reworked to fit the narrative. For example:

Books, movies, & other media

Emilie mentions reading David Sedaris' *When You Are Engulfed In Flames* in February 2008, but the book wasn't released until June 2008. Likewise, although she mentions her book club reading Dave Cullen's *Columbine* in March 2008, that book didn't come out until a year later, in 2009. She also mentions "the new Shrek movie" in February 2008, which came out in May 2007. Most of the classic movies referenced in the story were aired on Turner Classic Movies, though not necessarily on the dates mentioned. Emilie's book club read *Still Alice* in May 2008, yet although author Lisa Genova self-published the book in 2007, *Still Alice* wasn't in wide distribution until January 2009. Ethan mentions playing "the new Call of Duty game" in May 2008, although that specific version wasn't released until November of that year. Lindsay Shannon's blues program on KCFX runs from 8-10 p.m. on Sunday nights even though Emilie and Wade listen to it in the car at other times. Finn and Maggie see "Beverly Hills Chihuahua" in June of 2008, although the movie didn't hit theaters until October of that year.

News/historic events

Although the Virginia Tech massacre occurred on April 16, 2007, it was mentioned here as having happened one year later (April 16, 2008). And while several U.S. colonels were killed during Operation Iraqi Freedom, all news items that appear in this story are entirely fictitious, as are all other events involving the fictional characters in this book. For example, although the Mahdi Army was involved in acts of violence against coalition forces in Ramadi, Sadr City, and elsewhere in 2008, the incident described by Fakhir is entirely fictional. Emilie references the Military Spouse of the Year Award as if it's been in existence a while, even though the award was first given in 2008. In an email from April 2008 Emilie mentions burn pits even though the use of burn pits in Iraq and Afghanistan wasn't in the news or widely known until much later. Labor Day falls on September 8th here in order to fit the narrative when in fact it fell on September 1st in 2008. Although Emilie mentions the transfer of Anbar province from coalition forces back to the Iraqi government as happening in late September, the actual transfer happened on September 1st. While the Second Battle of Fallujah did in fact take place from November to December 2004, Wade's recollections of the battle are entirely fictional, as are all characters mentioned in that scene. Likewise, while the Battle of Khe Sanh did in fact occur from January to July 1968 during the Vietnam War, Joey's recollections of airdrop missions during that time are entirely fictional, as are all characters mentioned in that scene. Although Saddam Hussein's son Uday allegedly committed violent crimes such as rape, murder, and torture, the scene described by Fakhir is entirely fictional, as are all the characters mentioned in that story. And finally, the news item regarding a school shooter is entirely fictional. Buell City High School is not a real school, Buell City is a fictional town, and the local businesses mentioned in the story (restaurants, coffee shops, etc.) are also fictional.

Pop culture & miscellaneous other stuff

Will Ferrell's "The Luxury Spy" Jaguar skit didn't appear on Saturday Night Live until 2010 even though Emilie references it in 2008. Fakhir, Dottie, and Joey are mentioned drinking Boulevard Brewery's Tank 7

Farmhouse Ale in 2008 even though that particular beer didn't make its debut until 2009. Aunt Dottie mentions Katy Perry's hair being blue and purple in 2008 even though Perry didn't start using those hues until a couple years later. Emilie uses the phrase "sorry not sorry," which didn't come into popular use until 2011. Likewise, Lucia uses the term "ratchet," which didn't come into popular use until a few years later. Aunt Dottie mentions the girl in Greece with the partially absorbed embryonic twin in May 2008 but that story wasn't reported in the news until November 2008. Dottie and Joey want to get home on a Sunday night in time to watch "Dancing with the Stars," but this show actually aired on Monday nights in 2008. The process by which Rory received his learner's permit and restricted driver's license was modified to fit the narrative and does not reflect actual state law as it applies to teen drivers. Although Emilie talks about playing Words With Friends in September 2008, that game wasn't actually released until July 2009. "American Idol" season 7 premiered in January 2008 but Dottie mentions watching it in October 2008. Regulations involving licensing requirements for hair stylists vary from state to state; Lucia's journey as such is entirely fictionalized and does not reflect actual state law anywhere in the U.S.

Marine Corps Training & other Corps-related details

While the various aspects of life in the Marine Corps were portrayed as realistically as possible, it was necessary at times to modify certain details. For example, Cpl. Gibson's sniper training at Camp Pendleton lasted six months in the story when in reality the Marine Corps Scout Sniper School was originally a ten-week course (before 2009) and the Advanced Sniper Course (now called Team Leader Course) was originally a four-week course.

A note on visas & becoming a U.S. citizen

U.S. Citizenship and Immigration Services requires most immigrants to live in the U.S. five years before they can apply for citizenship; there is an exemption from this requirement, however, for those who served in the U.S. military for at least a year and who are applying for citizenship within six months of an honorable discharge. The fictional portrayal of Fakhir's naturalization process was sped up (and in some places, rearranged) to fit the narrative and does not reflect the actual time required to become a U.S. citizen, even for immigrants who served in the U.S. military. Also, while Fakhir's backstory is that he came to the U.S. on a Special Immigrant Visa for interpreters in late 2007, that program wasn't instituted until 2008, when it was passed into law as part of the National Defense Authorization Act of 2008. (The Iraqi SIV program was discontinued in 2014.) Likewise, the process by which Fakhir's mom & sisters receive their visas from Norway & the U.S. is fictionalized and does not reflect real-world visa processes from either of these countries.

A note on the VA

Similarly, Wade's interactions with Veterans Affairs are fictionalized to meet the narrative and do not reflect the actual process a veteran may experience at any particular VA facility. The Veterans Crisis Line was launched in 2007 but until 2011 it was called the National Veterans Suicide Prevention Hotline—hence, the characters in this story don't consider calling the Hotline in 2008 for non-suicide-related assistance. On a more general level, it's implied that Wade's therapists prescribe medication when in reality it is a psychiatrist (medical doctor) who prescribes medication and a mental health counselor or licensed clinical social worker who provides psychotherapy.

A note on style

Traditionally, the term "Marine" (when referring to individual members of the U.S. Marine Corps) wasn't capitalized until recent years, when news outlets such as the Associated Press, *The New York Times*, and the *Chicago Tribune* began capitalizing it. I use the modern, capitalized version of "Marine" in keeping with these recent changes.

Acknowledgments

With gratitude to:

Margaret Buell Wilder, author of the original *Since You Went Away* ... *Letters to a Soldier from His Wife* (Whittlesey House, 1943) and David O. Selznick, producer and co-screenwriter (with Wilder) of the 1944 movie adaptation of the book (also named "Since You Went Away"). Both served as inspiration for this modern-day story.

Mustafa and Asad, friends who served as Marine Corps combat interpreters in Iraq, for sharing their stories. Buddy Liston, who served in Vietnam as an Air Force C-130 loadmaster, for sharing his knowledge and experience, and for patiently answering my many questions.

Anne Stroh, who connected with my husband via Operation Paperback during his tour in Iraq and became a close friend of our family. An astute reader and witty conversationalist, Anne edited early versions of this manuscript as it was being written. Anne died in October 2020 shortly before the final book in the series was completed.

Carolyn Graan, longtime friend and early reader who helped me find my voice.

Gerarda Simmons, Patricia McCarthy, and Roger Laven, for their encouragement.

Dr. Amy Murphy, for answering my questions about high school administration. Sahar Chapuk, for answering my random questions about Iraqi language and culture.

David High of High Design for his marvelous cover designs.

Kevin Callahan of BNGO Books for his equally marvelous production work on the print editions and their ebook adaptations.

Kevin Callahan and David High for their collaboration on a thoughtful and lovely interior design.

Libby Hewitt for her perceptive and gracious copyediting and proof-reading on the final three books in the series. Faith Simmons for her insightful edits and commentary on the first three books.

My husband Pat, whose military service not only shaped this story but shaped who we are as a family. Pat also served as my sounding board and on-site consultant when I had military-related questions. (Any errors — military or otherwise — are my own.)

Our sons Ben and Coleman, who didn't ask to be born into a military family but who served nonetheless.

The Marines of Marine Corps Mobilization Command / Marine Corps Reserve Support Command, for watching over us while Pat was deployed, especially Maj. John Whyte.

All members of the military, past and present, who dedicate their lives to serving others, and to their families, who keep watch and wait.

About the Author

Nan McCarthy is the author of the *Since You Went Away* series, the *Chat, Connect, & Crash* series, *Live 'Til I Die*, and *Quark Design*. A former magazine editor, Nan founded Rainwater Press in 1992, initially working as a freelance writer for tech companies and trade magazines. During this time Nan also wrote and produced the computer book *Quark Design*. In 1995 Nan wrote and self-published her email epistolary novel *Chat*, which she sold directly to readers from her website. After the series garnered national media attention, Simon & Schuster published *Chat, Connect, & Crash* in trade paperback in 1998. Nan regained the rights to the series and released new editions under the Rainwater Press imprint in 2014. She began writing *Since You Went Away* in 2012, after taking a ten-year break from full-time writing to care for the family during her husband's frequent military travels. Nan and her husband, a veteran who served 29 years in the Marine Corps, are the proud parents of two adult sons.

10% of the net profits from the sale of digital and printed copies of *Since You Went Away, Part Four: Fall* will be donated to Hire Heroes USA. Founded in 2006, Hire Heroes USA helps transitioning military members, veterans, and military spouses find meaningful and lasting careers in the civilian workforce. (The unemployment rate of military spouses is four times greater than the national average, and 80% of discharged service members don't have jobs lined up.) By providing free job search assistance through personalized support, Hire Heroes USA helps transform military service into a successful civilian career.

Also by Nan McCarthy

Fiction

Since You Went Away, Part One: Winter
Since You Went Away, Part Two: Spring
Since You Went Away, Part Three: Summer
Chat: Book One
Connect: Book Two
Crash: Book Three

Non-fiction

Live 'Til I Die
Quark Design

You can find Nan online in the following places:

nan-mccarthy.com

facebook.com/nanmccarthywriter

instagram.com/nanmccarthy

twitter.com/nanmccarthy

pinterest.com/nanmccarthy

To reach Nan directly, please use the Contact form on her website: nan-mccarthy.com/contact/

Veterans Crisis Line: Call (800) 273-8255 and press "1" to talk to someone right away. Text 838255 from your mobile phone. Or go online at www.veteranscrisisline.net and click "Confidential Veterans Chat."

CPSIA information can be obtained
at www.ICGtesting.com
Printed in the USA
FSHW011142191120
75996FS